BLACKEST SPELLS

Edited by C. T. Phipps

Learning a trade is never easy. It takes repetition and involves endless trial and error to finally learn through experience. While a good mentor may speed the process, it really comes down to good, old-fashioned hard work and persistence. Some may be driven in their youth; they know what they want to do. Some may accidentally fall into their profession, finding an unknown talent and enjoying their trade. But, usually, young men and women are forced by circumstance to practice whatever skill, good or bad, that opportunity throws in their path. Jonathan was a quintessential example of the latter.

Salin was furious. Again. It seemed like he was always furious. "Damnit boy, I told you to summon a demon for threshing!" Jonathan dodged the blows from the Summoner's staff and searched for safety under the giant, mahogany table stacked with scrolls. The ritual beating wasn't scheduled for another three hours, so he'd attempt to save his bruised back until it was mandated that he comply. He immediately regretted his decision. The dark nether regions under the table were the dominion of Guul, Salin's pet demon. Guul skipped over and sunk his teeth into Jonathan's ear, leaving a semicircle of little pinpoints in his flesh.

"Owwww! You stupid little son of a b—" Guul giggled and jumped away before Jonathan could swat at him. The demon's laugh sounded like the tinkling of little bells as his leathery wings aided his escape.

"Boy, get up here. NOW! I asked for a Threshing Demon, and you summoned a Trashing Demon! It destroyed the entire ritual and knocked over six of the summoning braziers before I could dispatch him. How many times do I have to say it? IT'S IN THE INTONATION! That monstrosity almost burned the tower down. I rue the day that I agreed to take you on as an Apprentice."

CONTENTS

INTRODUCTION

Hey folks,
    I'm very pleased to bring you guys the second of my dark fantasy anthologies. Ever since I first read *A Game of Thrones* in 1996, I've developed an addiction to grim and gritty storytelling in fantastical worlds. This isn't to put down works like *DragonLance*, *Forgotten Realms*, or other lighter fare but to say I like it when my fantasy is dark.

The dragons and warlocks are just a bit more terrifying when you know the streets are filled with all-too-human cruelties. Conan the Barbarian was always evocative to me because he was a thief, pirate, and mercenary-for-hire in a world that contained both casual cruelty and eldritch abominations.

I remember when I first saw Conan.

One of the things I've always felt was a mistake in fiction, though, was the transformation of magic from a terrifying force linked to the gods (or Devil) to a practical tool. Harry Potter uses magic exactly like a computer command. You say the words and poof, something happens. This isn't a bad thing for stories more concerned with the action than the underlying philosophy of sorcery, but it does make magic a bit less terrifying.

I've always been a fan of evil magicians, whether they were Sauron, Ganondorf, Voldemort, the Wicked Witch of the West, Emperor Palpatine, or Snow White's Wicked Queen. Fantasy thrives on people who wield powers far beyond mortal ken and that might corrupt the user for their use. We all fear power and you'll find plenty of power within.

Blackest Spells is a book devoted to telling stories of terrifying sorcery, evil spellcasters, and malign magic. Blackest

Knights was a collection of short stories devoted to the concept of fallen heroes. Here, we have protagonists who are under siege by forces beyond their understanding. It's not just magic being used by evil people but evil magic.

I hope you all enjoy.

-C.T. Phipps
Agent G, Bright Falls Mysteries, Cthulhu Armageddon, Predestiny, Lucifer's Star, Red Room, Straight Outta Fangton, Supervillainy Saga, Wraith Knight

THE APPRENTICE

BY. C. H. BAUM

Learning a trade is never easy. It takes repetition and involves endless trial and error to finally learn through experience. While a good mentor may speed the process, it really comes down to good, old-fashioned hard work and persistence. Some may be driven in their youth; they know what they want to do. Some may accidentally fall into their profession, finding an unknown talent and enjoying their trade. But, usually, young men and women are forced by circumstance to practice whatever skill, good or bad, that opportunity throws in their path. Jonathan was a quintessential example of the latter.

Salin was furious. Again. It seemed like he was always furious. "Damnit boy, I told you to summon a demon for threshing!" Jonathan dodged the blows from the Summoner's staff and searched for safety under the giant, mahogany table stacked with scrolls. The ritual beating wasn't scheduled for another three hours, so he'd attempt to save his bruised back until it was mandated that he comply. He immediately regretted his decision. The dark nether regions under the table were the dominion of Guul, Salin's pet demon. Guul skipped over and sunk his teeth into Jonathan's ear, leaving a semicircle of little pinpoints in his flesh.

"Owwww! You stupid little son of a b—" Guul giggled and jumped away before Jonathan could swat at him. The demon's laugh sounded like the tinkling of little bells as his leathery wings aided his escape.

"Boy, get up here. NOW! I asked for a Threshing Demon,

and you summoned a Trashing Demon! It destroyed the entire ritual and knocked over six of the summoning braziers before I could dispatch him. How many times do I have to say it? IT'S IN THE INTONATION! That monstrosity almost burned the tower down. I rue the day that I agreed to take you on as an Apprentice."

"You think I like this? You think I had a choice? You saw that I had some ability to summon, and knew my family was so poor they just wanted to be rid of the extra mouth. They practically drooled over your four silvers and two coppers. That's barely the price of a stall mucking apprentice, and you swindled them out of *my* future."

"That's just it, boy. You *had* no future. A stall mucker would have been too good for the likes of you. Now get up here. Today's beating has just been moved up on the schedule. Over the barrel you go."

Jonathan stood up straight, determined to take his beating like a man. He walked over to the barrel, head held high right up until the point he had to bend over to grab the ceremonial handles. Salin readied the staff while Guul took his position at his little piano. That stupid, foot tall demon made a habit of playing his tiny piano while Jonathan received his daily beatings. The music was always played in B-flat, ominous notes of eternal sadness and damnation. He was a demon, after all. The tiny piano music made it seem like Guul was almost sorry for him, but Jonathan knew better. The tinkle of little bells accompanied the first burning strike across his back and continued for several minutes as Salin spent his overzealous fury.

A sweaty Salin finished the beating and dug his finger into one of the bloody lashings while breathing heavily. "Don't fail me again boy. I will beat this in to you until my arms fall off, and then I'll summon a Demon of Peeling to finish the job."

Jonathan screamed in pain, first at the scraping nail inside and under his flayed skin, and then at the unexpected bite of Guul. It left a matching semicircle of punctures on the opposite ear.

Salin laughed at his pet's behavior and directed a command at Jonathan, "Get out of my tower. I will call you tomorrow and you better not screw up again."

Jonathan gathered up his pain and shuffled off towards his room over the barn. At first, when he had been assigned the sleeping quarters, right after being purchased from his parents, he thought the smell of animal feces was unbearable. But after a few days on his new job, it was the only solace he found to lick his wounds and plan his next move.

One of his first procurements, or thefts, really, had been a summoning book. There were thousands upon thousands of demons and the book held some of the more popular summoning techniques. But fire was forbidden in the barn, so he had very little time to read before the light failed and he had to wait restlessly for the next beating.

Tonight, he let the book drop open at random, and Hell's luck was with him. It opened to the lesson on how to summon a Demon of Light. If he had a small light, he would read into the night and learn ever faster between beatings. Maybe even surprise his master with a particularly hard demon spell. So, he scraped away the thrushes from the floor, drew a summoning circle, and put a tiny bit of onyx in the bottom point of his pentagram. The smaller the onyx, the smaller the demon, and he was going for just a little bit of light to read by. He didn't want his master scrambling out to investigate unnatural daylight in the middle of the night.

He carefully reviewed the revisions to his circle, making the necessary adjustments to the lines and orientations, while squinting at the book to make sure it was drawn exactly as it was on the pages of the manual. Once he was satisfied, Jonathan began his intonation, "Gall Folinge Hackmarem. Bin Golish Bolemfaram. Demonius de luznimbus, acklolum."

The demon began to form in the pentagram, slowly materializing from the fires of Hell to kneel in the world of the flesh and blood. It was not what he expected. Black hair framed the most beautiful face he had ever seen. The reddish tint to her skin seemed to reflect the sinuous, dancing flames of Hell, even though she was in the land of the living. Her jet-black eyes glinted with evil knowledge and secrets. "Why have you called me, master?"

"To be my light, but you do not look like a Demon of Light."

Jonathan tried to mimic the confidence of his master when he first woke a demon, barely avoiding an adolescent squeak.

"I am not a Demon of Light. Even better. I am a Demon of Blight." She winked at him, sending a chill down his spine. He was very grateful she was still confined in the summoning circle.

"That was not your purpose as summoned, demon." Jonathan sounded less sure of himself with each passing moment. "I am your master, and you must obey, or return to Hell."

Her wicked, beautiful smile shook him to the core. "Make your attempt, Apprentice. Send me home."

Banishment was the only thing Jonathan had grasped quickly in his studies, so he made confident forms and signs with his hands while chanting, "Minik hollum DEMONIUS REDITUS!"

Nothing happened.

Plump lips split over fanged canines and she chuckled seductively. "I am yours. Forever. I cannot be banished, Apprentice. We will be inseparable for life as we are bonded in Hell. While I am yours, *you* are also mine." She stood, a full three inches taller than Jonathan, and rolled her delicate neck.

Jonathan couldn't help but notice her chest, the shape of her hips, and how sexy leather wings looked on a beautiful demon. The tight leather strips that served as her clothing barely contained her curves.

"Jonathan, master.....do not look at me like that. I am a Demon of Blight. Everything I touch, withers and dies. Would you choose to be impotent the rest of your days?"

"Ummm. No. I'd rather keep that as is." He glanced sheepishly at the floor, having been caught ogling a demon that wasn't a succubus. "What is your name?"

"Kaelish. I was elfin before I was damned."

"Well, it seems we are at an impasse. I want to banish you, but my chant is not working. You appear to want to stay, but you are stuck in the summoning circle until I give you orders and release you. I will be forced to leave you in the circle until you choose to leave on your own."

"Your master hasn't told you yet?" Her mirth shook her breasts as she laughed.

"Told me what?" Jonathan could feel the terror rising in his voice. Being the brunt of a very dangerous joke was not something he enjoyed.

"That each Summoner gets one demon familiar. But the pet chooses the master. It is always done when they are an Apprentice, when the intonation is weakest. I have chosen to be your familiar, and you my master." She began to trace the black acrylic of her nail along the summoning circle, dragging sparks and smoke where she touched it.

To Jonathan's horror, the sparks and smoke erased the binding circle, and she stepped out to stretch in the loft. The stretches gave Jonathan tantalizing views of the undersides of her breasts and he looked away against his baser instincts.

"It is time for you to sleep, Apprentice. The morning will bring surprises. Some desired, and some, ummm, not so much."

Jonathan woke with the light of the newly risen sun sliding slowly across his face. He stretched and started to climb down the ladder from his loft. He caught the hem of his rough robe on the rung and fell straight down to land on his back, knocking the air from his lungs. He blinked away unconsciousness and gasped for air while Kaelish stood over him laughing. The inverted vision of her form left him conflicted between desire and pain.

He wheezed out, "I'm not in the mood to be laughed at, demon."

"You should be excited to start your new life." She reached down, grabbed his hand, and pulled him to his feet with an unexpected strength.

A horrendous stench of rotting meat got stronger as they walked towards the front of the barn. Jonathan dry heaved from the smell, and asked, "What the hell is that?"

Kaelish pointed to the dairy cow's pen, and whispered, "In order to keep my blight at bay, I must eat each night. An animal sacrifice is required for my feast."

Jonathan poked his head around the slats of the pen and

retched. The dairy cow had been obliterated. All that remained was red gore smeared all over the inside of the pen. It was like the cow had exploded and only liquified beef, hooves, and smatterings of hair remained. The smell was overwhelming. It smelled of rot, death, and methane.

Kaelish shrugged, "It was one of the unpleasant things I warned you about last night. Let's head to your master's workshop for one of the more pleasant ones. I am much more powerful that your master, or his pet, so we will have some vengeance."

Jonathan covered his mouth, but even without breathing the stench, his eyes watered until they were outside in the light. "So how does this work? Can I kick him in the balls? Can I strap him to the beating barrel? Oh, even better, can you burn Guul's piano?"

"We will let it play out and see what happens. I need to warn you though. Your master will be furious that you've been chosen by a powerful demon. He will tell you all sorts of lies to get you to try and sever our bond, and to get you to stay as his apprentice. Do not believe his lies, or you will miss your chance at greatness."

"My chance at greatness?" Jonathan asked.

"Because of our bond, *your* bond to a powerful demon, you are no longer required to be an apprentice. You are a full Summoner and are more powerful than your master. He holds no dominion over you now. In his jealous rage, he will try to destroy us. But we will travel and offer our services to the Prince. There are many that will pay a hefty price for a control of my blight; the Prince more than any other. Prepare to live a life of luxury and hedonism as one of the Prince's prized associates."

Jonathan grinned more at the thought of hedonism than luxury as they walked the short distance to the Summoning Chambers.

Kaelish grinned as she reached the closed door and put a finger over her lips as a signal to remain quiet. She slowly lifted the latch, opening the door to reveal Salin bent over some scroll, preparing for the day's work. Guul was at the piano, tickling the tiny keys and playing some ominous march. The demon was the first to sense something was afoot and turned to take in Kaelish and Jonathan. Salin wasn't slow to react either, and turned around a second after Guul.

The vista of such a powerful demon must have been shocking, as Guul let out a high-pitched whine that sounded like a call to battle, while he half ran, half flew to the summoning circle drawn on the floor of the workshop. Salin scrambled in a panic to join his pet in the circle, looking like a bumbling idiot in one of the passing mummer's shows. He tripped on his robe and fell face first into the fist sized quartz stone at one of his points. He'd have a tender black eye tomorrow, for sure.

Salin gathered himself, straightened his robe, and asked, "What in the *Hell* have you done, *boy*?" His voice carried an indignant tone that belied his current position of cowering behind a summoning circle.

"I'm done with your beatings, I'm finished with Guul torturing my ears, and playing his stupid piano, and I'm done being your Apprentice." Jonathan spoke with more authority than he'd felt since being taken on in this miserable line of work.

Salin looked over Kaelish again, and responded, "You're a damned fool."

Jonathan knew his previous master was shaken and responded, "You only call me a fool because you are protected by your own summoning circle. You would not be so brave to call me names if you had to face me on even terms. This is my new pet, Kaelish. She is brilliant, beautiful, and powerful. When we are done here, we will be heading out of town to offer our services to Prince Torrek.

"You are a bigger idiot than I ever imagined. Do you realize the danger you're in?" While pointing at Kaelish, he went on, "*That* is an abomination. She is a Demon of Blight. How many times have I told you it's in the intonation? I bet you tried to summon a demon a Light, or Fight, or maybe even Might. But you got Blight. Do you know what blight does?"

"Yes, but she can keep it at bay if she eats sacrifices. So it's a weapon that can be unleashed whenever she wants, against whoever she wants. The Prince will pay through the nose for her services."

"She is lying to you. I warned you about never summoning

a demon without using my summoning circle. I can always banish, even the most powerful demon, if someone else uses my
circle. You must use your master's circle to summon your first
pet. If it is too powerful, too dangerous to be unleashed, the
master can send it back to Hell, and you can attempt to summon
another. If you had waited long enough to learn the process, we
could send her back and ask for something more controllable.
Now that she's here, you are tied for life." Salin wrung his hands
and paced back and forth inside the scribed shapes of his circle.

"You're lying to me. You always have. You saw that I had
some talent to summon, cheated my parents out of an apprenticeship fee, and haven't taught me anything but the pain of the
lash, and the dread of bite marks on my ears! The Summoner's
Council should send *you* to Hell." Jonathan had a full head of
indignant steam as he raged on. "I'm done here. Cower in your
circle old man. I'm beginning my journey that starts the rest of
my life."

Kaelish had been quiet up until that point, leaning up
against the doorframe. "Guul, come to me."

Guul's eyes glazed over, and he shuffled outside the circle
while Salin stared in horror.

"You, you shouldn't be able to do that. Guul, come back!"
Jonathan had never heard that level of panic in Salin's voice.

Guul ignored his master, and skipped over to Kaelish, hop-
ping on ungainly feet, and flapping his little wings. The little
demon was somehow susceptible to the compulsion, even while
inside his master's protections. Kaelish reached down, picked
him up by his neck, and bit off his entire ear. She threw him violently back into his master, hitting Salin the chest, and knocking
him to his ass. Guul remained eerily quiet.

She pointed at the duo while chewing the ear, and said, "If
you follow us, I will eat you both."

Jonathan and Kaelish turned as one and walked out of the
workshop.

Kaelish swayed her hips as they walked north and said, "You
did well in there. He did not deserve you. You will be the most
powerful Summoner in the Kingdom. Maybe even the world."

Jonathan smiled back. "This is the best day of my life so far."

Jonathan woke with a start, blinded by his small fire. They had walked all day, putting as many miles between them and his old life as possible. He had fallen into an exhausted sleep as soon as they found the small cave, and Kaelish told him she was going to hunt a sacrifice. "Kaelish, is that you?" He gripped a rock like a weapon and strained his eyes against the blackness at the cave mouth.

Salin stepped close enough to the mouth of the cave to be recognized. "No, she's off feeding on a farmer's livestock a couple of miles from here. It's just me."

Jonathan was suspicious of the visit and asked, "What do you want? Why are you chasing me?"

"You have your pet now, bonded for life. An extremely powerful and dangerous familiar. No one will ever threaten you again, for fear of her reprisal. Did I ever tell you the story of how I ended up with Guul?"

Jonathan felt like he was finally being treated like an equal, and so invited Salin in. "Sit, tell me the story."

Salin twisted his robes out of the way, sat down beside Jonathan, and warmed his hands against the flames. The light danced against the ugly bruise forming around his eye. "My master banished a couple of familars before I ended up with Guul. You remember that I told you it was all in the intonation. At first I tried to summon a Demon of Lust and got one that rusted everything within a few hundred feet. That demon had to be banished, because we couldn't keep any iron tools or braziers. Then I tried to summon a Demon of Rage and got another pet that just smelled like sage. My master explained that he would have made a fine pet, but that I was allergic to sage, and couldn't keep him. See? The sage was easy enough to control, but I couldn't concentrate with all the sneezing."

Jonathan nodded his head. "So the intonation comes out in our language as a word that rhymes, or sounds similar to what you're trying to summon...."

Salin nodded his head. "Exactly."

"So how did you get Guul? He just plays the piano."

Salin grinned, "I had a crush on a local girl and was trying to seduce her with my summoning prowess. Let's just say I was *not* trying to summon a twelve-inch demonic pianist."

Jonathan's eyes went wide with realization. "There's a spell for that?"

Salin used the distraction as an opening to shove a razor-sharp dagger in between Jonathan's ribs, slicing a deep gash that punctured clear through the heart. He gently leaned Jonathan back to the floor of the cave as his life bled into the ground and whispered, "The only way to dispatch her, before she kills everything in this world, is to kill her master. And yes, my apprentice, yes. There is a spell for that."

Twinkle, Twinkle

A Lucifer's Star short story

By C. T. Phipps

"What the hell is that thing?" I asked, staring at the image on the viewscreen.

The sight made me question if I wasn't the victim of an elaborate prank. It was an enormous glowing energy spreading itself out in three parts, splashing around (for lack of a better term) in the solar plasma of the Hephaestus system's sun. If that wasn't crazy enough by itself, it seemed to be absorbing the energy from the stellar body at a rate that would collapse the yellow sun into a red giant within hours. Something that I suspected the inhabitants of Hephaestus III would be less than thrilled about.

"It looks like an energy-based cosmozoan, sir. Sort of a big fire bat," Jun, my sensor officer, said. She was a blue-haired woman of Shogun descent and far too talented for her job.

"Or a phoenix," her boyfriend, Eugene, said. He was the communications officer and a good-looking man of mixed Crius-Xerxes heritage. "Can we name it the Space Phoenix?"

"That's not a scientific classification," Jun said.

"And this is a pirate ship," Eugene said.

"Smuggling vessel," Jun said. "We're not robbing anyone today."

"I think the Albion University Department of Interstellar Life Studies would find that reason enough to deny us credit for finding it," I said. "Assuming they believed us in the first place."

Jun looked despondent.

"It looks like a big blob to me," Clarice, my second-in-command and lover said what I was thinking. "One that's eating the home star of our customers."

Clarice Rin-O'Harra was a hard-edged mercenary of Shogun descent like Jun but with bright red hair that was equally artificial. She was taller than most men and fully capable of throwing them across the room when she was angry. I loved her but our relationship was complicated, not exclusive, and full of issues that made it as perilous as an untested warp jump. I wouldn't have had it any other way.

"Yes, that complicates things," I muttered, sitting back in my command chair. "Looks like we won't be getting paid this trip."

My name was Cassius Mass and I was the captain of the star galleon *Melampus*. It was a half-kilometer long ship with the population of a small town permanently living and serving onboard. As my crew said, it was both a smuggling vessel and occasional pirate ship. With the chaos in the Spiral, what humans called Orion's Arm, we did our best to make a living along the Border Worlds between human-controlled space and the Community.

Among the various jobs I arranged to keep the lights on and engines running was our yearly delivery of 100,000 tons of basic goods to Hephaestus III. It was a workhorse contract with little prestige or glamour but was dependable since no one else wanted to come out this far to deal with people who didn't even have any ships of their own. For a ship that operated in the ass-end of space, the Hephaestus system was the furthest we went.

"Has anyone actually ever seen a cosmozoan outside of a holodrama?" Eugene asked. "Especially one that, well, defies all the known laws of physics?"

"No," Jun admitted. "Though there's always legends—"

"There's legends about ghost pirates and space gods," Eugene interrupted. "That doesn't mean they're real."

"Some of those exist," I pointed out, watching the scene on the screen with a perverse fascination.

"Shouldn't we try and do something?" Clarice asked.

"Do what? It's eating a sun. It's not like our energy weapons will hurt it," I said, throwing out my arms. We were a cargo ship, no matter how heavily armed, and way beyond the boundaries of what was normally encountered during a routine junk haul.

"Sir, we're getting a hailing frequency from Hephaestus III's government," Eugene said. "It's the President of Hephaestus III."

"Mayor would be a more accurate summation," I replied. "Put it on screen."

Hephaestus III was a colony of about five thousand residents, possibly a few hundred more since our last visit. The planet had once been inhabited by another sapient species before the Elder Races had wiped them out. It had a mostly nitrogen-based atmosphere and they'd set up enough atmosphere processors plus enough plant-life to be self-sustaining. They were modern-day pioneers and I sometimes wondered who they'd pissed off enough that fleeing to the end of the universe was a better choice than someplace more civilized. My world, at least, had been founded by a weird ass cult.

The image that replaced the eating of a sun by a space monster, not something I ever expected to see in my life, was that of President Paula Lakshmi. She was a spectacularly lovely woman, the result of genetic enhancements, who'd made the somewhat bizarre decision to have her skin body-dyed purple as well as her hair made sparkling white. Paula wore a color-changing fabric that barely covered anything but it was more the fact the planet's temperature reached regular highs of 96 degrees on a cool day. Standing beside her was her bodyguard/lover Korbin who was bare-chested, equally magenta, and looking severe.

"How can I help you, Mayor...err Madame President," I said, staring at her. "It seems you are witness to a horrifying miracle."

I'd already decided to dump the cargo for the trip and gather as many of the colonists up as possible. It would be a tight fit and we wouldn't be able to save everyone. However, with the proper level of resource management, we'd be able to probably get a good four thousand to safety in the nearest starbase. I wouldn't want to be one of the people who made the decision of who to leave behind but it wasn't my first evacuation either: space was a pitiless mistress.

"There is no time for poetic flourishes, Captain Mass," Paula said, her voice hard and lacking any of the usual pleasantries we'd exchanged in the past few years. "We need you to kill the Fire Dragon."

"Is that what we're calling it?" Eugene asked. "I was thinking sun-eating whale."

"Shut up, Eugene," Clarice said.

"Yes ma'am," Eugene said, lowering his head.

"With all due respect," I said, using the code for 'you're out of your goddamn mind' when talking to people higher ranked thank you, "that thing is eating your system's star. I'm not sure there's anything we can do to it. We can, however, get your people—"

"It is the curse of the Technomancers," Korbin said, staring forward with a haunted expression.

"What?" Clarice and I said, simultaneously.

"Jinx," Eugene said.

"Shut up, Eugene," I said.

Paula looked embarrassed. "The Technomancers are a sect of Chel religious extremists existing on the fringe of even the Border Planets' space. They use a combination of Community and scavenged Elder Race technology to mimic...magic."

I processed that. "Any sufficiently advanced technology is indistinguishable from magic."

It was a phrase used a few times that no one knew the precise origin of. I'd encountered more than a few species that seemed to possess powers straight out of a fantasy holo.

"Did you say Chel?" Clarice asked, narrowing her eyes as she clenched her fists.

The Chel were a race of transhuman aliens. Their ancestors had gone above and beyond the normal genetic engineering humans did to work in space to make themselves barely resemble their parent race. They used advanced cybernetics to mimic telepathy and specialized pheromones as well as secretions to control emotions of people they touched. They were also, simply put, a bunch of assholes.

Clarice had fallen into Chel hands once during her soldier days and almost lost her sanity. After weeks of torture, she'd made a general habit of suggesting executing every Chel we encountered. I wasn't in the habit of summary judgements but so far, every Chel we'd encountered engaged in casual torture and mass murder of "lesser" humans.

Like I said, assholes.

Paula nodded. "Technomancer Master Akavma came to our planet and demanded that we turn over the relics we scavenged from the local Elder Race ruins. The Elder Race are—"

"I know who they are," I said, interrupting. I'd bought plenty of Elder Race relics from the locals. They were, in fact, the most profitable thing I acquired on these trips. Some of them I sold to museums and universities. Others, well, I sold to private collectors because they were buying food for these people and I was a pirate. Morals need not apply.

"Akavma got very upset and cursed us," Korbin said, pointing up to the sky. "He brought down the wrath of the Fire Dragon."

"Hold on a second," I said, turning off the viewscreen. Much to Paula's surprise as she realized what I was doing. "Okay, are we being had? Is there really a giant monster eating the sun, summoned by a freaking *wizard*?"

"Space is weird," Eugene said, shrugging. "Did you know I once met a guy with three—"

"Eugene, remember my earlier order?" Clarice asked. "It now involves slapping the shit out of you ever time you open your mouth."

"Heads?" Eugene said, grimacing.

Clarice raised her hand.

Eugene cringed.

"Is there any way this could be a weapon of the Chel?" I asked, looking around.

"No," Clarice said. "If the Chel had a weapon like this, they would have taken over the galaxy by now."

"Assuming they want to," I said. "Elder Race artifacts can

do almost anything, and they left them on worlds like this as refuse. Maybe the Fire Dragon is something this guy found while prospecting for their junk."

"Or something he knew was coming and is claiming credit for," Clarice suggested.

"Possibly. Send everything we have down to Doctor Hernandez and scan the system for signals around the sun," I said, pointing to the screen.

"That's going to take a while sir," Jun said. "Scanning is a long, painful, and annoying process."

"Hence why I have you do it instead of me," I said, smiling.

Jun muttered something suspiciously like my opinion about the Chel.

"What was that?" I asked.

"Nothing, sir."

"We're being hailed again," Eugene said. "Assuming I can speak now."

"Put it on screen," I said. "And don't say anything unrelated to the mission."

Eugene grumbled.

Paula glared at me. "We need your help."

"I'm trying," I said, staring at her. "But it'd be best if you prepared to evacuate the colony. I can get most of you away."

Paula looked down. "We can't. The colonists won't do it."

"I think they'll change their mind when the sun dies and they're freezing to death," I said.

Paula paused. "Perhaps, but by that point, I won't be President and the guns will have been drawn. This colony was founded on the principles of absolute freedom and the right to bear weapons."

"Uh huh," I said, avoiding saying what I thought about that. "So, they'd rather die than leave a planet they're squatting on."

"Yes," Paula said. "So they say."

"Fair enough," I said, staring. "We'll try and fix this. If we can't—"

"Please save my people," Paula said. "No matter what they've done to me for bringing this down on them."

"Try not to get too noble here," I said. "All of the stuff I bring you comes from Colonial Settlement Company (CSC) inventory lost due to a programming error."

"Or pirates," Clarice said.

"Yeah, hate those guys," I said before giving a fake smile. "Every pirate should be killed."

The rest of my crew returned my fake smile and looked at Paula.

"Right. Good luck. I'll find some way to reward you if this goes well." Paula signed off.

"Do you think she can afford to pay us for this?" Clarice asked.

"Not a chance," I replied. "But we've got a cargo hold of out-dated colonial rations, generators, and atmosphere processors. I don't know anywhere else to dump em."

"You're motivation to prevent planetary genocide is stir-ring, sir," Jun said.

"Thank you, Jun."

Ten minutes later, the image of Doctor Isla Hernandez appeared in a box to the upper left corner of the viewscreen. She was a lovely white-haired woman with alabaster skin and pierc-ing yellow eyes. Isla was a bioroid that had freed herself from involuntary servitude and taken up residence on our ship. She was also my lover, along with Clarice's—because it got really boring in space and there was only so much to do.

"Howdy, Doc," I said. "Do you bring us good news or are we going to be handling a bunch of homeless refugees soon?"

"Possibly both," Isla said. "I've managed to analyze what little data we have on the creature and have come to some dis-turbing conclusions."

"I take it your medical degree didn't come with 'creatures made of fire'," I said, cheerfully.

Truth be told, I was covering for a sense of deep sympathy for the colonists. I, too, had lost my homeworld to a disaster beyond my control. Crius had been pelted by mass drivers as part of the Archduchy-Commonwealth War. Tens of millions had died and hundreds of millions had been left homeless. This wasn't a disaster on the same scale but, costly or not, I was going to try to do something.

"We have to do something," Clarice said. "We have options."

"Which are?" I asked, looking back at the viewscreen. "I mean, our problems are starting with *planet-sized monster eats star.*"

"It's alive and capable of reproduction," Isla said.

I blinked. "That is in fact very bad."

"It converts the energy and gas inside the sun into whatever strange matter it's made of," Isla said. "By the time it finishes eating in a few hours, it'll have split off into dozens of more of its kind who will also feed from the sun."

"Okay," Clarice said. "This has gone from being a problem for five thousand people to an existential threat to the universe."

"Not really," Eugene said, forgetting he wasn't supposed to talk. "There's like a trillion stars."

"A hundred fifty-five billion at last count," I corrected. "Even then, if each of these things feeds off a star in a few days and breeds then that could rapidly grow out of control."

"That's assuming they're capable of reaching other star systems," Clarice said. "Without access to jumpspace, they'd take millennia to cross the void even at light speed."

"They're capable of entering jumpspace," Isla said. "In fact, I think they're made up of matter from that dimension. They could in fact devour the entire galaxy given a few million years—which is more impressive than it sounds."

"I'm pretty easily impressed," I said, imagining the end of everything. "Yeah, we should probably stop this if we can."

"Agreed," Clarice said. "How do we kill these things?"

"I'm not sure we can," Isla said. "However, we can possibly lure them back into jumpspace with a modified jumpdrive."

"Yeah, because we have a bunch of those lying around," I muttered. "Even if we can, that'll leave us at half-speed and make evacuation all but impossible."

"Other-dimensional entities turn out to be a problem requiring unique solutions," Isla replied, dryly.

Was everyone on my ship a smart-ass? Well, I guessed it was a requirement to be promoted to the bridge crew. In an emergency, I needed people who spoke my language. Still, her plan had merit. Sort of. If we could get a jumpdrive hooked up to a generator, it could create a field large enough to take the thing back into its dimension. The problem was, well, it was in the fricking sun. There wasn't a way we could get a jumpspace drive within a million kilometers of the place without destroying it.

Literally.

"There's more," Isla said.

"Oh joy," I said, feeling like our time was running out.

"This one you'll like," Isla said, smiling. "I think I've found our evil wizard."

I stared at her. "Tell me more."

"This is a terrible plan," I muttered inside my spacesuit. I was sitting in the cockpit of the *Engel*-class fighter that was slowly propelling itself through space despite its engines being offline. The thing about space was the absence of gravity meant that if you started propelling an object forward, it would continue going forever. There was no resistance to slowing it down.

With a single burst of thrust, we could send the starfighter moving toward our target and be almost undetectable. It was an old pirate trick and I knew it well even if I had a couple more decades before I qualified. I also had a cybernetic implant linking me to the starfighter's computer so controlling it was as easy as thought.

"It's *your* plan," Clarice said, sitting behind me in the co-pilot's seat. She was dressed in an identical spacesuit, though hers had a couple of emergency patches on them from the various battles she'd fought in them. Frankly, I was hoping we could use the money from this run to replace them but if wishes were fishes then Aquarians would rule the galaxy.

"Technically, it's Isla's plan," I replied, checking our instruments.

In addition to the starfighters, weapons, and shields that were not standard issue onboard a cargo hauler, the *Melampus* also had a top-rate sensor system. It came from being an ex-spy ship we'd stolen from the Galactic Commonwealth. The *Melampus'* sensor system was strong enough that it could pick up a cloaked Chel light saucer at short range. It was about the size of a small house and probably didn't require more than a single person to run it. I didn't know if it belonged to this Akavma guy but given it was the only other ship in the system, I was willing to bet on it.

"It's *a* plan, at least," Clarice said. "We exit out the ship, give a bit of thrust, and propel ourselves towards the saucer. We murder the guy and hopefully figure out how he summoned the Fire Dragon to the system."

"Maybe we should do the latter before the former," I said, amused. "Dead men tell no tales."

"I don't care as long as it involves murdering the guy," Clarice said. "We've only got a few more hours until that sun becomes a red giant. If we stop it now, then it'll be a few more million years of life. As insignificant as that may be in the life of a sun."

"In another life you would have made a brilliant scientist," I said.

"In another life, you a decent captain," Clarice said, good-naturedly.

"I wouldn't bet on that," I said, dryly.

"You know this is a really good thing we're doing," Clarice said, annoying me. "It feels nice to do something to help people rather than just spend all of our time robbing or cheating people."

"You shouldn't say anything," I said, faking looking at the dead instruments in front of me. "Akavma might pick it up."

"Sound doesn't travel through space, dumbass," Clarice said.

"Then maybe I just don't want to think about the fact we're doing charity work," I replied, shaking my head. "It never works out well. You think you're doing a good thing and then it blows up in your face."

"Is this about the war?" Clarice asked, referring to my past a soldier. I'd been involved in the biggest war in humanity's history and my side had lost badly.

I blinked. "Yes, Clarice, it's always about the war. I went into the conflict thinking I was a hero, got everyone I loved killed, and killed a bunch of other people who probably didn't have it coming."

"I'm pretty sure this guy has it coming," Clarice said.

"Destroying a star is some grade-A supervillain stuff."

"He's an evil wizard controlling a dragon and threatening to kill some (semi) peaceful villagers. You don't get much more morally unambiguous than that," I said, sucking in my breath. "That's why I'm hesitating to go forward. This seems all a bit too straightforward. You don't destroy a star to wipe out a bunch of settlers barely scraping by. We're missing something."

"Maybe he's making a demonstration," Clarice said.

"What?" I asked.

"Maybe he's going to show the galaxy what his Fire Dragon can do," Clarice explained. "Then sell it for a hundred trillion credits to whoever will buy it. Maybe he's just insane. Maybe he's a guy who tripped over some Elder Race junk and found it can summon monsters that eat stars like a dog whistle. Does it really matter?"

"Yes?" I suggested. "I think it does."

"I don't," Clarice replied. "Because in a few minutes he'll be dead, and we'll have a Chel ship we can sell for more than ten of these runs."

She had a point there. "I love your pragmatic mind."

"It's my third best feature after my eyes and homicidal tendencies," Clarice said.

"What's mine?" I asked, absently.

"You're remarkably pleasant company when you learn to shut up," Clarice said, pausing. "We're here."

My spacesuit's micro-binoculars were able to pick up the sight of the ship on visual as I lightly activated the thrusters to slow us down. The Chel light saucer was a sleek piece of engineering that barely looked made by human hands, possessing none of the usual lights or flourishes that decorated typical vessels made for our race. Instead, it looked like one solid piece of metal, floating in the darkness. There was something about it that made me feel a sick and I had to clamp down that feeling.

"Do we even know how we're going to get into that thing?" Clarice asked. "I don't see any airlocks."

"I have an idea," I said, simply.

I opened the cockpit up to the vacuum of space with the emergency lever and let the atmosphere escape around us. We were only a few meters away from the light cruiser and I fired a magnetic grapple from a pistol I'd packed ahead of time, tossing it to Clarice as it floated to her. The two of us then pulled ourselves to the side of the Chel vessel and attached ourselves to its side with our boots.

"Okay, so what's the plan?" Clarice asked.

I reached to the side of my space suit where an electronic sheath was attached to my belt. It contained a very anachronistic weapon which was a relic of my days with the Crius military: a proton sword.

"Oh no," Clarice muttered.

"Oh yes," I said, lifting it up and activating it. The weapon crackled with strange energies I didn't fully understand and yet which functioned perfectly fine in the vacuum of space. They were based on Old Earth technologies from before the Great Collapse and allegedly made the blades sharp enough to shear an atom in half. I doubted that since I'd yet to cause a nuclear detonation with my blade, but they were *really* sharp.

I brought mine down and cut a triangular hole, feeling Chel hypersteel fall prey to my weapon like it was paper, and exposed a chunk of the vessel's interior to vacuum. The chunk I'd carved floated away and I prepared to begin my assault on this so-called Master Akavma.

That was when a living shadow emerged from the hole and ate us.

"Twinkle, twinkle, little star, how I wonder what you are. Up above the world so high, looking down upon us as we die. When the blazing sun is gone, when the nothing shines upon, then you show your little light. Twinkle, twinkle in the eternal night," the voice that interrupted my dreamless slumber was soft, slick, and somehow slimy.

I recognized the nursey rhyme as the one they used on my dead planet of Crius. It was a reminder that space was a deadly and horrifying place that would eventually consume us all. Yeah, we were a messed-up people.

My wrists were tied to some sort of metal table and I could feel myself unclothed. There was always the sense of being violated when captors undressed you. On the other hand, you were always lucky to wake up when knocked out. I'd known plenty of people disabled by gas or electricity who hadn't woken up at all. Opening my eyes, I saw I was in an empty chrome room with no sign of Clarice. My captor was nearby, looming over me like I was the most interesting thing in the world.

He was over two meters tall with a sphere bald head, corpse-like papery skin that was covered in fish-scale-like splotches, and with a neck twice as large as a normal man. He was wearing robes and carrying a staff that I could tell had numerous devices built into it but, from a distance, could pass as a fantasy wizard's tool. His eyes were bulbous and completely black. Each hand had about six fingers with no thumbs.

"You are one ugly son of a bitch," I said, simply.

The Chel slapped me across the face.

"You stand before a Master of Eighteen Paths, an Enlightened Lord of the Red Lodge. I, Akavma, have seen the planes that lie beyond this realm. I have visited realities you could not begin to comprehend and know the secrets that lie in men's minds," Akavma said, raising his staff like he was on the stage.

"I've visited alternate realities too," I said, dryly. "Met a weredeer, a cyborg, and a supervillain. Are people actually impressed with this nonsense?"

Akavma frowned then shrugged. "You wouldn't believe how many people fall for it. I used to have a position as the special advisor to the President of Belenus. He paid 50,000 credits per session and that was in addition to the millions for the curses I laid on his enemies. Fifty million to kill the Prime Minister of Bridget."

"How'd that work out?" I asked.

"A freighter's toilet fell on her from orbit," Akavma said, chuckling. "Sadly, the President turned against me when the media found out about my use of his young attractive staff members."

"Yeah, they'll get you for that, Fishboy."

Akavma frowned. "You are Cassius Mass, Count of Crius. The Fire Count. The Butcher of Kolthas. The—"

"Guy possessing titles every bit as ridiculous," I replied.

"Yes, I know. Is the Hephaestus sun changed yet?"

"No," Akavma said. "Not yet. But soon. You weren't out that long. Changing the nature of a sun is by itself a great accomplishment but it's snuffing a healthy sun that will get me trillions."

"Money, really?" I asked, unimpressed. "Such a pedestrian motive?"

"Why do you kill people?" Akavma asked.

He had a point. "I still don't get it. Why here? To what end?"

Akavma shrugged. "My organization, the Technomancers, benefits strongly from the fact the Great Collapse left much of humanity a bunch of superstitious fools. Hephaestus III is a planet full of useful relics that could be used to make us a feared power in the galaxy. The locals resisted so I decided to teach them a lesson."

"And you think killing their sun was a proportional response?" I asked, trying very hard not to be sarcastic and failing miserably.

Akavma smiled. "It was one of the Elder Race objects I found on their planet that was still functional. When all you have is a sun-killer, a sun killer you must use. In any case, once my demonstration is done, I can loot the planet to my leisure. I probably won't need however much money I'll get from ransoming you back to your old enemies in the Commonwealth or selling Ms. Rin-O'Harra to the Shogun Syndicate, but I never turn down free money."

I smiled right back. "Of course. I don't suppose we could make a deal, Akavma was it? Is that your real name?"

"Dave Johnson," Akavma admitted. "But no, I don't think we can."

"Shame," I said, closing my eyes and checking to see if the Chel hypersteel blocked a transmission from my cybernetic implant. Given there was a big hole in the side of the ship blocked off only by a life-support barrier, it turned out it didn't. I ordered my starfighter to power up and fire its energy cannons.

"What are you doing?" Akavma asked.

That was when the starship rocked as I was smart enough to only fire at a quarter power.

"My ship has found you!" I said. "You have to release me to

tell them to stop before we're both killed."

Akavma hesitated before the second blast and reluctantly released my restraints, shouting curses. "You have no idea what terrible—"

I headbutted him in the face, grabbed him by the neck and snapped it in a single smooth gesture. His body fell useless to the ground as his staff bounced across the chrome surface of the floor.

"Wizards beat fighters at long range, not close," I muttered, picking up the staff. "Everyone who plays Star Fantasy Control Online knows that."

The staff wasn't a particularly complicated piece of machinery, being a basic control rod for a starship with a disintegrator built into it—expensive but not magical. Using it to open the door, I found Clarice outside my cell door, trying to force it open. She was wearing a hospital gown from what I assumed to be the ship's medical area.

"Hi," I said.

"Hi," Clarice said, blinking. "I see you managed to get yourself free."

"Likewise," I said, chuckling. "Ding dong! The witch is dead."

"Wizard, not witch," Clarice said.

I shook my head. "Whatever."

We found a weird Elder Race monolith with a computer-interface hooked up to the light freighter's central computer and did the only thing we could do in that situation by moving the ship around. It lured the Fire Dragon away to the next star system where Isla tried out her jumpspace generator trick. I had no idea if it worked since both it, the Fire Dragon, and the stone monolith vanished once they came together.

I hated using the Chel ship, but it was better to use its generator than the Melampus' own. We'd also cleaned it out of anything valuable along the way. It turned out the late Master Akavma a.k.a Dave Johnson, had been a collector of fine art as well as alien junk. Stuff that would fetch a high price on the black market once we got back to "civilized space."

As for the Hephaestians? Well, they were very grateful for what we'd done. So grateful that they believed me when I told them that the relics on their planet were all cursed and needed to be transported off at no charge.

We'd just have to figure out which ones were safe to sell and which ones needed to be dumped into a black hole.

THE WITCH QUEEN

BY MICHAEL POGACH

Long ago, when it was still good to wish for a thing, a black-bearded conqueror built a castle by the sea. With iron and grace he ruled his lands, and his subjects loved his unbending will, the more so when, after many years, it was announced the king's wife was with child.

The queen gave birth before dawn on a mid-winter morning to the blackest-haired girl the lands by the sea had ever known. Before the girl's naming ceremony, however, it was announced the king's wife had died of fever. Even so, the king declared the birth day celebration for the princess would last a year and a day.

And it did.

The king, all smiles despite his loss, hosted banquet and ball and masquerade. Hardly passed a day without celebration. Gifts were sent from the many corners of the world. Baubles from the cold lands to the north. Gold from the mountains to the east. Diamonds so clear they could be water from the coasts far to the south. And roses from the most distant lands of the dwarves, brought by seven of the stocky fellows who planted them around the castle walls.

It was said in whisper and in song, despite the king's loss, this year was the happiest any kingdom had ever known.

Like all things, however, happiness has its cycles, and soon the king returned to lordship and governance. The raising of the princess was left to the wise old crones who shuffled about the castle. Under their care, the princess grew bright and tall and inquisitive and headstrong, and she loved the crones and they loved her.

In time came the princess's twelfth birthday, the day a laurel crown like her father's would be fitted to her sable-haired head. She woke earlier than usual this day, before her father knocked on her door or the crones prepared her breakfast.

"Come, crones," she shouted, excited to finally see her crowning dress. "It's time. It's time."

And a-shuffling came the crones.

"Settle, princess," said the first.

"You cannot wind the clock faster," said the second.

"Patience keeps the Witch Queen at bay," said the third crone.

Though she was twelve and scoffed at the invocation of a childhood bogeywitch, the princess composed herself and let the crones attend to her. So enchanted were they, princess and crones, with their preparations before the large looking glass they never thought to open the balcony doors. Thus, none realized the time for dawning came and went without the sun.

Only when the king's voice bellowed through the castle, calling for his adjuncts and servants, did the princess break free of pins and yarn and spindle. Curious as ever, she ran into the hall and was nearly crushed by the press of servants rushing this way and that. Only the hands of the crones pulling her back into the room saved her.

"Prepare the guard," the king shouted, his voice carrying from the throne room. "Assemble the lancers. And bring torches!"

Torches? But it was day.

The princess flung wide the balcony doors. All the world was in gloom. Neither the distant mountains, nor the plains below could be discerned. Not even the rose vines which, in twelve years, had grown impenetrable around the castle, could be spied more than a few feet below.

The night was absolute.

Until a star shone upon the earth, at the edge of the plains, where the gold of wheat began to shimmer. Only it wasn't a star.

It was a woman, tall and radiant in a gown of white.

"The Witch Queen," said the first crone as they shuffled to the balcony beside the princess.

"The roses will keep her at bay," said the second.

"No, there will be war," said the third.

"War?" the princess asked, knowing the word only from the crones' tales, for few remained in the castle who had ever seen combat.

"Yes," said the king from the doorway, in his hands the princess's two best dolls: Hero, the woolen knight; and Mare, the wooden horse. "War."

Her crowning dress trailing uncinched behind her, the princess flew to her father. He raised her high and kissed her on the forehead and said, "I love you."

The princess knew from the crones' tales that a soldier off to war was to ask forgiveness of a cleric for his sins, yet there had been no clerics in the castle in her lifetime, and it was not her place to hear her father's transgressions. So, the princess said the only thing she could.

"I love you too, Daddy."

To the crones, the king said, "Protect the princess."

They nodded in turn as he placed his daughter on the ground.

"Don't go," she said.

But the king was already out of the room, calling like thunder, "Adjuncts, fetch my armor and arms!"

Back to the balcony, the princess went, her two best dolls clutched to her chest. Below, the Witch Queen's light blanched the plains.

"Will he win?" she asked the crones.

"If he is true," said the first.

"If his love is pure," said the second.

"It is war," said the third.

Curious and afraid, the princess watched as the vines opened below and forth rode her father and his army as if belched from the castle. Like ants to lines, they ranged upon the plains, men and boys barely older than their king's daughter, battle anticipation trembling their knees and releasing their bladders. Only the oldest among them remembered what it was like to parry death and to kill, and even these were memories of skirmishes not wars, for the kingdom had long known peace.

Flanking these soldiers, the knights aligned, their steeds pawing the earth until a great cloud rose overhead. These men, at least, knew of battle in their foreign service to their king who rode before them.

War is glorious, peacetime stories tell, but there is no glory in a girl watching her father die.

"You wicked ogress!" the princess cried when the dust cleared and the king's army lay scattered like so many of her toys, the king still before them, impaled upon a spear of night.

Of the Witch Queen's army, if an army she ever had, there was no sign.

"He deserved his fate," the Witch Queen said, her voice carrying like heat in the summer. She floated across the plains over the blood of the dead, her gown brilliant and unblemished. "As did the men who followed his treacherous authority."

The princess snugged her dolls between her elbow and armpit and climbed the balcony rail.

"Stop," said the first crone.

"It is dangerous," said the second.

"You'll fall," said the third.

But the princess would not fall. She knew her responsibility. With her stockinged feet upon the narrow rail, she announced in the custom of story and of the land, "In the name of the king, my father, I challenge you to battle."

The Witch Queen paused. If she hadn't been so far below, the princess would have believed she saw a smile cross her face.

"The king is dead," the Witch Queen said. "Long live the queen."

Her words struck the princess like a tempest gale. She stumbled and nearly fell, but though she was still young and still small, she was no weakling and no coward. And she knew her responsibility.

"I challenge you," she repeated.

"Think on your words, girl. Go back to your room and play with your dolls. Wait for my coming."

With that, the Witch Queen pointed a long finger at the castle. The rose vines below shuddered but did not part. The Witch Queen appeared neither surprised nor daunted. She stretched her finger once more, this time at the balcony, and spoke an incantation that scuttered into the princess's mind like insects seeking her soul. Frightened, the princess rushed inside and closed the doors, the vines swallowing the balcony behind her. A blast hit the castle, shaking it from foundation to spire, but it held strong.

"Wait for my coming," the Witch Queen's whispered voice repeated, prompting the princess to retreat into the castle's embrace.

Through corridor and hall the princess ran, seeking refuge. Seeking protection. But all the soldiers had gone forth. There remained not a single man with sword or shield in the castle. Only the crones and the squires and the adjuncts. And the princess.

Before long, she found herself in the throne room, weeping and clutching to her empty chest the laurel crown that had once been her father's.

"I can bring your father back," a little voice said.

The princess looked around expecting to see the Witch Queen come for her. She was, however, alone.

Again she heard, "I can bring your father back."

The princess looked deep into the corner shadows expecting to find a dove or a fairy or a talking mouse. She was, however, alone.

"If you love him," the voice said.

The princess's eyes fell to the crown in her hands. Entwined in its beautiful strands, flexed a tiny spider, its eyes glossy and wide.

Spiders, the princess knew from the crones' stories, were almost as dangerous as the Witch Queen herself, plundering the souls of the innocent with their many legs and eyes. But she could not resist the temptation of saving her father.

"Of course I love him," she said.

"Then you must do what I say," the spider replied, "but quickly."

"Tell me."

"First, collect the king," the spider said. "Bring him here so that I may work the few magics I have left."

"But the Witch Queen," the princess said.

"Even she cannot penetrate the shell of rose and thorn that protects this place. She has departed. The sun shines once more. Go, order the adjuncts and squires to collect the king."

And the princess did.

The king was lain upon a bed of gold and crimson within a glass coffin before the throne as was the custom of the lands by the sea.

"Now," the spider said when the adjuncts and squires had departed, "I cannot bring him to life just yet, but I can keep him from death."

"You promised," the princess wailed, fearing she'd been tricked by the enduring nature of spiders.

"And I will fulfill my promise. This is not storybook magic. It requires more than I alone can do. Tell me again, do you love your father?"

"Yes."

"Will you sacrifice for him?"

"Yes."

"Will you do as I ask, even to your own peril, if it can restore him?"

"Yes. Tell me what I must do."

"Fetch your crones," said the spider.

Though she couldn't fathom what help her crones could be, the princess left the throne room a-calling for the crones who came a-shuffling.

"Oh my," said the first crone when they entered the throne room.

"The king," said the second.

"It is done," said the third.

"Not done yet," the spider announced, revealing itself. From the crown, it wriggled. To the floor, it dropped. Before the crones, it rose upon its four hind legs.

As one, the crones gasped. The spider, quicker than any could prevent, threw filaments to the ceiling and swung upon them from one crone to the next, impaling the left of eye of each with one of its tiny legs.

"I'm blind," cried the first crone.

"It burns," cried the second.

"We are betrayed," cried the third.

A wind blew through the throne room, and the three crones collapsed. In their places, three piles of dust.

Came a second wind and blew away the dust.

"Now," said the spider when it had returned to the crown, three globules of eye jelly on one of its limbs, "I can save the king."

The words the spider next spoke, as it gesticulated with its many legs, made the princess's stomach quease and her head swim.

In time, silence returned, and the princess remembered where she was. She stood, wanting to find and squash the spider for its treachery, but when she saw her father in his glass coffin, his chest was rising and falling softly.

"He's alive," she said.

"He is," the spider said from the weaves of the laurel crown the princess still held to her chest. "But he is not waking. This is all the power I have. He will sleep for a hundred years. After that, he will pass beyond all magic and alchemy. To wake him, you must help me."

"Help you?"

"With my cauldron, I can distill a potion to restore your father, but the Witch Queen stole it long ago. Fetch it for me, and I will help you even before removing my own curse."

"What is your curse?" the princess asked, a fancy rising within her so ludicrous considering the situation, but she couldn't help its surge.

"Why, I am a prince, of course."

Of course! As all the stories told. As all the curses demanded. A prince in the form of a spider, awaiting a true love's kiss, no doubt.

"A prince," the princess repeated, surprised at the hunger in her words.

"With my cauldron and the Witch Queen's blood, I can

restore the king and remove my curse. Will you do as I ask?"

"But she is so powerful."

"Do not fear. She has returned to her tower on the other side of the Faraway Forest. She will never suspect your approach. Go and fetch my cauldron and a single drop of her blood, and all will be made right."

"But I am only a girl."

"You are the king's daughter!"

"I am the king's daughter," the princess repeated. A princess who knew she must one day marry a prince.

"Will you do this," the spider asked, "for my sake and for his?"

"Yes."

"Say it please, so I know your heart is true. Speak your name and say it."

"I, Zahra, princess of the kingdom by the sea, pledge to retrieve your cauldron and a drop of the Witch Queen's blood, so that my father and I can be together once more."

"You will be together," the spider said. "Now go."

The princess bid the spider farewell and made her preparations. She gathered a pack of food and water and her two dearest friends: Hero and Mare. Then, still in her crowning dress and stockings, she set out for the castle gates.

As they had for her father, the roses parted at her approach. On her way through, however, a thorn caught her pack, threatening to prevent her quest. She tugged until the bag came free, and then she was out on the plains, the roses sealing the castle behind her.

It was the first time the princess had been out in the world, and the size of it frightened her. Moreover, the smells—wisps she'd only noted before—came at her like tornados, and the brightness of the sun was like a thousand blades to her eyes. Upon the same plains which drank the blood of her father's army, she collapsed.

"Fetch my cauldron," the spider said, its voice falling to her like cold in winter. "For the king."

"Yes," she told herself. "For the king."

She rose and began her quest across the plains to the golden wheat fields. A week she spent through these fields before the boundary of the kingdom was declared by the Murky Swamp. Never before had the princess smelled such stink, but into the marshland she trudged, time ceasing to matter in the swamp's eternal shade. Days passed like hours and weeks like days. Seasons may have come and gone while the threat of sting-buzzes hung in the air the way the stench of the bog clung to her.

In time, the stingbuzzes grew bold, sneaking into the princess's camp at night to sniff at her and test her alertness. This continued until her crowning dress was blackened and tattered and her stockings no longer covered her feet. Finally, an audacious stingbuzz with knotty, stringed wings and a proboscis like a spear came for her.

"I wish I had a knight to protect me," the princess whispered, clutching her pack and bracing for the pain.

At her words, Hero leapt from her pack, alive and full grown, a knight armed with both sword and shield.

Wordlessly, Hero engaged the stingbuzz, slashing off its proboscis and stabbing it through its bloated belly. Thick ochre spewed forth, splashing the valiant knight. Wordless still, he shriveled and contorted until he was once more a doll, floating in the morass, torn and ruined.

The princess buried Hero upon a hammock of moss and mushrooms, and she wept until the din of night creatures gave way to the hisses of daytime ones. Sad but determined, she made a pair of boots from the stingbuzz's wings and kept on her quest.

The Murky Swamp gave way, eventually, to the Burning Mountains. Over their peaks, she trekked as the crags around her vomited up fire and molten stone. Here, years passed like seasons before she found the foothills on the other side. And from the foothills onto the wastes of the Endless Desert, slow and careful, wary of the snake's legend said moved beneath the sands like continents.

It was not, however, the snakes which caught her. It was the swallowing sands. They opened beneath her at midday when she knew she should have been resting. At first, she thought it was fatigue making the going difficult. Soon, however, she saw the sands had risen to her ankles. Then mid-calf. Then, at knee-depth, she understood. The sands were taking her.

"I wish I had a noble steed to pull me from this tomb," she cried.

At her words, Mare leapt from her pack, alive and full grown, a war horse determined and devoted.

From the higher sands, Mare lowered her reigns so the princess could grab them. With a strength the princess believed must have been love, Mare pulled. Inch by inch, until the princess felt herself coming free. But the sands betrayed Mare as well. Now, they were both sinking. Undaunted, the horse clutched and pulled, yanked and thrashed, dragged and hauled until the princess felt the firmness of earth beneath her.

Gasping for breath, she rolled over only to watch helpless as Mare sank deeper and deeper until there was nothing left but the hungry sands. And then, beside her lay the wooden doll, its legs splintered and its eyes closed.

She buried Mare beneath a stunted palm and wept. In the morning, she striped down Mare's reigns and re-stitched her dress and continued her quest.

Finally, the desert offered scraggles of bushes and hints of life, and then, before she knew it, the Faraway Forest wrapped itself around her like a terrifying embrace.

At first, she was thankful for the abundance the forest offered, enough food and water to sustain her a lifetime or more. Soon, however, she heard the scurrying of goblins around her. And after that, the guttural whisperings of the horrid things.

"It sounds human," said one.

"It looks like a princess," said another.

"It smells delicious," said a third.

Alarmed, and with no more companions to protect her, the princess ran, the clicking of goblin claws behind her. Tree branches stunk her cheeks. Brambles tore at her legs. When at last she thought she would collapse and the goblins would take her, the trees gave way. Into a clearing she spilled, and the sounds of her pursuers halted as surely as if they'd found a wall.

The princess turned, determined that if she was to die, she would do so facing her attackers.

But none came.

Their eyes glowed reds and greens in the shade of the trees but, like bats and beetles flitting at the edge of night, none dared pass into the clearing.

When she was sure she was safe, the princess turned to continue on her way. The clearing, however, did not stretch far. Across its grass rose a tower of ivory so tall and so bright the princess could hardly look at it.

"I have come," she whispered.

At the tower's base, a sliver of darkness split the brilliant façade. A door, swung wide, inviting.

Though the open door was surely a trap, the princess had traveled too long and too far to turn away now. With her pack slung over her shoulder, she entered the tower. It was as open as a cathedral. No corridors. No rooms. No fires burning to light the way. Yet light there was. And a staircase of white marble in the center rising clockwise up the tower.

Up, up, up the princess climbed. For hours maybe. Or even days. At last, she reached a door at the top. At her touch, it swung open to reveal a throne room not unlike her father's. In the center, however, upon the dais, stood not a throne but a great mirror, wide enough and tall enough to make the throne room appear twice its already vast size.

And in the glass appeared the Witch Queen.

The princess spun, expecting to face her foe, but she was alone in the cavernous room.

Turning once more to the mirror, the princess was shocked to again see the image of the Witch Queen. Understanding came slowly at first, then all at once like a storm. The woman in the glass was not her nemesis at all.

It was herself.

She was no longer small. No longer a girl. She was a woman, and her resemblance to the Witch Queen, to the villain who had slain her father, was so unsettling she retched all her stomach had to disgorge.

Then, beside her image in the glass, there appeared another. A twin.

"I did not expect you to grow so beautiful," the Witch Queen said, "daughter."

"I'm not your daughter," the princess said, steeling herself against the glamour that must be causing this hallucination.

"No? Who is your mother then?"

"My father's wife. The king's wife."

"Which one?"

The princess staggered as if she'd been struck.

"It's okay, child," the Witch Queen said. "What we know and what we don't is so often controlled by the men around us, is it not, Zahra? What, you're surprised I know your name? Who do you think chose it?"

"You're a monster!"

"Tut, daughter. I did not bring you here for insults."

"You didn't bring me."

"Of course not." The Witch Queen laughed. "It was your idea, wasn't it? Yours and the little spider. The cursed prince. Let me tell you a story. Once upon a time, there was a king whose seed was weak, so he slew men by the thousands to make himself feel powerful. And when the battles were won and there was no one left to murder, he built a castle and took a wife. But still, no children could he sire. So, as men do, he blamed his wife and cursed her and cast her aside. He took a new wife. Then another. Decades crawled by with no heirs. His fourth wife, however, knew some magics, and she did for him what no other could. She bore him a child. A beautiful dark-haired girl."

"You lie," the princess said, but her words were weak.

"Not to you. Never to you. Now hear me. The king loved his daughter, but feared his wife and her magics, so he cursed his wife the way he had his previous brides. But this queen would accept no such a fate."

"What fate?" the princess asked, rage and fear mingling in her the way only truth can inspire.

"He drank their lives until they were pliable husks of bones and regret. Crones to serve and raise his daughter."

The princess's vision spun. The two women in the mirror warped and wrapped until only one remained. She turned away, and found herself face-to-face with the Witch Queen.

"It can't be," she whispered.

"It can, Zahra. And we can get our revenge."

"But the spider?"

"The spider told you what I instructed. Oh yes, he was a prince once, and he hopes you will betray me and bring him his cauldron."

The Witch Queen motioned to a dark shape in the corner. The cauldron. A hope against death.

"But now that we are united," the Witch Queen went on, "perhaps I'll forget my pact with the spider. Surely, he deserves his jilted lover's curse. We could keep his cauldron, you and I. We could rule together, as we were meant. No king to own us. No men to control us."

On and on the Witch Queen went, speaking of liberty and power and glory, but the princess couldn't accept such a tale of the king. Of her father.

"I wish I had a sword to smite this evil bitch," she whispered.

At her words, her pack grew heavy. She reached in and found the thorn that had pricked her bag so long ago. Only the thorn had grown to the size of a sword.

In a single motion, she drew the sword and plunged it into the Witch Queen's belly. Through gown and flesh and organ and bone it slipped, like a sunbeam through soft clouds.

"It bites!" the Witch Queen cried.

The princess withdrew the sword, noting the streak of blood upon it, and a wind blew through the throne room. The Witch Queen collapsed so that only her brilliant gown remained crumpled on the floor. The princess lifted the gown and found beneath it a pile of dust.

"I am no witch's daughter," she said.

Came a second wind and blew away the dust. In its wake the mirror cracked so that a thousand broken princesses watched each other, glaring and vying for the center of the glass.

The princess traded the remains of her crowning dress for the Witch Queen's brilliant gown—it fit as if it had been made just for her—and with the cauldron in her pack, she left the tower.

The journey home took far less time than she expected, the goblins and the swallowing sands and the stingbuzzes giving the princess wide berth. She arrived at the castle at dawn one morning when the dew was cool and refreshing.

For her, the roses parted.

No one greeted her. No candles were lit. Dust coated the floor. The air was thick and stale. Here and there, skeletons lounged as if they'd died at their posts many years ago, loyal subjects to the end.

The princess continued deeper into the castle to the staircase. Up and up she ran to the throne room, worried too many years had passed in her absence, but there sat the crown atop the glass coffin, the king within, his chest rising and falling softly as if he'd only fallen asleep minutes ago.

"You have returned," the spider said from the crown, its voice so small the princess barely heard it.

"And I have brought you this." She produced the cauldron.

"Quickly then, the Witch Queen's blood. Then, when I am a prince once more, we can marry."

"My father first," the princess said. "As you promised, even before your own curse."

"As promised. Now, the blood."

The princess pulled the cauldron from her pack and set it beside the glass coffin. Next, she drew her sword and spit on the blade, wetting the blood streak, and wiped it into the cauldron. She backed away as the spider scrambled from the crown to the cauldron where it spoke words that made her stomach quease and her head swim.

She kept herself, however, and went to the coffin and slid the glass cover aside. Upon her father's chest, she laid her head. After a time, the king stirred.

"Where am I?" he asked.

The princess sat up and looked upon her father's open eyes for the first time in so many years. Eyes that widened in fear. Then hatred.

"You," he declared, as he tried to rise. "Witch. You have no claim on me."

And the princess—named Zahra by her mother—knew the truth. Of the king's lies. Of the crones. Of the Witch Queen.

With a gentle thrust, she slipped her sword between the king's ribs.

His eyes flashed. Then closed.

"What have you done?" the spider shrieked.

"He was a monster," the princess said.

She brought her foot down upon the spider. There was a cry. A crunch. Silence.

She lifted her foot to find no prince at all. Only a broken arachnid.

"He deserved his fate," she said, though none but the dead remained in the castle to hear.

Slowly, she took the crown and placed it on her brow. It fit. Next, she approached the dais and sank onto the throne. Her throne. For she was queen, and her subjects would love her unbending will.

Shadow's Promise

By Matthew Johnson

Rain poured into the flooded valley. At least a hundred and fifty feet of water covered all but the tallest tree tops. Thunder cracked, echoing through the valley, and lightning split the darkness. White fire scorched Hyman's vision, leaving behind a thin cowl to cover the horror of bodies floating in the rising water. The air tasted metallic, hairs rising across his body and a faint smell of burnt flesh rose from the dead. Lightning struck the bodies, setting them ablaze for a few moments until the water doused them. Hyman had never seen anything like it. Standing on the ledge, a hundred yards from the ground, fifty from the rising water, he knew he had to live. To continue spreading word of the evil sorceries those women used and build the resistance, before it was too late.

Nazglum's whores! Songs were meant for praising the beauty of creation and not destroying it. These Singers were given power from the Lord of Shadows for spreading their legs to spawn darkness across the land. They gave their fractured souls for the wicked gifts that no mortal should wield. Only the Silent Men stood against them, to put an end to their songs and restore balance across Gaia as the Creator intended. Twenty thousand of which were now corpses floating in an unnatural lake.

"What do we do now, Hyman?" Nathanael asked. The rain washed over the warrior's long black hair, matting it to his neck and back of his chainmail. At sixteen name-days, Nathanael was the youngest of the remaining dozen spared the fate of their comrades—they were sent to spy the battle from the ledge and report on the enemy's movement. Fear on Nathanael's face made him appear much younger.

"We climb," Hyman said, looking up at the edge of the mountain. They couldn't go back through the pass. It was choked with bodies and shattered evergrows. Twenty thousand good men, many of whom served with Hyman for many years, killed when the river suddenly diverted and they were unable to escape the onslaught of water. The vegetation had risen to create a giant green bowl, sealing off the valley basin. They had no warning, no chance to escape. Hyman and his men witnessed the evil spells defacing nature, twisting it to their will, from the ridge, but the rain kept on filling the valley, turning it into a lake of the dead.

"Won't we fall?" Nathanael asked.

"Do you want to swim?" Hyman began unbuckling his armor. "Only two ways out of here. Up or down."

"I ain't up for swimming with corpses," Frey said, swiping blonde hair from his face. He gave Hyman a knowing wink and kicked off his boots. "Once in a lifetime is enough for me."

Lightning sizzled into the water, causing more corpses to jolt and smoke. The rest of the men began to strip off their gear, until they stood in sodden tunics and wool breeches. A disparaged looking group hanging their heads, unlike the bawdy men who entered the valley, drunk on the prospect of slaughtering Singer Sympathizers. The bait that seeded the trap was the report of one woman camped against the steep mountainsides. Robin, whispers swept through Silent Men's outpost, the bringer of bad weather and cause of the rain storm. They said she would be an easy capture or kill. No escape for her, the scouts assured. The army of Silent Men quickly reached the Sympathizer's camp, but when they arrived, Robin was nowhere to be seen. She had abandoned her soldiers to be slaughtered at the rocky bluffs. Or so they thought. Watching the action from above, Hyman and his troop of eleven saw the trap unfold. But it was too late. The cursed songs echoed around them, sealing the twenty thousand Silent Men into the valley and drowned them all.

"Take it slow and easy," Hyman said. Water sluiced off the

rock's face. Fingers found holes and he dug in, lifting himself over the precipice, and reached up, feeling for more finger holes. The rock didn't crumble, but it wouldn't be much longer and the water would soak through the porous sandstone. Waiting wasn't an option. It was either climb a hundred yards straight up, or die.

Hyman's arms began to shake and his soaked clothes were a great weight, slowing him down. Halfway to the top, lightning flashed, striking the ledge where they'd stood. Men shouted as the rock exploded. One screamed as he fell, the terrifying sound dwindling the further the man dropped and then silence filled by a distant plunk sounding his watery end. Hyman pressed against the slick rock, eyes squeezed closed. More metallic taste and his bladder let loose, wetting his already soaked breeches.

"Hold on," he shouted, the white tendrils fading from his vision. He spoke more for himself than his men. The vision of his daughter's face, small and as fragile as porcelain, asked, "When will you be back, daddy?" The cluster of freckles surrounding Hyrian's button nose prominent under the midday sun. Her golden hair tied back in simple braids, making her blue eyes seem so huge, like puddles of water turned into bright, clear sky. "Soon," he had told her, but the response was as satisfying as a grain of sugar when one craved sweets.

Hyman's fingers slipped, the nail on his left ring finger tearing away in bloody, hot pain. His left foot lost contact. Water ran over his right hand, down his arm and fell away into the night. He grunted, swinging his left arm up, and for a moment found only slick stone, no finger holes, just smooth, wind polished rock face. Fingers scrambled for anything. His right hand cramped and the slightest shift, marking the long, deep plunge into oblivion.

This was not how he would end. He wouldn't leave Hyrian fatherless, or his wife, Glorian, a widow to weep over an empty grave like the thousands lost below.

Another shout signaled one more man lost his grip and plunged into death's waiting maw. Hyman tried to block out the screams, but they were the cry of a dark spirit foretelling his own doom. Desperately he searched for hold, but couldn't find one. His fingers were numb and he couldn't feel the stone beneath them anymore.

This is it! This is how I die. He cried out his frustration. *A forgotten man in a forgotten land, a—*

To the left, a voice whispered in his ear.

Splayed fingers scrambled along and the stone loosened under his right hand. His left gripped the rock, holding him up as the stone crumbled under his right. He grunted and pulled himself up, right arm slinging overhead and found more finger-holds. Reach and pull. Reach and pull. His life narrowed into the simple actions, when the holes ended, the rock crumbling away, Hyman's existence would end. Tossed into a black, watery grave, like returning to the womb, though more shocking. It wasn't the death he'd imagined, but the imaginations of men were limited by his experiences. This was an experience he wished he'd dreamt rather than face in the wakened world. Reach and pull. Reach and pull, a snail slithering up the garden stonewall. Any moment death could sweep down and crush him. Reach and pull. Reach and—nothing. He glanced up, the rock grazing his cheek, drawing blood.

The sky! A flash of lightning tossed among the clouds and he could almost stretch out a hand and pluck it from the air.

Heart pulsing in his ears, Hyman reached over the jagged edge and, limbs trembling, dragged his body across the flat stone. He lay on his back and laughed. Rain poured across his face, filling his mouth and he drank it. Drank in life.

"Alive! I'm alive!" He let out a loud shout, lost in the crash of thunder. "Dear Creator! I'm alive. Glorian, I'm coming!"

Nazglum's whores couldn't kill him. The Lord of Shadows could shove them up his ass and shit them out sideways. Next time he saw Robin, he would tell her. Right before he cut her throat.

"Help! Hyman!"

He rolled over onto his side. A hand waved over the edge of the rock. More voices joined in..

"Don't know how much longer I can hold on."

"Rock is breaking apart."

"Get the fuck over before I toss you over."

Hyman slid across the wet rock on his belly. The hand dipped and he feared the boy had fallen. Then it shot up again, and Hyman caught hold of the fingers, and then the wrist.

"I got you, Nathanael." Though it felt like his muscles were tearing apart in his arm and shoulder, he began pulling the boy up. The boy was a boulder, the rain making Hyman's grip tenuous and he began to slip. "Climb, boy! Pull for all you damn worth!"

Hyman dug his elbows in and braced against being toppled over the side. He didn't work so damn hard to survive just to be thrown off by some damn kid. Nathanael slipped, dragging Hyman forward, the skin tearing from his forearm. His head dangled over the precipice and he saw the terror in the boy's face. Beneath him were eight other men, all staring up at him, rain washed faces watching and anticipating what will happen next. They leaned away from the dangling boy in case he fell. Beyond them was the dark waters.

"Don't let go," Nathanael said, voice small and shaking.

"Trying, kid." Hyman skidded forward and Nathanael dipped. He saw two ways out of this: drop with the boy, or release him. He thought of Hyrian crying as he left her hugging her mother's leg. What would she think when he didn't come home? That he broke his promise. Hyman's fingers relaxed. "Sorry."

Nathanael let out a chocked cry and closed his eyes.

Hold him, the voice whispered. *Pull him back.*

A renewed vigor washed away the ache in his arms and Hyman gripped the edge of the precipice, shoving as hard as he could, screaming with the effort. Rock crumbled in his hand, but he moved backwards and Nathanael came up with him. Hyman's arm had grown numb, but he grunted and drove his palm into the rock and each shove brought Nathanael closer until the boy was lifted clear of the drop, pulling himself up the rest of the way.

Cheers accompanied the success and more men began to clamber over the side and they lay around like drowned worms, groaning and laughing hysterically. The rain had slowed.

"Look, Hyman," Nathanael pointed at the sky. "The sun is coming out."

"It cannot stay dark forever," Hyman said, closing his eyes and letting the warm rays shine golden through his eyelids. The voice had saved him, helped him save the boy. "Creator smile on us, we walk in His light."

Hyman slept and dreamt of being next to Glorian wrapped up naked in their fur blanket. He was shivering because she always stole it away from him, curled inside except for one bare shoulder poking out. Hyman reached for her, but his hand shook too much. When he woke, his teeth were chattering.

"Get up!" Frey nudged him with his bare toe. Where were his boots? Frey's tunic and breeches clung to his body, like he had gone swimming. Realization that they almost had all gone for one last swim set in and the rock became uncomfortable. "We need to find cover before night and get a fire started. Else we freeze to death."

Hyman rubbed the sleep from his eyes. His body hurt, like he had been stretched and stomped on repeatedly. Bare feet pattered on the cold, wet stone around him

"How are the others?" He cracked his neck.

"We are only ten, but a small number will be easier to move past the Singers and their Sympathizers," Frey said, helping Hyman up. "Most of us are good to walk many leagues, though Gillard sliced the soles of his feet on the climb."

Hyman saw Gillard, a small man, dark featured and built like a wine cask, leaning against two other men. Each step Gillard winced and Hyman let out a sigh. They would have to find somewhere sheltered to leave Gillard.

"He'll slow us down," Frey said, though the meaning beneath was clear.

Hyman shook his head. Carrying the man would be an annoyance, but better to be slow and careful than dead.

"Been more merciful if he'd died in the water." Frey laughed. "We could always toss him over and end his misery."

Hyman snarled and grabbed Frey by his wet tunic.

"Don't ever say that," he said, leaning in close enough to bite the man's lip.

Frey swept his arms down, disengaging Hyman, and took a step back.

"Just a jest." Frey held up his hands. "If we can't laugh in the death's face, when can we?"

"Save your effort for walking or else it's death who laughs at us."

Hyman walked past, slamming his shoulder in Frey as he began the long march from the barren cliffside. He could feel the man's eyes burning into his back. Frey had no family as far as Hyman knew, which meant he could be reckless. Reckless men tended to be dangerous to their companions.

Break his neck before he keeps me from seeing my home.

The rain had turned the dirt into mud. Mud that stuck between his toes, a sensation he usually hated, much like stepping barefoot in dog shit, but the mud soothed the cuts his feet had suffered on the climb. They'd have to bind their feet before they reached drier parts full of stone and hidden debris.

Nathanael slogged up to him. Hyman wanted to tell the kid to get the fuck away. Especially since he didn't want to see the look on his face when Nathanael confronted him about nearly letting him go.

"Do you think those men were left to die by the singers?"

That wasn't the question Hyman expected.

"They were already dead," Hyman said. "Basically, scarecrows set up around the camp fires." The scouts saw Robin walking among them and that was enough to make them shit bricks, hauling tail back to the outpost. Lucky they were part of the dead, or Hyman would have ended them for their impetuous stupidity.

"We almost died to kill dead men." Anger made Nathanael's voice crack.

"Seems as though we killed those men once," Hyman said. "It wasn't about them. It was to capture the woman, Robin. It was her song that has dogged us to the very ends with rain, snow, and blazing heat. She was worth the sacrifice of twenty thousand to save hundreds of thousands."

"But we failed."

"That's what happens in war," Hyman said. "Evil people don't play by the rules."

"I'm going to join up with our eastern brothers," Nathanael said. "They need to know about what happened."

They know. Hyman nodded. *This is our chance of getting out of a war we cannot win. As long as the shadow has those women to do his bidding, we'll always lose.*

Hyman had been fighting this battle for close to a decade and it has gone on much longer. When he was a boy, his father died in a flood caused by Robin. That was one bird Hyman swore to hunt and kill. Revenge burned hot in him, and he signed up for every mission attacking those women, escaping death more times than he wanted to count. He was prepared to give up everything, until he met Glorian. She was a seamstress working with her father and mother, both serving in the Silent Men army, as tanner and cook. Hyman remembered seeing her in the golden light on a scorching hot day, when the plantings had to be delayed because the sowing rains never came—caused by Robin and her Nazglum whores.

Glorian glanced at him from hemming a hole in a pair of black breeches. Hyman had a pair of his own that had a tear up the left side from a fall down a rocky hillside. He also had a pair of broken ribs and a bent nose. Not that he ever counted himself handsome, but then he felt hideous.

"Tavern brawl?" Glorian asked and motioned for him to put his breeches in a pile.

"No," Hyman said, a little annoyed. Rarely did the Silent Men engage in direct combat, unless brawling in the streets or smashing up the Leaky Bucket was their idea of a fight. He had been in two dozen battles, squared off against the Singers in at least half of those, if not more. Was part of the team to kill the one called Finch, a beautiful young woman who used her song to seduce men and break their hearts, literally. She died hard, taking hundreds of lives with her. He told her this story.

"Oh," Glorian said, her cheeks turning read. "I'm sorry to judge you so quickly."

"And harshly," Hyman said. "That means you are either my mother or my wife."

"Neither," Glorian retorted. "I have turned down the advances of men cleverer than you."

"Probably more handsome, too."

She laughed. A pretty sound that made him think of a

breeze rustling leaves in the sowing, rather than the blood and death constantly darkening his moods.

"You said it, not me." She set her sewing down. "Besides, my father has a hole dug behind his shop."

"For what?"

She shrugged. "Just because."

"Is it deep?"

"Very deep."

"It would have to be, because I'm an expert climber." Hyman took a seat in the chair across from her. "There was this tree taller, tallest thing I ever saw. Taller than a mountain, or, at least the mountains in my mind. At the top of the tree, on the branch furthest from the ground, grew a flower. I was a young boy and I liked this pretty girl. She promised me a kiss if I would climb the tree and get her the flower."

"Seems an awful lot of work for a simple kiss," Glorian said.

"You don't know the half of it," Hyman said.

"Go on." She moved closer to Hyman, eyes bright at the prospect of a good story.

"I began to climb this tree, moving from branch to branch like some squirrel after a nut, when I come across a gap between the branches. No matter how high I reached, I couldn't touch it. Down below, looking like a tiny ant on the ground was the girl. Her arms were folded and she shook her head in a way to say I had lost. So, I screwed up my courage and bent my legs. I leapt as high as I could, my fingers barely catching hold of the branch. I though for certain I would lose my grip and fall at any moment, but I held on. My eye still on the flower. I shimmied across the branch and plucked the flower. I forgot one important thing."

"How to get down?"

"Yes! Much easier putting yourself at risk going up, but the getting down part is always much harder. I put the flower in my mouth and shuffled my hands slowly back to the tree trunk. I knew I couldn't drop, since I chanced missing the branch directly below and break my neck before I got that kiss."

He thought Glorian would roll her eyes at that, but she watched him, leaning in.

"I hugged the tree trunk. Like a worm, I inched my way closer to the branch. The trunk got too wide to hold onto and my limbs were slick with sweat. I felt myself begin to slip."

"What did you do?"

"I positioned myself over the branch and let go."

"Weren't you scared?"

"Terrified, but I was bound to fall either way, so I made the choice to do it on my terms. Luckily, I did, because I hit the branch and had enough strength to hold on rather than bounce off. When I got to the bottom, I found the girl waiting. I was about to get my kiss but her father caught me by the scruff and tossed me down an old well. Took me better part of a day to climb out of there as well."

"I don't believe you." Glorian sat up straight, arms crossed. "You're some story singer, making up tales to impress a girl."

"I wish I was," Hyman said. From his pouch he took out an old handkerchief and handed it to Glorian.

Glorian unwrapped it and made a small noise of surprise. In the brown handkerchief was the perfectly pressed white flower. She tried to give it back, but he refused it.

"I never got that kiss from her," he said.

Glorian laughed and Hyman was about to leave, having embarrassed himself enough.

"Wait!" She put a hand on his arm. Before he could ask what she wanted, her lips were pressed against his.

"What if I did make it all up?" he asked when he caught breath.

"Does it matter?" Glorian replied. "You're going to have other ways to prove your story. Just keep climbing and coming back to me."

Hyman had promised and, so far, kept that promise.

The sun was setting, and a chill settled over them. They had scurried down the muddy ridge, a silent band of refugees escaping the slaughter. The men took turns supporting Gilliard as he hopped along on his torn feet, but they would grow tired, especially when the wounds began to seep pus and black vines crept up his legs. Hyman had seen it happen too often. Nathanael stuck close to Hyman while Frey walked off to the edge of the group, scrapping a rock against another and fashioning a primitive knife.

"Wish I knew how to kill one of them singers," Nathanael said, breaking the silence.

"They're women," Hyman said. "Stick a blade in 'em and they bleed just the same as anyone else. The problem lies in getting close enough to one without getting turned inside-out by their song."

"Didn't you kill one?" Eagerness raised the pitch of his voice, nearing the edge of excitement. He knew Hyman was part of the group of Silent Men to kill Finch. Everyone knew the ten men who had survived that expedition. Frey was there as well. Frey did things to Finch that turned Hyman's stomach, things no one spoke about afterwards. Nathanael was like all fresh recruits—he wanted to hear the glory stories while dreaming about making a name for himself.

"I was there," Hyman said, hoping to put off further inquiry.

"What was it like?"

Hyman shrugged. "Killing is killing. Messy business no matter if it's a man, woman, or child."

"Don't lie to the boy," Frey said. He had crept closer and gave a nasty grin. "Killing a Singer is like your first time fucking a woman. Satisfying, but over too soon. You always crave more, sniff out her blood like a hound sniffs a bitch in heat. Sometimes she bites back, but it doesn't stop you from hunting her down and wanting to bend—"

"That's enough," Hyman said. He glared at Frey who grinned even wider, revealing his yellowed teeth.

"Some men just aren't into women as much as others," Frey said and drifted back off to the side of the path.

Hyman thought about telling Nathanael that Frey was wrong, but that would be a lie. Killing a servant of Nazglum had a profound effect on a man. Made him feel closer to the Creator for doing the Creator's work of cleansing the land of such dark perversion. Though, Hyman preferred the death to be subtler, a slit throat like a sacrifice. He hated how Frey defiled the poor woman and how he stood back and allowed him to do it. Had he a chance to do it over, he would kill the woman before Frey got his hands on her.

"Sometimes the horror of it all makes you numb," Hyman once explained to Glorian while he was on his third cup of sour wine. "When one more shovel-full of shit comes your way, well, you were glad it wasn't dumped on you." He wanted to tell this to Nathanael, but the boy was lost in thought, staring off into the distance, and Hyman was too tired for more words.

They made camp in a grove of starfruit. Half of the men plucked the red fruit from the trees while the rest sought out dry brush and wood to burn. Hyman gathered fallen branches big enough to make several lean-tos. His body ached, muscles protesting as he wound the vines around each branch. After the camp was set and fires burned, Hyman stripped out of his wet clothes. He sat in his small clothes by a fire, chewing on starfruit. It wasn't entirely ripe, but hunger demanded his empty stomach be filled.

Eat too much and I'll waste time shitting my guts out on the side of the road instead of marching home. He tossed the pink core with seeds shaped like stars into the fire. It sizzled and caught the flames. He watched drowsily while it turned to ash.

Nathanael came, holding his tunic curled up like he was smuggling something.

"I found these over by the tree," he said, and unfurled his tunic. A dozen whitecapped mushrooms rolled out into his lap. "My mother used to cook these during the sowing."

"I doubt it," Hymen said, tossing the remains of the core of his fruit into the woods.

"She did. I used to help gather them when I was little. 'Snow on top, a good crop,' she would say." Nathanael picked one up and examined it in the fire's light. "'Grey under the cap, will make you crap and die.' This one's black."

"I wouldn't eat it."

"Your loss." He started to put one in his mouth and Hyman knocked it out of his hand. Nathanael glared at him. "What the fuck did you do that for?"

"Saving your life." Hyman pointed at the rest in the boy's

lap. "Those are called Death's Hood. Rub one of the tops and you'll see."

Nathanael ran a thumb over the mushroom cap. The white whipped away like a film, revealing the black crown. He jumped up, spilling the mushrooms out onto the ground and tossing the one in his hand like it had tried to bite him.

"How'd you know?"

"You see all sorts of crazy shit, like the time a man tried to eat one and his eyes grew big, empty as though he stared Death in the face, and he began to vomit out his guts. He was dead in less than a few breaths," Hyman said. "Can't trust anything out here in the wilds. Oh, ah, I would find something to wash my hands off, because that stuff can still get in you and cause you all kinds of hurt."

Nathanael ran off and Hyman chuckled. The boy would be dead in less than a moon if he wasn't here to watch over him. He could hear moaning from one of the lean-tos. Gilliard's back was to him, but Hyman could read the pain in the way his shoulders hunched and his head lay back like Gilliard wanted to scream at the moon. He'd seen men in worse pain in the exact same pose before their leg or foot was amputated. Crouched to the side of Gillard was Amyl, an herbalist, and married to Gillard's sister, Persimona. Amyl held Gillard's hand and said some words of comfort. Then he patted Gillard's face, giving a smile reserved for the grievously-ill, to keep their spirits up—Hyman had seen it too often in camp, and knew who would die hard by the kinds of herbs given to a man.

"Doesn't look good," Amyl said, approaching Hyman. He was dressed in his small clothes as well and raised goose flesh covered his skin. Hyman let Amyl talk. Listening was the best way to comfort a man. "The skin is cut too deep. I can't find any sphagnum moss to preserve the wounds and he's already got an infection. All these fucking trees and not one patch of moss, it's like the shadow knew we would be coming and tore it all down."

"What can be done?"

Amyl rubbed the back of his neck and then shook his head.

"Soon, we'll have to take his feet to keep it from spreading up his legs."

The unspoken problem hung before them. The feet had to come off, but they had no way to do it with Gillard bleeding out.

"Keep him comfortable," Hyman said. "We leave at first light."

"Maybe I'll find something on the way," Amyl said.

"If he can walk," Hyman said.

"He'll walk," Amyl said. "I'll wrap his feet and let him use me as his crutch. Else 'Mona will leave me to rot outside."

They shared a chuckle and Amyl wandered off.

"Try to sleep," Hyman shouted after him.

Amyl waved away his concern. The man would hunt for his herbs until he dropped in the middle of the grove. Hyman got up to check on the rest of his people. They were all huddled close to their fires, chewing on starfruit. He talked to them, offering encouraging words. Most were used to sleeping outside in the cold. Nothing new for seasoned veterans. He avoided Gillard, letting the man sleep. Only one he didn't see was Frey. *Knowing him, he probably set up first watch.* As much as Hyman disliked the man, Frey never shirked his duties as a soldier. Hyman chose another to stay up and watch for Frey, to wake Hyman when Frey returned. Then he returned to his own lean-to, discovering Nathanael fast asleep.

Hyman let him sleep, laying down on the opposite side. The ground was cold and hard, reviving every ache and pain.

Better than being dead.

Despite the discomfort, the weight of sleep was heavier, and he was no longer able to hold it off. His thoughts moved to Hyrian, his porcelain beauty. "Don't call me that, dad," she'd scold, hands on hips and looking up. "I'm tough and can kick your ass." Glorian didn't appreciate the language she learned hanging around soldiers, but he couldn't keep Hyrian away from the training grounds for very long, she'd always show up and watch them spar, spit, and curse. It wasn't much wonder where she picked up the rough tongue. At seven namedays, Hyrian was tougher than most boys and could sling a stone thirty yards to knock an acorn from a branch. She had yet to use her skill to hunt or kill, but it was still impressive. Hyman intended to teach her to use a bow when he got home. She'd soon trade in her dirty-old, rag doll for a quiver of arrows, and move from striking acorns to sticking arrows into strawmen. Glorian wouldn't be pleased, but—

A loud scream jolted him from his sleep. Hyman reached for his sword, to remember everything had been lost. He stood in his small clothes, moon shining through the trees, and grasped the branch used to hold up his lean-to. He wrenched it and the side collapsed. He held it like a club, searching around for the noise.

Weeping sounded off to his right and he saw Amyl outlined in firelight, kneeling before Gillard. Nathanael stood to the side along with several other men. They stared in shock. The only one absent was Frey. A quick glance and he found Frey laying under his lean-to, hands folded on his chest as he watched events from afar.

"What happened?" Hyman asked

"He's dead," Amyl said, though Hyman knew that before he saw the pasty face. He also noticed dried fleck of vomit and bruising around Gillard's neck and jowls. Death's Hood poisoning. The victim vomited up the first bunch, but then strangled to death as his throat swelled shut, drowning him in his own stomach acid.

Hyman reeled on Nathanael.

"Did you give him any?"

Nathanael took a step back, confusion on his face.

"Any what?"

"Mushrooms."

Nathanael shook his head.

"I didn't go anywhere near him."

Hyman glared over at Frey. Frey tipped him a finger salute. It wasn't a confession, but close enough to count. Hyman hefted his branch and marched over to Frey. His longtime war companion didn't move.

"Fucking bastard!" The rest of the words locked up in his throat. He wanted to bash Frey's head in, but doing so without proof would cause only more trouble, possibly a mutiny.

"The Creator brought him solace," Frey said, giving embellished sympathy.

"You murdered him." Hyman's body was shaking, the way it did on the verge of battle. "We could have helped him."

"He was helped," Frey said. "Only it wasn't by my hand."

"Don't you lie."

"Look to your own before you accuse me." Frey stood, all mock sincerity gone and his body tensed. "While you were sleeping and Amyl hunting in the dark, I kept watch."

"The boy was with me," Hyman said.

"Look to your own," Frey repeated, nodding at the turned over lean-to.

Hyman backed away and stalked over to where the boy had almost eaten the Death's Hood mushrooms. There wasn't a single one left, but that didn't mean the boy didn't sweep them away out of fear of accidently poisoning himself. The ground looked undisturbed. Even if they were here, he could have gotten more where he found the first.

"Was it him?" Amyl asked, motioning to Frey who was settling back into his lean-to. "If it was, I want the bastard's head to take back to Mona."

"I don't know," Hyman said. "Was there any growing by him, any he could have reached out and eaten unaware?"

"You think I'd leave my wife's brother where he could accidently kill himself?" Anger heated Amyl's voice. "Do you think I'm that foolish or careless?"

"No." *But weariness and worry make us overlook many dangers.*

"Do we beat it out of him?"

"We wait," Hyman said. "Perhaps someone else gave it to him thinking it would do some good."

"Who?"

Hyman nodded to Nathanael. The boy stared at the corpse.

"Might have been an accident," Hyman said. In his gut he knew this was planned. But as to which one did it, there was no clear answer. "I'm going to keep watch. I'll take the boy and see if he confesses."

"It doesn't make sense," Amyl said, close to tears.

"Nothing out here ever does," Hyman said and patted Amyl on the shoulder. "I'll find out what the boy knows and deliver the consequences."

Amyl stared off into the night, a hard expression, the kind a man gets before killing, softened and he sighed.

"I'll get a few others to help me dig up some stone. I won't leave him for the beasts to gnaw on." Hyman watched Amyl return to his brother by marriage and ask for help. Several men followed him and they laid Gillard out, forming a carrion for him. Nathanael was one.

Hyman dressed, though his cloths were still damp.

"Come with me, Nathanael."

"Where are we going?" Nathanael dropped a rock on the growing pile.

"It's our turn to keep watch. Get dressed."

"I want to help."

"You will be," Hyman said. "Let's go."

They moved away from the noise in the camp. Nathanael was sullen, like he expected to get a lecture. Hyman wasn't the lecturing type. Actions spoke louder than words. From what he saw of Nathanael, the boy was loyal. Hyman wanted a son and Nathanael was the closest he got.

"I should have left you at camp," Hyman said.

Nathanael's shoulders slumped.

"Then I would be left wondering if you died."

"I would have got word to you," Hyman said, "but here we are. You and I. The Creator put us in this spot for a reason. Up to us to make it work. Now, I don't know what happened to the mushrooms—"

"It wasn't me," Nathanael said. "I would never hurt one of our guys. Not Gilliard. He was nice to me. Gave me his extra ration of pudding, once."

"I'm not blaming you."

"Sounds like you are."

Hyman stopped and turned to Nathanael.

"You didn't feed Gilliard the Death's Hood?" He searched the boy's face for a lie.

Nathanael stared him in the eye and said, "No."

"That's all I need." He patted Nathanael and let him go. They walked further on and found a fallen tree to sit on.

"What happened to Gillard would have happened to me if

I ate those?" Nathanael asked. "You saved my life, again. You're right. I should've stayed back at camp. I'm more trouble than I'm worth."

"We all learn lessons in this life," Hyman said, repeating what his father had told him. "It's what we do next that's important."

When dawn broke, they spoke words for Gillard, ate a small meal of starfruit, and returned to their journey. Nine remained. Nine out of twenty thousand men. Hyman had trouble wrapping his head around that number. That would be twenty thousand or more grieving widows, mothers, children. All because of those women. They were the pox marks on the beauty of creation. Hyman knew they wanted to cast the land in shadow and bring Nazglum back to fuck up everything. There wasn't a damn thing he could do about it.

Hyman followed Amyl's advice. He mixed a plaster of mud and leaves and vines, slathering it on the soles of his feet. The impact of was less—he couldn't feel the sharp stones unless they were larger than his toes. What he wouldn't give for a nice pair of boots. He'd trade his home for some worn leather and a skin full of wine. Three more sunrises, he figured, and he would be home free. Let everyone else go back to fighting; he had a wife to fuck and a daughter to teach how to shoot a bow, alternating between the two. Everything else could go to the shadow for all he cared.

"How'd they do it?" Nathanael asked.

Not now, kid. Hyman held back a groan.

"How'd they bend those trees and flood the valley?" Nathanael was not one to sit on his questions. He always had more questions than there were answers Hyman could give. He chirped them out like a bird waiting to be fed by its mother.

"Their song," Hyman said. It was no different than the answers they gave on day one of training. 'If you're close enough to hear the song, then you're gone.'

"I sing and it doesn't bend trees."

"It moves my hands to my ears," Timonen said, mimicking the action. Timonen wasn't much older than Nathanael, but had

spent more time in the field. He joined their group not long after
the death of Finch, drawn to them the same reason moths were
to flames: because they burned the brightest.

"Stop fooling," Nathanael said. "Did anyone ever wonder
how the songs work?"

"No," Hyman replied, hoping to end the conversation.

"Why does it matter?" Timonen asked. "Our duty is to
silence them, you know, like our name means. Silent Men."

"I thought it was to keep you fools quiet," Frey said, coming
up from the side. "Especially since we're being followed."

"It matters," Nathanael went on, ignoring Frey and earning
a disapproving frown. "If we can disrupt the harmony, we can
find a way to counteract it."

"Followed by who?" Hyman looked back. They were going
down hill and could see nothing but the switch backs and rocks
they had passed.

"Not who," Frey said and pointed at his ears.

"We don't know if their ability comes from the words or—
Ouch!" Nathanael rubbed the arm where Hyman punched him.

Hyman held up a hand and they stopped. At first, he heard
only the wind blowing through the yellowed rag-grass. He
looked at Frey and Frey nodded. The sound was there, faint as
parchment rustling over a candle flame. Then he saw the shadow
and another. Over them flew two carrion eaters. Ugly birds that
looked like they had their heads bashed in from smashing into
a tree or three, their pale underbellies made them difficult to
spot unless you were looking directly at them, or their shadow
cast on you. If you saw the shadow, then it was too late to run.
Carrion eaters were not dangerous—it's what they trailed that
got them their meal that worried Hyman.

"Get ready to run," Hyman said.

"Will it do us any good?" Frey asked, his face going white to
match the carrion eater's underbelly.

"Some of us," Hyman said.

A faint cough sound beyond a rock outcropping, almost
like a child with a cold, except this was a creature with teeth
and claws that would tear out your intestines. Hyman's heart
raced as he scanned the lower rock outcroppings. He couldn't

see anything, but that didn't mean the ridge cats weren't lurking beyond them. Bold bastards that didn't care how much noise they made once they were in killing distance. Seldom did they hunt in more than pairs, or attack large parties of men. This felt like one of those exceptions because every-shitty-thing else was happening to them.

Traditional reactions to large cats was to stand tall, arms out and yelling to show you were bigger than they were. Hyman watched men die trying such maneuvers on ridge cats. They say not to run because you act like prey, but the truth was, you were prey running or standing still. Hyman quickened his pace, and he heard men grunt behind him trying to keep up. He couldn't out run, out climb, or out hide the ridge cat, no, he just had to be faster than the man they eviscerated. Hyman was half way to the bottom when the first screams began. The urge to stop and look back was strong, like the story of the man who looked back as Nazglum sucked the souls from the living and ended up the last victim before the Void was sealed.

Another scream and he stumbled, nearly teetering over the edge of a large drop. Nathanael caught him around the waist and kept him from going over.

"I got you," Nathanael said and yanked him back onto the path. The grade was steep, and Hyman slipped, skidding down on his heels and landing on his ass a few times. The screams didn't stop at two, but increased to three. Three of his men fallen victims to the fucking cats. He heard that sometimes they killed one and moved on, for the sport, before going back and feeding. He hoped this wasn't one of those occasions. To the left was an open meadow and he could run far enough where the cats would tire ad leave them for their meal. He took a step in that direction and stopped.

Go right, the voice from the mountainside said. When he looked in that direction, he caught a shape of a figure moving beneath a tall tree. He blinked and the figure was gone. Another scream broke his surprise and he began to sprint for the tree.

"Where are you going?" Nathanael stopped at the intersecting paths. "They can climb."

Hyman ignored him. The words of wife rung in his ears. *Keep climbing. Come back to me.* Hyman paused, glanced over his shoulder and witnessed three more of his men sprinting his direction. Behind them was a ridge cat, big as a small horse. Its orange face speckled red and it flowed through the grass like water in a river.

Hyman grabbed the lowest branch and pulled himself up. One branch, two, three and he felt the tree shake. Shouts and curses below drove him up higher. He found a solid branch and clung to it, drawing his legs up. A white flower bloomed with a red center. Hyman plucked it and stuck it in his shirt, because it seemed important, like a talisman of sorts. A heavy cough drew his attention back to the base of the tree. Nathanael followed by Fey were right beneath him.

"Get the fuck off me!" Amyl kicked at the cat's paw that had a claw caught in the side of his leg. There came a tearing noise and Amyl screeched. For a moment, it appeared he was going to slip, but Amyl recovered his grip and pulled up out of the ridge cat's reach.

Hyman looked around for anything to throw. He broke off thin sappers and tossed them, hoping to distract the cat. It stood on its back legs and leapt up onto the lower branch.

"Told you they could climb," Nathanael said. "What do we do now?"

Go higher. The same voice, the one of the cloaked-figure, he figured. It had served him well to this point.

"We go higher."

Hyman gripped the next branch up and pulled. He climbed until the branches became too thin to hold him. *Don't look down.* He kept waiting for the tell-tale scream that the cat caught his prey. None came. Hyman risked a look down, because there was no were else for him to go. Nathanael made it to a branch on the left and Frey below him.

"Amyl, you doing alright?"

No response. The ridge cat wasn't in view either.

"Amyl?"

"Here," came a faint, pain-filled response.

"Can you see the pussy cat?" Frey asked

"I think… it's gone." Amyl let out a cry. "My leg, my fucking leg! Nearly pulled it off."

"How bad is it?" Hyman asked.

"Bad," Amyl said. "I won't know until we can get back down where I can look better. It hurts like Nazglum is probing it with his forked tongue."

"Did you see if any of the others got away?" Nathanael asked.

"I was too busy running my own ass off to worry about any one else's," Frey replied.

"Timonen went the other way," Amyl said. "He ran to the meadow, like he was trying to draw the bastard away."

"It didn't work," Hyman said.

Amyl grunted.

"I hope he got away."

At least one of us will.

"What's the plan, now?" Frey asked.

"You tell me," Hyman grumbled. "Seems like everything I say almost gets us killed."

"We're alive because of you," Nathanael said. "You'll help us get back to the Silent Men. Then we can take our revenge on those bitches."

Frey began to laugh. The kind that was near hysterics. Close to breaking after surviving so many times when friends had died. Hyman was close to cracking, himself, but the thought of Glorian kept him glued together.

"That's the spirit kid," Frey said. Don't let several thousand dead men keep you from fighting back. While you are planning big, why don't you grow us some wings and fly us out of here."

"Shut the fuck up," Nathanael said. "Grow a pair of balls and skin the cat."

"I would take yours, but they haven't dropped yet."

"Shut your yaps, the both of you," Hyman said. *Come back to me.* "I'm going to climb down and see if it's still there."

"Let me," Amyl said, and groaned.

"Stay there," Hyman said and began dropping down to the lower branches. "Try not to fall, if you can."

"No promises," Amyl said.

The branch where Amyl sat had a large red spot and his torn breeches continued to drip. When Hyman got close, he saw

Amyl's face was pale. He wavered on the branch, like he'd been drinking and gave a weak smile.

"How are you holding up?" Hyman asked.

"I need to get down before I fall down." The drop was close to ten yards, enough to break bones if not outright kill Amyl. "I can't wait much longer. Damn cat almost nicked the sweet spot in my leg and then you would all be stuck while it feasted on me."

"Let me take a look around and then I'll come back for you."

Amyl nodded.

Hyman reached the lowest branch and waited. A breeze rustled the grass, but he heard no other sound. *They won't be heard unless it wants to. Creator, bless me, what am I doing?* He jumped down and made a widening circle, keeping the tree at the center. At the slightest noise he would scurry back up the trunk like squirrel escaping, well, a cat. He walked to the edge of the hill, smelling the air. Dry grass and the faint smell of blood. Five more companions were dead, maybe even six. Was that their blood he smelled in the breeze? Hyman returned back to the tree.

"It's safe," he said. He noticed the blood on the ground from Amyl, but it seemed too much. There was a boot print, one too small for his foot. The tracks went off to the east and Hymen followed them until they disappeared. *Mysterious shadow person? But he was here before we climbed the tree.* Of course, Hyman was a bit distracted, so the Shadow figure could have driven off the ridge cat. Lured it way, maybe.

"A little help," Amyl called from the tree, snapping Hyman's attention back.

"Where did you go?" Hyman asked he empty field, not getting any response, or expecting one, and then returned to the tree to help Amyl.

Going down took longer than going up. Twice Amyl almost slipped on his own blood and would have toppled off if not for Hyman. Amyl stripped off his breeches, hissing at the pain. Four gouges flayed the skin. They found some moss growing on the tree and, following Amyl's instruction, used it to pack the wound. Hyman tore the legging off and wrapped the wound.

Picking up a fallen branch, he broke it, giving to Amyl to use as a crutch.

"Don't let what happened to Gillard be my fate," he whispered to Hyman. "Otherwise 'Mona would kill me twice." Then he smiled, raising his voice. "It's only a scratch. I'll live."

Frey and Nathanael looked at him, neither saying a word.

"We'll get you home," Hyman said, "I'll do my damnedest to get you there."

They found Timonen, or what remained of him, less than ten yards into the meadow. Black flies buzzed around the red remains of the corpse, broken bones sticking out of torn flesh. No one said anything. Nathanael made it a couple of steps before vomiting. Hyman felt numb. In the end, they would all end up lumps of flesh with flies buzzing around.

"Explains where the ridge cat got off to," Frey said and began whetting his stone into a sharper point.

Amyl kept up with the three of them as best he could. The meadow was mostly flat, but the grass was high and hidden stones tripped him up. The herbalist didn't complain. The only one who did was Nathanael who groaned he was hungry.

"Plenty of grass to eat," Frey responded.

They found a clearing by a small brook. Amyl dropped next to it and began to drink.

"Is it safe?" Hyman asked.

"Safer than dying of dehydration," Amyl said, water dripping from his chin.

They all drank. Hyman unwrapped Amyl's wound. It had a slight, putrid odor. Like meat that had soured. The wound was still wet and runny. Hyman washed the rags off in the stream and then wrapped them around Amyl's leg.

"Too much walking," Amyl said. "Probably won't heal right until I am home in front of a warm fire."

"We'll get you there," Hyman said.

They slept out in the open, thirst sated, but stomachs rumbling. There was no food or anything edible. Huddled together against the cold, Hyman felt warmth pour from Amyl and the herbalist began to sweat, though he shivered, teeth chattering.

Hyman didn't sleep at all, listening to the snores and grumbles. *Probably won't sleep again until I get home.*

The next day was warmer. They followed the brook until it twisted west. They took another drink, knowing it could be their last for several days. Hyman guessed two more long slogs, unless something else slowed them.

That something else was Amyl. He fell a few times and Hyman helped him along. The heat from his skin was like standing next to a small fire. The smell from his leg wasn't any better.

"I think I've reached the end of my journey," Amyl said.

"Not yet," Hyman grunted, supporting his friend. "Mona is waiting for you, remember."

"Yeah. Don't want to disappoint her," Amyl said and gave a weak chuckle.

"No, then she will want to kill me."

Another moon rose, another day without food and water. Nathanael withdrew into himself, twisting the grass around in his fingers while Frey continued to scrape the stone against the other. Amyl slept fitfully, mumbling a name.

"Have you lost anyone close to you in the war?" Nathanael asked.

"My father," Hyman said, rubbing his sore calves. "Friends."

"What about you, Frey?"

"No one worth shedding a tear over," Frey said. "We all die in the end. What we do to fill up the time in-between, that's important. Crying over the dead won't bring them back."

"Well, both of my parents and a brother died last season," Nathanael said and tossed aside his piece of grass. "I cried, I'm not ashamed to say, enough to fill the moon and then some. Why I decided to do something about it by joining the silent men."

"No shame in crying," Hyman said. "It only proves you're human."

"I don't want to bring shame to them by dying before I kill the soldiers who attacked my village."

"Killing isn't all it's cracked up to be," Hyman said. "Like Frey said, nothing can bring them back. Taking another man's, or woman's, life doesn't fill the empty hole left by your loved ones."

"It sure does feel good trying," Frey said. "Almost as good as fucking a woman."

"So you said," Nathanael said.

"I stand by it, kid." Frey winked and set his sharpened stone aside. He lay down, arms crossed under his head. "After you've experienced both, let me know. Then we can talk about man stuff. Until then, I'm going to get some sleep."

Hyman planned on staying up again, to watch over Amyl. He got to thinking about Glorian. He could almost hear her voice singing their daughter to sleep. An old song, one his mother used to sing, about mountains floating in the clouds and cities made of gold that shimmered in the sun. The Creator watching over them, fatherly hands gathering them up and carrying them to the city in the mountains floating in the sky. Light and peaceful, to lay down by cool waters and eat at a bountiful table. Hyman could almost taste it in her words.

"That was beautiful," he whispered, wrapping his arms around her waist and kissing the back of her neck.

Glorian moaned, lacing her fingers through his.

"It's a sad song," she said.

"How?"

"It is the place my mother said where our souls go when we die," Glorian said. "I don't want to go anywhere without my loves."

"Well," Hyman said, and held her tightly against him. "I won't let you die. We'll live forever."

"How will you do that?"

"I'll find a way," Hyman said, leading her to their bed, "I will climb the tallest mountain for you."

Then he woke up. The first light broke through the gray clouds. Amyl had stopped mumbling.

"You ready for me to—" Hyman froze, staring at the bloody pulp where Amyl's face had once been. Next to the smashed head, covered in dried gore and bits of hair was a large stone. "Son-of-a-bitch!"

Hyman jumped to his feet, head swiveling from Nathanael to Frey. They were starting to wake, or pretend to at least.

"Who the fuck did this?" Hyman shouted, voice raspy and throat burning like he swallowed a sword.

"Oh shit!" Nathanael shouted and scuttled away. "Is he—"

"Sure looks dead to me," Frey said, stretching. "Head all smashed in, I guess we can rule out suicide. I think there's an easier way to kill a man than bash his face in with a rock, kid. Got to be subtler, like with the mushrooms. That was a nice touch."

"Fuck you! It wasn't me!" Nathanael wobbled to his feet. "I'm not a murderer or rapist like some."

"Watch your tongue, kid, else I'll remove it so you can see it squirm around in the dirt." Frey pointed his makeshift blade at Nathanael. "I sure as hell didn't kill him. Was sleeping here the whole night. See my mark in the grass?"

"You're always going on about being slowed and how its better to die than be a burden," Nathanael said.

"Yeah, but not like that," Frey said. "That's messy."

"Stop! Both of you!" Hyman squeezed his fingers into his eyes. A heavy pain was setting up shop and he couldn't stand any more noise. "One of you did it, and I know one has more reason than the other."

Frey narrowed his eyes. "What are you saying?"

"That you killed Gillard and Amyl," Hyman said.

"Why don't you include Timonen and the others," Frey said. "While we're at it, say I called down the storms and ridge cats to kill everyone. I'm fucking Nazglum in disguise!"

"You could never abide weakness," Hyman said. "Why you hurt the woman Finch before you killed her. She made you feel small, weak, and you wanted to take that back from her, from everyone who got in your way."

"Why didn't I kill you? Smash your head in while you slept?"

"I don't know," Hyman said, tossing his arms up. "Maybe I'm your witness to shit, like some village storyteller."

"Yeah, well, the boy gets to witness me kicking the shit out of you."

Frey moved quick for a man who just woke up. He dropped his stone-crafted blade, instead throwing a fist aimed at Hyman's ribs. Hyman twisted away, grabbing at Frey's arm. He missed and Frey kicked him above the knee cap. Pain ran though him like a snake coiling his leg. Frey was on him, sweeping an overhead blow that glanced off Hyman's temple, striking his collar bone. Hyman caught the ground and rolled away from another blow. Hyman kicked out, connecting a glancing strike. Frey caught his leg and dragged him closer. Then he dropped to his knees, pinning Hyman's arms beneath his knees. Fingers wrapped around Hyman's throat. Hot, stinking breath flooded Hyman's face for a moment, and then cut off his breath.

"I didn't kill them," Frey said, fingers squeezing Hyman's throat. They tightened and then the pressure relinquished. Hyman gulped in air, hot in his bruised throat. "I'm not a murderer. I only kill those bitches. They took everything from me. Every—"

Frey made a strangled noise and blood splattered Hyman's face. Eyes widened, his hands left Hyman's throat and reached behind. Nathanael stood there, arm extended, twisting the stone through the back of neck. Frey tried to turn, but Nathanael held him in place, like working a marionette. More blood spilled from Frey's lips, bubbling as he took his last gasps of air. Then he fell over, freeing Hyman.

Nathanael held the stone-knife, blood dripping from it. He stared at it, his face reverting to a small boy, who seemed surprised he knocked over his wooden blocks. He was distant, almost calculating, weighing other emotions and allowing nothing except surprise to show.

"Nathanael," Hyman said the name quietly. The boy's eyes shifted to him and he held up the stone knife. Hyman tensed to move, in case the boy decided to lunge at him. "Set it down, Nathanael."

Nathanael seemed to consider the knife.

"Drop it," Hyman said, using more force.

Nathanael nodded and bent, setting the stone knife in the grass.

"Back away."

"I didn't mean to," Nathanael said, stepping back. "He was…I tried to…"

Hyman relaxed a little, his heart still racing over the series of violent events. He sat up and moved slowly, picking up the stone knife. It was still tacky, covered in Frey's blood. *Does this mean he killed Amyl and Gillard?* Frey wanted Hyman to know he didn't kill the men, then that left Nathanael. *The boy acts like he never killed.* Though, it could be an act.

"Is he dead?" Nathanael asked, reaching out to Frey, but not moving any closer.

"Yes," Hyman said and whipped the knife across the grass, cleaning way as much of the gore as he could. "You sent him to the Creator's embrace."

Nathanael broke down and cried.

Hyman let him, walking away from two more dead companions. Two of twenty thousand remaining. The last leaves yet to fall.

Hyman still hadn't decided who he trusted: the boy or Frey? With the one dead and the other his last travel companion, Hyman decided he wouldn't take his eye off the boy until they got back home. Then the boy could go back to the Silent Men and Hyman would put all of this death and murder behind him. The meadow changed into more hills and the hills became a valley. They walked it in silence, stopping to forge berries and other fruit, some nuts that were hard to break open until Hyman used the stone knife. At night, he remained awake, holding the knife in his lap, watching the boy. Nathanael moaned and shifted restlessly in his sleep. He thrashed and kicked, crying out a name Hyman didn't catch in the boy's frightening shriek.

Hyman watched the boy wrestle with his demons.

The weight of the conscience is heavier at night.

One night he thought he heard the ripple of wind through a cloak. When he looked up, a shadow moved beneath the moonlight. It made no sound and kept a distance. A figment of his sleep deprived mind. Such omens were those of death, but Hyman believed he had seen enough death and this was the afterbirth still clinging to him.

On their last morning before they would cross the river and enter his village fields, Nathanael spoke.

"I have nowhere to go?"

"Back to the Silent Men," Hyman said.

"And tell them what?"

"You are the lone survivor of the flooded valley." Hyman walked on so the boy couldn't respond. All he wanted was to hold Glorian, the feel of her substance against him. Everything else could burn.

They crossed the bridge over the river as dusk settled in. A renewed vigor lightened his step and he walked faster. Nathanael complained about not being able to keep up. Hyman was close to home, he could almost taste the honeysuckle growing against his home. Inside, Glorian and Hyrian would be asleep. He'd wake Glorian up first, and then long after, Hyrian. They would eat an early breakfast and spend time together, doing nothing for as long as he could stand it.

After I have a soak in hot water.

It was a nice fantasy that ended when he reached the edges of the fields and saw smoke rising from houses. At a distance, the smoke appeared to be from chimneys, though the night was warm. As he got closer, he saw the fields were churned up and the homes that should have filled the edges were smoking ruins.

"Blessed Creator," Hyman said.

"What happened here?" Nathanael asked.

Hyman drew the stone knife. His heart sank into his gut. Not a single home remained intact. He sprinted through the fields, sharp stones biting into his heels. He ignored the pain, running for his house.

"Glorian!"

His own voice echoed back, mocking him by how shrill it sounded.

"No, no, no!"

Hyman fell to his knees in front of the charred remains where his house once stood. He crawled across the blackened grass, over the ash, cold touch, though he would have run through it even if it meant melting away his flesh.

Keep climbing. Come back to me, Glorian's voice so strong, so clear. He had never felt lower in his life, like he had fallen from the tree and kept falling.

Their bodies were under a collapsed piece of roof, burnt beyond recognition. The flesh had melted off, the porcelain skin, button nose and freckles gone. A shade in his memory. He held the small skeletal remains of his daughter, her hand fused against her mother's. In the instant before the fire consumed them, they must have reached out for comfort.

The voice led me here. Brought me home. Why are they dead?

"It doesn't make sense." Hyman felt his chest cinch and sobbed.

He laid Hyrain beside her mother and took out the stone knife. The edge was sharp against the inside of his wrist. A cool breeze blew ashes around him. Hyman felt a presence. The stench of rotting flesh wrapped putrid hands over his nose and mouth. Death had found him. The knife trembled and he imagined drawing it down the length of his arm, releasing his blood to the thirsty ask.

"You don't have to do that," the voice said, old and full of power, "to be united again."

The voice that guided him away from a horrific demise, to bring him home to witness the destruction of everything he held dear.

"Leave me the fuck alone and let me die in peace." Blood beaded around the tip of the stone knife

"A life you may have from the ashes," the Shadow figure said.

Hyman lifted the knife from his skin.

"Are you saying I could have them back?" His heart quickened and he turned to the figure looming over him. Grey, grave cowl was tilted down, but any face was lost in the dark beyond. The corpse stench was strong as the figure exhaled a single word.

"One."

Hyman's shoulder slumped. One. A single piece of his shattered being returned, but not whole.

"Do I get to choose."

"No."

He shivered as the cold knowledge sank into his bones. It felt wrong, tearing apart the natural order as designed by the

Creator. Life begat life and what was dead stayed dead. *Climb. Come back to me.*

"Did you do this to them?" Hyman's muscles tensed waiting for the response. He would drive the stone through the front of the cowl, damn the consequence.

"No."

"But you killed Gilliard and Amyl."

"Yes."

"Why?"

The Shadow figure gave no response. It seemed evident to Hyman. The others died to bring him home. A trail of blood and corpses. He even guessed the price the Shadow figure would ask in return for either his wife and his daughter, but he asked it anyway.

"What do you want?"

"Blood for blood, flesh for flesh."

A trade. One life for another.

"Hyman!" Nathanael shouted from a distance.

The boy was like a son. A son he could let live. Allow the natural course to continue unimpeded. Glorian dead. Hyrian dead. Nathanael alive until he wasn't. Easy to let it continue, but he had given up too much, climbed to high too just let it all go in ashes.

"Here," Hyman replied, his throat dry and sore. "Over here."

He could sense the Shadow's approval. Footsteps approached and stopped, followed by a sharp hiss.

"Blessed Creator," Nathanael said. "What happened?"

"The Singers." He didn't know if it was them, but it sounded right.

The Shadow figure remained silent and Nathanael acted as though he couldn't see it. *Maybe it's all a mad dream.* Hyman gripped the stone knife tighter, dream or not, he would see it to its conclusion.

"I'm so sorry, Hyman." Nathanael approached, standing beside him and placing a hand on his shoulder. "We will get back at them. You and me, taking on those Nazglum whores."

"Thank you, Nathanael." Hyman gripped the boy's hand, like he needed the comfort. "You were always like a son."

The boy smiled.

Let him die in joy. I can at least give him that much.

"I know you didn't harm those men," Hyman said. "You were loyal to the end. I am proud of all you did."

He wrapped an arm around the Nathanael's neck, bringing him in closer for an embrace. *Let go. Let him live. No! Climb!* Hyman plunged the stone knife into Nathanael's gut. He twisted it, tearing a wide gap. The boy grunted and pulled away. He looked down at the blood gushing through the hole in his tunic. Then he looked up at Hyman, and let out a horrific scream.

Hyman rose from the ashes and approached Nathanael. The boy tried to back away, doubling over in pain as he clutched his stomach. Hyman looked to the Shadow who gave him a curt nod, then pointed at the ashes. Hyman grabbed the trembling boy by the back of his head.

"It didn't have to be this way," Nathanael said.

"I know." Hyman drew the jagged edge of the stone knife across the boy's throat, holding him his body relaxed and dragged him to the ruins. He left him to bleed out.

"Good," the Shadow figure said and dropped his hood.

Hyman turned away. He couldn't witness what came next. The harsh words sounded like nails scraping bone and tearing off meat. The air turned foul and hot. Hyman walked away, sitting on the cold ground and stared at the moon. He wanted both, but would only get one. He tried not to think about it. About being disappointed at whoever returned, because he'd always be missing a piece of himself. Burnt away. Turned to ash.

I will not regret this. I climbed the tallest tree, scaled the largest mountain, and crawled from the deepest pit.

The night went silent. Hyman felt the presence behind him.

"It is done," the Shadow figure said.

"Daddy." The voice was small and lacked intonation.

"Yes, my love," Hyman said, turning and holding out his arms for Hyrain, "daddy is home."

What stepped into his embrace was not his daughter, though it wore her flesh. A cracked porcelain doll with lifeless eyes. She was his and he was hers. He would love her all the same.

"Daddy is home."

CITY OF GOD

BY RICHARD NELL

I read your letter, brother, though to be honest I wish I hadn't. At first I just drank and stared at it for hours and thought of old killing days I'd rather not remember, back when I had a few more bones and fingers.

Now I've waited, and maybe it was already too late to help your girl. I'm sorry, brother, I didn't know why you'd written. I don't know anything about near-grown women but if she's been taken here in this god-forsaken city then I won't lie and say it's alright. It might not be. I doubt it is.

And I never was a fuckin' war hero. I swear to God I'd better not read that again, even from you. The army ain't given me a thing except pain, a limp and a wooden medal, and I'll be damned if I'll hear any praise. But you're right—the old Fulvi, the man I used to be, he would have tried. You were always a good man, brother, and I'll help you. But don't call it honor.

You don't know what it's like in this city. Things got worse after the war. You can't live here now without being corrupted and befouled by it. Better to live in the country and take a family like you did. Better to live clean and away from it all.

To do what needs to be done I'll have to go places and see people you'd scrape off your boot with a stick, and they might drag me down before I'm done. I may fail. So I'm writing it down for you so at least you'll know what happened. Nightly reports, sir, as it happened! Just like old times.

Except this time instead of plunder and town-names and all

the boys buried or burned, I'll tell you what I'm up to, where I've looked. And if worse comes to worst when you find this at least you'll know what I tried, and how bad it is. You'll know Fulvi the turncoat, Fulvi the deserter, and whatever else he is, is still a fuckin' man of his word, at least when it counts.

Day One: Night report

I'm too old for this shit, brother. My hands are still trembling. My feet ache and my back is killing me and frankly I didn't walk a quarter as far as a standard march. But since I'm writing this it means I'm not dead, so that's a start.

First I go to Mogul town. I stroll through the cheapest, sleaziest blocks till I find what I need. It's cold, dark and dangerous so I wear an old, ratty army cuirass under my rattier wool coat, and I stuff all the spaces with knives.

Street-walking whores tell me to go bugger myself for all the disgusting filth I ask for, but eventually one gives a name.

"I don't do that, honey," she says. "You want to talk to Lip down at The Corner. And tell 'em I sent ya, yeah?"

She wouldn't ask for the name-drop if she knew my plan.

'The Corner' looks as good as an army shit hole, and it smells worse. I breeze past the stupid slips who pass for bouncers in this town, past the twelve year old girls in outfits that'd make my ex-wife blush, past the three old men who paw at the girls' chests as if there's anything there. I find 'Lip' behind the bar. I say hello.

"*Fuck*, man. What was that for?"

I knock his filthy ass off his filthier chair to set the tone. To me he looks like a rat that swallowed an orange, and maybe a rotten one judging by his breath. If you ever need to find him—he's got that squinty-eyed, pug nosed face that begs for a fist. His hair is greasy straw that sticks out and flops down his scalp to make spots on oily skin.

"Tell me where to find a depraved," I ask him. "I don't care who."

'Depraved' are what they call the men in this town who cater to sickening appetites. Yes, brother, they have names for men like that here.

The kid gets a look like an army camper stealing supplies—the kind of 'holy shit' look that condemns a man quicker than crumbs in his beard.

"I'm just a bartender, I dunno anything."

I crack his shin.

The old perverts and their pre-teen girls scatter at the sound like roaches in light. The boys acting like men up front come in to earn their pay, but they're all muscle and no brains. They see an old guy with a limp and dirty clothes and they put their hands on me like I'll just melt.

But I steal a little time. It's been years and never much at once since the war, and the magic damn near rips my old joints. But God brother, it still feels good. I break one tough's jaw, the other's nose, and let 'em lie there pretending to be out cold. I scoop 'Lip' off the slimy floor and beat the truth out, but I don't get my answer.

"Please, I dunno shit. I dunno who you are, but you can't hurt me like they can. They torture kids for *fun!*"

I work on 'em a little but Lip eventually cries and pisses himself, and I walk away. Cleaning up this city isn't my job, and God help the poor bastard whose job it is. There's other ways, I know, other dark places these 'depraved' lurk for victims. And sorry, brother, but that's what your girl maybe is.

Men and even women here snatch country girls like your Roxxy and sell 'em to the highest bidder. Sometimes it's at the auctions and it's just slavery, or if you're lucky more like servitude and in a year or so they work their debt off. But it can be worse, brother, much worse. So I start at the bottom.

Before he breaks down Lip at least tells me if a man pays up with the right people he can grab bums off the street, or even poor folk from their beds. He tells me the usual haunts, the cheapest neighborhoods, though I'd already guessed where. Unless you have protection in this town, your life's not worth a damn.

I leave 'The Corner' and go downhill. In the holy city your trek to hell is almost literal. The lower down you go, the more muck you'll find, the more misery spreads like disease and festers in deep, sunken places. I ignore the beggars and whores. I flash a knife at the thieves just to let 'em know 'Yeah, I see you, kid', and 'Yeah, I'll kill you.' God knows I've done worse.

I smell the rot that stinks up every street, pollutes every nose till otherwise healthy folk tear at their faces to block it out. It's like being back working for rich nobles who don't give a shit about life or rules or pity. Except in the city it's not just mercs and scoundrels doing dirty deeds in shadows. It's in broad daylight. And it's not just men like me working, it's God damn everyone.

You can't spit in this city without hitting a crook who calls himself a priest or a merchant or a guard. You can't cross the street without tripping on orphans that'd cut your throat for your shoes and pay up to a gang of kids just as poor. And that's the good part of town. That's three districts and a hundred degrees prettier than the hellholes I need to see.

I head down and down till my legs burn from holding my weight. I see a plaque on a burnt out building made from rock so old it's rounded. It spells 'Riverside', not that anyone here can read, and the wall it's on is the only one left standing, a few half-burnt support pillars resisting the slow rot of time and rain. Everything else is torn apart for the wood and nails. Mostly it all gets burnt for warmth—it gets cold at night here—or maybe to cook the few scraps of meat the locals can steal or catch.

The name's a joke now. Back before I was born, Old Dusty exploded and choked off the river. Now the poorest live in the old dry bed in shanties, maybe hoping one day the water comes back and the land is worth something. But it won't.

People just can't handle change. They'd rather starve and beg and whine than get up and risk a move, and now whole generations of cowards huddle in a dried up trench the world forgot, slowly going extinct. If you ask me, they deserve it.

In Riverside the festering stink and heat of massed up poverty hits me as the road goes flat. There's no ruts from wheels, not even animal shit. Merchants don't go in or out and anything with four legs gets eaten. Miserable eyes on miserable faces stare at me, too pitiful to be afraid. I pick my way around them, around the tents and burn-pits and men in circles with nothing but who still find something to gamble with.

I'd tossed my last few copper chits before I came in, and if you're ever here I suggest you do the same. The sound of jingling can get you mobbed and shanked in the Riverbed—nevermind your limp, nevermind your dirty clothes, or your size.

I look and look but don't find much action. There's no shouts or moans or haggling voices. And I figure people are too hungry and sick to fight or fuck in a place like this, but I keep looking. I see all the dirt and misery of God's city. I crunch it under my boots, feel it on my skin and taste it in my mouth. I wander for hours sometimes forgetting what the hell I'm doing here.

A soldier's daughter is missing, says the voice. You know the one—the angel that whispers over cannon fire, the Goddess of fortune who for whatever reason speaks to some men when others just stand there, lost and alone, petrified and dead.

So I keep moving, and keep alert. I trudge all night through the misery of others, but I don't find what I'm looking for. I give up when the night turns so black I'm slipping on garbage. I decide tomorrow maybe I'll pay for a few names. Maybe I'll steal a few bigger coins and make myself presentable and try to look like a client instead of a drunk. I'm sorry brother, one night wasted, and every night counts. But I'll try again tomorrow.

Day Two: Afternoon report

I realized today your girl would stick out like a sore thumb. I went through the city to the North and tried to see if anyone sold her something, or put her up somewhere, or just spotted her. From your letter I'm not sure exactly what the hell she's doing here, but I guess it doesn't matter. Stupid kids. They've no idea.

Truth is I've not been North in a while—I've not been anywhere. I stay in my own block with the other drunks and frankly I prefer it that way. Here they look at me as if I'm odd—some dangerous stray to be avoided, to be repelled.

I suppose it's true. Last time I was here I damn near killed a priest. Back when I found out about my Suzie I tried to pay the Dead Priests for a cure. In the war I'd seen at least a few of 'em knit men's flesh like fucking cloth, and here I am with a healthy girl—a girl who just maybe coughs a bit too much with a bit of blood, and this man shakes his shrunken head and says god damn 'nothing to be done'. So I broke a bone, or maybe two, and I tell the other pricks to heal him. Sorry brother, I digress.

Anyway I guess it's been five years. Sad truth is the Temple District is the place kids get taken the most. No doubt they come looking for something, looking for help, desperate and distracted, mostly run-aways without a chit.

The place looks welcoming and clean enough. You see all kinds outside the temples. Young or old, pious or profane, all come to make their peace with the gods, one way or another.

I take my moment for the Grey Lady. Like most time thieves I know who butters my bread, but to be honest I never did take to the old spinster. If I'd had my choice I'd have taken the Whore—at least the Coin-Men and Fortunate Boys looked like they had a bit of fun before their luck ran out.

Anyway. We don't get to choose. We just bear our lot and play our hand. I played mine, and you played yours, and here we are, God damn heroes.

It's early when I get to the district. Men and women I wouldn't trust to shine my shoes offer salvation and divine tokens on every corner. And they don't just sit quiet, neither, they yell out like fishmongers—'Blessings! Get your blessings!' The bloody arrogance. But in the end I don't blame them none. If folk are stupid enough to pay then who's really at fault? If you're a fool you'll get robbed, and it might as well be a priest. At least a priest gives back a little hope, a little comfort, and maybe even builds a temple with whatever he doesn't spend.

Anyway. I check every temple and ask about your girl, then I try the alleys and the shanties and eventually the inns. Everyone acts like I'm crazy—like the idea of a young country girl alone and chitless and in danger is something they've never heard of. Damn them all to whichever hell you please. They're all so worried about the gangs and their own necks they don't just ignore me, oh no, they have to lie. Some are so wrapped up in it I swear they even believe.

In the end it takes the worst kind of monster to tell me the truth. I wind up in the Rest Stop. It looks cleaner than the rat-holes around it, which no doubt draws the naive like candles in the dark—stupid kids who think beauty's the same as goodness. I ask about your girl, and the sleazy prick's kindly-uncle routine slips until he shows his fake teeth.

"You're a bit late, brother." Yeah, he's a god damn ex-soldier, and I nearly kill him just for that. "I sent word to the gangs three odd nights ago when she came in. Already collected."

I take a long, deep breath, and he reads it wrong.

"Sorry, brother, she was a fine one, too. Nice little chunk of chits."

He winks, and for a minute I warp my rage into a grin by picturing what I'll do to him.

"How much?"

"Oh." He shrugs, and winks again. "You boys are fair, I always say. No complaints."

"Enjoy spending it?"

He laughs a desperate, ugly laugh. "Always. Thank your bosses for me, eh?"

I close the door.

"Hope it was worth it," I say low and mean, and he goes quiet when he sees the knife. But he screams when I show him how the army handles traitors. I dump him in one of his nice, clean rooms with the spotless floors, the sheets so clean even the sergeants would be proud. I wipe his blood on them.

It might not even be your girl, brother, but I think it is. And I'm sorry again. But what's done is done. I'm worn down to be honest but tonight I'll see what I can find. She might be older and harder when I find her, but she'll be alive. And if she is, I'll do what I can.

Day Two: Night report

I saw some shit tonight. Just a few more memories needing a good drowning when time and coin allows. I didn't find her, and best be thankful for that. I think I know where she is. But I'm ahead of myself.

First I rob the richest man I find in the city center. It's not really hard to steal in this city, just hard to get away with it.

Someone always sees you, always knows, and word spreads like rain dripping through the cracks until it pools at your feet and soaks you to the bone. You can't escape. And I suppose there's a certain justice, at least for the rich, and if a man like me takes what's yours than sooner or later he'll pay for it. But it won't be quick, certainly not tonight, and I need the coin.

It cleans me up and cuts my hair and buys me a cane—gives the shine of respectability. Underneath it I still wear knives and even the last oiled up flintlock I didn't sell, and I still keep some round-shot under my eyepatch. Maybe I even look like a veteran with more than the two coins he flashes at the door.

Anyway. I hit the Fields—the strip of watering holes and whorehouses and God knows what else on the outskirts. I tell 'em I want good, clean country girls, and of course every bastard shouting on the corner tells me they've got exactly what I need. I try a few but the girls seem too experienced, too *employed*. Slavegirls are frowned on by decent folk, even here. So they're kept in the back rooms and the basements—the special clubs. I know a few by reputation.

By the time the night's dark as sin I'm underground exchanging words with a greasy lizard of a man. He keeps licking his fingertips and it makes me wonder where they've been. He winks like we're conspiring, and all the while I'm sweating under this thick wool coat and sizing up his three thugs with cudgels and wondering how the hell I'll see all his girls unless I take them on.

"We have a deal?"

The lizard's name is Ren, from the Red Skirt, and he promises a country virgin for five gold chits. Even if I hadn't spent an ounce on clothes or drinks or bribes I'd only ever have had four.

"Maybe," I tell him. "But I've gotta see her, first. Won't be paying unless I like what I see."

He doesn't like that. In these sorts of places, brother, when you're this deep the time for walking out is gone, and one way or another, you're gonna pay.

But he says "Of course," like he's not about to walk out and set the bruisers on me. I smile. I let him turn. When he goes to move I drop a hand to his round, skinny shoulder. I raise my pistol and point it at a bruiser's face, and I blow it clean off.

Things get pretty red after that. The other boys freeze like any civilians who hear powder flare, and I get my knife out and start stabbing. They don't deserve it, but I don't care. I picture them standing still while little girls parade past them—these big, brave boys never saying a word, just collecting their chits. The stabbing comes easy after that.

"Where's the girl?"

I'm panting now and just trying not to slip on the blood. My left hand's cut up because I can't hold for shit since Baker Ridge. But it works well enough.

"She's...she's..." The lizard's gone white as a sheet, so I slap some sense into him. "Second door on the left! No one's touched her. Not yet. I swear to God!"

It's the wrong thing to say, so I cut off one of those fingers he can't stop licking. I tell him if I have to come back he'll remember this moment fondly.

I step out into the hall and already old men and young girls are running. If it had just been the pistol shot, or just the screams, folk can stick to their business. But put the two together and folk always panic.

I stumble across re-loading my pistol and kick the door, and for a moment I swear to God I see her. No, not yours, brother— my Suzie. But I shake my useless, blurry eye in its socket until the girl becomes a stranger, her arms hugging her knobbly knees. I see the hair and the skin are wrong—she isn't yours.

"Let's go." I hold out my best hand, but she screams and scuttles as far back as the room allows, and I know there's nothing I can say. So I go back to the lizard.

"It's the wrong girl," I tell him. "Who else has one? A recent grab. No more than three days. Light brown hair, lighter brown skin. Taken from the Northern district. Fifteen years old. I know you scum all know each other, now tell me, or I'll make what I do to you the worst thing I've ever done in my life."

He looks me in the eye and sees I fucking mean it. He talks. He tells me about a warehouse more like a prison where the snatchers take their slaves, and from there they go to the whorehouses or private buyers—says he only knows of two like mine, and he thinks they're both still there. I threaten to take another finger, but I believe him. I leave him alive and when I do I realize I don't plan on coming out of this thing. But it's alright, brother, it feels good. It feels peaceful.

I rob the place of a few meager coins before I go. I wouldn't bother except I'll need some help. I'll need a saber and maybe more guns—pistols, long-stocks, doesn't matter, and if I'm lucky another man or two to carry 'em.

Next I hit some veteran drinking holes—Old Saggy and Irongut. I flash a bit of stolen coin and get a few toothless brothers with more booze than blood in their veins. I get lucky and hear there's men asking after me already, no doubt gang-thugs who found my handiwork at the Rest Stop. Someone must have seen me, just like I knew they would. Someone always bloody sees. What matters is I'm running out of time.

So I get sloppy. I club another few rich men in alleys and hurt a few more bruisers without using up any gift because I'll need it. I buy four cavalry sabers and a whetstone from an antique shop, plus a few old wheel-locks—even a bloody crossbow. It's not much, I figure, but it'll do, and I give the boys my instructions.

This'll likely be my last report, brother, and thank God for that. I hope when you read it you won't blame yourself because the truth is, I should thank you. I've drunk down every chit and more since I left the army. I've done things, brother, things I'm not proud of. I've used up near every ounce of the Lady's gift left flowing in my veins, stolen every scrap of time until I've wrinkled and puckered like an opium slave.

But at least I'll have this. You've given an old, useless drunk one more purpose—one more thing to do and maybe even a good reason to die. It's more than I expected. It's certainly more than I deserve.

I hope I've saved your little girl, brother, when you read this, and that she's home safe and sound. But if not, well, I promise you this: tomorrow will be what the Ridge should have been. It'll be my very last thing. I'll steal every second I've left in these bones, brother, and do the regiment proud—Under-Sergeant Fulvi Keydu. South Army. Formerly 17th division. Final report.

Post-Script

Hello, father. I'm sitting on a sweat-stained chair worried about fleas, and I've been drinking. There's blood on my hands and on my dress. But no, none of its mine, though I wish maybe it was. It took me awhile to stop shaking enough to write this, but then I needed it anyway to think of what to say.

First things first: I'm sorry I left in the middle of the night. It was stupid and if I was going to leave I should have done it in the day with kind words, or with an argument, but in either case as a woman grown and not a scared little girl.

We've never been close, you and I, surely you know that. And when mother died...well, that's no excuse. I don't know why I left when I did except I didn't want to live on the farm my whole life and marry the Thacker boy, and I thought in the city I could change who I was and be...something more.

I know you always talked about the world and how hard it was, but I guess I had to see for myself. Maybe in the end I'm more like you than I thought, or maybe I'm just a little girl. At least I used to be.

I didn't understand you or the things you'd seen and done. But now I've seen girls my age so worn down and used by life they stopped washing themselves. I've seen human beings treated worse than any animal on even the Lister farm. Some of the girls here...they just gave up. They stare at the walls and don't say a word no matter what you do. They're breathing corpses. I didn't know a person could be dead but still alive.

And tonight...I'm sorry if this is hard to read my hands are still shaking...tonight, I saw a massacre. I saw a man like you, I mean, another version of you. You'd spoken of him, I think, just once or twice—I didn't remember his name until I heard it, but I remembered 'the hero of the ridge'. When I saw him I admit that thought never entered my mind.

For the last three days I've been locked in a filthy attic waiting to be sold, but they didn't hurt me. A lot of the other girls they did.

Many times I'd imagined you or maybe some stranger

coming for me, stopping this and putting the world right again, but no one ever did. There's not even a lock on the door because there's always, *always* men outside watching, sitting in plain daylight without a worry in the world.

I'd sit at my grated window and imagine escape. Or I'd think of being back at the farm and all the stupid little things I hated like waking up before the sun, or sharing a bed with Lisbet. Time went on and pretty soon all I was praying for was to be sold to a man who wasn't too old, or too cruel. And when a savior finally came, I was almost embarrassed.

All I saw was this old, dirty man stumble into the street. He looked drunk and worn down and hardly able to hold himself up. He looks up like he's just remembered where he is. Then he calls my name.

"Roxxy," he says, not even Roxanna, but 'Roxxy', just like you would. His voice is like a chimney and he coughs after he yells.

I couldn't understand it. I watch this toothless, hunched old man lean on his walking stick and scratch at his fleas, and I don't know why he should know my name, or call it out.

The men holding me watch him, too, and they just laugh. These hard, young brutes playing dice seemed ready to ignore him, knowing he's maybe here for a daughter or a grand-daughter—that he's helpless even though she's just inside. And God forgive me, I didn't say anything. But he doesn't move, even when they threaten to run him off like a wild dog. He just calls again.

I felt like two people, then. The first wanted to hide away and accept whatever came, as if my life weren't mine anymore and if I just kept my head down then maybe I could bear the weight of that. But the other knew this moment mattered. Maybe it wasn't even me, just a voice in my mind telling me to find my courage, right now, to seize it, or my whole life would be misery and regret. And there was something about him, something strange, something familiar.

I put my face to the grate and screamed as loud as I could. "I'm here! Up here!"

His face turns up, angled, like one of Uncle Tymen's hunting dogs. And in a blink he throws his ratty cloak back to show pistols and knives and maybe armor, and suddenly it's like the old man was just an illusion, some mask worn by another man.

Three more men step out from the darkness beside him and they've got walking sticks, too. Except the old man props his up and holds it with one arm, and I realize it's really a brass-handled gun just like you store in the basement. He braces it against his chest.

Some of the young men stand and start calling out, but before they've taken a step there's a click, and just like that, without another word, the old man shoots.

Father, I...tonight. Tonight, I saw four broken down old men stand against ten half their age. They came to that place, that awful place, and they came ready to die. They came just for me, and the first man fought like the men in your stories. I guess I never believed it, not truly, but he moved like some magic hero in a myth.

As I watched I think I imagined he was you. I pictured the glorious endings, the beautiful victory, all the battles won for the old dead king. But that's not how it was. It was loud and horrible, and the men were all screaming. The old man fired his pistols one by one and every bang meant a young man screamed and fell in a cloud of blood and smoke.

Then he used the sword, and they hurt him, even as he killed them. These brash, cruel brutes who'd threatened me with more vile words than I knew existed stabbed him and clubbed him but he just wouldn't fall. Covered in blood he killed them, killed them one by one, and I felt like I killed them because I'd imagined it so many times.

Before it was over I got up and I ran. I ran out into the night and one of the other old men took me and told me to 'stay put, darling'. Then he re-joined the fighting, and I stood there and watched the street run its gutters red, until finally all was quiet except for a few dying men.

Your friend was one of them, Father. Your friend died tonight.

The other men told me his name was Fulvi. They told me where he lived, and that they were supposed to bring me there.

I came thinking I'd find walls covered in honors and medals. I thought a man like that must be celebrated, accomplished, and proud.

But the walls here are bare. The floor is dirty wood covered in empty bottles, and all I found were a little bag of chits, these letters, and a note that said 'Go back to your father, girl. One day you'll know the loneliness of love'.

I cried a long time, I think, when I read it. He knew he'd die, and that I'd come here and see.

So I'm bringing his letters with me. I owe him that, and more, much more, though I don't know how I'll ever repay him now.

The men are telling me we need to leave. They say the gangs will be out and they'll 'be damned if we let you get killed after Baker done what he done.'

And they're right. Fulvi saved me, father, and he died for it. I don't know what that means or what to say except I'll never forget him. He did it for you, and maybe for him. And I don't care what happened and if he deserted the army, or if he ran away. He's still my hero. Just like you.

I'm coming home, father. These men will help me; they said they owed Fulvi that. Maybe they can help us on the farm and things can be better, for us, and for them. I don't think they can come back here. But I'll read you these letters myself.

Your Roxxy.

SOOTHSAYER

By Matthew P. Gilbert

I had just broken into a furious, uphill sprint when I ran into the Soothsayer. He had already tossed the rope over an abandoned lantern pole and was just starting to hoist his kill. Cussing and muttering under his breath, he hauled on the rope, throwing all his weight into the task as he inched his burden higher and higher. His victim, a large man, dangled a few feet from the ground, suspended by his ankles, belly open to the elements. The scent of stale fires and fresh death hung in the air like incense. The blackened, charred frames of the surrounding buildings, backlit and limned in the pale moonlight, seemed like skeletal fingers pointing in accusation at the grim scene before them.

Switching from the euphoria of running to the cold sweat of a potentially lethal encounter isn't as jarring as one might think. Adrenaline is adrenaline, whatever the source. Still, it can be disconcerting. I tried changing course to avoid running headlong into the grisly pair, but shock, speed, and fortune conspired to humble me. I lost my footing on a loose cobblestone and went down face first into a pile of something warm and smelling of death. I felt bile rise in my throat as I realized just what I had blundered into.

Cursing myself for a fool, I leapt to my feet, ready for a fight. He spun to face me, his smoldering, feral eyes staring at me from behind a tangled mass of stringy hair, his intent unmistakable. With a hiss, he released the rope, letting the corpse drop to the ground, and drew a blade from his belt. It was no ordinary weapon he held. An eerie, green light, as bright as a torch, oozed like blood from runes carved along its length. He brandished it in my direction, his free hand clutching nervously at the dirty, bloodstained robe he wore. His lips moved, making sounds like words, but in no language, I recognized, a chanting, whispery, sing-song string of nonsense syllables.

He was not a large man. I stood a head taller, and had a damned good weight advantage on him, but I had no idea what that knife of his might do to me. Somehow, I suspected it had many uses beyond simple illumination.

"Soothsayer, I presume," I said, as we began to circle one another.

"The man who fights without a blade," he answered, as if he recognized me, too.

"You're not what I expected," I told him, still judging his capabilities, summing him up before I struck.

"And you're just what I expected," he cackled, his voice a hissing, whisper-chant. He slashed the knife in a vicious half circle, carving out his personal space and showing me he knew how to use his weapon, was ready to use it if I came close enough. "It's just a shell, you know, just a form, a life support system to keep the brain supplied with nutrients. No meaning in it beyond the mechanical."

"That's how you think of people, just parts?" Waiting for an opening, for a gap in his attention.

"Just parts," he agreed, repeating the phrase several times. "Some useful, some not. I separate the wheat from the chaff with my little knife. You think I don't know you, Lucian Lenoir?"

I felt something cold in my gut as he called my name, and he knew it. He raised his free hand to his face and twisted his features into a fright mask, then cackled and slashed the blade again.

"We're no different."

"We're about to be—"

"'You'll be dead. That will be different, won't it?'" he said, completing my sentence with a chuckle. "Stole your words, didn't I?"

"How—?"

"Heard you say them," he whispered, his face serious once again, eyes blazing with purpose. "In the guts of an older specimen. He was in poor shape. A pity, really, how they break down in this environment." He jerked the dagger in my direction, punctuating his words. "It's the alcohol, mostly, damages the digestive system and the liver over the years, lets too many poisons slip through. They wear down, less reliable. They'll have to be younger from now on."

I said nothing. I was troubled by the familiar pattern of his speech, but it was something I could consider after I had dealt with him. To hell with his knife. It would make a fine souvenir. I tensed, ready to spring. *Keep talking, fool.*

"Now you're going to try to kill me," he said. "But you can't."

"I don't think you can stop me."

"We are all dust blown in the wind of merciless fate!" he told me, as if imparting some terrible truth. "I've seen these things before! Accept it! It's not to be!"

I leapt at him, but he was ready. He scuttled aside, then turned and fled, shucking his robe on the fly, his mocking and gibbering echoing from the blackened, crumbling walls. I should have known better, should have realized there was method to his madness, but his taunts nettled me, and I gave chase.

He was damnably fast. I chased him for nearly a mile, closing the distance between us inch by agonizingly slow inch. By the time I came close enough to lay hands on him, we had left the burned-out area far behind and come into the wharves. No matter. This was as good a place as any to finish this dog. Just as I reached to grab a fistful of the long, tangled hair that trailed behind him, he turned and ducked into an alley. Damn him! It was as if he had rehearsed this!

I turned with a drunken lurch, backtracked the few feet I had skidded past the entrance, and charged directly into his trap.

Pain ripped through me in jagged, flashing thunderbolts as a padded club smashed against my chest, and I staggered backwards out of the alley. Three bruisers in stocking caps were headed my way, all sporting stout cudgels. I rose quickly, trying to clear my head and evaluate my situation. My ribs were intact, and the Soothsayer was sprinting merrily away, still laughing. As for my would-be assailants, their stances and form marked them as hopeless amateurs, the type who relied on brute strength and size to carry the day for them. They would be no match for me, but they could damned well waste my precious time.

"Hey, what about the little guy?" one of them asked.

"Forget him, this one looks like he could pull an oar better," replied the one who had hit me. "Come on, I'm gonna need some help."

"That man's a murderer, you fool!" I shouted.

"Yeah, well, so are we," said the third, a veritable mountain of flesh. "So don't give us any trouble."

I have no time for this, I thought, as I surged forward and slammed my fingers, stiff like a board, into his throat. He went down with a gurgling cry. The next swung at me and missed as I ducked, then hammered a foot into his jaw. I heard the crack of bone as his head tilted to an impossible angle. The last simply stood, stunned and mouth agape, as I struck. I grabbed him by the neck and slammed him against the wall. He clawed at my grip as I ground my thumbs into his throat, our faces so close that our noses nearly touched. Terrified, confused eyes, stared back at me, unable to understand how it had come to this.

"It seems we all have something in common!" I said as I released him. He slid down the wall, still clutching at his throat, slowly realizing that he would never draw breath again.

I rushed to the end of the alleyway, but there was no sign of the Soothsayer. He had known, somehow, that these men would be here, had known just where to go to delay me. I realized, with a chill, that he must have known he would meet me before I had ever arrived.

There was no point in trying to pick up his trail. He could be anywhere by now, and at any rate, why should I even care? Let the Soothsayer kill all he wanted. Until someone offered me enough money to make it worth my while, it wasn't my concern.

I spent a while walking off my anger. It began to rain, and at first, I welcomed it, but before long, it became simply miserable. After an hour or two, cold, wet, and in a foul mood, I decided I had been sufficiently punished for my stupidity, and I made my way to Thull's. Warm, yellow light from the oil lanterns and roaring fire spilled from the open door, lighting the weather-worn shingle and beckoning all fools and mad dogs to take solace from the downpour. I walked in and took my usual seat at the end of the bar, leaving a trail of muddy footprints behind me.

Thull was standing watch, polishing a glass with a towel, his huge hands making the sturdy pint mug he was holding seem more like a child's cup. He was built like a moose, an inch or so taller than I, and close to three hundred pounds, all of it bone and muscle. He was in his fifties and long retired from the army, but unlike most old soldiers, he had kept himself in fine shape. I could have beaten him in a fight, mind you, but I wouldn't have arm-wrestled him, not even with heavy odds. As I slid onto the stool, he looked my way and grinned, exposing perfect, white teeth that fairly glowed against his almost black skin.

"You look like shit, Lucian," he said, his deep, rumbling voice filling the room. He wiped his towel over his glistening, bald head, then tossed it my way. I snagged it out of the air and made use of it.

"Thanks."

"No problem." He poured a shot of vodka and brought it over. "Little late for you tonight, ain't it? You out running in that mess?"

"Every night." I traded him the towel for the vodka and knocked it back. It was just what I needed. "Had some thinking to do, took a long walk afterward. What's new?"

"They say the Soothsayer got another one tonight. What's that, like thirty now?"

As they say, bad news travels fast.

"Thirty-three," I told him, scowling and gesturing for a refill, not particularly happy at being reminded that the bastard had outfoxed me. Thull shook his head and poured another.

"Somebody's got to do something about him," he said quietly.

I stared down at my drink, saying nothing.

"I seen him, ya know," called snaggle-toothed Sal from across the room.

"You ain't seen nobody, you liar," another patron retorted. "Everybody knows the Soothsayer is invisible. How else ya reckon he creeps up on people?"

"Fuck you, I seen him!" Sal bawled, angry now. "Seen him grab a feller down the canal last week! He ain't invisible! Some guys I know even follered him home one night! He's a man, like you and me!"

Before long, they were all arguing over it. The Soothsayer was a demon, or a vampire, or an invisible spirit. He could fly and walk through walls. He could see into your soul. He could walk on water. But one thing they all agreed on was that Sal had definitely not seen him. The poor old drunk turned to me for help.

"You believe me, don'tcha, Lucian?" His eyes implored me to impart some measure of credibility to his story. Well, there was no harm in it, and it was important to Sal. Perhaps, later, he would be grateful and do me a favor in return. At least he had the time scale right. The Soothsayer had murdered a bum about five days before. Maybe he had thought his lie out well enough to have an entertaining story to tell.

"You've never lied to me before, Sal, not that I know of anyway," I said. That much was true, for what it was worth. "Tell us what you saw."

"Well, like I said, I was down the canal—"

"Ah shut up, ya old windbag," suggested the patron who had started the whole mess.

I heard a whistle in the air behind me, but I was not concerned enough to turn. I had been a regular here long enough to know the sound. One of Thull's heavy mugs streaked across the bar and slammed into the chest of Sal's heckler. The man fell over in his chair and spilled onto the floor, gasping. One of his companions tossed the mug, none the worse for wear, back to the old barkeep, who took a bow to a round of applause.

"Next time, I'm gonna put it upside your head, boy," Thull admonished once the clapping was done. "Now shut up and let the man speak."

Sal cleared his throat, waiting for total silence, then continued. "So I was down there, tryin ta hit up the sailors for some rum or maybe a few coppers, and one of em give me a bottle of sumpin, I dunno what it was, but it warn't bad. I drank most of it, and, well, then I decided to have me a nap, so I climbed up in a stack of tarps they had layin along the pier.

"Well, I wake up, and it's real late. I dunno what time, but late. And I hear some kind of scuffle, so I peek out, just my eyes, and I see him. He's got this old feller slung over his shoulder like a sack o 'taters, and I couldn't tell if he was dead or asleep, but he warn't fightin him none."

"How'd you know it was him, Sal?" Thull asked, interested despite himself.

"I'm gettin to it," Sal said. "So anyways, he flops this guy on the ground next to a lamp pole, and then I can see him good, and he's cut wide open like the rest of em. Then he pulls out a knife. It's glowin all green, like some kinda evil thing. And he starts cuttin out the poor bastard's...." Sal's grimaced, obviously distressed, took a swig of whiskey, then continued, "You know what he does."

Everyone nodded. The Soothsayer gutted his victims, and left the entrails in curiously arranged heaps near the bodies, hence the moniker.

"Well, I just couldn't stand it. I come out from under them tarps and I yelled out, 'Here, you! What're you doin?' just as loud as I could. I reckon it was stupid, but I did it. And he stops and looks at me, and he just *laughs,* and he says, 'I'll be comin after you soon enough, Sal'. Knew my name, I tell ya!"

"Oh, bullshit!" someone yelled from the back of the bar.

"Shut up!" I shouted. The speaker ducked his head and tried to present as small a target as possible for Thull, but the barkeep, now fully caught up in Sal's tale, was too distracted to do more than wave a glass menacingly in the air while waiting for Sal to continue.

"What'd he look like, Sal?" asked the first heckler, who had either been converted, or was trying to regain Thull's good graces.

"He was ugly, that's for sure. Raggedy clothes, and tangled up hair all hangin in his eyes. Looked just like a bum, mostly, like me I reckon, but younger. He was all whisperin and grabbing at his shirt, and he had eyes like some kind of fiend, crazy eyes, like he'd pull out your soul if you looked in em long enough."

The scream came just as Sal finished his sentence and was drawing breath for the next. It rattled the windows in their frames, and the teeth of every man in the place. I am certain that at least one reveler lost control of his bladder, and the rest of us were closer than we would care to admit.

My mind shifted immediately into combat mode, categorizing the scream, and calculating angles: female, terrified, unmoving, perhaps twenty yards away, too coherent for an attack. Over and over she screamed, and then, as suddenly as it began, there was silence.

Sal gave voice to my suspicion. "A silver says the Soothsayer's been out in this storm."

I rose and headed for the door, with most of the clientele and Thull following behind me. Almost exactly twenty yards from the bar, in a darkened alley, we found them, two dead.

No, I corrected myself, one was still alive. She was lying unconscious on the ground, most likely fainted from screaming. There could be no mistake about the second, however. Several drunks, already struggling to keep their stomachs, gave up their dinners on the spot.

She had been slaughtered like game, slit from crotch to chin and gutted. She dangled upside down, nude, a rope cinched about her feet and looped over the arm of a lantern post, just like all the others. Her long, once blond hair was now red, drenched in her own blood. It dangled gently against the ground, blood dripping from it and mixing with the dirty water as she swayed to and fro in the light breeze.

The worst, by far, however, was the sight of her eyes, flung wide open in horror that had not dulled even in the glaze of death that hung over them now. Her features were forever locked into a final mask of the agony she had known in the last moments of her life. Though I could not be certain without a more complete examination of the body, the wound edges suggested she had been alive and conscious through most of it. It was the most brutal killing I had ever seen, and I had seen far more than my fair share.

"Ilaweh give us strength," Thull whispered.

I bent to examine the living woman. She appeared whole enough, so I tossed her over my shoulder and carried her inside. Thull led me to his back room, where we laid her on a table and roused her with smelling salts, then pumped some strong liquor into her until she could speak.

She was a whore, not very surprising considering the locale and her dress. Her name was Alicia, and she was a pitiful thing, perhaps fifteen, and absolutely terrified. Young, indeed, but in her eyes was that hard, bitter glint that street people, especially whores, acquire early in life, a keen awareness that death, in one guise or another, is a constant neighbor: random violence, disease, starvation, and lately, the Soothsayer.

I felt an uncharacteristic pang of guilt as I considered the life to which these people were condemned. I had been there once myself, twenty years before, struggling for survival in the pitiless streets. I had known their desperation first hand, yet, for months, I had stood by while the Soothsayer had butchered them. Had I truly surrendered so much of my soul, I wondered, that I could not expend the effort to hunt down and destroy this unnatural predator, this thing that killed without rhyme or reason?

"Her name was Cheri," the girl said softly, head bowed, as she ran her fingers through her fiery red tresses. She spoke mechanically, the words seeming to hold no meaning for her. "She was nineteen. She looked after us, ya know, called us her little sisters. She had friends and stuff, people who could keep pimps like Hammer in line." Then, as if suddenly awakening from a nightmare, her head snapped up, eyes clouded with rage and grief as she glared at me, tears leaving tracks in her thick makeup, throat working as she swallowed.

"*Why?*" she whispered. "Why don't somebody stop him?"

Her voice rose to a shriek, and she tore her hair in frustration. "'Cause we're easy, 'cause nobody gives a fuck if we live or die!" She doubled over and put her arms behind her head, rocking back and forth in a frenzy of anguish.

Was she a reader of minds, this child, that she hurled my own thoughts back at me like stones? But no, she was simply voicing her misery to the skies, at no one in particular, or perhaps at everyone.

Looking back, I remember this single, powerful moment as a turning point in my life. I will not make the claim of having ever been a good man, but I have certainly been more evil than I am now. As I listened to a child far too wise for her age crying against the wretchedness, the savagery of the world I had come to accept, I was forced to re-evaluate a few things.

I pulled a coin from my pocket and regarded it for a moment, admiring the graven image of a kris piercing a crown. It was my own design, my calling card. I took it between my thumb and forefinger and gave it a thump, setting it spinning on the table.

"How much money do you have, girl?" I asked at last.

She eyed me with distrust, the street in her telling her not to answer. The coin slowed, drawing her gaze as it flipped on its side and gyrated a moment, then stopped. Her eyes widened in alarm as she recognized the image and made the inevitable connection with my own grim stare.

She swallowed again and stared at the floor, doubtless wondering what retribution I planned to take upon her for her disrespect. "Not enough," she whispered.

"A hundred crowns?" The sum was so paltry to me as to be meaningless, yet I knew it was a fortune to her. So be it. Death should never be cheap.

She looked up at me then, her eyes deep green wells of hope and sorrow, not quite daring to believe I was serious.

"But—" she said, then swallowed hard and continued. "I heard you charged millions...."

"Do you have the money or not, girl?"

"I got fifty," she said. She drew her purse from between her breasts and offered it, pleading. "But I can get *more!*"

I took the purse and emptied the contents into my hand, five silver coins, most likely a month's earnings for a woman in her business. The pimps took most of what they made, leaving them with just enough to survive.

"Half in advance, the other half payable when the job is finished," I said. "Gods help you if you don't have it."

"I'll have it!" she assured me, her eyes once again filled with hatred. "You make him suffer, make him *fear* like Cheri before he dies!"

I put the coins back into the little purse and hung it on my belt. As little as it meant, it bound a contract. I was her instrument, and could kill in her name, a purely professional distinction, to be sure, but one that had always been of great import to me.

"Name your proof," I told her.

"I want his head," she replied without the slightest hesitation. "I'm gonna have it stuffed and mounted on my wall."

I bowed to her and said, "It shall be so, madam."

As I turned to leave, she said gently, "Sir? Mr. Lenoir?"

"Yes?"

She was crying again, the hot tears welling in her eyes and streaming down her cheeks. "Thank you," she whispered.

I nodded and left her to her grief.

Thull followed me into the street, where at last he spoke.

"It's a good thing, you're doing, Lucian."

"But I should have done it before, shouldn't I?" I shot back. "I should have killed him months ago. Too little too late, that's how it feels."

Thull stared at me as if he had never seen me before, then shook his head in amazement. "It's never too late to turn things around," he said.

"You offering me salvation, bartender?"

"Just a drink before you go, if you want," said Thull. "I ain't no savior."

I waved off his offer and turned to leave. "Neither am I."

Murmandimus pulled the sheet back over Cheri's face, done with his reading. "Why?" he asked. His voice was calm and soothing, as always, but with the hint of some deeper motive now.

"I need to see it," I told him.

The mage eyed me with a curious stare, the dim firelight reflecting from his metallic, pupilless eyes as he considered the issue.

"It's very disturbing. I could just describe it to you, you know."

"I can handle it."

With a shrug, he leaned forward, reached his hands toward me and placed his long, delicate fingers against my temples. I felt a slight shock as each touched my skin. He paused, his eyes now a pale green.

"I'm not exaggerating. Are you *certain*? This could cause you some trauma."

"Just do it."

He nodded. His eyes drained of color, back to quicksilver, and the world about me faded to elsewhere.

It was perhaps ten minutes of experience that Murmandimus had pieced together during his brief reading of her body, the final moments of her life. As his power coursed through my mind, I lived those moments as Cheri, saw the Soothsayer again, through her eyes this time. I saw the blood, heard the screams, felt her horror, her pain, all of it. I knew every aspect of what it was to suffer her fate. Darkness closed in upon me, and I gasped a last, feeble cry, feeling my own life slipping away in a haze of agony beyond anything I had ever known. Then, there was nothing.

When at last I came to my senses once again, I found myself lying on the floor. Murmandimus, inscrutable, sat comfortably in his chair, watching as I shook the fog from my head and rose, my own body feeling strange and unfamiliar.

"Was it worth it?" he asked. "Did you find what you seek?"

"There was no way to tell where the place was," I said. "The windows were boarded."

"That's not what you were looking for," Murmandimus noted. "Have you found your justification for your intended action? Your motivation?"

"I don't know what you're talking about."

Murmandimus shook his head in mock sadness, his hair

ruffled by some unseen wind, flowing as if he were a man underwater. One could have almost believed it as a living thing unto itself. He fixed his hypnotic stare on me and said, more seriously, "Why are you doing this?"

"Because it must be done," I told him, "and no one else is going to dirty their hands to set things aright."

I rose and walked to the fire, busied myself by poking at it, stirring it to life again. I welcomed the rush of warmth from it on my face and arms, the memory of Cheri's death still close in my mind.

"Is it an issue of morality for you?" he asked.

His question irked me. "Morality is for philosophers and weak minded fools."

"And yet you choose to put yourself at great risk, for no obvious gain."

"Killing a rogue is good for everyone, including me," I told him. "He's killing people for free, after all. That could well be money out of my pocket."

"Now you *are* grasping at straws," Murmandimus said with a wry smile. "Why is it so difficult for you to admit that you want to destroy him for his evil?"

"He's not evil," I snapped. "What *I* do is evil, if you want to use those silly terms. What *he* does is monstrous." I paused, looking him in the eye. "It's inhuman."

Murmandimus nodded as if I had confirmed something he had long suspected. "How many men have you killed, Lucian?"

I returned to my seat and stared into the fire again, watching the shadows skitter over the bricks. The hand of darkness reached for the burning flame, recoiled at the heat, then, like a stupid child, tried again. But the darkness is not foolish, merely tenacious. It always wins in the end.

"More than you," I muttered.

"How many mages?"

"None," I said, nodding in understanding. The familiarity of the Soothsayer's speech made sense, now. The bastard really *was* a sorcerer. "If I had never met you, I'd not even believe such things were real."

"And you are one of perhaps five men in the world who

know of me. We are few, and reclusive. One becomes...." He considered a moment, then continued. "Distant. The Soothsayer is a classic case of what we can become. We are all, even I, vulnerable to obsession, even monomania." He shrugged, as if somewhat embarrassed. "It's a self inflicted wound, a necessary evil in the all important search for truth."

"I need specifics: motivations, patterns, projections. Do you know why he's doing this?"

Murmandimus shrugged. "It is his field. He is interested in the truth of life, as I am in mind." He shook his head sadly, sighed, then continued. "He was once a brilliant man, you know. The work he has done with tiny machines is simply amazing. He claimed, given time, he could create a sort of artificial life with them, self replicating devices that could repair living creatures, even remake them." Murmandimus turned to stare at the fire, his eyes glowing orange from reflected flame. "Heal wounds, fight diseases, even turn back time for a man. Imagine, an immortality serum of tiny, living machines. What a pity that all his work will be lost."

I stared at Murmandimus in disgust, cold anger rising within me. "You know him?" I asked, appalled. "And you have stood by and done *nothing*?"

The mage turned emotionless eyes of quicksilver upon me, and in that moment I understood just how little remained of his own humanity.

"Most of us know one another. And what better example of aberrant psychology to study?" he asked, without a hint of guilt.

"Is that what this is about? Fraternal loyalty? Protecting your 'specimen'? I should kill you where you stand."

"Bah." He dismissed my threat with a wave of his hand. "He was once an interesting subject, but there is little more to learn from him. I merely regret the loss of his capabilities. In any event, I am hardly alone in doing nothing when the opportunity presented itself."

I clenched my jaw, accepting his rebuke. He was right. I was in no position to judge him. "Tell me what I need to know to kill him."

"Oh, he'll die as any other man will," said the mage. "But the issue is getting yourself into a position to strike. Of all the rumors about him, one is certainly true: he *can* see the future, to a limited degree."

"What else is he capable of? Can he call down lightning? Can he command spirits to kill me?"

"Of course not," Murmandimus said, waving his hand in derision. "It's not his field. You could easily defeat him in single combat, but don't imagine he would be foolish enough to confront you on anything approaching fair terms."

I sighed, feeling suddenly very powerless and alone. "How do I fight such a man, who knows my every move?"

"He can't know *every* move. He has to look for specific events, and even then, he can only see so far into the future," Murmandimus reassured me. "Still, it will only be a matter of time before he finds you in a moment of weakness. Fortunately, there is now a period, a *brief* one, during which he *won't* know what you're doing."

"How can you know that?"

"Because he no doubt cast for his future in the entrails of the woman he killed tonight, and finds you hunting him. But he will question the result."

"That's absurd," I said. "I assure you, the man has a high degree of confidence in his work."

"Yes," said the mage with a patient nod. "But now he will have reason to distrust his craft, because this will be the first time he has received a contradictory result. You see, there is a reason I am interested in your rationale for all of this."

I stared at him, uncomprehending, and he positively grinned. "You have *changed*, Lucian," he said at last. "Don't you understand the significance?"

"Could you damned well *please* just spell it out for the ignorant savage, you smug bastard?" I shouted.

"Of course," he agreed, smiling at my frustration, but perhaps a bit embarrassed, too. "Understanding is as much a weapon as a sword, man hunter. Understand your enemy." Murmandimus rose and clasped his hands behind his back, pacing in front of the fire as he spoke, a professor lecturing a student.

"For a man to perform such loathsome acts as he commits, he must acquire a mindset that permits any action, no matter how depraved," he told me. "This manifests itself as a conviction that men are nothing more than complicated machines, their behavior merely appropriate, automatic response to various stimuli." He stopped pacing and stared intently at me as he drove home his point. "That there is, in point of fact, no such thing as *free will*."

"'Just parts,' as he put it," I said with a nod. "'We are all dust blown in the wind of merciless fate.'"

Murmandimus nodded. "With such a world view, the deviant is free to rationalize all things as not merely permissible, but inevitable. A machine cannot change its destiny, cannot suddenly choose to be something other than what it was yesterday, or the day before. It must behave according to its function.

"Now, consider. You only just tonight made your decision to stop him. You have had a change of heart. Something in you has awakened that was not there before, and you have made a choice. You have *changed the future*, Lucian, by your free will. By now, surely, he's made use of that girl's innards, and is seeing a very different fate than he saw previously. He can't accept that they are both true without admitting free will, and that would force him into direct confrontation with his madness. His mind will reject that explanation. But he will be highly confused and agitated."

"Then time is of the essence," I said, rising.

"Oh, it certainly is," Murmandimus agreed, features hardening, eyes darkening to blood red as he stared intently at me. He raised an eyebrow, and the door to the street opened at his silent command. "He is confronting an assault on his reality. He will not rest until he resolves this, and that requires confirmation. A great deal of it."

I nodded, understanding him all too well. I turned and bolted for the door.

"You mentioned friends who followed the Soothsayer."

Sal fidgeted with the sole button that remained on his worn coat, struggling with himself. I knew what he was thinking. It was the custom of street people to answer no questions regarding others of their kind, an unwritten code of ethics among people who, by necessity, occasionally resorted to crime as a means of survival.

"Well, there's a couple of guys I know what said they follered him one night," he confessed at last. "I don't know if they was telling the truth, but I wouldn't put it past em. They ain't got no sense about things." He paused and looked about the alley where we stood, as close to home as it came for him. Satisfied that we were truly alone, he continued in a conspiratorial, near-whisper, "They said they figured out where he lived, and was trying to get some of us to go burn him out, but we warn't fixing to get mixed up in that. No telling if it was even the right place, and if it warn't, there'd be hell to pay. And then, well...." Sal paused briefly, looking embarrassed. "Well, you know there's folks what say he's a demon. Some of em said that fire, it'd just make him smile a little bigger when he was rippin our guts out."

"Take me to them."

Sal gaped at my words. "I can't do that! I gotta *live* with these folks. I can't go putting the touch on em, or they'll fix me up!"

"The Soothsayer is coming after you one by one. If I don't end this tonight, he's going to kill a lot more people, Sal. He knows I'm coming, and he needs to know what will happen, and that means dead people, a lot of them. I'll bet you what you like that he knows about those two who followed him, as well. He'll try to cut that link before I get to them, if he can. Those two are dead men if I don't find them, and quickly."

Sal began to sway and hum, looking back and forth and trembling. He chewed his lip hard enough to draw blood as he tried to come to a decision.

"It has to be *now*, Sal."

He looked at me with undisguised terror, his whole body quivering. "Can you take him, Lucian? You're real good at that stuff, ain't ya? Killin' a man, I mean? You done took down a lot worse than him before, right?"

I considered lying, but he deserved better. "It depends on how quickly I move."

He looked at me a moment, then gave me a curt nod, and as

he did so, he seemed to find some inner reserve of strength. He stopped trembling, stood up straight, and looked me in the eye as an equal, as a man rather than a wretch.

"Alicia told me about what you said. I don't know much about money or figures, but I know a man like you don't even notice if he loses what she's paying you. You're puttin' your ass on the line, and this ain't even your fight. I'll put my ass on the line with you."

He reached out a hand, and I shook it, surprised that, despite his frail appearance, his grip was strong and sure.

"Let's go then," I told him.

Tubbs spat on the ground and stared daggers at Sal, refusing to make eye contact with me.

"I don't know nothing."

I pulled some coins from my pocket and tossed them to the ground in front of him.

"What does that jar loose?" I asked.

"I said I don't know nothing," he said, more belligerent now.

I turned to look at Sal, who shook his head to indicate that the man was lying. From the corner of my eye, I saw Tubbs draw his finger across his throat at Sal.

There are two universal languages. Tubbs, it appeared, spoke only one of them.

"You should have taken the money," I told him.

I lashed out, a striking snake, to grab him around the neck, squeezing like a vise. With my other hand, I seized one wildly flailing arm by the wrist and turned his elbow near to the point of breaking. He writhed in pain, unable to scream, hammering at me as best he could with his free hand, but he could only reach my shoulder. He had no leverage to actually injure me. As his face began to turn a dark purple, he shifted to attempt prying my hand loose from his throat. It was almost amusing, watching him try to break a grip I had trained for years against unyielding stone. He might as well have been trying to bend iron bars.

Sal watched, growing more agitated with each passing second, as Tubb's struggles grew weaker. "You're gonna kill him!" he yelped. "Look, he ain't my friend or nothin, but he's all we got. I don't know where to find Billy Boy! The Soothsayer might've already got him for all we know!"

I said nothing. I knew what it took to strangle a man, and Tubbs still had a few minutes. I held on long enough to let him feel consciousness slipping away, then released him, shoving him hard. He fell to the ground with a thud, where he remained, cradling his arm and sobbing between gasps.

I walked over and stood above him. "The Soothsayer is killing people even as we speak. I have no time for games," I said, punctuating the statement by slamming my boot into his stomach. He gave a heavy wheeze and curled into a fetal position for a moment, then rolled over onto his hands and knees, retching, trying to recover the wind I had knocked out of him.

I grabbed a handful of his hair and hauled him to his feet from behind, pulled his head toward me so that his ear was at my mouth. With my free hand, I drew a dagger from my belt and put the point against his throat.

"Let's try again," I whispered. "Where does the Soothsayer live?"

It wasn't what I had expected. Somehow, I had prepared myself for a charnel house, but the location Tubbs had given me turned out to be a nicely appointed country estate, discreetly nestled in a grove of gnarled trees, very private. I wondered if Tubbs had been foolish enough to lie to me, but dismissed the thought. He knew full well I would be back to kill him if he had sent me on a fool's errand. No, this was the right place, just far enough from town, in fact, so that no one would hear any screams that might come from the place at odd hours of the night. The Soothsayer had chosen his lair well. This was fine with me. For what I had in mind, there would be screaming aplenty.

I did things by the book, checking my few weapons. The bandoleer of shuriken I wore across my chest seemed secure enough, as did the pair of daggers at my waist. My hair tied in a bun, black on my face and hands, tools of the trade wrapped in muffling cloth and hooked on my belt, I set out for the house. I crawled on my belly like a snake, creeping ever so slowly from the edge of the property toward the house, looking for tripwires, listening for dogs. Nothing. He had no traps of that kind laid, I decided. No doubt, he would have considered them a waste of his time. I rose to my hands and knees to move a little faster, still low and quiet.

It took me ten minutes to reach the back door. It felt more like centuries, but this is how it must be done. Speed kills in a situation like this. After a quick check to ensure that all of my equipment had arrived with me, I rose and peeked through a window in the door. It opened into a kitchen, a fairly large one at that, with various pots and pans hanging from hooks. I lowered myself to a crouch again and tried the door. It was locked, of course, but this was no problem. I pulled a lock pick from my belt and set to work. Within moments, I was on the other side, easing the door closed with perfect silence.

I waited for long minutes, listening in the dark for sounds of breathing, or the skittering of claws on hardwood, anything that would indicate someone or something nearby. From elsewhere in the house, I could hear a man's voice, but I couldn't make out the words.

It appeared I had the kitchen to myself. On my belly again, I went, snaking along past the inner doorway and into a sitting room. I could hear the voice more clearly now, coming from somewhere upstairs. Though I still could not make out the individual words, I could tell that the speaker was not actually having a conversation. He was singing, chanting.

I made my way up the stairs, low, alert, and quiet. At the top, I paused and listened again, at last able to make out the words.

"Snake a slipping 'bout my house,

Come in here to catch the mouse.

Thinks he's clever, he don't know,

We saw him coming hours ago."

The bastard was mocking me again! He had known all along! Boiling rage swept over me, but I held it in check, refusing to act on impulse. The last time, he had led me right into a trap. He would have expected me to find any he had laid outside, but if he could nettle me into carelessness, I might miss one here.

I inched forward, searching, and indeed, there was a

tripwire across the floor. I followed its path with my eyes, the Soothsayer all the while continuing his mad little ditty, over and over.

"Snake a slipping 'bout my house—"

The wire ran through the banister, up, and to the ceiling, where it attached to an enormous, scythe-like blade. The device appeared to be hinged so as to swing down in front of the entrance. It would indeed have been the end of me if I had rushed the door.

"Come in here to catch the mouse—"

I moved cautiously toward the wire and removed a set of clippers from my belt, then took a long second look at the blade before I brought it down. Miscalculating its path could prove disastrous.

"Thinks he's clever, he don't know—"

Satisfied, I clipped the wire and drew my arm back as quickly as I could, standing as I did so. The blade swung through its deadly trajectory, and I watched it carefully, timing its impact as best I could.

"We saw him coming—"

Just as the blade hit the floor, I let go with a scream fit not merely to wake the dead, but to kill them with fright a second time.

The singing stopped. For several moments, there was complete silence, and then I heard him begin to move, a slow, nonchalant sort of gait, stopping, as near as I could tell, directly in front of the door.

"Let's have a look at our present, shall we?" I heard him say.

Let's do just that, I agreed.

I hurled myself at the door and slammed a foot into it. It burst from its hinges, splinters flying in all directions. The Soothsayer screamed as the wall of wood exploded inward upon him and sent him crashing to the floor beneath it.

I followed and leapt forward, landing atop the door with my full weight where I presumed his head to be. I was on the mark, save for one crucial detail. My feet hit farther apart than I had intended. As the Soothsayer howled in new misery, the door, already damaged when I had kicked it, was simply levered too well atop the fulcrum of his skull. It snapped in two, and the pieces rapped my ankles sharply as they flipped to the sides. I staggered forward, gasping at the shooting pains in my legs, my arms pinwheeling, struggling to regain my balance.

I caught myself against a set of shelves holding a variety of organs preserved in jars. In another place, it would have been quite normal, a laboratory with specimens. Here, knowing their likely origins, it was repulsive. My impact had already tipped the shelf slightly. I deliberately gave it a shove to finish the job, sending the entire contents to shatter upon the floor. So much for *that* grisly collection.

I turned my attention back to the Soothsayer. He had moved the pieces of the door aside and was on his knees, chuckling and grinning like an idiot. He licked at the blood pouring down his face from a nasty gash in his forehead.

"Amused by your own demise?" I drew my dagger and advanced, intent on finishing the job.

Still laughing, he raised a hand and twisted it into a claw. A curious gesture of defiance, I thought. Then I felt something wet and cold grab my ankle.

I looked down in horror to see that my attacker was a severed human hand, one that had been safely in a jar not moments before. As I stared in shock, the nails of the thing lengthened and sank through the tough leather boots I wore and into my flesh, penetrating deeply enough to scrape against bone.

I stabbed my blade into it, not bothering to hold back my own screams. The demon hand struggled furiously, but at last, I pried it loose and knocked it aside. Even as I dispatched the first attacker, a new one, an intestine, rushed toward me, propelling itself with the gyrating motions of a serpent. The mottled, fleshy cord bunched into a knot, then leapt from the floor, trying to wrap itself about my neck. I managed to get a hand beneath it before it tightened, allowing me just enough room to slip my knife past and cut the thing. Even so, I nearly opened up my own throat in the process. The pieces fell to the floor and thrashed about like a severed worm.

I tried to kick them away, but before I could do so, the hand, recovered, took the opportunity to resume its attack. As I bent to fight it off, the two sections of gut lengthened, coiled, and struck again.

I was beyond revulsion now. I was fighting for my life. I bit at the pieces as they slithered over my face, splitting them once more. A second hand began ripping at my other leg. The intestines, four of them now, all sprung upward and continued their assault. From the corner of my eye, I saw dozens of other organs and viscera slithering, loping, and oozing toward me.

As I fought a losing battle against those monstrous attackers, panic rising in my chest, I noticed the Soothsayer, grinning and waving his hands as if he were directing an orchestra.

I snapped a shuriken from my bandoleer and sent it flying his way. Not surprisingly, my aim was a bit off, and it hit him in the arm instead of the throat, but it was effective, nonetheless. He cried out and grabbed his wound in pain, then turned and fled through a door in the back of the room.

With his departure, the animated gore fell to the ground, lifeless once again, mere specimens preserved in formaldehyde.

I looked to where he had disappeared, and felt my blood run cold. I could see through the doorway and into the room beyond, and I knew the place. It was in that room that Cheri and I had died. Now, I am a strong man, but I must confess, at that point, I felt the urge to turn tail and run, to find someplace safe to hide and sob like a child for a while. Still, I knew if I could not face this now, I would never be able to do so in the future, and in any event, I could never live down such an act of cowardice. I thought of Cheri's body, gutted and hung up like a side of beef, and I felt the horror and pain subside, displaced by an overpowering lust for vengeance.

I mocked him as I stalked through the rear door. "Is that all you have, little man? It wasn't enough!"

It was a small lab, with several long counters and a worktable about the size of a large man. The table was covered with an incredibly fine, sandy material, the likes of which I had never seen. As I passed, I laid a hand upon it, and it began to creep along my fingers and up my arm like a living thing. Disgusted, I brushed it away and continued looking about.

Various beakers and tools were scattered haphazardly about

the place, but there was no sign of the Soothsayer. There were no doors or windows that I could see. Surely, he was hiding somewhere. "Come out, you cowardly bastard, so I can wring your neck!"

"Oh, I don't think so," he called back from behind one of the counters. "Don't think so, no, don't think so at all. Time for us to parley."

"Miserable wretch! We'll parley in hell!" I vaulted the counter and landed directly in front of him, blade in hand, and froze. He had a hostage.

He was crouched in a corner, holding a terrified, naked girl as a shield, that glowing, rune engraved knife pressed against her throat. She was no more than twenty, and naked, her skin mottled with bruises. Her eyes, wide with terror, stared pleadingly at me, and her lips moved, but there was no sound, only a rush of air. I noticed with loathing the recently healed scar on her throat, lit by the eerie, green light of his blade, and I knew he had taken even her voice from her. How like this monster, I thought, to strip every last ounce of dignity, of humanity from his victims.

"Back," he hissed, chanting it over and over as he rose. I had little choice. He would certainly kill the girl if I rushed him. I retreated to the other side of the counter, keeping a combat stance, my own dagger still in hand and poised to strike the instant an opportunity presented itself.

He stared at me over her shoulder, leering, his mad eyes like windows into hell. Blood dripped from his chin as he twitched nervously, like a fly. The girl shuddered and almost fainted. He pricked her throat with the knife point, just breaking the skin.

"Don't move, my darling," he told her. "Don't move a hair." He kissed the top of her head, never letting his gaze leave me.

"I know what you're thinking," he said to me. "You're thinking, you could throw the knife, but you'll need an instant kill. Only one good way to do it. You'd have to throw your knife hard enough to penetrate my skull. It's got the length, and you're strong enough. You'd be almost certain to damage the proper motor controls. Or, perhaps, perhaps if you're good enough, in through the eye socket, but it would be difficult to get the right mix of power and precision necessary." He trailed off in a hiss, grinning, beyond insane.

"You squander your last moments by telling me my trade? Let the girl go, and I'll make it relatively painless."

"Oh, no nonono", he chattered, breathing heavily, speaking in short bursts between gasps. "You can't do it that way. As I said, I know what you're thinking. Right now, you're asking yourself, 'Self, how fast can he move the bitch's head into the path of the oncoming dagger?' And you're answering, 'Self, I really don't know, but I don't think he can do it fast enough." He shook his head violently, the twitching seemingly too mild an expression to suffice for his nervousness any longer. "And it's true. Axons can only transmit a signal so quickly. Dendrites can only release motor control chemicals in a finite period of time. I have to see you throw the knife, and then react, move my hands like this." He shifted the girl's head in front of his, then looked back with a grin, a macabre peek-a-boo game, back and forth, never leaving quite enough room for me to get what I felt was a clear shot. I began to sidle around, but he moved with me, and we began to slowly circle, he keeping the bulk of the counter between us.

"Physically impossible," he declared. "Can't be done. You're too close. Nerves don't work that quickly. A pity, really. Wouldn't it have made so much more sense if our nerves were made of gold, good fast, non-corrosive conductors to handle our impulses instead of pitiful flesh?

"But, you know, I know when you're going to throw the knife, I do I do, seen it before. That gives me enough time. So you don't really want to kill this pretty thing, do you? Just to get to me?"

"You're bluffing," I said. "You wouldn't warn me if it were true. You'd just do it."

"And then where would I be? Dead is dead. She dies, I die, right? So it's smarter for me to keep her alive, yes, much smarter."

I stopped circling and considered. He could well be telling the truth. He had been fooled by the door, but who could say what he knew? Murmandimus had said the Soothsayer could only see what he specifically looked for. Maybe he had simply looked to see how it would end. With the girl in the equation, I couldn't afford to risk it. I had to get her out before I could finish him.

Such thoughts were alien to me, enough to make me question

my own sanity. Where was my conviction, my resolve? Why was I hesitating? From a dark corner of my mind, I screamed at myself, *What the hell is wrong with you? This is your chance! Kill him now and the girl be damned!* But I could not. Something stayed my hand, something new, something powerful and frightening, and yet undeniably a part of me. I felt sick with the knowledge that this was not some vile sorcery, but my own will preventing me from sacrificing his hostage. I cursed Murmandimus for his manipulation. This was his fault!

"What do you propose?" I asked at last. "I am a man of my word. Make me a realistic deal, and I'll stand by it."

"A realistic deal." He licked his lips and shook his head again. "You let me go tonight. Tomorrow, resume your hunt if you like. In return, I let the girl go."

"Not good enough," I told him. "You'll kill another tonight, maybe more than one."

He nodded. "True enough. I'll give you my knife. It's very special. I need it for my work, and I can't possibly make another tonight. It takes time and energy for my little machines to assemble themselves into a form as complex as the blade."

"What are you nattering on about? What machines?"

"You saw them," he said, inclining his head toward the work-table and the living sand. "The knife is composed of them, too, a permanent form. It took a week and the life force of three strong men to charge it with power. It's a prize, to be certain. It can cut through anything, if you move it slowly. Surely, that's a reasonable deal, reasonable yes, the girl *and* the blade to spare me for a single night."

I had no idea what he was trying to lecture me about, but getting the knife from him was the most important thing. And there was nothing in the agreement about not following him. I would do that, and kill him the instant the sun topped the horizon. "Agreed," I told him.

"Back up, then. I'll slide it over to you and let the girl go."

"That's not part of the deal."

"I *will* kill her!" He pricked the girl again, drawing more blood. "Show me some good faith!"

The girl's eyes convinced me. I stepped back to the doorframe, my own blade still held for throwing.

He moved slowly from behind the counter and made his way to the worktable. The living sand rippled with purpose, and I realized something was amiss, but I was caught out now. "Slide the knife!" I ordered. "*Now!*"

He looked at me with an angelic, innocent expression, and asked, "You are a man of your word?"

"I am! Get on with it."

He began cackling maniacally. "What a pity I am not!"

He ran the knife across her throat in a slow, gentle movement. With no effort at all on his part, it sliced cleanly through her neck. The girl's hands rose, faltered, and fell lifelessly as her head rolled down her chest and into the pile of sand amidst a river of blood.

I leapt for him then, but a tentacle-like swath of the sand rose and struck me in the chest with the force of a sledgehammer, slamming me to the ground. The Soothsayer's laughter rose to a shriek as I watched through a haze of pain, trying to force myself to some degree of movement. He buried his arms to the elbows in the churning, growing pile as it boiled like a mud pit. Another tentacle formed, reached out and pulled the rest of the girl onto the table and into the sand, where she was quickly and completely absorbed. I struggled to my feet as the strange material, now red as blood, rose over the Soothsayer's shoulders and enveloped him like a new skin.

Before my eyes, fangs erupted from his gums, and new muscle rippled over his crimson body. Talons sprang from his fingers, and the knife slipped from the claws they became to clatter upon the floor. His robe fell away, dissolving before it ever struck the ground, consumed to fuel this monstrous transformation. He was the demon the street people claimed, now. Only his eyes remained unchanged, the same brilliant, mad gleam burning within them.

I charged forward and rained a flurry of blows against his chest, but they did little more than daze him. Fine, I'm adaptable. While he was still reeling, I followed up the punches with a kick to the side of his head that should, by all rights, have cracked his skull. He staggered back briefly, and I was certain he would fall, but it was not the case. He shook his head, groggy, then advanced toward me again as I stood, slack jawed to realize he was not yet dead.

With a low, guttural cry, he lunged forward, slashing with his claws, but for all his new found bulk and weaponry, he had no training. I sidestepped his attack with ease and tripped him, sending him sprawling. I leapt upon his back and drove my knife to the hilt between his shoulder blades, heartened to see that at least the bastard could still bleed.

"Die, damn you!" I pulled on the blade, trying to free it for another strike. As I worked, I realized with dismay that what I had thought to be blood from the wound I had dealt him was in fact the same material that had transformed him! I continued struggling with the knife in desperation as the red fluid erupted and flowed upward, dissolving and absorbing the blade right out of my hands. There was no sign of a wound when it was done. Frustrated, I beat the back of his head with my fists, to no avail. The Soothsayer laughed, then leapt to his feet, sending me flying into the air like some unfortunate, green horseman.

I landed hard on the opposite side of the worktable, dizzied from the impact, but still alive, and hoping to remain so. I cast my gaze about frantically, looking for something, *anything* to use as a weapon. As it happened, the Soothsayer's lovely knife lay right where it had fallen moments before. Surely, it would prove useful now! Invigorated by my find, I snatched it up and rose slowly, feigning injury. I leaned heavily against the table, my right hand, holding the knife, blocked from his sight as he approached.

"Vertebral damage, or a broken rib, perhaps," he noted. "Either way, no more dodging for you now, is there?" I stood my ground as he approached, keeping an expression of pain on my face, letting him get as close as I dared before striking.

"You know," he said with a monstrous chuckle, "You were right. I was bluffing."

"I thought you could see the future," I said in a weak, husky voice, even going so far as to feign a swoon.

"I haven't had time to fetch any new parts," he replied, gloating, savoring his moment of victory. "But isn't it delicious, the anticipation of not knowing how things turn out?" His grin was a nightmare of teeth as he moved in for the kill.

"I know how it turns out," I said, and with every bit of strength and speed I could muster, I brought my weapon up in a searing arc and buried it in his gut. Sparks erupted from the blade, accompanied by the sounds of rending metal and the Soothsayer's own shriek of agony as I drove it higher and higher, laying him open like a fish. The red demon skin exploded from his body in a cloud of the curious, red sand, filling the air around us. I gasped in shock, unintentionally drawing in great lungful of the stuff. As the Soothsayer fell to the floor, I could feel my chest convulsing. Tears poured from my eyes in torrents. Blind and paralyzed by the choking and coughing that wracked my body, I seized the edge of the worktable and held on with all I had left as I rode out the storm, praying that this time the bastard was truly dead.

After long minutes, the fit passed, and not slowly as one might imagine, but instantly. One moment, I was doubled over and strangling. The next, I was fine. It was damned peculiar, but I gave it little thought. I had other, more pressing concerns to address.

I looked about, frantic, uncertain of where the Soothsayer had fallen, fearing he had somehow escaped. With grim satisfaction, I saw him splayed upon the floor scant yards from me, looking like nothing so much as one of his own victims.

I stood over him, covered in his blood, and watched him twitch as the life seeped from his body. He still lived, was still conscious.

I squatted beside him and caressed his neck with the wicked, glowing blade, my gesture communicating more certainly than any words precisely what I intended, and that I wouldn't be buying him even an instant's respite by doing it before he was well on his way to hell.

His eyes were no longer lit with any hellish purpose. In the end, as my employer had requested, they were filled with the same horror he had inflicted upon so many unfortunates.

"Just parts," I hissed.

It took him quite a while to die.

I made it back to Rellith just as the sun was rising. Sal was waiting where I had left him. When he caught sight of me limping his way, he flashed a snaggle-toothed grin.

"You got him, dincha?" Sal asked, barely able to contain his excitement. "Izzat his head in that bag?"

I answered with a nod and kept moving. I was too tired to chat. Sal whooped and shouted with glee, then ran off to tell his friends the good news.

I, however, had one more point of business to conclude before I could call it a night.

The ache in my muscles had begun to fade by the time I reached the red light district, and I found myself in surprisingly good spirits. I had decided that I would forgive Alicia the rest of my fee. I had been forced to move more quickly than I had expected, and it was unlikely she had raised the other fifty in a single night. What purpose would it serve to terrorize her over the money?

I come upon a group of whores plying their trade on a street corner, and asked after Alicia.

Everyone fell silent. As they looked back and forth at one another, nervous and reluctant to speak, I felt my high, fine mood slipping away, replaced by a sick, glacial feeling in the pit of my stomach. My intuition sang like a bowstring. There was more here than simple, streetwise reticence.

"What?" No answer. I singled one out and confronted her. "Tell me."

"She's—" The woman licked her lips, and continued, "She's dead. She came home short last night and Hammer—" She looked down at the street, unable to meet my eyes. "He beat her to death. They found the body this morning. Everybody knows what happened, but nobody saw it, so nothing's gonna get done." She lowered here eyes and stared at the ground. "You know how things work down here."

I stood long moments in silence, my jaw locked as if welded in place. When at last I found my voice, the words fell from my lips like sleet from a gray sky. "Where is he?"

I stood in silence over the mound of freshly turned earth, the wind whipping my long hair about my head and into my eyes.

Thull, Murmandimus, and Sal were just behind me, respectful and quiet. The sack I held in one hand, now soaked through and dripping with blood, seemed doubly heavy. The cold part of my mind, the calculating part, chuckled that 'doubly' was, give or take some minor weight variations, literally true.

It was a good grave, as far as graves go. I had paid for the best. But in the end, it was still a just a hole with a dead girl inside. She had no family. We four were the only ones to mark her passing.

I thought of offering some words, but what was there to say? I loosed the drawstring on the sack and dumped my grisly trophies on the ground in front of the tombstone. Soothsayer's cold, lifeless eyes stared up at us, his face contorted in agony that he no doubt still suffered, wherever his soul had gone. Hammer, it seemed, hadn't the nerve to face us. His head was face down in the dirt. It seemed fitting.

And yet, there was something undone, something important that I was loath to do. I looked over my shoulder at the mage. He nodded his approval, his quicksilver eyes reflecting blue, but otherwise giving no sign of emotion. It galled me that he had so easily guessed what I was contemplating. No doubt, he would poke and prod at me about it later, damn him.

I wondered what dark work the Soothsayer's tiny machines were up to as they coursed through my body. Murmandimus had assured me there was nothing to fear, that I should count them as spoils of war, a fortunate accident of unimaginable value. I had no such illusions. He claimed they would make me immortal, and I believed him. But it seemed to me that this was no blessing. Rather, it was the Soothsayer's final curse, my sentence to witness forever the pointless suffering and death of innocents. Was it any wonder that creatures like Hammer and Soothsayer prospered in such a garden of apathy?

I envied Alicia her peace, even as I resolved to ensure it. She had given me a pouch of coins. I took it from my belt and tossed it to the ground in front of the tombstone.

"Rest well, child. This blood is on my hands alone."

Stonebound

By Damien Wilder

A sharp whistle pierced Desdemona's ears, and she winced. If she had to say anything for Matron Alys, it was that the woman could whistle like a tea kettle. She turned to face the other woman, fixing her pale blue eyes on the brunette behind the desk.

The older woman stared, brown eyes narrowed and one brow cocked. Desdemona licked her lips and shifted side to side, fingers tightening around the book in her hands. "Yes, Matron?"

"Bring. Me. The. Regional. Maps." She enunciated each word as though she'd said them more than once. Probably she had.

Desdemona shoved the book she was holding back onto the shelf and scurried to the corner where the maps were stored. After a frantic search, she rushed to the desk, a roll of vellum in her hands. She spread it on the desk and stepped back, dutifully folding her hands at her waist and keeping her eyes averted. A little averted anyway. No way she'd completely turn away from her mistress.

As Alys slid her finger over the trade ways and roads, Desdemona twisted her white robe in her hands. It had been two years since her powers kindled, six months since she'd used them to sneak up to the sixth floor and spy on Matron Alys conducting a diplomatic meeting with King Majendra of Ashet. As far as punishments went, reverting back to a servant, and only for Matron Alys, wasn't so bad. Better than the flogging

Lady Bellis took for allowing a then fourteen-year-old to steal her power. Desdemona got off light with what amounted to an apprenticeship with the matron. Evidently, she felt it was ambition that led Desdemona to her actions and wished to reward it.

Biting her lip, Desdemona inched closer and leaned to better see the symbols. After a moment, Alys shifted and glanced over her shoulder, one dark brow raised. Heat flooded Desdemona's face, and she quickly looked to the ceiling. With a chuckle, Alys gestured for her to come closer.

"You're too inquisitive for your own good." She touched a shaded triangle over Loreth. "I'm working on setting up an alliance with the people here. They will send us skilled laborers to help expand our village, and we will send the lanterns we create to make their lives a little easier. What do you think of that deal?"

Desdemona was quiet for a long while, lips pursed to the side. Finally, she sighed and said, "I wonder why we're sending anything to them. They should give us what we ask for because they fear us, and men are good for nothing better anyway."

Alys frowned, her brows coming together. She scooted her chair back and folded her hands in her lap. "Desdemona, we aren't wanting to use our allies like slaves. Men are certainly good for many things."

Desdemona snorted. "Bedroom things. That and going Vuli. They're good at that."

Alys and Desdemona locked eyes for a brief second, long enough to see the smolder in the brown-eyed woman's gaze before the palm of Alys' hand struck Desdemona across the face. The younger woman staggered sideways into the desk, lips parted in a gasp. Warm blood oozed from one side of her nose, and she lifted her hand to press against it.

"You are a child, barely past your first bleeding, and I will not have you speak in that manner." The matron stood, towering over Desdemona.

Alys was taller than most of the other Embers; she even stood a good half foot taller than King Majendra. Staring up at the giant of a woman, blood slicking her top lip, Desdemona certainly felt like a child and not like a woman of fifteen. The matron arched a brow, and the younger woman lowered her gaze, slowly straightening until she stood respectfully in front of her mistress.

"Men are good for many things—labor, love, ruling even— and some have trained their Flame enough to use it for good as well. Most of the farmers of Vendith are chloromancers and use their power to grow better crops."

"I understand, Matron," Desdemona said past her bloody hand and then promptly ground her teeth together to stop from saying anything else. Tears burned at her eyes, but she was determined not to let them fall.

"Good." Alys sat again and pulled her map closer. "Go to your room now."

Desdemona offered a bow of her head before striding from the study and down the hall to the little room she called her own. She closed the door and leaned against it, eyes closed. She counted to ten. To twenty. To fifty. With a growl, she pushed away from the door and stormed to the tiny desk, gripping the back of her chair until her knuckles were white.

"What does she know? Born in the citadel, raised among nothing but women. Nothing!" She flung the chair to the side, and it skittered its back into the wall. "If she spent more than a few hours with a man…" If she'd been alone with Majendra rather than with her guards…

Desdemona sank into a crouch, hand sliding over her face and nails biting into her hairline. She squeezed her teary eyes closed, but in the darkness of her mind, his blue eyes pierced into her soul. Dark hair tumbled around his face to brush her shoulders, his strong hands knotted in her dress…

She shook her head and jerked to her feet. She spun, eyes scanning the tiny room, the windowless walls, before slapping her hands to the cold stone. "Stone. Be cold and unfeeling. Don't let it out." She pushed out a shuddering breath and moved to sit on the cot in the corner. "Made of stone."

After a moment, Desdemona folded her arms around her soft belly, pushing at the fat that had plagued her since…She tore her hands away from herself and slapped them against her thighs. It was two years since her old life, two years since her Flame kindled, two years since she'd joined the Order of Obsidian Embers as the youngest with active magic. There was no use for tears anymore.

Alys could say anything she liked, but Desdemona knew better. And if she had anything to say about it, there would be no alliance with any man.

All feeling was gone in Desdemona's fingertips. Everything but prickling pain, anyway. Like she'd been holding her hand under a frozen puddle, but, with a hiss, she just ground the heel of her palm into the other woman's chest, eliciting a yelp of pain.

The woman's balefire—blue and cracked—slowly dimmed until nothing was left but a faint haze around her body. Desdemona jerked her shaking hand away and cupped it close against her body as the other Ember stumbled back, her own hand pressed to her chest.

"See?" Desdemona breathed, shoulders trembling. "That wasn't so bad."

"Wasn't so bad?" The woman shot Desdemona a scathing look. "It felt like you ripped my soul out through my chest."

Pain burned along her fingers, and she shook her hand, teeth clenched. "Stop being so dramatic. All I did was make a copy of your Flame. It hurts, but you certainly still have a soul."

With that, Desdemona turned away and strode down the garden path. She stretched her hands to either side and trailed pale fingers along the soft leaves on either side of her, eyes turned up to watch the gentle drift of orange blossoms overhead.

The tips of her fingers cooled, and with a grin, she dropped her gaze and watched as frost crackled over the leaves. When she mimicked a new Flame, the exploration of it was always her favorite part. And today, she would explore in a most delicious way.

Desdemona hesitated at the head of the stairs, squinting into the red-lit passage below. Enchanted lights drifted lazily along the ceiling, fireflies of magic. She watched them, breathing deeply to gather her courage. Though she'd been a full-fledged Ember for a while now, she'd never ventured lower than the dungeons.

She'd listened to other women talk, of course, knew what to expect, but that didn't stop her heart from pounding.

She closed her eyes and focused on her breathing, on the pain, until the staccato against her ribs lessened, if only a bit. These men were not him. She was stronger now, different.

A shriek split the silence, and Desdemona gasped, taking the first step down and shooting a wide-eyed stare over her shoulder. One of the men in one of the cells was not having a good evening, and if she lingered here too long, she wouldn't be either. Desdemona skittered down the stairs, the fireflies sparking and twisting over her head.

When she hit the bottom of the stairs, she stopped again. More of the enchanted lights drifted along the ceiling, their shadows playing with those from the flickering torches. Rows of doors just like those in the dungeon above marched off into the darkness until the end of the passage where the hall split. Each door was etched with one or more symbols, something to tell what region of the world the men inside were from.

Desdemona was almost to the end of the hall when she found the symbol she was looking for: a sun with a stylized eye inside. The symbol of the nomadic desert tribes' god, Sabha Memakon, The All-Consuming. Why they would name the sun something like that was beyond her. Why they would worship something called that too.

She wrenched the door open. A bevy of multicolored fireflies bathed the room in a soft rainbow of light. Large, blue pillows, big enough to be beds in their own right, lay in each corner, and on them lounged four men, each attached to the wall by a sturdy chain around their necks.

As one, they turned to look at her, straightening as they took in her white robe. Desdemona paused to examine them in turn, eyes sliding over their bare, tawny chests. Her gaze couldn't rest without fear speeding her heart, so she took in the oddest details: the black dusting of hair over their legs and chests, the uneven cut of this one's hair, all four of their upside-down Flame brands, the glint of light off the man in the corner's nose ring.

Her eyes flicked up from his nose ring to follow the chain

attached to it over to his ear and then back to his honey eyes. In the center of his forehead, a raised scar stood out stark against his dusky skin: the same eye that adorned their sun imagery. A smile curled Desdemona's lips, and she strode toward him, chin high as though the proximity to the other men didn't unnerve her.

The man straightened and shifted onto his knees, hands resting on his thighs in the well-practiced show of subservience. "How may I serve you?" he asked in accented Atheran.

Desdemona waved her hand and knelt. "Drop it. You're new here; your loyalty isn't that good yet. You're Kiran, right?"

Kiran relaxed just slightly but remained in his same position, giving her a silent nod.

Desdemona gave a tight smile. "I've done some research. That symbol on your head, the eye of your god, your people believe it lets you communicate directly to him. So you were a shaman before being brought here. Correct?"

Again, Kiran nodded, a slight raising of his brow the only indication he cared about what she had to say.

Desdemona shifted and tilted her head a bit to the side. "I've read that your people tend to possess fairly violent magics, or if not violent, then often rare. I want to know, if you weren't locked in this magic negating room, what would your Flame be?"

Kiran snorted. "If you let me out, I would be gone like that." He snapped his fingers, not quite in her face, but close enough to be annoying. The man grinned at her scowl. "Sand. I can turn myself into sand."

Desdemona's brows shot up, and she leaned forward. "Truly? You have a weak baelfire, but it must still take a huge amount of energy to use a power like that. That will definitely be useful." She leaned back and tapped her hands against her knees. "What can you do with it exactly?"

"What can't I?" Kiran shifted off his knees and sat cross-legged. "I can dissolve my body into sand. What I do after is limited only by my imagination." He kissed his fingertips and lifted his hand, palm up, to the sky. "It is a wondrous gift from Sabha Memakon that I should become what his kingdom is made of."

Desdemona rolled her eyes and slapped his arm down out of the air. "Yeah, okay, but specifically, what could you do to, say, kill or incapacitate someone?"

The man lifted his gaze to her, eyes wide, before sitting back on the cushion. He idly toyed with the delicate chain connecting his nose ring to the one in his ear, watching her with intense eyes. "Many ways. Who are you wanting to kill?"

With a shrug, Desdemona grinned and said, "For starters, the matron."

Kiran guffawed and slapped his thigh, bending and practically burying his face in his own knees. His shoulders shook with suppressed laughter. Desdemona narrowed her eyes, grinding her teeth as she watched him. After a moment, he sat straight again and wiped imaginary tears from his eyes.

"Funny. Look at you!" He waved his hand in her direction, a smirk curling his lips. "You're a child! I will not hinge my escape on someone who likely hasn't even bled yet."

Desdemona shot forward and wrapped her fingers around the chain where it touched his check, and with her other hand, she slapped her palm on the collar around his neck. Ice crackled along the metal, fanning out in intricate patterns until it spread to his skin.

It was beautiful, but his pained groan was more so. Kiran tried to twist his head away, whining as he did. The chain pulled away from his cheek just slightly and a ragged piece of stiff skin came with it, blood bubbling at the edges to slide in fat, slow drops down his jaw.

"Maybe you're a little blind and can't see the robe." Desdemona nodded down to her own body. "Notice it's white. That means I'm an Ember, not a servant, and not a child. So watch your tongue or I'll freeze it and break the pieces down your throat."

With that, she released him. Kiran scrambled forward, pressing his forehead to the cushion in front of him and stretching his fingertips toward her. "A thousand apologies. I'm a stupid man. Command me as you will," he said, half muffled.

Desdemona swatted his hands to the side. "Get up." She grinned as he shifted back onto his knees, one hand pressed to his ripped cheek. "Lilia said you were obedient. I'm so glad to see she was right."

She settled back and gestured for him to relax again, though he declined her offer. "Now, let's talk about what I want from you. First, I'm going to release you. It will hurt. Then we will walk together through the servant's passage. Once we reach the fifth floor, you will use your Flame so that you can accompany me to Alys' personal floor. You will incapacitate her ability to speak as that's how her Flame works, and I will kill her."

Kiran opened his mouth to speak, but Desdemona flipped her hand up, narrowing her eyes until he shut his mouth again. "I don't trust the task of killing her to you. You're a man, after all, and men are weak and treacherous. If you try to betray me, I will destroy you." She lowered her hand, brow raised. "Do you understand?"

Kiran's tongue darted over his lips, honey eyes shifting in turn to look at the other dark-skinned men around the room. Desdemona could see the thoughts as they turned in his head, and logically, she knew she couldn't stop him if he dissolved and flew away on the wind. She sighed and offered a little shrug when his gaze settled back on her.

"I'm not an ungracious woman. If you assist me willingly, then when I become matron, I will offer you protection." She swept her hand to encompass the room, and the other men shrunk away from her gaze. "Your people have always held many places in our rooms. With your dark skin and exotic features, not to mention your heathen beliefs, many of our women find you appealing. When I'm matron, your people will never fear being taken again. I will ensure that all those who follow The All-Consuming will be free of our cells as long as my rule lasts."

She offered her delicate hand and leaned forward, a smile gracing her lips. Kiran stared at her hand, his fingers brushing over the symbol burned into his forehead. With a slow nod, he grasped her wrist. "Deal."

"Excellent." Desdemona started to lean back, but when she tried to pull her arm away, he squeezed, eyes narrowing. "But what of these others?" He nodded toward the man directly across from him. "When I am gone, they will torture them. I won't have that."

Desdemona jerked her hand free and stood, brushing herself off as she turned. "I'll take care of it. Just be ready tonight."

The door swung open, and Desdemona braced her hands, fingertips extended to catch it before it could hit her. She let her breath out slowly so it pooled on the wood in front of her face, masked by the footsteps of the person entering.

The woman crossed into Desdemona's line of sight, never looking back as she swung the door closed. She ran her hand through her short, blonde hair and quickly made her way to one of the nightstands in the shared room. Desdemona followed her, hands raised as she watched the woman pull a little box from the drawer.

"Those things will kill you, Isana."

Isana jerked around, match halfway to the sigara in her mouth. She shot her hand up, and Desdemona slid back into the wall, pressure like an invisible hand pressing her throat closed. Through the spots in her vision, she watched Isana approach as the woman casually lit a new match and touched it to her sigara.

Pain blossomed in the middle of Desdemona's chest, a burning in her lungs. Isana stopped and grinned before taking a long drag and letting the smoke out to billow in Desdemona's face. The pressure relented, and she sucked in a breath, smoke pooling in her lungs. She bent at the waist, hacking until she was trembling as she fought to pull air in.

"Bitch," she murmured and straightened up, wiping a hand over her mouth.

"Creep." Isana sidled back to her bed and hiked her robes up to her knees so she could sit. "Why are you in my room?"

"First off," Desdemona said as she sat on the bed across from her, "this isn't your room. You can't call a room yours and share it with five other people. And second, this whole place belongs to the matron, so you can't own any of it."

Isana rolled her eyes and riffled through the drawer again until she pulled out a shallow, clay dish. She tapped the ashes into it, and shot the other woman a sideways glance. "Technically.

What are you doing in this room in which I share space?"

Desdemona chuckled and smiled, though briefly. "I want to offer you a promotion. You know, when I depose of Alys, I'll need a trusted guard."

Isana choked on her smoke and shook her head, pounding the center of her chest until the fit subsided. "What?" she hissed, leaning across the gap between the two beds. "You can't be serious."

"I absolutely am. We came in together. You're the only one in this place I know I can trust, and I know you share my opinions on the men."

Isana ground her sigara into the clay dish and rapidly shook her head. "You're mad. It's one thing to talk about how wrong she is. It's another thing to talk of overthrowing her. Nothing she's done has been that bad."

Desdemona scooted to the edge of the bed and reached across the space to take her friend's hands. "She spent the morning talking about trade deals with Loreth. One that involved an exchange of our goods for male services, and eventually, the leaders of that city will ask if some of us Embers can come help them tend the fields since our magic is so much better. Then, it will be us women in service to the male authority of Loreth, and who knows how many cities after that?" At the slight widening of Isana's eyes, Desdemona squeezed her hands and leaned closer, dropping her voice to a whisper. "If someone doesn't stop her soon, we'll end up with men coming to learn here, wearing the white robes, and going Vuli in the hall when the pressure is too much for them."

Isana pressed her lips together until they were no more than a white line. Her eyes glinted in the lamp light, anger in the depths of her oceanic eyes. "What do you need from me?"

Desdemona grinned and squeezed her hands once more before releasing them. "Guard me, as I said. There's a man in the brothels who can dissolve himself into sand. I'll use him to stop her Flame." She brushed her fingers over her own neck. "To slide down her throat so she can't use that powerful voice of hers."

Isana arched a brow and shifted back, mouth open to speak,

but Desdemona widened her eyes and halfway shrugged, staring at the other woman until she huffed and waved at her to continue.

"I don't like working with him, but it's hard to find magic that can stop hers. Just this once. I want you there to stop him from running or trying to turn on me."

Isana bit the corner of her lip, brows together as she considered. After what felt like ages, she finally nodded. Desdemona pushed up from the bed and offered her friend a genuine smile before putting her porcelain mask back in place. "Meet me in the brothels tonight one hour after the final bell. Your powers will come in handy getting the guards out of the way."

Isana gave her a tight smile, and Desdemona turned to go, pausing by the door to turn and look back at her. "You should get back to your lessons before it looks suspicious."

With that, she slipped out of the room, letting the door click closed behind her.

Desdemona gripped the edge of the door so tight her fingers ached. The tapestry in front of her puffed dust into her nose every time she took a breath, and it was all she could do not to sneeze. On the other side of the hidden door, a small group of Embers gossiped about the men they'd just spent their free time with. She leaned away from the opening and scrunched her nose, blinking rapidly against the burning in her nostrils.

The women's voices faded until they were gone altogether. Desdemona slapped her hand over her nose and mouth and let out a snorting, choked sound that echoed softly through the hidden stairwell. She widened her eyes and stared into the darkness, hand still clamped over her mouth. When no one came to investigate, she let out her breath in a whoosh and fanned herself, eyes rolled back to stare at the stones just above her head.

After a quick ten count, she shoved past the tapestry and made her way to the red-lit staircase, eyes fixed on the guard. Isana slipped from a side passage, falling into step beside her. They walked in silence, Desdemona's hands clenched at her sides. The iron-clad Ember standing at the top of the stairs narrowed her eyes, gaze sweeping over their white robes. She lifted a hand when they got close and glared until they stopped.

"Last bell rang an hour ago. No one should be out of bed but those returning to their quarters from prayer or from here. Turn and go back before you get in trouble."

Neither woman acknowledged her words, all three of them eyeing each other until the older woman frowned and reached for her dagger. Desdemona rammed her shoulder into Isana's trembling arm, jolting the other woman from her trance. With a snarl, she lifted her hands and shoved the air, and her Flame complied. The woman staggered backward, heels hitting the edge of the stairs and, with a yelp, she tumbled backward.

Isana rushed to the edge and closed her fists, stopping the woman's fall before she could hit the ground, but she still groaned, eyes closed. With one more sideways look, Isana shifted her hands, using her telekinesis to move the guard to the bottom of the stairs and over to a corner. She stayed there, hands closed tight to keep the woman immobile, as Desdemona strode down the hall.

This time, she didn't hesitate at the entrance. The men jumped as the door bounced off the stone, scrambling back to cower in the corners. Kiran, though, rushed to the end of his chain, standing on his toes to get as close to her as he could.

"You came back. We had thought you would not." He pressed his fingertips to his collar, eyes pleading. "We're going now?"

Desdemona slapped his hands away. "Don't touch it unless you want more pain than necessary. Now hold still."

She wrapped her hands around the chain where it connected to the metal ring around his neck, focusing all her new powers into it. Frost spread across the iron, crackling and hissing as it thickened and lightened. Kiran pressed his eyes closed, breath coming fast and trembling, misting in the chilled air. The ice inched across the front of his collar, and he whined, hands shaking with the urge to try and pull the freezing metal from his flesh.

With a resounding crack, the metal fractured, the chain falling to pieces on the stone floor. Kiran shot away from it and across the room to stand near the door, eyes fixed on the cushion which had been his home for the last months. The other men stared wide-eyed at Desdemona as she panted. After a moment, they crept to the ends of their own chains, whispering words of encouragement to her as she caught her breath.

One by one, she freed the other three until there was no one left. She leaned against the wall near the door, eyes closed and body trembling in the cold room, gooseflesh prickling along her skin. It was more magic than she was used to wielding in one burst, but she had to recuperate. She needed to take care of Alys tonight. There would be no other time.

"Des?" Isana called down the hall.

"Coming." She pushed away from the wall and shot a look at Kiran where he still stood beside her. "You didn't run while I was weak."

"A man keeps his promises no matter the person he promised them to." He offered her a tight smile and tilted his head, indicating the door.

Desdemona slipped past him and quickstepped down the hall, Kiran not far behind. She didn't stop when she reached Isana, but rather nodded for her to come with them. When she reached the top of the stairs, the guard grunted from below, and Isana rushed to join them.

The other woman eyed Kiran as they moved back to the tapestry, a scowl on her face.

"You understand your place in this?" she asked softly, her words harsh.

"Do you?" he shot back. At her glare, he shrugged one shoulder. "Be sand. Take out her voice. I understand."

Desdemona swept the fabric aside to reveal the partially opened door leading into the servant's stair. She shot a look over her shoulder and hissed at them both, nodding toward the door when they both turned to her. Isana crossed her arms and lifted a brow, watching Kiran until he rolled his eyes and moved past her into the darkness.

The women followed behind him, and Desdemona pushed to the front. Without a word, she started up the stairs, cursing Kiran's heavy, slapping footsteps. At least he wasn't wearing shoes. It would be so much louder then.

They followed the spiraling stairs up one floor at a time, silent as they could be, Desdemona's wide eyes staring at every door they passed until it was out of her sight. Her chest tightened until breathing was hard, her stomach roiling like a mad cat was trying to claw its way out. She pressed her lips together and clenched her jaw. She must look calm, in control, stone.

Desdemona slowed as they neared the top of the stairs. She extended a hand behind her and waited until she heard the other two stop. Kiran panted in the darkness, his breathing uneven.

"A few stairs got you breathing hard?" Isana whispered in the dark, stifling a chuckle.

"I come from the desert. There are no stairs." Kiran leaned against the wall and wiped his hand across his forehead, eyeing the door in front of them. "This is where I change?"

Desdemona shifted so she could look at him. "Yes. This is the doorway to the fifth floor. The servant's passage doesn't go up to Alys' private floor. Higher level Embers live here, so we're still not supposed to be here, but we'll get in less trouble if you aren't visible." She waved her hand, tilting her head to the side. "So, why can I still see you?"

Kiran pushed off the wall and shot her a glare. "Give me a moment to breath." He carefully stepped around her and touched the wood of the door. He was still for a moment, eyes closed.

His skin cracked in delicate lines starting at his fingertips and moving up until he looked like mud on a scorching day. Desdemona and Isana watched in awe as flesh dissolved to golden sand and swirled in the air around them until there was a sandstorm in the hall. Isana buried her face in her arms, eyes squeezed closed, but Desdemona only covered her nose, squinting through the maelstrom to watch as only his eyes remained, and then nothing.

The sand calmed until it was suspended in the air, and then it slowly trickled into Desdemona's pocket, filling it up until it was full and heavy. Isana lowered her arm, eyes wide as she stared.

"That was...really something."

Desdemona nodded and pressed her hand to the door. "Truly a marvelous talent indeed." With that, she pushed the door open and strode into the hall.

The guard on the other side of the hidden passage stumbled forward, spinning when she regained her footing, one hand up and her iron gauntlets already forming a blade. Her gaze quickly took in the two girls, and she shook her head, straightening up and releasing her magic.

"Girls, you know it's far past your bedtime. Come, I'll—"

Isana flung her hand up, and her magic caught the woman in the chest, bringing her to the ground in one swift motion. She writhed as Isana stood, feet on either side of the woman's hips and hands pressed to the air above her chest. Desdemona moved to the side and watched, eyes fixed on the woman's metal breastplate as it sank in until a loud crack sounded in the hall. The guard sputtered, and blood welled from her mouth, pouring down her cheeks to the stone.

Isana nodded toward the stairs farther down the hall. "Let's go. Someone was bound to hear something."

Desdemona didn't need to be told twice. She hiked her robes and sprinted, eyes fixed on her goal. There would be another guard at the top, one of Alys' personal ones, and she would need to overwhelm her fast. They took the stairs two at a time, and when she burst onto the landing, the woman was already ready.

She made a grab for Desdemona, but the girl ducked and halfway slid around her, hands up. Icicles pieced together in the rapidly cooling air, growing to a wicked point in the span of a heartbeat. The woman turned, and Desdemona propelled her makeshift missiles through the space between them.

Isana skittered forward as the woman fell, catching her, if barely, and lowering her to the ground where she gasped for air, one hand pressed to her bleeding throat. Desdemona took two deep breaths—there was no time for more—and stepped up to the dying woman. She crouched and laid her hand on the woman's chest, eyes closed.

For a moment, Desdemona's skin cooled, and then the ice magic dissipated. The spot where it had previously been warmed until there was no trace she had ever possessed it. But she didn't focus on the feeling. Instead, she touched the pulsing throb of the other woman's Flame, the magic stretching out to her living energy even as its owner perished. She opened her eyes and watched as the guard's baelfire faded and then, with her last breath, disappeared altogether.

A coldness of a completely different kind settled over Desdemona, a stillness that only came with the grave. She let out a shuddering breath and flexed her fingers against the corpse's chest. With a gasp, the body shot up, eyes darting to take in Isana where she stood with her hand over her mouth and the girl crouched over her.

"You can't do this. I have a daughter. Victoria. Don't kill me." The words gurgled out of her mouth almost too fast to understand.

A slow smile curled Desdemona's lips. "It's already done. You're dead. Thank you for these remarkable powers, though. I'll give my regards to your daughter."

She jerked her hand away, and the body hit the ground like a puppet with its strings cut. Desdemona stood and shot Isana a glare as the girl's harsh breathing filled the hall. "Be quiet," she hissed.

"Yes, you probably should do that."

They both turned, Desdemona's hand hovering near her pocket, to stare at Alys where she stood just outside her bed-chambers. She wore nothing but a thin, knee-length nightdress, one brow arched at the girls standing over her dead guard.

"I see." She straightened, hands loose at her sides.

Desdemona flicked her gaze to the woman's baelfire, watching as it twisted and coalesced in a funnel in front of her mouth. Her eyes widened, and she hit the ground, hands flying to her ears. "Isana!"

Alys shrieked like a hawk, the force of it vibrating the doors in their frames, sending pain shooting through Desdemona's head even though she was outside the cone of her magic. Isana wasn't so lucky. She fell to the stone floor, writhing in pain as blood trickled from her ears. Alys took a few quick breaths and refocused her attention to the girls where they lay. She opened her mouth and filled her lungs.

Sand exploded around them in an instant, filling the corridor in swirling, choking clouds. The matron let her breath out in a whoosh and pressed a hand to her chest, gagging on the scratching particles filling her throat. Her nostrils flared as she tried to draw in breath, eyes watering.

Desdemona crawled to where her friend lay and grabbed her arm, shaking until the other woman looked at her with red, tear-filled eyes.

"Do it!" She gestured at Alys.

Isana stared at her for a moment, fingertips trembling as they wiped blood from the side of her face. Finally, after what felt like ages, she blinked and shifted her gaze to the matron where she gasped and coughed. Her lips formed into a perfect oh and she scrambled to her feet.

She thrust her shaking hands toward the woman, and the matron slid across the stones, slamming against the wall hard enough to send what breath she had left rushing out. Desdemona stood and watched her struggle to breath, struggle to move her arms, to do anything. For a moment, seeing the giant of a woman she had apprenticed under so long laid low gave her pause.

Think of what she wants you to do. Desdemona's lips thinned, and heat flooded her face. "I will never have a man think I owe him anything. Not again. Not ever. No man is ever worth my time, or any woman's in this citadel for that matter."

She walked toward her former teacher, eyes hard like frozen puddles. "Not as long as I'm in control."

Alys tipped her chin back and looked down at Desdemona, jaw set, eyes hard. There was nothing she could do to stop what was coming, not in her current position, and she knew it. Desdemona laid her hand on the woman's cheek, gazing up into her face.

Pain flared in Alys' eyes as Desdemona used her new powers to pull her soul away. It was like holding a hot coal in her hand, the intensity of the woman's spirit prickling at her palm and sending heat racing through her veins to pool in her chest. She closed her eyes, her breath rushing from between parted lips as the sheer force of Alys' life pushed into her.

With a gasp, she staggered away, taking a few steps back before falling to her knees. She slumped forward, hair obscuring her face. The thump of the former matron's body hitting the ground dimly registered, but she didn't move, not even when Isana crouched beside her. She didn't try to speak, just squeezed Desdemona's shoulder until Kiran knelt beside them both.

"I did not expect that to work. My congratulations on your new position."

Desdemona finally lifted her head, and her vision swam just a bit. "Thank you for your assistance, Kiran. I'm a woman of my word." She pushed to her feet and held her hand down to help her bloody friend stand, Kiran following suit. "I'll draft up our agreement right now. Though I have many plans of subjugation for the men of my own country, your desert tribes will remain untouched."

Desdemona squeezed Isana's hand and nodded back toward the study, her study. She offered her friend a small smile, one that Isana returned, albeit pained. "Come. It's time to set our own plans in motion."

The two women walked down the hall, Kiran following behind. Desdemona let the smile linger on her lips for a moment, just a moment, before forcing it away. She would never have to worry about being weak again. Never be subject to the whims of others. She would be strong. Like stone.

HALDIOM

A *Crater* Short Story

By S. D. Howarth

Mellar's whistling grated on my nerves. Not because of the atmosphere, or the location, or even the tune. He was just shite at it. Every single lift down and it was the same bloody tune. It was beyond irritating and I realised my subconscious had been harbouring the urge to hurl him into the shaft for some time.

"Quit it."

"Huh?"

"Desist, or you'll force me to feed you something blunt."

"You wish, darling. What if I pick another one?" He caught the look I gave him out of the corner of his eye and shut up. I waited and his lips puckered as though for another tune. My hand moved. Grinning sheepishly, he spread both hands and hooked his thumbs onto his belt. I released my pistol and let out a long breath, expelling my irritation. It wasn't entirely him, or the lift, or travelling up to the back of beyond without an army. It was everything. Maybe I'd been doing this too long. Mellar give me a considering glance and cleared his throat.

"What?" I snapped.

"I think you're being unreasonable, your holiness."

"Are you making me reconsider shooting you?"

"Hah, no, but we have been on the trail for a while. I appreci-ate The Order's pay, Topan, but we are beyond your city empire

and denying a man the right to whistle is just mean." Giving
him a flat stare I received one back. "I agreed to guide you to
Mid Rim, Investigator. That was over a day back."

"We *are* Mid Rim, why do you think the lifts descend? As
I suspected, there's a highway inside the caldera wall. For a
mountain guide, you can be thick."

"Piss off."

Exasperated, I held out my hand, palm up, fingers raised to
form a dish. I stabbed the middle. The Hub. "Crater city and the
environs with the surrounding lake, you loathe." He grunted, I
suppose it was better than his fucking tune. I tapped my palm
heading towards my ring finger. "Farmsteads, factories, found-
ries for the iron caterpillars sprawling to your new frontier with
its coal. You make plenty of coin guiding folks, don't you?" He
gave me a 'what the fuck are you on about look', but he deserved
my lecture. I tapped an arc on my ring. "Mid Rim. The iron
mines and forests. Guiding those caravans and lumber trains
between settlements is risky. Isn't it?" Mellar's disinterest evap-
orated, and he jerked his nose to my fingertips.

"Your order has driven many vampyres and other beasts
into the higher wilderness. We clash when monthly caravans
return hub-wards. If that interests you, why head here? No one
lives on the High Rim. The air thins and the weather's abysmal.
You're lucky we've missed the avalanches."

"The mine is here for a purpose. The location matches the
rumours where something dark forms. We spent two weeks
climbing up, I bet you that bonus we cover the same distance
down in as many days."

"Then what? Of course it's fucking dark, it's been abandoned for centuries. Call it ancient history. Call it a mistake
by the founding fathers, or haunted—who gives a fuck? You'll
never persuade folks to work here. You are wasting your time
and I mean it about the bonus for entering here."

"Yes, I doubt inners will live here and you will receive your
coin." I tapped the middle of my hand. "Civilization *is* here,
twelve hundred ovoid miles of avarice and flaw." I circled my
finger around my hand through the middle knuckles, touching
my callouses randomly. "Rumours exist here. And here. And

here. Mid Rim, where industry wishes to flourish on roads of iron and stone. Where merchants seek their fortune, yet fear to tread. Why?"

"You're asking *me*? Now? By the Seven Gods, Inquisitor, either you trust me, or don't? No-one knows what's happening." Mellar's voice rose, and the first flush of anger ruddied his nose in the lantern light. "Not one body has been found. The last incident was a column of militia from Low Crag. If they took off, they are still running. I heard in Bend before you hired me that vampyres are also scarce. Can you tell me if something connects them?" He flicked a lopsided sardonic smile my way. "No vamp' bounty, makes the rimfolk unhappy, 'specially when high and mighty inners come calling."

"Unhappy as folk vanishing without a trace?" I could also be sardonic.

Our little cuboid world lurched, and something overhead gave a strident crunch and echoing screech. There was a rustle, then silence as we undulated. I exchanged a grim look with Mellar and shrugged. Conversation forgotten as we wouldn't be progressing by lift. Still, we weren't falling which was always a relief.

"Reckon they fed the ferrets?" he smirked.

"They'd need to be big fuckers to haul this mine crate up and down. Ogres perhaps, or worse. Are you hankering for a stroll?"

"We may not have an option. The timing's bad as I dropped one before the clatter."

"Gods! Not your guts again, that *will* attract things. I've been making regular prayers on your behalf for two days since we passed through the gorge. Could you not stick a rock in it?"

"Don't be daft, do you want a lump of ore pinging around in here?"

I tapped the scuffed blackwood sides of the swaying chamber and conceded he may have a point. Stains and tiny scratches merged in mottled abrasions. Either it was damn hard stuff to resist mine workings, or this deep had irregular access. That much that I could discern in the lantern light.

"Stay, or go?" He pushed, breaking my thought. He withdrew a thin neck-slicer and poked at the seam between two close-fitting boards. Good luck prying them out I considered and looked for options.

"Deliberate, or accidental?" I tossed back to make him pause. The squeaking of his blade was grinding my nerves worse than the whistling.

"Either. We're going down with a light load, so either a failure or someone pulled a lever." Steady dark eyes bored into my own. "The hatch?"

"The hatch, better anchorage. I'll proceed first."

"I'm wounded."

"Not as much as anyone near your arse. If we don't remove the rumoured cultist threat, Crater will revolt."

"Ha, what's new. Four riots this year with iron and food shortages?" he muttered as he cupped his hands. Bracing himself, he waited for me to climb up him to the hinged square furthest from the gate. As our faces became level, he yawned. The utter bastard. I could taste, never mind smell the spiced crab he'd wolfed before our descent. Unable to resist, I kissed him. A light one, brushing my greying beard into his stubble. A mockery of a distant memory.

"What if it's trapped?" he asked, pulling his head away.

"A little late to ask? Let's crack on." Leaning hard on his shoulder, I heard him grunt as I stretched, scrabbling for the chill iron. My fingertips brushed it before I clamped in a wanker's clasp.

I screamed. Jerking and shuddering as though possessed, he dropped me like an anvil, his face ghost-white. An inopportune colour when two miles underground. After several seconds, I whooped in a breath and laughed, the pains in my back and arm fading as my voice rolled around the chamber and up into the shaft. *Oops.*

"Bastard! You diseased godfucker of a bastarding bastard. Your order will always be bastards, worshipping that whorish bastarding bitch!" He paused, lost for breath, his face flushing like ink spilt on parchment, darkening the weather-lines on his narrow face. It was a stupid thing to do in the dark when we may not be alone, but I laughed louder.

For once in maybe half a dozen occasions over thirty years of service, the rumour and location whispered into my ear for coin proved true. We found the last remains of a dark temple. Unknown hands had carved and caressed stone into angular forms when smoothing the contours. To civilise the rock. They'd also directed the seepage trickling in patters and streams on the walls towards the lift shaft in a neat central channel. It suggested habitation continued deeper and perhaps my superiors were wise to be cautious. *To send me.*

The tunnels here were older than the spent seams of iron, copper and coal a mile above and suggested a worrying organisation of labour considering we could breathe almost normally. I estimated we'd descended five miles below the High Rim entrance. More worrying, it was as cold as a brisk winter's day. The earth gave off no heat and perhaps rimworkers were right to complain mine-work was cold work. *Why?*

Someone. Something. Some party, had made a deconstructive effort to collapse the tunnel leading to the portico we glimpsed in the swaying light of rolled glow globes. Once, might be the fickleness of age. Three separate locations suggested efficiency, or someone failing to drop the outer sprawl onto the subterranean temple.

Only the central collapse concerned me. The furthest I could see through an irregular gap led to an elaborate anticline, with a short flight of steps to the void. Half the roof had come down but tumbled into an airway instead of forming a final blockage. Once we cleared several large boulders, it would be navigable. The first rockfall we'd encountered took a quarter hour to clear. Backbreaking sweaty work, with every second an eternity as stretched nerves waited for the assault which never came. It never became easier trailing after obscure hunches, but I knew we were close to the source. I could taste the tension. We eased the smaller rubble aside with deft scrapes of shovel and gauntlet. A caress too kind for this place.

Once we shifted the detritus, we moved onto the principle obstructions. Higher than a man, there was no way we could move them stacked as they were. Sorcery was a lost art to humans, and a banned one to non-humans. I knew about the latter more than most, I'd hunted and executed enough until the scant few who embraced their dark art abandoned their obelisks and fled.

Working in silence, I wondered who'd performed the sabotage while we spread alchemical cutter paste with iron scrapers. We'd both lugged the canisters on our backs down the lift shaft, through winding passages and perspired up too many hogs backs to count. Silent of activity and barren of workers, the only noise was the echo of our laboured breaths. Every so often I felt his glance, but I kept my own counsel.

Crater was the pits, and we were well outside the arsehole, yet a million souls depended on the sanctuary and sanctity The Order provided. Twice that including The Rim. Archaic traditions married pragmatism, racism, religion and secular control. It could have been a paradise if humans controlled everything. We didn't, only the base of the bowl and we needed the resources on caldera cliffs.

The land was ours, the skies a mystery and the depths the domain of every other denizen we sought to purge. There lay the problem to pardon the pun. For each mine we had to fight, scheme and betray. We had numbers, factions, but older creatures existed, whose survival depended on their cunning, speed and skill. Where people expanded and innovated; they dug and grew stronger. My thoughts turned as dark as to what might exist through that doorway as the paste etched its way to the heart of each boulder. Gods, it was diabolical stuff. We backed off a hundred feet just to gulp in breaths of foetid air, the acrid taint a barrage on our senses.

"I'm not liking this brain-fart of yours, Topan. I presume you've a plan beyond crawling into dark holes?" Mellar groused, tossing his scraper aside. I'd been smarter and left mine jammed in a crevice between two boulders. Taking care to tilt my wide-brimmed hat back with the back of my gauntlet, I saw his eyes crinkle at the crash of rock, shattering across the smoothed tunnel floor. Pings and pops followed in a discordant symphony of echo and vibration, with dust clouds holding onto their coattails.

We backed off another dozen feet to a widening in the

corridor as though the dust cloud was alive. In reality, the particles could still contain active cutter and it could eat through us from the lungs outward. Neither of us chanced it, as there was no way either of us could haul the other back into daylight. A swift jerk of blade in flesh and that accompanying moment of white-hot agony wasn't what either of us sought. Not this far from the light. I owed Mellar half his payment on purpose to maintain his vested interest in my return. Only the dead trusted another fully.

"It is what it is," I shrugged. I'd needed a guide through the mountains. He was reliable muscle, with a passing familiarity with the area where the secluded adit overlooked the clouds and sheer cliffs down to Mid Rim. If I was guessing, things, he wouldn't know the story of the mine, would he? People talked to the Caravanserai Guild, and it was slow, profitable work, built by decades of word-of-mouth business. I'd chosen him over two younger men and he'd earned my coin.

Yet someone *was* down here. Mellar's lack of curiosity was odd now we'd descended. He'd gave me a slow nod and offered his price with nary a question, nor quibble in Bend. Someone had lit the lantern and disabled the lift and opened the hatch on every lift below. If disused, the chains around granite counterweights would have rusted long ago. Someone *had* applied the brake on the passage far above. A quiet and cunning sort. *What was I missing on top of the delay?* The climb down to the next lift had knackered us, yet we'd seen no-one. No spoor. Nothing. I looked hard at him and his humour faded.

We worked well together, knew the moves and survived the risks. That was it. We'd been deliberately exhausted. Exposed to claustrophobia and the humid depths. The caress of the unknowable as the earth pressed down. An invisible and inexorable threat, just like the cult. A day in the mine acclimatised me to the air becoming so stuffy, breathing was like swimming. So why the sidelong glances? *Expose and trap us?* I heard a coin drop. Not us, *me*. Had the rumours of a distant cult been a ploy? Shit.

My hand moved of its own volition, snatching the butt of

my flintlock from my hip and dragging the hammer back with a deafening click. Mellar's eyes widened in resignation and became huge as my arm drew up. I fired. He threw his glow globe. A grunt and a flash as I punched out in reflex. The pistol missed. The bastard elongated around my shot. *Elongated!* I saw the flash occur as though in slow motion as the lead ball slammed into the wall behind him and sparked orange and blue filaments. Our shadows danced. Fuck, he was close—way too close! Then I screamed as a hammer-blow crashed into my side, slamming me into the wall. Words formed on my lips, but the coppery tang of my blood bubbling cut me off with the suddenness of a noose. Darkness enveloped me, my light snuffed away like a candle.

Thwack. Thwack. Hard slaps nearby returned me to the land of the living. I pried at my eyes, but only one worked. That would be enough. Head buzzing and breathing shallow, I moved my arm through the dust. Soft, like a hand into a velvet glove and touched bruised contours. I rotated my eye on the noise which disturbed my enforced slumber and saw Mellar slapping the flames chewing through his right knee with my gauntlets. Ha! My wild swing had flicked the globe and the vicious contents back on him. How I hadn't gone up in the inferno as he poleaxed me was a miracle to which I could only credit the great lady.

Why wasn't he screaming? In the fading embers, I saw him for what he was. A vile image burned into my eyeballs past the smoke and leather and charred flesh. Brittle-looking, more like rotten wood than meat. Grey, the grubby colours of stone. Mellar wasn't a human.

"You never were good at keeping tabs in these mountains of ours. Your precious religion never cared for anything beyond Crater Lake. The Hub will learn their mistake. The Darkness will see to it. We've prepared for a century while feeding the edifice. Learning the masters' desires, while your holier than shit attitude stagnates throughout your inbred squabbling surface dwellers. Stifling change. The world beyond the rim could grind you to dust and you'd still be unchanged. Crater is no volcano and we've barely begun scraping a path to the light."

"I can't believe I kissed you!" I snarled, my mind whirling at his admission as my body sought an out. He might be right, as it explained the frigidity I felt from the unnatural cold. I reached under my chest and clasped the hilt of my short blade. Felt the warmth as my feet sought purchase.

"Is that what bothers you? You small petty man," he scoffed as his face contorted into a long venomous sneer. He became taller, more feral until his head brushed the tunnel roof. His eyes glittered golden, all seeing.

"A shifter, for how long, heathen?"

"Long enough to remember our cozy night trapped by the blizzard in that old tower. Our progeny are destined for greatness when Darkness ascends." He gave a malicious smile which vanished as I rose. Light illuminated the tunnel, reflecting his sudden fear back into his iris. "No! That's not fair!"

"Inquisitor to the Lady of Illumination, not investigator. Your clan of wriggling bottom feeders slipped up." I raised my long dagger as though wagging a chiding finger and the golden spine with its sigils irradiated a garish orange light. Faith suffused the tunnel. Blooming. As I prayed, pouring forth my cant, he diminished. For all his physical prowess, he seemed smaller, unable to face the light, the glory of my mistress in melic radiance.

He cursed, his words unintelligible, and we cast together. A hammer of purity punched from the tunnel roof into his head, blasting eyeballs and brains over my feet as he flopped limp with a wet splat into the puddle of dissolved rock. I looked down, expecting to see a steaming hole through my chest. To my incredulity, I remained intact. Being the practical sort around miracles, I gulped in a deep breath, grimacing at the stench and lurched to retrieve my gauntlets.

I bless my equipment, yet for one reason or another, I'd neglected on buying the gauntlets with hustling before a storm to meet the wagon train into Bend. Crater city is sheltered by distance, yet the rising land and Rim mountains are brutal when the weather turns. It made a seasoned guide a necessity and Bend has plenty, being a major trading town. A soldier worships the God of War, or in rare circumstances, the God of Healing. I'd sought knowledge instead. I'd needed to find logic in the world—answer every why. It was a mutual marriage of convenience. My sect within The Order needed rid of corruption and I needed a cause, which I hadn't realised at the time. I became the hammer on their anvil. Common, utilitarian and effective.

I raised my dagger and peered towards the temple, squinting and probing with my senses. There was something, an eerie hollow dread I couldn't shake. Shit, he'd sacrificed himself for a summoning—the cunning bastard had reached out to his unseen master.

Then I felt it. I shook, and that was before I saw a tiny mottled octopus on four stubby legs crawl out of Mellar's neck where the flesh still sizzled. I stamped, swallowing bile. I wasn't taking a chance with the sickening sensation I experienced, as I'd done that and been played like a harp. What could dim my goddess? Piss-poor perspicacity for an inquisitor. *For me.*

From the depths of that dark entrance, a cry echoed until it roared like all the hives of hornets in the land released together. Darkness exploded between those all too close columns, swerved over the partial collapse and split around my blade. I felt chilled to the marrow as the light dimmed to a pitiful mockery of its former self. I spun on my heel, coat billowing as the ground tremored and ran as the glow globes died. My only illumination was my dagger, irrepressible and enfeebled.

I scooped up both pistol and smoking gauntlets and barrelled down the passage, past the unworked rich rider of coal we'd come across when having a breather. It extinguished a cheery flicker of reflected light out as I wheezed past, skidding and sliding through turn and syncline. Adrenaline clutched my weariness and wounds and flung them behind as mouth gaping, my heart pounded, and legs pistoned.

The pitch of the roar shifted, becoming pure malevolence as I fled through crossroads and side tunnels, past abandoned carts and hurdled discarded tools. Hidden eyes followed my every move, boring into my back. I caught glimpses of pursuit out of the corner of my eye, but with the dark drawing in, they were distant flickers.

My subconscious ran amok as I hit my second wind, seized it in a vice of determination, clenched my teeth and bit. A promise of unstoppable despair caused frosty tendrils to seize my spine and compressed my bladder in unadulterated fear. The short blade became the symbolic fragment of my goddess—a spark in the dark. Her residual touch might save my soul and if she so desired, my life.

Whatever followed me, Crater, and The Rim was unprepared for it. My temple and The Order hadn't faced something of this magnitude. Black, white, purple and blue, the old and young of humanity needed warning. I stifled a sob, feeling powerless as my second wind faded and the pressure increased on my trembling steel, with just the sigils glowing. The lift appeared, empty and lit by the lantern we'd dimmed. I could have sobbed a prayer to luck itself if I'd the wind.

Wheezing, gasping, I tottered on rubbery legs as it lurched to a halt. I heard the crack of the brake being released and redoubled my pace. Snails passed me as I saw it rise, inch by painful inch. The blood roared in my ears as it ascended. *I wasn't going to make it!* I hurled myself on, willing more speed, throwing myself at the opening, punching out my arms to grab the gate— and missed. My pistol flew inside as my armpits rebounded on the threshold. My tattered gauntlets snaked through the dust where we'd stood, fingernails gouging. *No!* I clutched nothingness in a despairing grip and plummeted, spent. My hat flew off, and I caught a brief flicker of it spinning end over end into the shaft as I somersaulted. Shit, I'd see it again soon enough.

Pain. A bastard motherfucker of a pain seized both my wrists as I swung dumbfounded and dragged me upwards. I became a howling human pendulum a foot beneath the dusty floorboards and an inch from spreading my nose on the centre beam. A pale face, with a halo of dark curly hair the colour of midnight smiled down with the warmth of a winter blizzard.

I half expected my hands to explode from the force of her grip as elongated teeth and red featureless eyes turned my bowels to ice when she licked her lips. A languid curl and twist of promise. When terrified beyond your wits, this isn't a sensation to relish. Like a babe, she hauled me into the lift before the rock face smeared me flat. Like said child's toy, she deposited me under the still open hatch with a chaste kiss that had my cheek prickling and my cock tingling against my thigh.

I blinked, face now burning like the searing pain when thawing from frostbite. My hand darted for the gun, seeking reassurance in empty arms as I shuddered away. Her touch, sent my soul writhing. I took in a deep shuddering breath, summoning professional civility and holstered the flintlock. I missed my hat. It surprised me I had the energy to conceive such inanity.

"Lady Jezebel, fancy meeting you. My thanks, your timing was impeccable."

"Grand Inquisitor, Luthir Topan, forgive my imposition, but Baal awakens." I would have laughed at her dry formality, here of all places, but I didn't have it in me. Not after experiencing the thing below. I leaned against the wall and started. It was no small relief to see the light on my blade brighten and the lantern flutter on the ceiling pivot. Jezebel stared, and I was thankful to see her eyes become mithril mirrors. Instead of pupils, I saw my blade reflected. "This concerns all races. Unchecked, it will envelop everyone for an eternity of unimaginable despair."

"Wouldn't the long-lived like yourself appreciate mankind being consumed? This Old One, Baal—is the Darkness?" I took no particular pains to conceal my incredulity.

"Yes. I am here by choice. My choice, Priest. My coven, my race, will not become mindless pawns. If we do not stand together, that will be our fate, before being consumed. Assimilated and eradicated from existence."

"A nice thought considering our not insubstantial differences. The tunnel, was you?"

"Yes, I failed. It was too strong."

"Fuck."

She was a cool one, and I could not remain to stand. I could feel the world pulling me down. I slid onto my backside to sit on my holster. My eyes became heavy and the last thing I saw was the sigils of Pansoph fading from my blade as vampyric eyes scrutinised me, then the rock face beyond the opening.

"Wake up!" Her voice came from far away. I moaned as her boot probed the side of my chest. It didn't take much imagination to feel the enmity behind the pain. My backside ached of sitting on my pistol, but I felt fewer aches than I may have expected, so I couldn't have been out long.

"What is it?"

"The Baalim are coming," she bit her lip, but there was nothing sensual in the mannerism. No obvious diabolical deception. She peeked over the gate and flicked a sideways glance my way. "We have a few minutes at most."

"Right." My mind whirled, too gummed for melancholy. I moved my leg and decided I may as well reload. "Do we have a truce?"

"For now, yes. We can arrange a concord later *if* we get out." He eyes emitted a glow like coals and I gulped. I rammed the ball down the barrel and felt my wrists sting. I muttered a prayer and checked under my cuffs to see dark weals in the angular shadows. She sensed the movement and my surreptitious shield prayer and rolled a throaty chuckle to my ears.

"It appears we are not compatible. A simple touch between us remains unclean. You are not the only one with trust issues, Inquisitor. Self-righteous purple-skinned bastards like you have hounded non-humans for millennia. You reap what you sow, but this entity is as old as the land and its minions will not drag my brethren down with your kind."

I grunted. I couldn't disagree with anything she'd said and my clever plan to sneak in for a preliminary look had unravelled. I looked at her, small beautiful and determined and shook my head. We were almost a match in our arrogance and failure.

Only a Vampyr would wear a silk ballgown in a mine and not appear stupid. Her lip curled, and she wriggled her fingers. I saw flesh through the charred burgundy velvet and that answered one unasked question. With a sigh I stood, fingering my ankh and split my gaze between the hatch and the gate. Neither inspired confidence as the sounds of pursuit reached us. Form an alliance with a devil to fight a different hell. I shuddered and not from the chill.

She moved in a blur, a feral hiss bursting from her throat as
shadows loomed. Her punch sent one figure and the gate back
down the shaft. I struggled to see the Baalim as darkness and
shadow undulated in misshapen humanoid form. They dwarfed
Jezebel who'd stand five-foot-four when not in heels to match
my six-foot and the shapes were a head taller than me.

I lashed at one squirming past her and it snarled as it came
into proximity of my nimbus. I seized the imperceptible hesitation and thrust my blade in its throat and twisted. Jezebel spun
on one exquisite leg and buried her heel in the amber eye of a
creature launching itself from the roof. I chanted at the one following to blast globs of brains and flesh over both combatants
as she struggled to extricate her foot. She gave me a look. *A look
to wither a man.* Sighing at her dress, she pivoted, throwing the
corpse into another pair clawing inside.

I glanced up, my instincts working faster than my mind and
saw a face in the hatch. I fired. A howl, a thump and scraping
splatter as it tumbled between lift and shaft. No time to reload
as another javelin'd inside and clobbered me before I could flip
my gun. I owed my goddess another prayer as I careered into
the back of the lift, somehow keeping my grip on the blade and
pistol. I ducked and slammed the heavy butt into a kneecap. It
shrieked so loud I felt blood run from my ears. I hit it again, and
again, infusing myself with divine power. It howled, I smashed
the fucker in the mouth, shattering its jaw and silencing it.
Jezebel grabbed it by the back of the neck and tossed it out. No
clatter.

More dropped, and we fought back to back. Each time we
touched I felt nauseous, and she hissed. Bumping and twisting
I stabbed, clubbed and chanted, but my strength was draining.
I could not maintain the tempo as lean bodies piled around our
feet. A punch felled me and only the flick of her hand into my
hair kept me from a long trip downwards.

Another punch rocked me where Mellar had struck, and I
toppled, lungs voided. I felt myself fade out as a figure pounced
to tear out my throat. Eyes like coals drew me in; empty, merciless and I accepted it was my time. Jezebel darted in but darkness

clamped fangs around her thigh. She shrieked, in pain and the anguish of having her gown ruined. Hammering its head, the vampyr twisted and attempted to drag herself forward and reach me. Instead, it punched a talon between the floorboards and pulled her backwards.

With a curse, she tore free her necklace and threw it at the roof as she barked something guttural. I stabbed. A last pathetic act of defiance. The lift shook as though caught in a hurricane. The weight on me vanished as stickiness gushed over my arm. Frustrated rasps and thuds swirled as everything went white to a clarion chime. Agony exploded, as though an unseen hand grabbed my life energies and sought to tear them away.

Her boot prodded me again, thankfully on my uninjured side. I rolled over and threw up, feeling weaker than a day old kitten. I knew the taint of sorcery and it repulsed me to my core. I hauled myself onto my haunches in a suddenly empty car and spat into the shaft to clear my mouth. Other than the small hole in the floor and patches of sulphurous scorching as though something had ricocheted around, it appeared we'd been ascending alone. I wiped my mouth and cursed. All the corpses had vanished, and I'd wanted a head as evidence.

I caught her as she fell, light, yet somehow solid and grimaced at the amount of thick black blood pouring over my coat from her leg. I could let the unholy bitch die. Be righteous as holy Pansoph decreed and my reputation dictated.

My goddess commanded me to cleanse the world of the impure, but I couldn't end her. Not here. Still. *I yearned to do it.* The spell formed on my lips unbidden as I shook with indecision, frustration ripped across my face as I watched her breathe. A regular in, out of blood mottled silk. I slammed my knife into the boards and summoned light. Moving with a purpose, I tore free my neck-scarf, rolled and wrapped it tight around her thigh. Ignoring the smell was more difficult, and I felt my gorge rise as her blood stank like old coffins.

I sat when finished, applying pressure on the wound, using one paste eaten gauntlet as a pad and applying pressure while wearing the other. Idly, I fingered the shard of jewellery she'd used to save us. Felt the energies through my fingertips. I had a premonition and didn't like where it led. I'd have to suggest it. Be the one to persuade her to darken our light, and grant mankind greater power for an unprecedented cost. For a moment, I felt lost, as sick as when she'd stolen my life force. I'd felt the pursuit, the wrongness below and couldn't imagine how to stop it. It was not owing her my life that stayed me, nor humanities need, but a question. *What the fuck were we fighting?* I laughed until the jerk of the mechanism stilled my bitter tears.

Even exhausted, it took me a moment to drag her into the next lift and lower the battered one so I could stand on the roof. I imagined the things that almost killed us—the Baalim—as I fingered the vial on my belt. If honest to myself, I was glad to escape her taint. If I destroyed the lift, it'd delay whatever was emerging. It'd prevent a return in numbers for a counterattack as a trade-off but returning to gather the forces and resources would consume precious time—possibly months.

I didn't have the time to spend and what fucking inspiration would prayer grant? Shit and shitter, two scales to balance fate and future. A bad hand to roll on, to temporise upon but I took the easy option. Call me a coward, but I cracked the wax seal and tipped droplets of cutter on the roof shackle, then the chain, before jumping to the passage and kicking the brake. I didn't look back, I knew nightfall lay ahead.

The King and the Wizard

By Frank Martin

I pushed open the hatch above my head and was instantly met with the relieved faces belonging to my personal guard.

"My king!" exclaimed one of the excited knights. "You're back!"

The men helped me up the last step and into the wine cellar. One of the knights then looked down into the tunnel I just emerged from. It led into a secret passage that had been used by royals and knights to sneak in and out of the castle for centuries.

"Where is Lady Grace, my liege?" the knight asked.

He was referring to my bride-to-be. She ran off tonight, on the eve of our wedding, to the Black Witch of the dark forest. I didn't have the time to explain what happened when I found her, though. Our predicament was dire, and there was only one thing I needed to know.

"Where is Wyland?"

The same knight scrunched his face confused. He didn't understand. But he didn't have to. He just had to answer the question. "In his study."

I fled from the cellar so quickly the puzzled knights couldn't react swiftly enough to follow. I sprinted through the castle's halls as fast as my armored body would allow. I found no one awake at this late hour. Everyone was probably asleep and resting for what they presumed would be an eventful royal wedding tomorrow.

Everyone except Wyland.

I knew he would still be awake. It was rumored the wizard had conquered the necessity to sleep as a youth and now spent his nights refining spells and concocting potions. In all my family's royal history, I never read about a wizard so skilled at such a young age. I only hope he was strong enough to help solve this crisis I've stumbled upon. Otherwise, the whole kingdom would be at risk.

As king, I wasn't necessarily required to knock on any doors of the castle before entering. I usually did, though, out of respect and courtesy. Not now.

I barged into the wizard's study without breaking my stride and spoke even before spotting him. "Wyland, I need your help."

The wizard looked up from an ancient tome he had his head buried in and squinted at the sight of me. "My king? What's wrong? You look frazzled. Are you anxious about tomorrow's nuptials? If you require a calming potion then I'm sure I could—"

"It's the Black Witch."

Wyland's squinted eyes grew wide. He stared at me a moment before asking a question threw gritted teeth. "What does she have to do with this?"

I shamefully lowered my gaze to the floor. "Grace is dead. The witch transformed my beautiful fiancé into a dragon and compelled me to slay her."

"That devious hag!" he shouted while slamming the tome shut. "Is it revenge you want?"

"Yes." I looked up, eager to plan our next move, but then caught my excitement when I realized there was more at stake than my vengeance. "I mean…I do, but there are greater matters to worry about."

Wyland walked around his desk to approach me, his grey robe swaying across the floor. "What could be greater than avenging my would-be queen?"

I had to tell him what happened, though the memory, still fresh in my mind, was painful to recall. "The witch tricked Grace into entering a blood rite. They were bonded as family. And now that Grace is dead our betrothal has passed to the witch. She is set to be my queen."

"That fiend!" Wyland clenched his fist and sneered. "How am I just learning about this now?"

My back stiffened at his sharp-edged words. I wasn't accustomed to people speaking to me in such a tone, especially since becoming king when my father and brother perished in a shipwreck those few months ago. I was willing to overlook Wyland's temper, though, given the circumstances. The young wizard, barely two decades old, was my only hope to stop the witch's machinations.

"We didn't want to cause a panic," I answered. "I thought I could handle the witch myself, but after I learned of her trickery I ran straight back here to you."

"You should've notified me the second you knew the Black Witch was involved."

"I can't marry that monster, Wyland. If she would become queen then—" I shook my head in disbelief, stopping myself before imagining such a future. "I don't even want to think about it."

Father always told me to display authority in front of my subjects. To never let them see me waver. Only my wife, my partner and confidant, would be allowed to share the burden of my doubts. I wanted Grace to hold that role. Sadly, she cannot.

Now hear I am, succumbing to weakness and fear while begging a wizard that had been anointed less than a year for help. "Please. You must stop this wedding."

Wyland stared at me, unsure how to respond. His face then widened into a smile as if a glorious idea had entered his mind. "Blood rites aren't spells. They can't be reversed or broken."

It was a strange comment to make while looking so enthused, but Wyland elaborated while heading deeper into his study. "They can, however, be prevented."

The distinction puzzled me. "I don't understand."

The wizard replied while scouring the woven baskets of magical totems scattered around the room. "Time magic is very difficult, unstable, and potentially catastrophic...but not impossible."

The enigmatic response only compounded my confusion. "Time magic?"

Wyland's hooded head emerged from one of the baskets. He held a small jar of red powder between his fingers, happily staring at the substance like it was some sort of intoxicant. "I've been saving this for an emergency."

"What is it?" I asked

Wyland walked over to a bookshelf in the corner, his eyes still fixated on the glass in his hand. "Dehydrated dwarf liver. Very rare, considering most dwarves are reluctant to part with theirs. I traded a druid for it when I was still a magic student. Cost me nearly every gold coin I had."

Now I was less interested with what it was than what it was for? "What ever would you want with such a thing?"

He removed a small scroll from atop the shelf and then tossed the jar upwards, shattering it against the stone ceiling. "We're going to use it to turn back time and stop Lady Grace from running off to the dark forest."

I shielded my face from the falling glass as the red powder scattered to every corner of the room. It lingered in the air, slowly falling like bloody snow. Wyland was oblivious to it as he opened the scroll and began chanting in a strange, foreign language. An aura of green light manifested around him, extending out to cover the entire study.

I watched anxiously, hoping Wyland's spell would work… until something he had said struck me as odd. "Wait. How did you know Grace ran off and wasn't abduc—"

I was interrupted by a thunderous boom against the wall. Wyland didn't stop, though. He kept on chanting, even as a large section of the stone wall started moving backwards. The green light throughout the room grew strong along with the volume of Wyland's voice. The retracting wall was now removed completely, opening the study to the outside world. The Black Witch herself then emerged through the crude entrance she had created.

A hooded ebony cloak covered her humped frame and she spoke with contempt upon seeing Wyland's spell. "What do you think you're doing, youngling?"

The Black Witch reared her arm bank, a bolt of lightning forming in her hand. She prepared to throw it at Wyland when the green light encompassing the room suddenly roared with energy, exploding in a flash of light that blinded me completely.

I barged into the wizard's study without breaking my stride and spoke even before spotting him. "Wyland, I need your help."

The wizard looked up from an ancient tome he had his head buried in and squinted at the sight of me. "My king? What's wrong? You look frazzled. Are you anxious about tomorrow's nuptials? If you require a calming potion then I'm sure I could—"

"It's the Black Witch."

Wyland's squinted eyes grew wide. He stared at me a moment before asking a question threw gritted teeth. "What does she have to do with this?"

I opened my mouth to answer when the stone walls around the room started to rumble. Wyland reacted by chanting while making a series of hand gestures. He was casting a spell and appeared far less confused by the shaking walls than I.

After a moment of rattling, the walls began to crumble into dust, exposing us to the moonlight. To my shock, the Black Witch entered through the opening she created and immediately threw a ball of fire at Wyland without saying a word. I expected the magical attack to strike him down, but the fireball struck an invisible shield around the chanting wizard and extinguished into steam.

We were under attack, and although I knew I couldn't match her in a battle of the supernatural, I had other means to combat the witch. She continued to launch fireballs at Wyland's shield while I was drawn to a cabinet behind me and the silver sword I discovered inside. I couldn't explain how I knew of its presence but was grateful all the same.

I grabbed the blade by its handle and took a fighting stance. "You've invaded the wrong castle, witch!"

"You fool!" She cursed at me. "If only you'd wait a moment we could—"

I wasn't going to give the hag a chance to deceive me with her tongue. I struck down with the sword straight for her head. The Black Witch lifted her feeble arm far quicker than I expected her to, catching the blade with one hand and freezing it to ice.

I was in awe of her ability, and she capitalized on my shock by ripping the frozen weapon from my hands and hurling it at Wyland.

I was unsure if his shield would be able to deflect something physical in nature, but before the sword reached him, the wizard abruptly shot his hands out, sending out a blinding green flash of light throughout the room.

I barged into the wizard's study without breaking my stride and spoke even before spotting him. "Wyland, I need your help."

The wizard looked up from an ancient tome he had his head buried in and squinted at the sight of me. "My king? What's wrong? You look frazzled. Are you anxious about tomorrow's nuptials? If you require a calming potion then I'm sure I could—"

"It's the Black Witch."

Wyland's squinted eyes grew wide. He stared at me a moment before asking a question threw gritted teeth. "What does she have to do with this?"

I never had the chance to think of an answer. As if planning her arrival for the perfect moment, the witch passed through the wall of the study like a spirit. I was stunned at her magical entrance. Wyland, however, was not.

He wasted no time conjuring a spell, almost like he had been waiting to use it. Several daggers of light manifested in front of him and shot straight towards the witch. She swirled her hands in a circular motion, generating a portal of darkness to engulf the daggers.

As Wyland continued his spell to summon more weapons of light, I noticed another dark portal forming behind him. I stared into the blackness and saw a vision of the daggers emerging from within it. Where such a premonition came from I do not know, but I felt compelled to warn the wizard.

"Wyland!" I shouted. "Behind you!"

It was too late. The daggers soared through the portal and straight into Wyland's back. He gasped in pain and stumbled forward onto his desk, a look of agony on his face.

I took a step forward to help him but was interrupted by a wave of green light exploding out from Wyland's body. The flash was as bright as the sun, and I failed to raise my arms fast enough to shield myself from being blinded.

I went to barge into the wizard's study when I was suddenly paralyzed in place. I couldn't move. My joints were locked as if frozen mid-stride.

This strange sorcery intensified when I felt myself pulled through the floor and into the dungeon below the castle. There I found the Black Witch standing before me, anticipating my arrival.

"You!?" I bellowed in anger.

Her grotesque, wart-ridden face snarled in frustration. "Shut your mouth."

I could barely hear her raspy voice under the howls of the prisoners locked in their cells. I couldn't tell if the collection of drunkards and vagrants were wild because of my presence or the witch's, but they behaved like animals.

"All of you," the witch commanded them. "Be quiet!"

I was unaware if the witch had casted some kind of spell or merely demanded them to listen, but the prisoners obeyed by quietly sulking back to the corners of their cells.

"You kings are all the same," the Black Witch said, turning her attention back to me. "You think you can solve all the problems in the world by talking when sometimes all you need to do is listen."

It took every ounce of will I had not to lunge forward and attack the wench, but I was no fool. She had the advantage, and I had to keep her talking if I were to turn the tide in my favor. "You will pay for what you've done."

Buried within her dark hood, the witch's sunken eyes shot upwards towards the ceiling I had magically just passed through. "You need to be more concerned with the wizard above us."

"Wyland? Why? I was just about—"

She waved her hand to silence me as if I were nothing. "You weren't just about to do anything because you've already done it. Many times before."

I clenched my fists, fighting back the impulse to strike. "I'm so sick of your lies."

"Then don't trust me," she said, removing her hood to reveal a grotesque visage underneath. "Trust yourself."

Again, the witch persisted with her riddles. "What are you talking about?"

"Think," she uttered with a soft, encouraging voice. "What do you remember of this day?"

At first I resisted the urge to comply. I wasn't about to give in to the witch's schemes. But I couldn't stop the flashes from entering my mind. They were brief and scattered, but as vivid as if I lived them only moments ago.

My eyes drifted to the dungeon's cold, wet floor as I relived the images in my head. "I arrived at the castle then...I told Wyland about Grace and...he suggested we go back in time..."

The vibrant visions stunned me, and my glaze shot back to the witch. "What kind of trickery is this?"

She slowly shook her head, denying my claim. "It's not a trick."

"Then how do I remember something that never happened?"

"It did happen," she explained. "Those are memories buried deep within you of time that had been erased."

I looked back again and recalled our plan falling apart. "The time spell didn't work, though. You interrupted it."

The Black Witch shook her head once more. "No. It worked perfectly. Just not the way you hoped."

The more she revealed the more I was lost. "What do you mean?"

"Your wizard didn't want to travel back in time. He wanted to create a time loop that allowed him to relive this moment over and over again until it reached the outcome he desired."

"Which is?" I asked, both curious and concerned as to what her answer might be.

"Presumably my death," replied the witch as plainly as possible.

I couldn't rule out the possibility that the Black Witch was trying to deceive me, but something about her tale seemed right. That no matter how hard I could deny it, the pieces of her puzzle fit together perfectly.

Still, I had to remain skeptical and fill in the rest of the blanks. "How can you remember what happened so easily while my memories are suppressed?"

The witch scoffed at my question. "It's going to take more than some novice time incantation to manipulate my mind."

"But in my memories, it appeared as if Wyland didn't remember casting the spell either. How could that be?"

Something had attracted the witch's focus. She began slowly looking around as if sensing a presence that I couldn't.

"He does," she responded while scanning the dungeon walls for some unseen threat. "He's just pretending not to manipulate you."

"Why?"

"I don't know and we don't have much time to find out. It's only a matter of moments until he wonders why you haven't entered his study. I intercepted you before—"

The thick metal entrance to the dungeon slammed shut, interrupting the witch and grabbing both of our attentions. It was Wyland. He stood on the other side of the long, dark passageway, his hands clasped in front of him. "Very clever, witch."

He left his position to approach us, his pristine robe sweeping across the grime of the dungeon floor. "Though I assumed you would find a way to get to him eventually."

"Wyland!" I roared. "Is what she says true? You've trapped us all in some sort of time loop?"

He laughed at my question. "I was hoping to have avoided this conversation. Unfortunately, the Black Witch has proven to be more difficult to vanquish that I anticipated."

His lack of a denial only increased my suspicions.

"That wasn't the plan," I protested. "We were going to go back and save Grace."

Wyland stopped his approach and again chuckled to himself, this time rocking his head back in a conceited cackle. "Oh, please. I never cared about that pretentious harlot and you shouldn't either. She hated you and would do anything to get out of your wedding. She came to me for help, but it was all too easy to convince her to go see the Black Witch instead."

I couldn't believe what I'd just heard. The court wizard,

appointed to the post by my very father, had orchestrated my betrothed's demise.

"You betrayed me?" I uttered, more out of disbelief than inquiry. "Why?"

"To defeat her." Wyland raised his robed arm to point a finger in the Black Witch's direction. "For as long as anyone can remember, every court wizard has sought to rid this living plague from our kingdom, and every one of them has failed. But I won't. You see, I knew if I could somehow lure her out of the dark forest and battled her on my own terms I could beat her in battle."

The witch snorted in what seemed to be some kind of wheezy laugh. "I see that's been working well for you thus far."

"There have been some problems," Wyland admitted, "but with every skirmish I grow closer to beating you."

Although I had flashes of memories in my head, the complete picture was lost on me. Wyland and the Black Witch spoke of each other as bitter rivals. To me, this still all seemed so new. It made me wonder a curious question. "How many times have we done this, Wyland?"

"It doesn't matter," he replied, shaking his head. "I would be locked in this loop for eternity if it meant—"

"How many?!"

He was quiet a moment and raised his chin to me, hiding his shame. "Seventy-six cycles."

Could it be possible? Had we truly replayed this moment seventy-six times? I'm the king. I'm supposed to be in control of those around me. Instead, I'm nothing more than a bystander, a prisoner locked in someone else's story.

"End this now," I commanded the wizard.

"No" Wyland replied. "Not until she's dead."

I restrained my anger to a subtle scowl. "I order you as your king."

Wyland's shoulders bounced as he mocked me with laughter. "You think I care? Your father was a real king. You're just some weak brat unable to keep his own wedding from falling apart. Once I kill the terrible Black Witch everyone will see my power for what it truly is and it is I who will wear the crown."

I clenched a fist at my side, grinding the armor covering my hand. "You traitorous swine."

Wyland lifted his hand and a green aura steadily circled around him. "Go ahead. Call me what you wish. Because the truth remains that none of this ever happened."

The green light suddenly exploded throughout the dungeon. It shot out in every direction, and I was so focused on its approach I failed to notice the Black Witch had slipped beside me. She was soft, quiet, and placed a long, scraggly finger against the side of my temple just as the wave of light completely engulfed my being.

I barged into the wizard's study without breaking my stride and spoke even before spotting him."Wyland, I need your help."

The wizard looked up from an ancient tome he had his head buried in and squinted at the sight of me. "My king? What's wrong? You look frazzled. Are you anxious about tomorrow's nuptials? If you require a calming potion then I'm sure I could—"

"It's the Black Witch."

Wyland's squinted eyes grew wide. He stared at me a moment before asking a question threw gritted teeth. "What does she have to do with this?"

"Grace is dead." I left my position by the door to approach the wizard with steadfast steps of conviction. "The witch transformed my beautiful fiancé into a dragon and compelled me to slay her."

I lunged forward upon reaching him, swiftly latching my armored hands around his mouth and throat. "Just as I'm now compelled to do the same to you."

I twisted my wrists before Wyland had a chance to react, snapping the young wizard's neck like a twig. His body instantly grew limp in my grasp and I let go just as quickly, allowing the heavy corpse to fall to the floor.

It felt odd, staring down at the dead wizard before me. I had essentially been his prisoner, locked in an eternal cell of his own design. The memories were now all clear to me. A gift from the Black Witch so that I could break us both free from his grasp.

Still, the decision to kill Wyland was not one I made lightly.

I had watched his ascension with hope. He was young like me. We could've grown old together. In fact, I often imagined what it would be like to live out my reign with his consult. A court wizard and king. A friendship forged through the decades.

Alas, he did not feel the same way.

"Did I do the right thing?" I asked to the presence I felt behind me.

"There are no right things," the witch's raspy voice replied. "But you're allowed to believe that if it helps you sleep at night."

I didn't turn around. I refused to. That meant I had to accept the truth of my situation.

However, the Black Witch wouldn't allow me to forget it, gently placing her wrinkly, decrepit hand on my shoulder. "Now come, my groom. Our wedding awaits."

THE BANSHEE

BY JESSE TELLER

24 Years Before The Escape

Itook my hat off and ran my hand across the slick, sweaty skin of my bald pate. I fought not to gag and fought not to laugh. From atop the cliff, I could see the entire farming village and what was left of it. The houses had burned to the ground. Survivors tried to clean the bodies from their town proper. They were all dead. A thousand men, if one could call them that, completely eradicated by one man—the man I was here to see.

Laughing was poor play. My friend had suffered terribly for this victory, if he even was alive at all. But as I looked down at Herask's ragged battalion and their rotting corpses, I remembered the things Herask had promised he would do with all his men and all his power—the horror the warlord had boasted would follow his march—and I smiled.

A murder of crows, hundreds strong, hung fat and greedy in the air above the town. As I made my way through the bodies, every crow I passed squawked and screamed at me. Men and women, drenched in blood to their elbows and knees, hefted one body after the next to the wagons and they drove out of the city. This was hard, bitter work, with no sign of complaint or grumble. Every citizen here was grateful to be alive.

The children did not run and play. They carried buckets of water and dippers to the workers. They beat the crows back and watched the scene in horror. All save one, a beautiful, soot-smeared blonde girl I knew as Ladonna stood in the burned out shell of a house staring at the char in wonder.

I stopped near a water-bearing boy and smiled down at him. "Water for a thirsty traveler?" I asked. The boy looked up and smiled. He took the battered dipper out of his bucket and held it out.

The clean water was cool and sweet. I nodded to the boy and smiled. "You're Thrak, are you not?"

"How do you know my name, sir?"

"You have a brother, is that correct? And a sister?"

"I do. A ma that loves me, and a pa I haven't seen in a while," the boy said. His accent was thick but refreshing. These were good people. I knew exactly where this young man's father was, but there was no mercy in telling him.

"Well then, I guess you're set, aren't you?" I said. "Sounds like a lot of people that love you, young man. Can you see me to the church?"

"Hecatomb's church?" the boy said.

"Is there another one?"

"There is one in the woods being built. The man building it says it will house wonders," Thrak said.

"He is not to be trusted. You stay away from that building. I do not mean that one. I am for Father Hecatomb's place."

"I'll show you," the boy said. He turned and I followed.

When we reached the church, we found a few low-ranking warriors of Hecatomb standing guard at the door. Not from this village, they had just been called in from Wrathe. One of them stepped forward and shook his head.

"Church is closed, stranger. I'm sorry. We are in mourning. I cannot allow you to enter."

"I am expected." One guard nodded and the other walked into the church.

The door opened.

The idol at the front of the room was modest and wrong. The face was too thin, the nose too large. The man who had crafted the statue obviously loved the god, but had never seen him. However, two marks he could not miss: the lack of legs and the missing eye.

The candles burned soft and few, cloaking the room in shadows. A man in black laid atop the altar. I spoke a word in prayer and a priest met me.

"Welcome to my chapel, Bard. We were told you could answer a few questions for us."

"I'm sure I can. May I see him?"

The priest ushered me forward. I stopped at the altar, stared down at my friend, and held back tears.

Ky's ruptured throat was swollen like a black pumpkin, larger around than the man's head, and his skin had split in many places. I placed a thumb on an eyelid and opened it gently. The whites of the eyes were blood red. Every vein had burst. Looking at the ruin of a mouth, I could not tell which scraps of flesh had been lips and which were gums. The teeth were gone, every one, and the mouth trickled blood slowly.

"Tell me what happened. Tell me everything you know."

The priest kneaded his hands together and nodded. He drew me over to a pew, his words less than a whisper.

"A few weeks ago, a rider came through this place. He was frantic and terrified. He asked for water and food, and we gave. He warned us of an army of monsters headed this way and begged us to run for our lives. We were able to ask very few questions before he was back on his horse, riding to warn others.

"We went to our lord. We told him what we had heard and begged for his help. But he would not waste his resources on the word of one man who hadn't even stayed to be questioned. He told us he had no knowledge of this army, and he sent us away. When we demanded more, he drew a whip and we ran for our lives.

"We sent our own men in the direction of the warning. In but a few days, we had confirmation this horde was bearing down on us and we were doomed. Why they were coming for us, I couldn't tell you. We have nothing. No treasures, save our people, and nothing to steal except a crop of corn and soy. We held meetings to discuss our future and came up with two options.

"We could gather what arms we had and fight, or we could

hide in the forest and the caves. It was our best option, but if they wanted to find us and were willing to search for a small time, we could not escape them. Then he showed up.

"He rode a gray stallion, a magnificent beast we have never seen an equal to. He wore robes of black that flowed when he walked, and a sword with a crystal blade. His hair was black, his skin pale. He walked into our town hall and we followed him in. He pulled out a scroll and quill and wrote this letter to us.

Your village will be destroyed. An army comes for a treasure you do not even know you have. Its master will take it and defeat the world with it.

I am here to help. Gather your things and hide. Take your families and what food you can grab and flee. Go into the forest. Go into the caves. Hide and leave this army to me.

"We asked him more questions, but he would not answer. He went into the woods and came back with a large branch. As we packed, he crafted a bow. Not a hunting bow like we have here in town, but a war bow—too large for any fair aim and too heavy to run with. He carved two enormous arrows, only two, and wrote another note asking for arrowheads.

"Some in our numbers did not want to give this man control of our town. Many of our people thought him part of the army itself, here to trick us out of a fight. But the rest of us knew. We knew the only hope we had was the man in black, and we obeyed.

"The last we saw of him, he was standing on the peak of this building, looking west, in the direction of the army, and praying.

"Two days went by. We had not run out of food, but the army had never come looking for us. We set out scouts, and the tales they brought back led us here to this slaughter.

"We found the bodies as they are. No wounds except head wounds. All their heads ruptured, and their bodies contorted into forms of terrible pain. Every one of them was dead. In the very center, as if he were a drop of death that had contaminated an entire pool of people, he was laid out exactly like this. We stared down at him and wept. Many thanked him, and I prayed over him, in the name of Hecatomb, for his sacrifice. We were going to give him a hero's funeral before little Ithyryyn cried out that he was still alive.

"Imagine our horror. There was much talk of taking his life, ending his suffering. This is no way for a man to exist. I prayed about it, asked Hecatomb what I might do. I was told you would come, that you would tell us what to do and explain what happened. I have been waiting for you to make any sense of this for me."

"His name is Ky," I answered. "He once had another name, but he set it aside. It was of another life, a life taken from him, a life he can never have back. He was at one time a Trimerian Knight. If you ran a hand along his forehead, you would find a third eye hidden in the flesh of his head, though his kind is not well liked among your people.

"My story is from eons ago, a time when a child needed a hero and Ky came to his cry..."

Ky hit the ground outside the tower of the Reese Wasteland with the slamming of lightning and a showering of stone. His white robes billowed out around him, tossed in a flurry by the terrible wind of the storm. The ground hissed and popped as it let out its noxious fog. Ky did not tarry to allow its work on his body. He pulled his sword from his hip and strode to the tower. Black-smeared stone, stained green and yellow from the smog at its base, it looked as if the structure had been built on infection and rot. The sharp, pale spires that rose from its peak were carved from the body of a fallen god. The building, an epicenter of hate, stood a stain on every land save this one. It was the hub of a diabolical coven tolerated nowhere but here. The Reese Wasteland was home to few beasts, and no other races. The creatures that did walk this land were monsters, more akin to insects than any animal, and as dark-hearted as the land they crawled upon.

Ky called on the power of his blade with the singing of a song, and he slid it into the side of the stone building. He slid the blade in, to the hilt, slicing a perfect circle in the tower. He grabbed the stones and, with a wrench of his might, ripped the wall free and stepped inside.

The Breakion Coven had found, after much searching, the last of the Terakin bloodline. They had bound the last of the immortal seers and were, even then, sitting to make a meal of him. This boy had the power of first sight, the ability to see an outcome before it happens, to see the end of a struggle before it begins. They had gone to much trouble to find the boy. Now that he was in their clutches, they could become the most powerful force in the known world.

Ky walked straight into their dining hall and, while they toasted the meal laid out before them, Ky slowly chose his song. He was a lyric smith, a mage who learned a song for every spell. He looked the boy in the eyes and smiled.

The boy lay naked on a table before the coven. They each had long thin blades and were preparing to devour him alive. He whimpered when he saw Ky, and the table looked up. Ky lifted his song high and deadly in the air, and his sword began to dance.

The spells of the coven were mighty and terrible, and they brought their magic to bear as Ky leaped atop the table and crouched over the lad. He touched the boy's chest so no spell would strike him. He sang and moved among them. Blood followed every verse and every swing.

The Trimerian Knight knew few rivals. Within moments, the entire coven had either died or fled. He laid a kiss on the boy's forehead and encased the lad with a shimmering, impregnable globe. Ky promised he would return and rushed after Sister Killion, the most powerful of the order.

He found her in the upper reaches of the tower, in a room enchanted with darkness. Ky entered, glowing white and unafraid. He stepped into the middle of the room and found death all around him.

Sister Killion, one of the dread Witches of Deem, had grown up in the cemetery nation of Eloo. Death was hers to command. Bones rattled around Ky, rotting flesh and gasping undead at every turn.

Necromancers were evil almost exclusively, and Ky had not known he would face one that day. He chose a song and began to sing, and death stepped out to greet him. With every swipe of his sword and every word of his song, he dropped them all to steaming parts of unlife. He sang his mightiest spell and the darkness in the room shattered. The woman before him, dressed in black spider-web lace, carried a silver goblet.

"The Trimerians sent a singer to us. We know now that they fear our coven and my order."

Ky had nothing to say. He knew no pride, no reason to defend the bravery of his order. He shook his head. "I came for the boy."

"You have him. Nothing can stop you from taking him now." She took a long drink of her goblet and, when she pulled away, a dark fog crawled out of the glass to cling to her face. As it moved across her features, Ky saw her skull, her jawbone, and her spine, all through the skin of her face and throat. She grinned and he stepped closer.

"I came for the boy, but I will have you, too. Sister Killion is too corrupt, too vile to allow to live when I have her under my blade."

She dipped her pinky in her goblet and smiled as she licked it. "Have you heard of the banshee?"

Ky desired to kill her then, but he held back, allowing for any information he might get. He wanted the Witches of Deem eradicated. If she was about to give a clue to their mysteries, he would give her a chance to spill it.

"It is a terrible story, the banshee, a woman of noble birth who dies after losing a loved one. The poor soul cannot rest. She roams the lands of the estate, bemoaning her loss. She will, for generations to come, scream when she hears of the death of another in her family. Her scream is so terrible to hear that all who lay ear to it die a painful death. To hear the banshee is to know her loss, and to perish in the knowledge."

"This, I already knew," Ky said. "The tales of the dead are known to my people. The fate of the banshee is an ill one for sure, but why talk of this in the hour of your death?"

"It is not the hour of my death, Ky. It is the moment." She

stepped forward and tossed the contents of the goblet into his face. The black ichor gripped his face and held. It slid its way up his neck and across his lips. The liquid death sought his nose and mouth, and he choked and coughed. He opened his mouth to sing, but loosed such a hideous racket as to soil a soul. He fought to speak, but only a scream would come. His voice poured out into the air, and the Witch of Deem before him dropped to the ground, her head breaking open as she wept.

"Ky killed every one of those men, women, and other creatures out there in your village with the sound of his voice. His people tried every spell they could. They sought to write spells that might free him of the banshee's voice. But he will carry it around with him until the end of his life. He will kill anyone who hears his voice, as he killed the enemies of your village."

The priest looked at me, then back to Ky. "How do we help him?"

"No magic or god can heal him. He must pull through, if he is to live, by himself and his own strength. Starve him. Any food will be his death. Give him tiny sips of water, but do not pour it down his throat. He will drown. But before all else, you must whisper. Whisper the names of every man, woman, and child he saved. Remind him how much you love him, because right now, Ky is wishing for death. He knows one day this curse will take his life. He desires that death, an end of all his suffering. Remind him he is loved and needed, and Ky might come back to us.

"Tell him I came to see him. Tell him I said he did a fine job."

Pock and Cock

vs.

The Necromantic Circle

An Ashen Fells story

By Paul Lavender

Visalon walked slowly along the streets of Ashen Falls, each alternating footfall punctuated by a crack of her silver tipped cane. The limp and the cane were an affectation that she could easily have remedied, after all she was a necromancer.

She thought the limp gave her a certain look, made her look like one of those preposterous villains from those human fairy stories.

She spat onto the cobbles made wet with the light rain that had been falling for the last half an hour.

Human!

That word was like poison on her tongue, they were like furless, tailless rats. Well, like rats, they would soon find themselves being killed without mercy.

Visalon looked at the shadowy parts of the streets as she walked along, and her eyes soon found the sleeping forms of children sleeping in the doorways and gutters.

She spat again. This city had once been great, full of elvish love and laughter. Before the coming of man had began to dilute the pure elvish bloodlines.

The irony of a necromancer wanting to bring back an age of purity and elvish enlightenment seemed to be completely lost on her.

She spat for a third time. *Half-elves!*

Soon Ashen Falls would be free of both humans and half-elves. It would start here and then it would spread, until there were none left in Esterada.

Visalon was snapped out of her reverie by the faintest of touches, the sensation of a finger sliding in to one of the pockets in her robe. Looking down she saw the dirty face of a street urchin looking up at her with big brown eyes. He looked so sad...and vulnerable, "You really shouldn't have done that boy."

Even as she spoke, the skin from the boy's brow began to slide down over his eyes, and the boy started to open his mouth to scream even as his upper lip slid down to join his lower lip and seal his mouth closed.

None of the other nearby children heard a sound as Visalon's enchanted robe absorbed the boys muffled screams. A robe that Visalon had created herself, allowing her to taunt her victims but allow her to avoid their pitiful mewling and whining.

Flesh continued to slough down from the boy to create a puddle on the cold cobbles of the street. A sudden flash of lightning revealed the sign that hung from the side of the nearest building—Butcher's Row.

How apt, she thought and laughed to herself, before leaving the pile of pink sludge and sticking out bones where they lay.

So much to do and so little time to do it!

Cock tilted his head up and took a long, deep sniff.

His brother, Pock, looked over, "Aye, I can smell it too."

Both men stood well over six feet tall, with short hair and black eyes. Pock's face was covered in old pock marks, but Cock's wasn't. Other than that, the two men looked eerily similar.

They were standing at opposite sides of the entrance to The Dove's Head Inn, which was where the two men worked as bouncers. They were both, if they were to be believed, gods.

Pock was god of, unsurprisingly, pockmarks and Cock was the god of...no, not that. Get your mind out of the gutter! No, Cock was the god of fowl.

It's a well-known fact that on Esterada humans have so many gods and goddesses that they are pretty common. This doesn't mean that they go around doing crazy god-like shit twenty-four seven. After all that wouldn't pay the bills... unless you were Cash, god of wealth or Gold, god of even more wealth.

And anyway, as there are so many of them, they have less power for each to use, unlike the seven elven gods and the one orc god—Shatak.

So on a list of magic using folk human gods are basically between battle mages and dragons, and to be fair there is a huge gap between battle mages, dragons and elven gods. This gap was made even greater when the elven god, Octarion, killed all the dragons to make magical items, but that as they say is another story!

Cock made a face like someone sucking on a lemon, "Fucking necromancers, I fucking hate necromancers!"

Pock turned to look at his brother, "I know you do, but we need to find out what they're up to."

"Why?" Cock asked.

"Why what?" Pock asked back.

"Why does it have to be us? I mean I'm god of chickens. Why can't the god of cats sort the shit out for a change," Cock replied indignantly.

Pock hated these arguments. "Because you fucking hate necromancers."

"Oh yeah! Good point."

Pock looked on as Cock's mouth began to smile. "What?"

"I'm just thinking of Kitty lay in the sun with her legs in the air licking her..."

"All right, all right. Admittedly, it's a good power, but yours is pretty good too!"

"It is?" Cock asked.

"Yeah, running around flapping your arms for ten minutes after you've had your head cut off is pretty spectacular."

"I suppose so." Cock rubbed his chin, deep in thought, "Wait…"

"Don't worry about it brother." Pock slapped Cock on the back, "Let's go and get those necromancers!"

"I fucking hate necromancers. I really do.."

Pock turned and opened the door of the inn, "Half hour break!" He yelled to no-one in particular.

A disembodied voice sighed theatrically, "All right!"

"C'mon, lets go."

The two men followed the stinking trail through Ashen Falls, they could have cast a locate spell, but decided that they really didn't need it. They wended their way down dark alleys and across empty squares until they came to where the stench was the strongest. Butcher's Row…here the stench was almost overpowered by the residual tang of butchery and blood. By the acidity of offal and crushed hope.

They paused and took a deep breath of the relatively fresh air and then stepped in to the street. The brothers knew that they were taking a big risk, as the gods of Butcher's Row had become unhinged over time. Not as much as the gods of Tannery Square, but still…Too much pain and blood had addled their brains and no-one knew which way they would go.

"Fuck it!' Pock took another step in to the street.

Nothing happened and the two brothers began to edge further and further along the cobbles. Here and there small pieces of flesh lay amongst the stones or in small pools of light red liquid where the blood of the slaughtered animals was being slowly diluted by the rain. A rain, it should be noted, that didn't seem to want anything to do with the two men.

Several more steps in to the street and they came across the fleshy lump that had once been a boy.

Pock sighed, "Bastards! Bastards! Bastards!"

He stopped suddenly realizing what he had done, his brother looked at him with wide eyes even as a tapping noise came from the darkest part of the street. It was Cock's turn to sigh, "Now why did you go and do that for?"

Pock looked slightly abashed, "Sorry brother. It just kind of slipped out."

"Even I know not to say words in threes, especially not in the likes of Butcher's Row."

"I said I'm sorry, didn't I."

The tapping had become louder and the brothers were sure that they could see a figure in the dark. Pock suddenly held a long knife in his hand whilst Cock had produced a crossbow with a huge bear bolt slotted in it ready to fire.

"Those won't do you any good boys." The voice came from behind the two men, and it was a voice both youthful and aged at the same time. It reminded the men of summertime and winter all at once. Turning around the boys took in the sight of a figure that was a young girl and then an old woman, then a young girl again. They squinted at the figure in the hope that it would make it easier to look at—it didn't.

"You've summoned the lord of this street and you know he's going to demand a sacrifice." The girl/woman shook her head, "How could the two of you be so stupid, I thought I raised you better than that?"

"Sorry, Mum." Said Pock even as Cock said, "He did it, mum, not me."

By now the figure was close enough for the three to see and what a sight it was. The Lord of Butcher's Row certainly wasn't human. He stood on the hind legs of what looked to be a goat, his body was that of a bull, his head was a pig's and where his arms should be where chicken wings. From the top of his head sprouted two huge antlers.

"Who has summoned me!" His voice boomed like a mountain avalanche and echoed of the houses and down the street. For all that, none of the figures sleeping in the street seemed to hear anything.

Pock gulped, "Well 'summoned' isn't exactly the word I would use."

"Bwaak! Thrice a word was used, so summoned I was!"

Cock's eyes narrowed as an idea started to form. Perhaps he could save them.

"Sorry! I really didn't mean to summon you. You can go back now."

"Brrk! Buck! Buck! I demand a sacrifice!"

Pock was about to say something when Cock stepped forward, "As your god I demand that you go back to whence you came!"

Beady eyes stared at Cock, "Technically you're only one fifth of my god."

"Isn't that enough?"

"Not really, but I tell you what...Urgh! What the fuck is that gloop at your feet?"

"Necromancer victim."

The Lord of Butcher's Row spat to one side, "I fucking hate necromancers!"

Cock gave an evil smile, "Me too!"

"Not surprising really. I hate the way they kill animals for no purpose other than to attach different animals together and bring them back to life. Bloody disgusting and a mockery of the sanctity of life."

The two brothers couldn't help noticing that their mother had disappeared, and that the creature before them was made up of several animals that looked like they had been stuck together.

"Yeah! Us too." Said Pock whilst giving his brother a look that seemed to say *Don't say it!*

"Well it looks like today is your lucky day then doesn't it? Instead of a sacrifice you can find this necromancer and kill them...slowly...even slower than that if you can manage it. Moo! Oink! Bwaak!"

"It's a deal!" Pock yelled as the figure began to recede back into the darkness.

"I know. Now don't let me down."

"Good thing we were going to do that anyway, eh brother?" Whispered Pock.

Cock draped an arm over Pock's shoulder, "You're not wrong there, brother. Now, a simple tracking spell should be enough to follow the trail."

A set of tracks began to glow on the cobbles and the two men put their weapons away and began to follow them.

Life watched the two figures walk off, and then turned her attention to the pile of gloop on the cobbles. Pointing a finger, the gloop began to rise like a pig's bladder being filled with air. Soon the boy was standing as if nothing had happened to him.

Life held out a few copper heads, "What's your name boy?"

The boy looked at the nice old lady that stood in front of him, unable to see the constant battle of youth and age. He frowned as he realized that this wasn't the person that he had tried to pickpocket from, but he couldn't seem to remember what had happened. His memory was hazy and he had to claw out his own name, "Alder, my lady."

The old woman smiled, "Here Alder, take these few coins."

Alder didn't need telling twice and grabbed the proffered coins. He quickly spun and began to run off before remembering his manners. He looked over his shoulders as he shouted, "Thanks, you stupid old cow. Hope your fucking cats eat you alive!"

Luckily for potty-mouthed Alder, there was no one there.

Pock was scowling as the two brothers followed the trail of glowing footprints.

"Are you worrying about mum turning up?" Cock asked. Truth be told he was worried himself.

"You fucking know I am. She's gotten free and that means that we have to put her back, in fact she may even be responsible for all this. Even if she isn't she might get in the way."

"Yeah, Life has a habit of doing that."

"That's not even remotely funny."

Cock sighed, "I know."

Visalon removed her cloak and shook off the accumulated rainwater, behind her two sturdy, wooden doors lay closed at an angle to the ground. She removed her dry cloak from a peg and hung her wet cloak up, smiling to see that the other pegs were already occupied. The Circle was complete with her arrival, the others would all be in place in the lower chamber, below this basement entrance. Opposite the angled doors another, less pissed door stood and she made towards it. The door opened without a sound to reveal a small landing followed by a set of stairs spiraling down in the depths below.

Visolon hoped that her compatriots were ready for what was about to happen. She descended the spiral stairs, here and there glowing skulls had been placed in niches to allow the Circle time to make the journey safely. None of them wanted to fall and break their neck.

Zombiefication was so not a good look for a necromancer.

At the bottom of the stairs Visalon entered a large, round chamber. The rest of the Circle were already in their rightful positions, ready to begin the ritual that would deal with the human problem once and for all. They all wore black clothing with black cloaks, their cowls were pulled up over their heads to hide their faces from each other.

With the arrival of Visalon the Circle consisted of three men and three women, other than that Visalon didn't know anything about them except that they were all elvish. Their mistress had been most insistent that the members of The Circle did not engage in conversation with each other, that familiarity would lead to mistakes being made.

Visalon took a deep sniff of the air, the metallic tang of blood flooded her senses. The other members of the Circle had already sacrificed a chicken to appease the gods for what they were about to do.

One last chicken watched Visalon approach with its beady eyes. Its head moving so that the bars of its cage would be no impediment to its line of sight. She paused as she reached the cage door. She had heard rumors of chickens that were really demon possessed killing machines. Visalon shook her head in disgust at herself, demon chickens…it was absurd! She quickly opened the cage door and reached in to grab the chicken within.

Cock stopped outside the front door of a medium sized house, "This one."

"You sure?"

"I can see a half dozen chicken ghosts… or are they ghost chickens?"

"I have no idea."

"Oh, it's alright for you. You don't get ghost pockmarks…or is its Pockmarked Ghosts?"

"Maybe, but I do have a lot of people praying that I don't come knocking on their door."

"I'm not sure that's a good thing."

"Keeps me amused."

"Yes, well I suppose it's good to have a hobby. Now, we have ghostly chickens and we have blue footprints going off around the side of the house…Ooh, that's interesting!"

"What?"

"They're underground."

"Are you certain?"

"I've just seen a ghostly chicken come up through the earth so I'm pretty sure."

"Round to the back then. C'mon let's go."

Pock took a few steps and then turned to his brother, "I do see dead pocks…and spots…and pimples."

"You do? When do you see dead pimples?"

"All the time."

"Really?"

"Yes. There are so many of them though that I've had to learn to block them out."

"How the fuck do you learn to block them out?"

"Time, brother. Lots and lots of time. Come on, let's go and sort out these chicken killers."

"Yeah, bastards!"

The two brothers continued to make their way to the back of the house.

Visalon threw the carcass of the chicken across the room where it landed amongst the remains of several of its kin.

"You are all doing very well, but my friends, time is short."

All the members of the Circle bowed low as the figure appeared in their midst.

"Mistress!" Visalon's voice wavered with emotion as she spoke, "We merely await the sacrifices arrival and then we will wipe the human scum from Esterada forever!"

"I have brought you all here to make history. Outside of this chamber you are all high-ranking members of elven society, well regarded by your peers but you live such sad, lonely lives whilst the humans laugh at you, point at you and now even dare to fornicate with you. Soon two will arrive that will free you from their filthy touch and their mocking gaze...I sense them above. You must deal with them forthwith!"

"Oh great Mistress don't leave us in our very moment of triumph."

"I fear that I must as I'm quite parched and fancy a nice cup of tea but have no fear for I will be back after I have visited the second circle."

Visalon blinked, "Wait...what sec..."

All the other members of the Circle bowed low again and intoned, "Yes, Mistress!"

The figure vanished before them all.

The entrance to the underground sanctum had proved to be no match for the two brothers. Pock had started to cast a spell of opening when Cock bent down and ripped the doors from its hinges.

"Well, that was subtle."

"Fuck subtle, Pock, they're all chanting something down below and wouldn't notice if a large rock landed on their heads."

"I think they fucking would notice!"

"Alright they would notice, but not until their brains had been splattered in all directions."

"Good point well put."

The brothers crept towards the chanting and soon came to the room with the circle of necromancers within. Cock's mouth turned grim as he saw the sacrificial chickens lay discarded about the room, "You know I fucking hate necromancers and yet even they can do one thing that I fucking love."

"What's that, brother?"

Cock raised his crossbow, took careful aim and fired. The bear bolt flew straight and true. The head of the first necromancer simply exploded like an overripe melon being dropped from the sky. Even before the body could hit the ground the bolt smacked into the left eye of a second necromancer. The momentum of the bolt forcing the body back where it pinned the corpse to the wall, "They make for an easy pair of kills."

Pock stepped into the room with his long dagger in his hand, "Which one of you fuckers wants to die next?"

The four necromancers that remained stopped their chanting and as three of them drew daggers the fourth started pointing at the chicken corpses.

Pock flinched as a bear bolt flew just centimeters past his right ear to explode another necromancer skull, "Oi! Watch what you're doing with that thing."

Then a necromancer was swinging his or hers, Pock really couldn't be sure, dagger down and Pock brought one hand up to grab the arm even as he stabbed forward with his own blade. His foe doubled over as eight inches of steel pierced through their robes and into their guts, puncturing through flesh and intestines. Pock let go of the body and it flopped to the floor groaning as it bled out, "That's what happens when you spend all night raising dead people and not learning how to use a fucking dagger properly!"

Pock gave the necromancer a kick in the head for good measure and to stop the groaning and moaning. The fifth necromancer lay slumped against the wall with a bear bolt sticking out of it's chest. Which just left one.

Suddenly he felt a pain in his left ankle and then his right one, looking down he started to laugh as several undead chickens pecked at his feet, "Fucks sake. Cock get in here and sort this out!"

Cock stepped into the room, his crossbow aimed at the last necromancer. Looking at his brother he scowled, "That's not even remotely funny."

"Just stop them from pecking me. They're beginning to irritate the fuck out of me."

"He can't help you for I, Visalon control the dead. They will peck you to death even as you beg for mercy!"

Both of the brothers blinked a few times before they burst out laughing, "Fucks sake! I haven't got all century to be pecked to death by chickens...Well, actually I have but that's not the point. You cannot kill people with zombie chickens. Quite frankly it's ridiculous."

Visalon had the sense to look abashed, "It's all I had available at the time alright! I couldn't raise the two necromancers you'd already killed because of the cranial impaction."

Cock scratched his head, "Cranial what?"

"She means head trauma, bro."

"Oh, right."

Suddenly there was another person in the room and she was standing next to Visalon, "Well done my disciple. You've kept them busy long enough for the other Circle to nearly complete the ritual. Soon Esterada will be free of all humans."

The figure lowered the hood of her cloak.

Pock, Cock and Visalon gasped aloud.

"Mother!" said Pock and Cock.

"A human!" said Visalon.

Then another voice came from behind the brothers, "Don't be silly boys. I'm your mother, that over there is my twin sister, Death."

Cock rubbed his forehead, "Fucks sake, I think I'm getting a migraine."

Pock clapped him on his shoulder, "And I've still got chickens pecking my ankles."

"Oh yeah. Sorry about that."

The undead chickens flopped back to the ground.

Life stepped forward and between Pock and Cock, "You have to stop this Death."

"Never! Imagine the power I'll wield when I destroy humanity."

"But.."

"Do not 'but' me! You're just jealous. You've always been jealous of me, because I'm better looking and had more handsome boyfriends!"

"Sister, we're identical twins!"

Pock felt it was time to say something, "Err…auntie, you do realize that you're the human god of death don't you?"

"Do you take me for an idiot, child?"

Cock couldn't help himself, "Well…"

Pock quickly interjected, "If you kill all humanity you won't gain power, you'll cease to be."

"..."

By now Visalon was halfway to the city of Illirium, flogging her horse for all it was worth and vowing to set up a home for waifs and strays (but that's another story). No one back in the room had noticed that she had slipped away.

Now, where were we? Oh yes!

"..."

"Oh shit."

"Indeed, sister. You're going to have to go back and stop them."

"I can't!"

"Why not?"

"They're my friends. I made them promises, I can't break my word."

Pock looked at his brother, "She has got to be shitting us!"

Cock sighed, "Just let us know where they are and we'll deal with it."

"They're under Butchers Row. Under Chops the Butchers."

"You have got to be kidding!", Pock shook his head, "Mother can you take us there?"

"Of course I can. Anything for my boys."

Suddenly Pock and Cock found themselves back at the entrance to Butchers Row, there was no sign of Life or Death even though this was a life and death situation.

Cock sighed, "Tell me you have a plan and that it won't take long to implement."

"Oh yes. And for once we won't get bloody."

The two brothers hadn't gotten far, before Pock staggered to one side and started to dry heave. Cock rushed over and started to rub his brothers back, but to no avail. Pock's face started to turn blue. Then the screams started. Close at first and then seeming to expand out in a circle from Butcher's Row.

Pock grabbed at Cock. "Get the Lord of Butcher's Row. Only he can help us now."

Cock gently pushed Pock away and ran into the alley, "Hey, Lord!"

Nothing happened.

Cock pointed down to the sewers, "Necromancers! In the sewers."

Still nothing.

At the alley mouth, Pock had fallen to the ground with froth coming from his mouth. Tears started to run down Cock's cheeks, "Fuck!"

And then he heard it. The tap, tap sound from before and the portal opened and out strode the Lord of Butcher's Row, "Who dares to…"

"Yeah, yeah. We haven't got time for that shite. There are necromancers in the sewers below and they are about to kill all mankind."

The Lord blinked, "Really?"

"Yes, fucking really! Look my brother's dying and only you can save him."

"Why should I?"

"Because…err…because they are evil as fuck necromancers, and they have been killing chickens left, right and center."

"Good point. Hang on a moment and I'll be right back."

The Lord of Butcher's Row walked back into the portal and seconds later Cock was sure he could hear screams coming from below.

Serves the fuckers right, he thought.

From behind him came a groan and he whirled around to see Pock up on his hands and knees. Life helped him to his feet, and as she held him his strength seemed to return, "Mother, what the fuck is going on!!?"

"Sorry, lads. I have to keep hunting my sister or there's no telling what mischief she will get up to."

"How the hell did the two of you escape The Vortex Prison?"

Life sighed, "The barriers are breaking, my boys. A boy is coming with a black bird on his shoulder and the Orcslayers are returning to Ashen Falls, and when they do you will know that it is time."

"Time for what?"

"Why, time for The Eight God, of course."

"Of course they—" Pock stopped talking as his mother was no longer there.

Cock came and stood next to his brother, "I need a drink."

"Me too."

"What did mother want?"

"I'll tell you on the way to the inn."

WHAT IS STOLEN
AND WHAT IS LOST

AN IMMORTAL TREACHERY STORY

BY ALLAN BATCHELDER

The girl was his penance and his salvation—his penance because he'd inadvertently caused her parents' deaths, and his salvation because she gave him reason to live. His conundrum was that being a Shaper burned his wick a deal faster than most men's, meaning that he might not be around long enough to see her grown and married. It was a fear that kept him up at nights, stewing and fretting until he eventually succumbed to exhaustion.

But how *was* he to deal with the Burning, the ever-present, painful cost of doing magic that all Shapers felt? Some of his colleagues, he knew, dosed themselves with sedatives or hallucinogenic herbs. Others drank to excess (he'd certainly given that strategy a lengthy trial). Some few tried to sleep away their days and nights together. And some went mad. On the other side, there were Shapers who became addicted to the pain, who became as emaciated and fiendish as any vampire. And then there were those, like the Queen's Shaper, Cindor, who had learned to use his Shaping to control the very burning it generated. Chyrin envied such men, for he had no idea how such a thing was possible. It was like feeding one's hunger by eating the air.

If he could just find some new approach, though, he could blunt his agony and slow his own premature aging, which would then allow him to see Mellie grown.

If.

What a world of hope there was in that little word. How it could contain so much emotion, possibility and import was yet another of life's mysteries that remained frustratingly beyond Chyrin's reach.

Better Shapers, he was sure, could glean the answers. Alas, he was not of their quality. Chyrin had come to his magic late and, as a result, had not enjoyed even half the financial success of his peers. He'd never been able to secure the patronage of any of Lunessfor's nobility, and even its wealthiest merchants looked elsewhere for their arcane assistance. Thus, Chyrin was relegated to helping the working poor; his clientele paid him not in Royals or Merchants, but in Shims, in fish, and in bread of questionable provenance. For all that, he was a master of a few particular spells—none better!—and it was in this ability that he hoped to find his sought-after answer.

The question vexed him like a recurrent rash, or a cough that simply would not leave his lungs. The only cure for this torment, he knew, was to focus less on himself and more on his child, Mellie. She amazed him. Her ability to find or create playthings out of next-to-nothing was endlessly surprising, as was her commitment to whatever narrative she'd chosen for her games. He was, he suspected, in awe of her. And the more he watched, the more spellbound he became. He adored her riot of honey-colored locks, the spray of freckles across her nose, her silly, gap-toothed smile. And her radiant blue eyes (his were brown)! Ironic, the thought, that he should be the one enchanted. After watching her for several minutes, his mind returned, inevitably, to himself.

Chyrin set down the bowl of soup he'd been eating and stepped in front of the mirror on the room's western wall. He was not given to vanity and could certainly live without encountering his haggard visage, but the glass was useful in his magicks, and so he kept it. Today, it showed him the face of a man in his middle years who might as well have been seventy.

Mellie had even taken to calling him grandpa in jest, though it rarely brought a smile to his face.

How might he reverse or retard this rapid aging?

He watched Mellie pouring soup from his bowl into her own, and suddenly he had an idea. It was not an entirely pleasant idea, but as it was the only one he'd had in weeks and as he was getting increasingly desperate, he had to entertain it. The trick, as he saw it, was to essentially pour someone else's youth and vitality into himself and then to pour his own increasing frailty into the other person. There were apocryphal tales of magicians draining the thoughts from others' minds, and even one outlandish story of a body-swap. Surely, what Chyrin imagined would be easier. It would likely do nothing for the pain of the Burning, but if it could add years to his life, he was willing to make the attempt.

Oh, but to steal another's youth and burden him with Chyrin's age! How abhorrent it was to him, how it shamed him to think of it, and yet he could see no alternative if he wished to remain by Mellie's side into her adulthood. Unconsciously, he sought reasons to justify his eventual actions, telling himself that he'd done more good than harm in the grand scheme of things, and that, perhaps, he was owed a little leeway in this instance, especially as his ultimate purpose was to continue his care for a child who would otherwise assuredly be an orphan.

That night, he dreamt of the fire in which Mellie's parents had died. It was the custom, the expectation, throughout the city that whenever a fire broke out, everyone would help after his own abilities. Most folks participated in bucket brigades, but there were always a few A'Shea—healers—on hand to attend to the wounded, and certainly every available Shaper was expected to do his part. It was just that Chyrin had done his too well and too quickly.

He'd been out strolling when he smelled smoke and, seconds later, heard the general hue and cry of citizens addressing a building on fire. He'd been close enough that he'd had no reason to Jump to the scene and, anyway, he wanted to save his energy for the fire itself. The building was an old pile of a thing, subdivided into numerous homes, the top floor of which was already roaring with flames and past saving. A number of women and children had gathered across the street, whilst their neighbors did their best to pitch in however they could.

Now, there are any number of spells a Shaper might use to extinguish a fire. The actual choice typically depends upon that Shaper's comfort and skill with his repertoire. Chyrin was not terribly adept at summoning large quantities of water, and so he usually opted to suck all of the air out of a burning structure, thus suffocating the flames. This time, to his everlasting regret, he neglected to check if there were any people still trapped inside the building when he cast his spell. The fire went out with a great whooshing sound. The only slightly-burnt bodies of Mellie's parents went out with no sound at all. When he learned what he'd done and discovered the dead couple's child sobbing uncontrollably in the arms of an old woman nearby, he swore that if he accomplished nothing else in this life, he would see that girl raised properly.

He spent days and then weeks visiting all the necessary authorities, filling out endless paperwork, and enduring more interviews than he could remember, but at last he was given custody of the girl. He wanted only to make things right. It was his fear of failure, then, that haunted him in these dreams, dreams that could only be banished by lavishing more love and attention upon his sweet Mellie.

In the ensuing weeks, Chyrin worked day and night, experimenting with the spells he knew and borrowing spell books from the few friendly colleagues he had in order to develop the magicks necessary to accomplish his task. Like many a Shaper (or alchemist) before him, he tested his findings on rodents, on stray cats and dogs, and even on the city's street urchins. With every incremental bit of progress, he became more and more obsessed, until he inevitably abandoned all pretense of morality and began taking whatever and whomever he needed to fulfill his vision. He suffered only occasional fits of conscience, but he pushed them aside, over and over, with his fervent belief that it was all justified in the service of his beloved Mellie. Finally, he was convinced he'd created the necessary spell-work; his challenge now was to find the right subject, someone of abundant health and vigor and someone, too, whose expedited demise would not be mourned.

Days passed and only his usual customers came by, looking to rid their homes of pests, spy on their spouses, or locate missing objects. The truth was, Chyrin hated this kind of work. It was so far beneath his abilities, it was almost embarrassing. The greater truth was that no work would satisfy until he'd found his victim and stolen that person's youth. After days of frustration, the ideal candidate walked through his door, and the Shaper could barely mask his elation.

The fellow in question was a strapping specimen, hirsute, toothy, with chiseled features, sunken eyes and a shelf-like brow. Chyrin could almost feel the young man's strength radiating off him and found it difficult to contain his excitement.

"Welcome to Solutions," he told the man. "What can I do for you?"

"Can you...can you make someone love me?"

It was a common request, but one more asked by young women than large, gangly men. "Of course," Chyrin lied, although it was far more complicated than that. What he did—what he knew how to do—was to create compulsion that looked and felt like love for a time, but was really far worse for the mental health of both people in the long run. No one had ever come back to complain about his efforts, but he suspected that was more out of fear than desire. And, in any case, he was prepared to respond if they did.

"You can?' the man asked, hope and relief comingling on his face.

"I said so, did I not?"

The other man nodded enthusiastically.

"Now, what do you offer in exchange?" Chyrin knew that whatever the man might pay him would be worth far less than the vigor he would also surrender, but he'd appearances to maintain, and so he pretended to barter.

After several minutes, the Shaper and his customer struck an agreement: the young man would give Chyrin a copper ring that had belonged to his mother—or so he claimed — and a large sack of apples, and the Shaper would enspell the young man such that the object of his desire would, by gradual degrees, find it necessary to be in his presence at all times. Once the promised goods had been handed over to Chyrin, he said, "Now, I need you to come behind the counter, here, and sit in this chair."

The man awkwardly made his way to the chair specified and sat. It was sturdy but sparsely upholstered, and he struggled to find a comfortable position for whatever was to come. Chyrin offered him a small glass of quince wine—as small, in fact, as might deliver the required reagents without cutting into the Shaper's supply. He was thrifty of necessity, but not where his quince wine was concerned. Rather, he purchased the best his limited budget could afford, and he didn't like wasting too much on his customers.

After some minutes, his client, whose name he still did not know or wish to know, drifted into a gentle sleep, whereupon Chyrin rubbed his own palms with Theulia resin, the better to channel his magic, and grasped both of the sleeping man's hands in his own. Chanting words of focus (a crutch he often wished he was powerful enough to avoid), he felt a new energy surging into his breast, even as his subject seemed to shrink and grow pale. He was not shrinking, of course, but his dwindling vitality certainly made it appear so. For his own part, Chyrin felt by stages invigorated, exhilarated, virile and, lastly, mildly alarmed. Was this truly how it felt to be young, healthy and strong? Had he fallen so far, or was the young man simply exceptional?

Whatever the case, Chyrin felt as if he might live for a hundred years more, now, and the prospect thrilled him. Turning his attention back to the other man, Chyrin saw that his breathing had become more shallow, his skin, blotchy, and his hair, dry and brittle-looking. He shook the man gently but was unable to awaken him. Frustrated, he pinched the fellow, with no better result. Finally, he shouted at him, causing the man to bolt upright and launch into a prolonged fit of coughing.

"I don't feel s'good," he complained.

I imagine not, Chyrin thought. "That's to be expected with such demanding spells," he said. "You'll feel better by this evening, tomorrow at the latest." And, of course, he had also delivered on the compulsion spell he'd promised. Even if his victim had not recuperated by then, he'd probably be too preoccupied with his intended's attentions to bother returning. And what could he possibly do to Chyrin, anyway? The Shaper was now at the height of his powers, and the other man was no match for him.

With a little tut-tutting, he was able to urge the man out of his shop, after which he heaved a great sigh of relief and no little satisfaction. His spells had worked! He couldn't remember having felt better.

Thus, it was with great joy that he took Mellie on a stroll through the city's parks the following day, stopping in Market Square for a rare picnic lunch, doing a little light shopping for trinkets that caught the girl's eye, and then taking in a masque at day's end. Now, *now*, he felt like the kind of guardian the girl deserved. *Now*, he was truly worthy of the girl's affections and trust.

Except, of course, that he'd stolen another man's youth.

He pushed the thought aside like unwelcome relatives dropping in unexpectedly. Stolen wasn't exactly the right word, he decided. He'd given the man something in exchange, after all. Somewhere in the city, the poor sap was receiving all the attention he could handle from his would-be lover.

And there was Mellie to think of. Never had he seen her happier than she'd been today. Never had her eyes lit up with such wonder, never had she smiled with such abandon, never had her laugh seemed so lighthearted and carefree.

That night, Chyrin slept well, comfortable with and proud of the good he'd done for the girl. His daughter. There it was, and he might as well own it, for she'd no one else in the wide world but him. She was his, and he, hers. It was bliss.

The following morning, Chyrin fairly bounded from his bed, feeling both jubilant and famished. Ah well, that was to be expected, now that he'd been refilled with the energy of youth.

"What would you like for breakfast, dearie?" he asked his Mellie as she shuffled, sleepy-eyed, to the table where they shared their meals. "If we don't have it," he said impishly, "I'll summon it!" He waved his fingers comically and added, "Or I'll send out for it!" Nothing could dampen his humor.

And how Mellie laughed to see him in such spirits!

They ate like royalty. Or he did, anyway. Mellie ate as she always had, but Chyrin was positively ravenous, devouring everything in the cupboards and still searching for more. "Not to worry," he said, "I promised more, and more we shall have."

For the second day in a row, they ventured out into Market Square. It was such a rare occurrence that Mellie hardly knew what to make of it. Chyrin, however, relished the chance to consider a broader array of groceries than he typically allowed himself. Yes, he would spend a bit more today than was perhaps prudent, but his new-found youth needed fuel, and it was hightime, too, that he put a little more meat on Mellie's bones. The girl had always been slight and likely always would, but there was no harm in feeding her more. With this in mind, the Shaper bought sausages, cheeses, a ham, a goose, two loaves of bread and a small pot of real butter. There were fruits and vegetables to be had, as well, but, for some reason, they didn't excite him as much. Oh, he bought a small bundle of berries for Mellie, but he spent not another Shim on produce.

During the day, a few customers entered Solutions, and he addressed their needs as well and as quickly as he was able, accepting their meagre payments and shooing them away before turning his thoughts to other things. As was his custom of an afternoon, he read a few fables to Mellie and asked her what she thought of them. Often, he derived great pleasure from doing so. Today, though, he felt an odd urge to return to the parks, perhaps even to climb a tree. Wouldn't that be something? How many decades had it been since he'd last tried?

Chyrin ate a large lunch, focusing mostly on meat, while leaving the bread, butter, berries and the sack of apples for Mellie. He was surprised how hungry he was—an obvious side effect of the youth he'd stolen—but wasn't unduly concerned about it. He vaguely recalled having a monstrous appetite as a young man, himself, so it didn't seem completely unwarranted now. Too, he'd noticed his skin seemed firmer and his muscles, more pronounced. He'd even gotten a bit hairier since the previous morning. At this rate, he wouldn't have been shocked if he looked and felt like a man in his early twenties by week's end.

At one point in the meal, he found his daughter staring at him as if he'd turned into an exotic animal of some sort.

"Oh!" he laughed, "I must seem a trifle odd to you, eh? It's simple, really: I was ill for the longest time, and I'm finally healthy again!" It seemed a harmless enough lie. He really had not felt himself for a decade or more, and now he felt...wonderful! He made a silly face and Mellie giggled. "Shall we go climb a tree?" he crooned.

In fact, they climbed several, or at least he did. Mellie joined him in the first tree, but Chyrin seemed downright obsessed with it, trying tree after tree, until one of the constables came by and ordered him to get down and stay down. He complied begrudgingly, but made faces at the man as soon as his back was turned, to Mellie's delight. Well, Chyrin concluded, by the time they'd walked home, it would probably be time for supper, and he wanted a bite of that ham in the worst way.

He had more than a bite, though. He devoured the whole damned thing as if he hadn't eaten in ages, licking his lips, sucking his fingers, and he was still hungry. Mellie, understandably, was unenthusiastic about returning to Market Square for the third time in two days, so Chyrin instructed her to stay in her chair, playing, until he returned. He'd only be gone a few minutes, he promised.

And that was what he'd intended. Until he set eyes on a woman so beautiful that he became immediately aroused and felt if he didn't at least speak to her, his suffering would be unbearable. The thing was, he'd never been the sort of man to sidle up to a woman and win her over with confidence, charisma and wit. He was no courtier, he. No; he was, he had to admit, more of a skulker, someone who admired ladies from afar and tried to impress them with generosity and kindness. Today was different, though. Today, he felt possessed of an uncustomary swagger, an unfamiliar degree of self-assurance that seemed to propel him towards the woman. As she reached for a bolt of fabric in a nearby merchant's stall, he bumped into her, accidentally-on-purpose.

She turned to look at him with dark eyes, wide as saucers.

"So sorry," he said, offering what he hoped was a humble yet winning smile.

Apparently, it was not, for the woman backed away, a look of mild distaste on her face.

This irritated Chyrin. Who did this woman think she was, to sneer at him so? He took a step towards her, and she began to turn from him. Further annoyed, he accessed his talent, the better to compel her attention. It was not normally something he would have done, but the woman had effectively spurned him— yes, she had!—and he insisted she hear him out. Unfortunately, the moment he began to Shape, she cried out for help in the most powerful, strident voice. Chyrin had no choice to be leave the market immediately.

He Jumped to another, smaller market, halfway across the city, where the prices were much steeper, but the wares were also typically of finer quality. Shrove Street Market, it was, and served the wealthy North Hill District. Everything here was well beyond Chyrin's budget, but as he was still famished, he supposed it wouldn't hurt to purchase a little something to tide himself over.

In short order, he happened upon a street vendor, hawking sausages right off his grill.

"I'll take five," Chyrin told the wrinkled little man. "No, better make it ten."

The vendor was delighted to make the sale, but his joy dwindled somewhat as he watched his customer wolf the still-sizzling sausages down one-by-one in less time than a normal man might eat an apple.

"I need more," Chyrin complained.

"It'll take me a few minutes to cook 'em up good."

"I'll have them raw, then."

The vendor, keenly attuned to the attitudes and expressions of his clientele, then offered to sell the Shaper his entire supply, though in truth he was less eager to make money than to close up for the day and make as much distance between himself and his customer as possible.

"Good, yes," Chyrin mumbled, around a mouthful of sausage.

The other man hefted a small crate of meat in the Shaper's direction, doused his grill, and patiently/impatiently waited for his coin. Chyrin, focused almost entirely on his meal, fished a handful of lesser coins from his ubiquitous pockets and dropped them into the sausage seller's waiting palm. He didn't even notice when the other man bowed briefly and walked away.

Once he'd finished the sausage, Chyrin straightened up and wiped the grease from his face with a rumpled sleeve. That was when he became aware that he'd attracted an audience of horrified on-lookers.

"I've been busy working," he snapped at them. "Working for days without food, drink or sleep. I'm certain that none of you would understand!"

Again, he was forced to Jump away. And he knew just where to go.

He'd satiated his hunger—for the time being—but his sexual appetite remained unassuaged, and if he couldn't win his way into a woman's arms and charms via old-fashioned flirtation, then he would bloody well have to buy his way in. He was that desperate. Appearing just outside of Lendy's Love Nest, he straightened his robes, tousled his hair, and slunk through the front door. Once inside, his senses were bombarded with exotic odors (both intoxicating and unpleasant), décor, and music. He hadn't been there for thirty seconds before he was approached by an impossibly tall, possibly male madam, who gave him a sultry greeting and asked what he fancied.

"I'll need two girls," Chyrin replied, with a slight tremor in his voice. "Or three. Might even need more."

"Really?" the madam asked in barely concealed disbelief. "I admire your ambition, friend. Have you the coin, though?"

He had, though he was fast-exhausting his funds for the month. He did have magical means of reconciling his debts, however, and was not remotely concerned that he'd fall short. Consequently, he poured another handful of coins—these of higher denominations than he'd given the sausage vendor—into the madam's hands.

"Would you like to peruse my girls?" she asked with a satisfied grin.

"Yes. No," Chyrin contradicted himself. "Any two will do. To start."

The madam chuckled condescendingly, but she was willing to take his money all the same.

She ushered the Shaper into a bedroom of sorts that smelled of sweat and worse, only partially masked by a cloying mixture of perfumes, oils and incense. There was a large, lumpy thing in the middle that looked more like a bag of corpses than a mattress, but a colorful quilt had been thrown over it, and Chyrin didn't figure the aesthetics of the place mattered much, given what he'd come here to do. Nevertheless, he took a moment to delouse the place with one of his more common spells. No sense in making things messier than they needed to be.

After a short period, two women came into the room, smiled seductively at him, and began to undress one another. Chyrin wore them both out in less than an hour and sent them limping away, whilst requesting several more be sent in. Gods, he felt like a beast! Never in all his life had he known such potency, such animal passion. More girls arrived and departed, spent like yesterday's fireworks. Chyrin got rougher and rougher, biting several of them during climax, until, at last, he took a large chunk out of one poor girl's shoulder, causing her to scream as if she'd been stabbed. She might as well have been, for all the furor and uproar that came of it.

The madam burst into the room with two muscular bruisers by her side and demanded an exorbitant sum of money and then his immediate departure, never to return.

Chyrin might have Jumped away again, he knew, but this was the sort of happening that got around, the kind of thing even the High Constable took an interest in, and so he resigned himself to settling with the woman, despite the cost.

"I haven't a great deal of cash on hand," he began.

"Not my problem," the madam responded. "And don't try to Shape your way out o' this, neither! These men are my witnesses."

"Yes, yes," Chyrin sighed. "Have you a paper, a bond I can sign for the monies I owe?"

The madam snorted derisively and glanced at her

bodyguard. "You think you're the first man likes a little rough-and-tumble? 'Course I have a paper!" She pulled a document out of the bosom of her dress and presented it with a flourish. "There's quill and ink in the bed table."

The document attested to some ten Monarchs the signee agreed to pay one Lendy Lascivia for damages done to her girls and/or property. So, it was not an uncommon occurrence. But ten Monarchs! Alheria's fiery bush! It would take him months to recoup that amount, and he had Mellie to think of…

Suddenly, he was beyond anxious to sign and be out the door. In his hunger and his arousal, he'd quite forgotten about his beloved charge. He'd promised to return shortly. How much time had passed?

Chyrin rushed through the agreement, his contrition, and even his getting dressed. He needed to get out of Lendy's Love Nest and Jump home. Oh, but he looked a terrible mess and smelled worse. For all that, he still felt as strong, as vital as any three men. If his new appetites were the only consequence of his stolen vigor, he supposed he could manage, especially if it meant more active, meaningful years with Mellie.

He could see she'd been crying the instant he walked through his front door and set eyes upon her. Mellie being Mellie, of course, she did her best to hide the fact, so as not to seem ungrateful or suggest that she didn't trust her beloved 'nuncle. His heart nearly cracked with shame. As he drew nearer to embrace her, she recoiled just the tiniest bit, and, again, he realized what a frightful picture he must have presented.

"I fell into a pile of offal," he lied, "at the market, whilst shopping for mutton and pork. Let me have a quick bath, and we'll magic up a bit of supper. Would you like that?"

The girl's eyes sparkled. Despite his half-hearted attempt at breakfast the other day, Chyrin never really used his shaping to conjure meals. It wasn't worth the subsequent Burning. But to Mellie, a magically summoned meal was a treat, indeed! She clapped her hands and bounced on the balls of her feet, so excited to have him home and promising such wonders.

Chyrin excused himself to the back room, where his tub was located. He kept it empty at all times, lest Mellie should fall in and drown when he wasn't looking. But he had several rain barrels on the roof of his place, which he accessed by means of a wooden pipe that he was able to pour into the tub whenever he wished. He was not given to bathing frequently, so there was plenty of water for this occasion.

"Would you sing for me, dearie?" he called out as he began using his magic to heat the water.

From the other room came the soft, sweet and slightly off-key voice of his child, singing a silly little tune about the Sod Man's Son.

"*Bring-ee in ee sod,*
The cart's so heavy, so
The sheep they 'gin to nod
The Sod Man's Son must go..."

It was a wicked pleasure, summoning the food Mellie wanted, for, in his Shaping, Chyrin simply called it from someone else's plate or table. Yes, it was stealing. Yes, it was wrong. But he did it so rarely, and surely those from whom he filched could endure the loss. And, anyway, why should such as they begrudge his darling Mellie a fine repast now and then? Both man and child marveled at the fine roast his spell-work had called in, along with stuffed quail, two or three kinds of oven-fresh bread, several tarts, and some egg creams. How Chyrin loved to watch his girl enjoy a good meal! And how he loved that meal, himself!

A part of him, of course, felt mounting anxiety at his ever-growing hunger. He understood it was all a part of his renewed youth and vitality. Still, he couldn't help hoping he'd reached the limits of his appetite—both for food and for sex. He couldn't afford another scrape like the one he'd been in earlier—not financially, and not spiritually. He was, had always been, a man of thoughts and ideas, not appetite, not lust. He enjoyed his newfound strength, but he worried where it might lead if left unchecked.

As he watched his child gobble down tart after tart, he resolved to find the man whose youth he'd stolen and learn more about him. It was what he should've done from the beginning, but he'd been too eager to be rid of his infirmities. Yes, he'd find the man and discover the origins of his insatiability.

He didn't know the fellow's name, didn't even know which district he called home, but being a Shaper had its advantages. He searched the city for traces of his own magic and came upon a small apartment above a chandler's, at the back of the building. Chyrin went out at mid-day, once more instructing Mellie to entertain herself with books, drawings and whatever toys she might make.

Chyrin found an external stairway in the alley behind the building in question and climbed it to the second floor. There, he found a door that stood slightly ajar, and he opened it and went inside, into a short hallway with doors on either end. So: two apartments. He was able to detect his own magic behind the door on his left. Without waiting another moment, he strode towards it and knocked with authority. After a minute or two, a young woman cracked it a handspan wide or two. She was pale, gaunt and had large, riveting eyes. If Chyrin hadn't known better, he'd have taken *her* for the Shaper and himself, the target. But no, she was the object of the compulsion he'd laid upon his customer, and now she was, clearly, deeply in its throes.

"May I speak to the man of the house?" he asked.

"What's this about, then?" There was a thin sheen of sweat on her forehead, and her hair hung limply and greasily around her shoulders.

"I..er...I am his Shaper."

"Are you?"

What an odd question! Why should she doubt him?

"Wait here," she said in a dull monotone.

After what seemed hours later, the door opened wider and the woman again stood in front of him, her arm around the waist of a frail older man.

"There must be some mistake," Chyrin sputtered. "A young man came to see me the other day..."

"That was me!" the old man cackled.

Impossible. The man in front of him was easily into his

seventies or eighties, withered, stooped, and with hardly enough hair to cover a mouse. But his eyes were the same.

Chyrin gulped air, tried to compose himself. "I just came by to...to see how you're feeling."

More cackling, following by a bout of wheezing that seemed destined to end in death. "How am I feeling, you ask? Never better!" the old man leered. "And you, my friend? How are *you* feeling?"

Chyrin looked from the man to his mate and back, baffled and terrified by the other man's condition and, even more, his attitude. Without so much as a fare-thee-well, he turned and fled from the fellow's doorway, raced down the hallway, rushed out onto the steps and hurried down to the street below. Only then did he pause to collect himself and slow his breathing. What in Mahnus' name had he gotten—*taken*—from the other man? He began to shake almost uncontrollably and sat on a nearby stoop whilst the episode passed.

What had he done?

Almost before he knew it, he was wandering the streets, frantically looking for something, for...food. For sex. For diversion. He rounded a corner and came upon a small white cat, basking in the sun. He pounced on it and wrung its little neck before suddenly realizing he might have been seen. He glanced all about himself and, comfortable he had not been witnessed, carried the cat deeper into an alley, where the shadows were nigh onto impenetrable. He held the cat up to his face; it was still warm. The next thing he knew, he'd buried himself in its innards and was gobbling away as fast as he could swallow.

He was repulsed by his actions, and yet the cat tasted so damnably good. Too late, he saw that he'd spattered his robes with blood and other, less desirable fluids. He ate the cat's bones. Sucked its brain right out of its broken skull. Lastly, he licked his fingers clean, just as a cat might do when finished with a mouse.

But he wanted more.

And that was when he smelled it; the unmistakable though new-to-him odor of a female dog, a bitch, in estrus. His stomach rumbled, and his loins became tumescent.

He howled in frustration at the night sky above, scarcely recognizing his own voice; once again, he'd forgotten his promise to return home soon. Mellie would be so, so disappointed with him, the poor thing. How could he have allowed himself to be so selfish a second time?

He dashed home, as fast as his hands and feet would carry him, his tongue lolling lazily out the corner of his mouth, and the wind ruffling through the hair down his shoulders, back and arms. He sprang through his door, sailed over the counter, and landed on the far side of his front room. Cautiously... stealthily, he peeked into the room he shared with his daughter and found her lying on her side on her little mattress.

She looked so innocent. So vulnerable.

And so delicious.

SWORDMAN'S HOLIDAY

BY MARTIN OWTON

Out of the corner of his eye Aron scrutinized the man who had been watching him. He was so powerfully built that it seemed his shaven head sprouted directly from his shoulders. He was plainly dressed, carrying no weapons openly, yet there was a sense of menace about him as he watched as Aron teach his afternoon class of basic bladesmanship in stable yard of The Spotted Cat.

I haven't been in Laranda long enough to upset anyone, so I wonder what he wants? Of course he could be Caldon's man, or even Sarazan's.

Aron had arrived in Laranda just under a moon ago, chasing tales of Saxish clansmen. The tales had proved false but he'd stayed, attracted by Laranda's wealth and the easy going reputation of its ruler, Duke Falis. His face and name were too well known in the Holy City just now for him to return, and he had nowhere else to go.

He'd taken lodgings at The Spotted Cat; cheap enough that he could afford to pay for several weeks, but not so cheap as to make him look disreputable, and passed word around the city of his availability as a personal escort and tutor of bladesmanship. Business had been slow. His class today had comprised only three pupils, but there was plenty of time for things to improve as word spread of his abilities. He had been looking forward to a long carefree summer, maybe even a little romance to help him forget the ladies of Nandor; then the man had arrived.

A little knot of tension began to tighten in Aron's stomach

as he took his pupils through the basic drills with their wooden practice swords, and the stranger's silent vigil continued. Aron dismissed his pupils and turned to face the watcher. The watcher stood up and nodded in Aron's direction. *If he were here to harm me he'd have brought more men.* Nevertheless Aron's right hand sought the hilt of the throwing knife he wore in a sheath in his left sleeve as he approached.

"You can teach, I'll give you that," said the big man, looking Aron in the eye. "But can you fight?"

"I believe I can back it up," said Aron, still on edge. "Perhaps you should ask Mikael of Sarazan."

"So that was you." The big man smiled. "I saw that fight. You're exactly the man my boss is looking for if you're available." He held out a meaty calloused hand. "The name's Tyrone. I work for Theodis of Laranda. He's a successful merchant in the city."

Aron took his hand. "What's the job?" said Aron, the tension draining out of him.

"His daughter was abducted yesterday. If you come along with me he'll tell you the details."

The warehouse of Theodis was filled with goods and much activity despite the lateness of the day. Tyrone brought Aron through to the office upstairs where they went straight in.

Theodis was a short plump man with greying hair and beard. The rings on his fingers spoke of wealth, the deep shadows under his reddened eyes spoke of worry.

"This is Aron of Darien, boss," said Tyrone. "He is the swordsman I told you about."

Theodis stood up and offered his hand. "Theodis, merchant of Laranda."

"Aron of Darien, Bladesman of the Academy," said Aron. "Tyrone tells me your daughter has been taken. How can I help you?"

"I'm gathering a team to get her back. She was taken yesterday morning in the market. Two men picked her up, put her into a large basket and made off. The maid she was with tried to chase them but she was tripped from behind. When she recovered her feet they were gone." Theodis told this with his fists clenched all the while. "There's only five of them. I'll pay whatever is necessary to get her back. She's only sixteen."

He reached into his desk, withdrew a small bag and dropped it on the table with a heavy clink.

"How do you know there's only five?" asked Aron.

"A wizard found them for me," Theodis said grimly.

"Has there been a demand for money?" said Aron.

"Not as yet. It will not be long in coming I'm sure."

"Have you approached the Constable?"

"Useless. He told me that Ghislaine had probably eloped. The man's an idiot and sober for less than half the day." The bitterness in Theodis's voice almost smothered the words. "Fortunately I have some friends in this town. They told me of you. I have a few good men, but none of your qualities. Were you truly at the Academy?"

"I was, indeed I am still. I'm merely on extended leave."

"Then I hope you will join us."

"How many other men do you have?" asked Aron cautiously.

"Well, there's Tyrone there. He's my caravan master. There's Brin, he's an archer. Nicoll and his brother Colam, they are my kinsmen. With you in the party, I am sure we have enough to deal with five bandits." Aron's heart sank as Theodis named his relatives. He hoped they were tough fellows, able to handle themselves in a fight, but he had a strong suspicion they would turn out to be callow youths with big ideas about adventures. Aron was minded to decline the proposal, but two things stopped him: firstly the fact that Theodis had already sought out a wizard, precisely as Aron would have done, and secondly Tyrone's air of muscular competency.

Aron wondered whether he might have misjudged Theodis. He was clearly a successful merchant and someone like Tyrone would not work for a fool. Perhaps the good men Theodis had named would be exactly that. There was little harm in his finding out more. If Theodis was right, and the rescue was straightforward, then the money and improved reputation would be most welcome.

"I think I would like to talk to Tyrone and your kinsmen

before I commit myself," said Aron. "I'd like to meet this wizard too. Is that acceptable to you?"

"Of course. I would have had grave doubts about you had you not wanted to know more," said Theodis evenly. "I'll take you to him myself."

Aron felt uneasy; he had passed some test without being aware of it and he had misjudged Theodis again.

"Is there anything else you can remember of the place?" asked Aron. "The smallest detail could be crucial." He and Theodis stood in a dimly lit room behind a pork butcher's shop in a poor area of the town. Heavy curtains covered the windows and the scent of cheap incense filled the air. Master Alberic, the wizard, was a short man with a luxuriant beard. He wore a long purple robe which Aron reckoned would have appeared moth-eaten in stronger light.

"Who are you to question me in this manner?" said Master Alberic, glaring at Aron from beneath bushy eyebrows. "Do you doubt the truth of my words?"

"Master Alberic. The young man means no offence," said Theodis soothingly. "He seeks only the last scrap of information."

"I'm the one who'll be going into this cave to fetch Ghislaine out. Any surprises, and I'm the first man in line to receive them," said Aron, answering the wizard's glare with a hard look of his own.

"Come now gentlemen. Let us not fall out over this. Surely we are all on the same side. Master Alberic, I would consider it a personal favour if you could visit my daughter once more. I am desperate to know that these bandits haven't harmed her, and of course if you should see anything else of use to Aron." Theodis left the sentence hanging as he dug in his belt pouch. Gold glinted between his fingers.

"Very well," said the wizard with an oily smile. "The fee is the same as last time. Do you have the girl's comb?"

Theodis passed over a tortoiseshell comb and Master Alberic drew from it a few strands of red hair. "Please sit down while I prepare. Do not speak to me until I speak. I need complete silence in which to concentrate."

Aron and Theodis sat on a couch which puffed out a cloud of dust as it took their weight. Master Alberic settled himself cross-legged on a rug with a woven pentagram in the middle. He sat in the precise centre of the pentagram, placing the palms of his hands on two of the points. Aron sneezed as the dust filled his nose.

"Hush," said Master Alberic fiercely. "I must have complete silence."

Then he began to rock gently back and forth humming a monotonous low chant. Aron watched the performance in silence. He had seen this magic worked before, but with far less theatre; it did not increase his confidence in Master Alberic.

At length, Master Alberic ceased his chant and noisily took a deep breath. "I am with Ghislaine," he said.

"How is she?" asked Theodis, his voice hoarse with anxiety.

"They are holding her in a cave. She is chained by her ankle, but otherwise unharmed. The men have not touched her," replied Alberic in a dreamy sing-song voice.

"Thank the Gods," sighed Theodis, his fists clenched tight. He asked no further question so Aron felt it was his turn.

"How many men guard her?" asked Aron.

"Four. There was another, but he left before they reached the cave," replied Alberic, still in the strange voice.

"What weapons do they have?"

"Knives and swords. She hasn't seen anything else."

"Tell me what you see when you look out from the cave."

"There's a flat area before the cave, beyond that there's a slope down to the stream. There's a little hill on the other side of the stream with trees on it. I can't see very far away to the right because of the bend in the valley. To the left the stream broadens and there's a rock face at its edge. I'm losing the contact." The last phrase was spoken in Alberic's normal voice.

"Do you have enough? We already know where this cave is," Theodis said, his first words for some while.

"I think so," said Aron after a moment's consideration. "If it is not all some showman's trick."

Master Alberic glared at Aron but said nothing. Theodis hurriedly opened the door to usher Aron away from the wizard before another argument began.

Nicoll and Colam, Theodis' kinsmen, turned out to be tall dark-haired men in their late twenties with an air of brawny solidity that reassured Aron greatly. No callow youths these two, nor Brin the archer. He was a muscular shaggy-haired hillman who would look stocky until you realised how tall he was. Tyrone nearly broke Aron's hand with his handshake and called for ale for all of them when Aron told him that he would join the rescue party. Colam wanted to know if Aron could join straight-away as they intended to leave in the morning. If the wizard's vision was accurate, then with these fellows, Aron thought, the rescue would be money easily earned. One thing only troubled him; Theodis had still not received a ransom demand.

Theodis had maps of the region and, with Master Alberic's information, had located the cave in a small area a day and a half's ride from Laranda. The five rescuers rode out in the mid-morning, with enough supplies for eight days in the wild and a spare pony for Ghislaine to ride back. They made good time through the morning and, as the day aged, they turned off onto a smaller lane that wound towards a ragged line of purple hills. As dusk descended, they arrived at a country inn and took lodgings for the night.

"Mind what you say in here," cautioned Tyrone as they approached the inn. "We are close enough to the area where the kidnappers should be that someone might carry them warning if we arouse suspicion."

It was easy to avoid loose talk in the tavern as there was almost no-one else there. The tavern keeper was interested in only the quality of their silver and, once satisfied, he showed them to their room in silence. The rescue party were the only diners at supper. Later in the evening three or four farmhands, as Aron guessed them to be, came into the taproom taking to a corner to play some obscure game with cards and dice. After one mug of the sour ale Aron could understand why the tavern was not more popular. He returned to their room leaving Nicoll,

Colam and Brin, who were clearly more used to the local brew.

Tyrone was sitting on his bed sharpening a dagger which he put aside when Aron came.

"I'm glad you've come back. I've been wanting to talk to you about tomorrow," Tyrone said. "That is assuming we catch up with them tomorrow."

"As you wish. What's on your mind?"

"It's this. I have known Colam and Nicoll since they were children, Brin almost as long. You, I met yesterday. I know I can trust the others in the tightest corner, but can I trust you?" Tyrone looked Aron squarely in the eye as he said this. "I've seen you fight in the arena, and you're a fine bladesman, but can you, will you, kill when the moment comes?"

Aron relaxed. If that was what most bothered Tyrone, then he need not be concerned. "I've probably killed more men face-to-face than you have, though I do not needlessly seek it. You need not worry about that."

There was a moment of silence as Tyrone studied Aron.

"What do you intend to do with any of the kidnappers we take?" asked Aron, more to break the silence that had descended than because he wished to know.

"No prisoners. I'm not the Constable of Laranda to be fetching them back. They'd only hang anywise, so we'll save ourselves the trouble. Have you any problem with that?" Tyrone looked hard at Aron again.

"They're no family of mine," said Aron. He'd have been surprised if the answer had been different. "It's a hard world. They've made their choice."

This seemed to satisfy Tyrone. "I'm sorry to doubt you, lad, but I've known Ghislaine all her life. She's like my own daughter. I can't risk anything that could put her at any more risk." He picked up his whetstone and returned to work on the dagger. "So you reckon you killed more men than me eh? You must have been a busy fellow."

The rescue party left the dreary tavern shortly after dawn, continuing towards the hills on a narrow and rutted track. The countryside changed as they rode into the hills; in the early

morning they had passed through pasture land with cattle grazing. By midday rocks were showing through the thin soil and
the cattle had given way to sheep. In the middle of the afternoon
they came upon the first of the landmarks that Master Alberic
had seen in his vision. Tyrone pulled out the notes that Theodis
had made. After a few moment's reading he directed them away
from the track across through the rough scrub of the hillside.
Every so often Tyrone would nod or grunt in approval and consult the notes. From this Aron understood that Master Alberic
knew the countryside well or, just possibly, had the true sight.

As the shadows lengthened the five rode in single file following a rough stony path down a valley that narrowed between
the outstretched arms of a limestone height. Hoof prints in the
dust showed that others had passed this way since the last rain.
Aron felt the muscles in his chest and shoulders tighten in anticipation. A stream chattered over the pale stones beside them as
they came to where two shoulders of the ridge closed in, creating a gateway across the valley. Here they dismounted, tether-
ing the ponies in a thicket of young trees whose foliage gave
good cover. Tyrone drew out Master Alberic's notes once more
and gestured to the others to draw near.

"If I have it right, then they lie just beyond." Tyrone pointed
to the hill at their backs. "If we climb this hill then we should be
able to look directly into the cave. There should be woods on the
far side of the hill so let's use the cover. Master Alberic said they
keep no lookout, but that is no reason to be less careful."

Tyrone had it right. From the crest of the hill they crouched
in the undergrowth and were able to look across the narrow
valley into the cave unobserved. But instead of three or four ruf-
fians guarding Ghislaine, the slope below the cave was crowded
with armed men all wearing dark full-length robes. Aron's heart
sank. The area immediately before the mouth of the cave had a
great pile of wood on one side, on the other side a stake taller
than a man was driven into a crack and between the two a white
circle had been inscribed on the flat rock. As they watched two
men stepped forward from the cave and looked down the valley
to where the sun was sinking towards the horizon.

"Fuck the bastard!" swore Tyrone . "Eberlan!"

"Who's Eberlan?" said Aron.

"The shorter man there, " said Tyrone. "He's Duke Falis' cousin. He tried to overthrow Falis fifteen years back. The revolt was broken, but Eberlan got away. I think the big bearded man in white with the golden belt is Arathaxis, the death cult high priest. He matches the description I've heard. He's under a death sentence from the High King."

"There must be two hundred of them," said Colam.

Aron spat a whispered curse in reply. "Well done, Master Alberic."

They retreated to the bottom of the hill where they had left the ponies.

"Does anyone have any ideas?" said Tyrone.

"The white markings on the rock before the cave look like a conjuring circle," said Aron. "I fear they have seized Ghislaine as an offering."

"They're going to sacrifice her?" gasped Colam, clenching his fists. "Why?"

"Because that's how you bind a demon," said Aron.

"Can you really do that?" said Nicoll.

"I'm afraid so," said Aron. "You summon a demon, offer it a sacrifice and if it accepts it, then it is bound to serve you."

"Why her?" said Colam.

"Who knows?" said Aron. "I've heard it said the stronger demons can be very specific in what they will accept. Perhaps there's something about her that fits the requirement."

"How can we fight a demon?" asked Brin.

"We can't without a couple of strong wizards," said Aron.

"With two hundred men and a bound demon there's nothing to stop them between here and the Holy City," said Tyrone. "They'll overrun Laranda in no time."

"What are we to do then?" said Colam, his voice breaking. "We can't just leave her."

"I can take down that priest anytime you want," said Brin.

"How many arrows do you have with you?" asked Tyrone.

"Twenty five," replied the archer.

"Then that would leave us with at least one hundred and seventy five enemies between us and Ghislaine. I do not like those odds," said Tyrone grimly. "But we cannot return without her. I could not face Theodis."

There was silence for a while as they all considered the situation. Then Aron spoke. "We have rope do we not? Brin, you have spare bowstrings." Brin nodded.

"What's your idea Aron?" asked Tyrone.

"The timing is all important, but I think we can cause enough distraction to give us a chance to rescue Ghislaine. I'm guessing that they will wait for moonrise before beginning whatever their ritual is. It's a full moon tonight."

"Then we have a while to wait," said Tyrone. "What are we to do?"

"My poor Ghislaine," whispered Colam. "I cannot live if we don't rescue her." Nicoll and Tyrone shared a knowing glance at these words.

They filled all the waterskins they had brought, lugged them up to the top of the hill and made ready as the dusk deepened into night then sat down to wait for the moon.

Far into the night, the cultists fired the stack of wood which roared up to a fine blaze sending leaping shadows through the little valley. The rescuers then got their first sight of Ghislaine as she was dragged cursing and screaming from the cave and tied to the stake a few paces from the fire. She was attired in a long flowing white gown secured with a silver belt and her hair fell loose about her shoulders. Her screams were drowned by the voices of the cultists chanting in unison as the full moon rose through a gap in the hills then Arathaxis stepped forward from the cave to begin his ritual. Tyrone, Colam and Nicoll each silently embraced Aron and Brin before they slipped away down into the valley to get into position.

Aron watched from the hill as Arathaxis stepped forward to the edge of the chalk circle and raised his hands. His followers stopped their chant and even Ghislaine fell silent. He threw a handful of powder into the fire which burst into blinding white flame for a moment and then he began to declaim in a harsh tongue that Aron did not recognise. The breeze dropped and the air in the valley grew very still as if everything was holding its breath. The knot of tension in Aron's stomach tightened even further.

At first Aron thought it was a trick of the firelight, a twist of smoke caught in an eddy perhaps, but as he watched something began to take shape within the circle. Ghislaine saw it too and screamed again, but her shrill cries made no difference to the priest who carried on the spell without faltering.

"Iduna, help me," whispered Aron, even though no-one would have heard him at this distance. "Guide our hands tonight."

In the circle the twist of smoke thickened and began to glow orange-red like the heart of the fire. The glow expanded until it filled the cylinder defined by the drawn circle, then it darkened abruptly as if something had stepped into the light. The priest opened his arms wide in welcome, and his congregation let out an awed sigh of triumph as a huge figure materialised. Three times the height of the priest, it stood within the confines of the circle, its skin glowing as if it burned from within with the fires of its home. From within the great horned skull red eyes fixed upon Arathaxis as its lips drew back in a snarl of greeting and a forked tongue flicked out to taste the air. Its impressively muscled body writhed as it sought to burst the spells that bound it to Arathaxis' will.

"Now, Brin," called Aron.

Aron cut the restraining ropes and with a creak and rustle of leaves, the tied-back saplings launched the waterskins into the night sky. Brin's longbow sang softly as he sent his first arrow on its way.

From their position in the bushes beyond the firelight, Tyrone, Colam and Nicoll had a good view of the events. Firstly Brin's arrow took the priest in the centre of his broad chest; moments later the waterskins landed on the area between the fire and the circle. The skins burst on impact spilling water across the stone, some splashed into the fire, hissing away instantly into steam. More flowed into the circle, washing away the chalk line and wetting the clawed feet of the demon. A gasp of dismay rose from the cultists.

The moment the circle was broken the demon was free. With a howl of triumph it surged forward, seizing the stricken Arathaxis as he stood transfixed by Brin's arrow. One great arm lifted him from his feet and delivered him to the beast's many-fanged mouth. Tyrone, Colam and Nicoll watched in horror as the demon flourished the headless body at the crowd then bounded forward howling and slavering. The cultists broke and ran in panic, scattering into the night. The demon gave chase, splattering Tyrone, Colam and Nicoll with the Arathaxis' blood as it passed by their hiding place.

Ghislaine had fainted in terror. Tyrone's battle-axe made short work of the ropes that bound her to the stake. Colam lifted her free of her bonds and carried her to the mouth of the cave where he cradled her limp body in his arms sobbing her name over and over.

Up on the hill, Aron and Brin watched the chaos unfold as the cultists fled from the demon. Most headed down the valley but a handful started to climb the hill. Brin picked them off and Aron did not even need to draw his sword. The demon stormed off down the valley in pursuit of the cultists and, as the noise faded into the distance, Aron relaxed.

"I think it's safe to rejoin the others now," Aron said. Brin grunted his assent and they began to pick their way down the hill. The cultists' fire had burnt down and, in the depths of the valley hidden from the moon, the night was now very dark. The sharp thorns exacted a high price from Aron and Brin for their passage through the dense undergrowth.

Tyrone met them at the stream.

"How is Ghislaine?" asked Aron.

"Tearful and very shaken," said Tyrone. "She'll survive, and time will blur the horror of it. Colam is sitting with her."

"Is she fit to be moved?" asked Aron.

"She is. I think we should get away from here in case the cultists come back," said Tyrone looking around. "Or the demon." As he spoke the silence of the night was broken by a huge roar and the ground shook as if pounded by a gigantic hammer.

"Too late," shouted Tyrone. "Into the cave."

They scrambled up to the cave as a dark-robed man burst through the undergrowth pursued by the demon. Halfway up the slope the beast caught the cultist, casually scooping him up with one paw before ripping his head off with the other.

"What's happening?" squeaked Ghislaine, looking up from Colam's embrace.

"Get as far into the cave as you can go," ordered Tyrone. "The demon's back."

Colam picked up Ghislaine and carried her into the dark interior followed swiftly by Nicoll, Aron and Brin. There was another bellow, much louder than the first, and Tyrone scrambled into the cave.

"It's right outside," he gasped. Then, with a dreadful snarl, the demon filled the entrance of the cave. It stretched out a huge arm and reached for Tyrone with a clawed paw that carved grooves in the rock floor of the cave as Tyrone leapt back. The demon screeched in frustration as the narrow entrance prevented it reaching its prey who cowered as far back as possible, gagging as the demon's foul breath washed over them. Brin's bow sang as he loosed arrow after arrow at the beast, each one finding its target, but seeming only to provoke it more. The demon threw itself at the rocks around the entrance, dust and pebbles fell from the roof but the rocks held.

"What do we do now?" gasped Nicoll.

"Pray, if you have a god," said Aron. "And wait for dawn. Some demons can't stand sunlight."

"Is there any chance it'll just of this and go away?" said Nicoll.

"Not really," replied Aron. "Without that priest's control, it's simply a random destroyer. It doesn't possess the intelligence to get bored. It'll attack anything that catches its attention."

"So that's why it didn't attack Ghislaine, she wasn't moving," said Tyrone. "How do you come to know so much of demons?"

"Mastery of weapons isn't the only thing taught at the Academy," replied Aron.

They huddled together for warmth in the darkness with the beast's claws relentlessly seeking them. After a while no-one seemed to have anything to say, so they sat in silence; each busy with their own thoughts or prayers. Some may have slept, Aron did not.

Grey morning light showed around the massive form of the demon as it continued sweeping its claws across the rocky floor an arm's length short of the prisoners. Aron watched the sky behind the demon lighten in hope, but the demon stayed right where it was completely focused on its prey; dawn brought no change. The only thing that had changed was that they now had enough light to see the walls of their prison.

"Like a cat before a mouse hole," said Aron. "It has fed too well here to return to its own world yet."

"And we're as helpless as mice," replied Tyrone. "There's no way we can fight this thing is there? Yet we can't let it run loose to ravage to countryside." He turned to the others. One by one they shrugged and shook their heads.

At the far end of the deep cave, where the roof descended to less than waist high, the wan light revealed a cleft with a rough blanket stretched over a rough wooden frame.

"What's behind that screen?" asked Nicoll.

"I don't know, but there's a draught that comes through there sometimes," said Ghislaine. "That's why they put the screen up; to keep them warm."

"That sounds promising," said Tyrone. "Tear it down and let's see if there's a way out through there."

Colam and Nicoll pulled down the screen revealing a narrow passage. Nicoll threw the screen at the demon which seized it eagerly. It bit into the wood and old cloth and then screamed in frustration. Colam crawled forward into the narrow space. "I can feel a breeze on my face," he called back over his shoulder. For a short while the others could discern the sounds of Colam's progress over the noise of the demon but, after that, they sat in a huddle watching the demon, silently praying Colam hadn't got stuck in some narrow place.

A nailbiting eternity later a rattle of stones announced Colam's return. He scrambled into view, face scratched and hair full of dust.

"There's a way out," he called, as he crawled the last few

feet to them. "It comes out on the top of the hill. It's narrow, but passable."

"Right, let's get out of here. You lead Colam. Nicoll, you look after Ghislaine," ordered Tyrone.

"But," said Colam.

Tyrone cut him off in mid complaint. "Colam. Go. You know the way."

"What about that?" Aron pointed at the demon which still clawed the cave floor in vain attempts to reach them. "What's to stop it coming after us once we're outside?"

"We'll be far enough away that it won't see us," said Colam. "It comes out right on top of the hill."

"That's not certain," said Tyrone. "And it leaves the demon loose in the countryside."

"The slope above the cave has got plenty of loose rocks," said Colam. "It'll be easy to start a landslide. We can wall the thing up in here."

"That should do," said Tyrone. "But we have to keep it by the cave entrance while we get out."

"Then someone has to stay here to keep its attention until we can bring the rocks down," said Aron.

"But they may get trapped," said Nicoll.

"I know," said Aron.

One by one, the others slipped past Aron down the passageway. Each one stopped for a moment as they came by him. Tyrone grasped his hand firmly. "See you up top, lad," he said gruffly. Colam and Nicoll took his hand similarly and wished him the Gods' protection, Brin embraced him and said something in the hillmen's tongue that Aron took to be a blessing. Ghislaine kissed him and then snuffled tears down his neck before Nicoll took her hand and led her after Colam

The demon still scrabbled its claws mindlessly on the cave floor and walls trying to grasp the man who sat just beyond its reach. Aron needed to keep in its sight so could not retreat to the back of the cave. He had faced danger and death many times before, but always the outcome had turned upon his own resources. Whether facing a swordsman in single combat, or climbing a sheer rockface, his fate was in his hands; sitting shivering in a cold gloomy cave waiting for the roof to fall in tested his nerves in an utterly different way. Cold fingers of fear gripped his stomach and refused to be dislodged as he thought about how much damage the rockslide would do. Would bring down the roof of the cave? Would he be able to get out, or would he share his last hours with an entombed demon?

Rather than dwell on his situation, Aron focused on keeping the demon within the cave mouth where the rockslide would trap it. To hold its interest he cut at its paws with his sword from time to time. This caused no more damage than Brin's arrows, but kept the demon's attention.

Aron felt the rockslide before he heard it. The rock trembled around him and the demon howled in response; the rumble drowned the howl and ended in a crashing roar. Then there was silence broken by a couple of small stone slides. Dust filled the cave but the roof held. Aron whispered a prayer of thanks to Iduna as he fumbled with his flint and steel to light the makeshift torch he'd prepared. As the torch lit, the demon burst out in an ear-splitting fury and attacked the rocks that imprisoned it against the cave mouth. Aron crawled away down the passageway, which appeared undamaged, and breathed a sigh of relief as he began to climb up into the hill leaving the trapped beast to its fate.

"So what'll happen to it?" asked Ghislaine. She'd been the first to hug Aron when he emerged from the cavern, and now walked beside him as they found their way back to where they had left the ponies, Colam just a step behind her.

"When it weakens it'll dematerialise and return to wherever it came from," said Aron.

"Are you sure it can't get out?" Ghislaine said, turning to look back .

"Who knows what a demon can do, but I think we've walled it up pretty good," said Colam. "Once we reach the ponies we'll get you right away."

"What do you suppose happened to all those men?" asked Ghislaine.

"Scattered to the four winds and still running," laughed Aron. "Those that the demon didn't catch. I hope they didn't find our ponies, or we've a long walk ahead of us."

"I hope the demon ate every last one of them," said Ghislaine fiercely.

They saw no sign of the cultists as they made their way back over the hill to the ponies. Aron presumed that they had all taken the fastest route away from the demon up the valley, which made it easy for the beast to hunt them down. The ponies were in the thicket where they had left them and, after they had been fed and watered, the party loaded up and rode out.

The sun was sinking into the west as they left the hills behind. Nicoll lead the small procession as they rode in single file. No-one talked much as they rode along, each tired and busy with their thoughts of the days' happenings. There was one thing that still stirred Aron's curiosity; he moved his pony forward past Colam to ride beside Ghislaine.

"Have you any idea why they picked you out?" Aron asked Ghislaine. "Did they say anything that would give us some clue?"

"It was my hair," said Ghislaine. "They said they took me because I was the first girl they saw with red hair."

Colam reached over and lifted up her heavy tresses, pointing to the blonde roots and laughed. "I'll wager that'll be the last time you dye it red."

"I thought you liked redheads," said Ghislaine with a toss of her locks. "I know Nicoll does."

THE LOINCLOTH MASSACRE

BY CHRISTOPHER KEENE

K essler breathed in the bitter air and imagined the symbol for enhanced sight. His vision changed so he could see every detail of the city of Tyria spread out below him, allowing him to survey the dark, mortared towers looming over thatched slums. Squat buildings were crammed between towers tall enough that the splash from an emptied chamber pot could still hit the bottom windows. It was a fly-ridden corpse of a city, dead but not yet buried.

Perched on a high roof, Kessler watched as one of his target's guards, who would have appeared as a mere speck to any normal human eye, entered his enhanced view. He was a man in white armor who was swiftly making his way down the stone path toward the whoring district.

Not the best place for a cleric to be found dead.

He knew that the guards in the Loincloth brothel would be trouble even having *wift*, the symbol for speed, planted in his mind. Despite this knowledge, he did not hesitate before stepping over the roof's edge. Falling, he watched through enhanced eyes, blurred from the rushing wind, as the guard beneath him walked under the veiled archway of the brothel. Kessler envisioned the symbol to decrease his weight, *ari*, lowering his speed to that of a drifting feather. Just as the white-clad man vanished inside, Kessler slowed in his fall, the tail of his black cloak billowing out behind him as he landed.

Looking up, he saw the Loincloth's two bouncers staring at

him, their mouths agape. Kessler envisioned the *wift* symbol and drew out his two Sai-Blades. He bounded between them as the blades landed in the bouncers' necks and they fell limply on either side of the archway. Piercing skin with a Sai-Blade killed in an instant.

Kessler hadn't seen the bouncers fall. Dashing forward, he leaped and landed in a crouch on the long wooden table in the middle of the brothel's bar. Men of all classes and creeds looked up as silence came over the room, some at the table wearing the same white regalia as his target. He flung his arms back and envisioned the symbol which manipulated the Sai-Blades, a crossed arrow known as *zex*. The daggers dislodged from the bouncers' necks and flew toward him, spinning onto his index fingers as he brought them up. He heard seats fly back and tip over from men's backsides as the cleric's guards stood and drew steel.

Kessler spread his arms, his Sai-Blades stabbing directly into the white cloth between two of the guards' armored plates. The blades of the other two guards' swords slashed down in his direction, but they only bit the wood of the table. The bewildered fighters looked up to see Kessler above them, his body spinning in the air as his cloak trailed behind his every movement like a flag. As the symbol for *ari* faded from his mind it was quickly replaced with the crossed arrow before he changed the arrow-head's direction. The daggers flew up into his waiting hands before shooting out again to seek new victims. He flipped back onto the floor behind the table, his Sai-Blades once again return-ing to him. He counted six dead already, four spread across the floor in front of him and the two bouncers behind, a hefty load for the corpse-cutter to collect.

Kessler rose slowly and envisioned *uon*, the symbol for strength. At the mere flick of his hand, the heavy table flew from his path before smashing into the sidewall of the bar. People ran screaming from its path. He began to walk, his black cloak stained with the ale he had crouched in. Having been hidden in a corner of the room, the guard in white he had first seen entering the brothel ran screaming out from behind him with his sword raised. Kessler envisioned the symbol for *uon* again and kicked out. His foot crushed the man's breastplate like a tin can. He assumed the kick would kill the guard but had not predicted the man's corpse would fly through the plastered wall of the brothel and into the street. Kessler smirked and strode toward the stairs that led up to the private rooms. No one was rushing at him now that they could see the almost perfect circle of dead guards spread around where the table had once been. As he arrived at the staircase, the single remaining white-clad guard seemed to weigh his odds for a moment and then fled through the archway.

A better option than through a wall.

Feeling he would no longer need them, Kessler sheathed the Sai-Blades under his cloak. Climbing the stairs that led up to two separate balconies, he envisioned the symbol for hearing. He was suddenly blitzed with a myriad of sounds which, when he had been new to this ability, had been overwhelming and confusing for him. Over time he had trained himself to focus on only what he wanted to hear.

The familiar voice of the cleric was blurred with every other sound at first but soon became clear to him. *"Did what to my men? Here?"*

From the same upward direction he had heard the voice, Kessler noted heavy footsteps approaching. He looked up as the white-robed man came into view on the landing above and looked down on him. Ptolemy was even fatter than Kessler remembered, his second chin alone showing the wealth he had gained from his betrayal. This thought quickly made way for the symbol of *ari*. A single symbol needed complete and utter concentration. He leaped up onto the staircase's banister, jumping off it and landing with a flip onto the second floor. The fat cleric cursed and retreated back into his room, his flowing robes no longer belted to hold in his fat, wobbling body. Kessler followed him through the sliding doors, seeing the young, frightened boy lying on the room's sleeping pallet. As he entered he saw, not Ptolemy in the darkness, but the flash of steel in the light of a flickering candle.

If Kessler hadn't kept his ears enhanced the ambush would have undoubtedly finished him. However, his knowledge of the trap wasn't going to make it any easier to avoid. As quickly as his mind could work, he used *wift* to dive away from the strikes. Rolling up onto his feet, he turned to face the two remaining guards in the darkness. It appeared Ptolemy was paranoid enough to keep them even in his bedding chamber. Replacing the symbol with *uon* Kessler ran forward, throwing the men through the sliding doors and off the balcony with a single push.

On instinct, he leaped up as he heard the broken doors hit the bar floor below. His instincts served him well, for as soon as he jumped, Ptolemy stumbled under him with a thrust from his own Sai-Blade. The symbol of *ari* that looked so much like the letter 'i' was replaced by the crossed arrow once again. The look of horror that came over Ptolemy's chubby face when his Sai-Blade flew from his hand was highly satisfying for Kessler. His expression didn't change until he turned to see Kessler landing behind him with the very rare and sought-after weapon now within his grip. Even then, it only changed into a look of bewilderment.

"Now give that back. You may be a killer but you're not a petty thief, are you, Kessler?"

Kessler was surprised by the effect a few dozen pounds could have on a man's voice. He turned to the young boy still in the room with them, unmoving, as though frozen in fear.

Sliding the extra Sai-Blade under his belt, he murmured in his gravelly voice, "Get out."

As though taking any opportunity he could find, Ptolemy turned to leave.

"Not you!"

The boy awoke from his trance, jumped to his feet, and ran out of the room. Ptolemy stopped and shrugged, giving him a whimsical grin that reminded Kessler of older days.

"You can't really blame me for trying."

"I can!" Kessler snapped. "And I do blame you... for everything that has happened to this country. You must've been relieved that they kept their promises. After all, you're a cleric and can get all the young boys you can lay your sticky fingers on."

Ptolemy poked out his bottom lip and raised a fat finger. *"And* a lordship, but I assume that promotion is still being decided upon considering how long it has taken the earl to summon me."

"The earl..." Kessler's already heavy voice rumbled with hatred when hearing that title.

"We couldn't have won, Kessler. This land would have been the Avaani's within a year anyway, even if I hadn't—"

"If you hadn't betrayed us?" Kessler's interruption cut through Ptolemy's words like an ax through wood. "Have you seen what he has done to the land? What you allowed him to do?" He walked over and pulled aside the thin drapes of an open window, pointing to the barren wasteland that was visible over the city walls. "Look! Do you see any trees out there? No, because they cut them all down to make Sai-Blades! You sold them this land and they have destroyed it! How can you be proud of that?"

Ptolemy was unaffected by Kessler's words, his face turning solemn. "My pride was never as strong as yours, I'm afraid. If Lord Ganarak had won his duel maybe we could have kept fighting, but—"

Kessler held up a hand to stop him. "But he didn't and so you sold us out?"

As though still content with his decision, Ptolemy nodded. "This is a different world we live in now, Kessler. I was simply the only one with the vision to see it coming, and yes, I took advantage of that. I saw the changes for what they were and acted upon them for my own benefit. What's really so wrong with that?"

Kessler turned on him, jaw clenched. "Not a thing. Though I wonder if you'll have the foresight to see this coming also."

He stalked forward and Ptolemy raised his hands.

"Wait, what are you doing?!"

Kessler envisioned the *uon* symbol and grabbed Ptolemy by his shoulder.

"Kessler, come on, no, don't!" the fat man cried, struggling against Kessler's rock-like grip as he carried him to the window. "Kessler, no!"

Catching Ptolemy's ankle up in his other hand, Kessler threw the fat cleric through the opening. He watched the man's quick fall end with a sudden stop as he hit the rock pathway in front of the brothel. It was a clean defenestration and didn't make as much of a mess as he had expected. Despite this, he was surprised at how quickly the guards posted in the area rushed to see the cleric's dead body. They had obviously been warned by the one guard he had let go and were now being ordered to storm the place and find him. Kessler had no intention of waiting around for them. He had done what he needed to do here.

Taking a few steps back into the room for a run-up, he envisioned *wift* again, the symbol for speed. He sprinted toward the open window, launching into the air as he swapped it for *ari*. He soared over the open street, between two of the high towers, and landed softly on a tiled roof before he began running again. No one could catch him now that he was in free-flight unless they were on horseback. Even if they were, he could always take them out in a similar fashion to the guards he had killed.

Although being chased was always more interesting to him no one seemed to be following. It didn't matter. His mind was calming again, wandering to other issues and goals ahead. Revenge on the betrayer was only step one. Step two was the drawing together of those who still remained true to Tyria, those who would fight like him if given the power. He hadn't been collecting these Sai-blades for nothing, after all.

From up on top of one of the high towers Kessler could see the hills. Their green was always a bitter reminder for him of what used to surround the Tyrian city during his youth. Now the green and tall trees were gone, replaced with the cracked and dead hardpan of the wasteland. With it the animals had gone, the shade had gone and the minor storms that used to gently caress the trees now ripped at the city and the desert sand in cyclones, unperturbed.

Despite all this Kessler was grinning, because even though he could see the reminders of the green hills in the distance, he could also see the events that were happening in the street below him. They showed him yet another occurrence of a tipping in the balance of power. Those he had given the Sai-Blades to were taking back the city, kill all those that stood in their way. The knights could no longer stop them, after all, they no longer had their weapons.

Everyone's death belonged to someone his master had taught him, so said the gods. To him, of all things his master had taught him, the idea of the gods was the least convincing aspect of the Lunari beliefs. But when the exiled Minaaya had taught him of it, he had never let his skepticism show. If he was to believe all that how could he suppose to do what needed to be done in this city?

He stood up on the edge of the high pointed roof, like standing on the edge of a spear jutting into the sky. He cleared his mind and envisioned the symbol similar to the shape of spectacles for sight and watched as those under him began advancing on the castle.

Kessler would give them no more assistance. He had taught them the crossed-arrow symbol first because it was the least overwhelming on the senses, making it easier to learn. However, *zex* would only work on those with Sai-blades. The next group he would teach the strength symbol, they would need to keep the castle when the Avaani tried to take it back. Either way, it should still be enough to keep them alive.

His dark cloak-tail lifted as he sprinted around the edge of the roof for a run-up. He then envisioned *ari*, jumped off the roof and began to soar through the air, so high up that anyone from below could have easily mistaken him for a crow flying in the sunlight. As always he was pleased with the sense of freedom given to him by his powers, but he knew he had to apply the correct focus or he was more likely to get himself killed.

The next step in his plan was already in motion which meant he could move onto his other schemes in the governing system for what was to come. Like in the Imperial Capital of Nasaia he had already set up his noblemen's identity in the court. It wasn't hard with his pale complexion making him look like an Avaani northerner. It wouldn't be long before he was invited to their formal gatherings.

Things were falling into place far too easily.

The Aptet
of Tchatcha-em-Ânkh
By David Niall Wilson

Rebecca York was a woman of ritual. Her father had taught her at a very early age to treat every moment of every day with the significance of a final ending, and a great rebirth. To do less was disrespectful to the powers that created the heavens and the Earth. The end of her day was no less to her than the beginning, and in some ways, far more important.

She had expanded on her father's wisdom over the years, caring for her mind and body with equal parts of her attention. At 5'9" she was taller than most women. She was slender, which accentuated her height, and wore her hair in one long braid, normally draped forward over one shoulder. She kept to herself—evident in her choice of homes—and her clothing was usually dark and plain with only a few meaningful ornaments to set off the glitter of her eyes.

You would not know from looking at her that she'd traveled the world, or the mystery that had surrounded her life since a very early age. If you didn't know her, you would not suspect the power she was intimate with, or the iron will with which she controlled it. Not unless you met her gaze full on. That was an experience none could ever forget. Rebecca York might appear unassuming, but that appearance was the epitome of the old adage about books and their covers. And despite her best efforts to hide it, she was beautiful.

Her cottage was tucked in among rolling foothills of the Great Smoky Mountains, just west of Asheville, North Carolina. There was a road leading in, but it was closed off by a series of gates she locked carefully each time she drove in. She had other ways out, but they were not shared with the world at large. As far as anyone was concerned, she was the crazy lady who lived in the woods, and that was fine by her. Those who knew her often kidded her about taking to the North Carolina hills. Born in Israel, she'd lived in France, England, Tibet, and several other even more exotic places over the years, which made her choice of a rural mountain home seem odd. Rebecca always explained it the same way—she did not choose the place, it chose her.

If the person questioning her had the proper background, she'd explain about the lines of power, and their convergence. She'd tell them how this was the single place in all the world she'd found completely in line with her energies. In this small cottage she could reach levels of concentration that were impossible anywhere else, and for her work, concentration was essential.

As the sun dropped toward the line of mountains to the west, she walked through the small home, tracing symbols of protection at each window, checking the wards at the doors, and setting things to rights. Her books were perfectly aligned. The small fountain in one corner of her den trickled with just the right amount of clear water. There were no stray papers on her desk, or pencils laying askew on the blotter. Among other interests, Feng Shui occupied her mind on a constant basis. She was keenly aware of any shift in energy, and quick to correct it. She abhorred imbalance.

Her bedroom lay on the eastern side of the cottage where the morning sun could slide over the sill and invite her into each new day. The room would have looked strange to most, with the bed centered between walls hung with tapestries and lined with shelves. The floor was inlaid with concentric circles, each band of which contained a carefully placed ring of esoteric characters and symbols. At the head of the bed, the foot, and to either side, centered between the widest of the circles about five feet from the frame, four wooden stands held cast-iron bowls. Directly behind her pillow, a stouter stand held a large, ceramic bowl of white stone.

Rebecca walked slowly around her bedroom, stopping momentarily at each of the stands in the circle, sprinkling small handfuls of powder into each shallow burner, as well as some leaves and twigs. When they were filled to her satisfaction, she walked to the head of her bed and peered down into the ceramic bowl.

It was filled about halfway with clear water. The interior of the bowl was mirrored. It was a relic she'd brought back from a trip to Europe—very old. She'd followed a map so old it had threatened to crumble before she could photograph it through mountains and down tunnels to retrieve it. The hiding place, a larger pool of water, had been deep, and protected by water spirits. It had taken her nearly a week of careful preparation to brave that pool, and all for this apparently unremarkable bowl. Of course, it was—in every way—remarkable. It was said to have belonged to Morgana herself, though Rebecca was loathe to believe such tales. She knew what it was, and what it was used for, and that was what mattered.

The sun had completed its circuit of the sky and fallen behind the mountains as she moved about the room. The shadows were deeper, and she turned, just for a moment, to stare out her window at the fog-wreathed hills and the darkening sky beyond. It was a place of power, a place that attracted those with creative spirits, and those with dangerous hungers. Secluded as she was, she was far from alone.

Before building her home here, she'd spent weeks walking the forest paths. She'd lived in the mountains. She'd spoken to those whose families had lived there for centuries, learned their ways and studied their myths. She had found other powers in the hills. Some she'd contested, others were allies. All the while, she'd carved her place, carefully creating the proper boundaries, negotiating the wards and digging in roots. It was home now, more than the sand and rock of her homeland, or the high peaks of Tibet where she'd learned so much, or the deep glens and rolling hills of Europe. As much as possible, she had made herself a place of absolute tranquility and peace. The madness that was her life required it.

From her nightstand, she pulled out a long, slender joss stick. It was sandalwood. She had many scents available to her—cabinets filled with herbs, spices, leaves and tinctures of all sorts—but it was the Sandalwood that brought her peace. It was the Sandalwood that strengthened her vision.

She also pulled out a small box of wooden matches. Working in a counter-clockwise direction, she made a circuit of her bed. She lit the scented powders and leaves in each brazier. When all four were smoldering, tendrils of smoke wafting in slow circles in her wake, she lit the joss stick and stood at the foot of her bed, facing North. She held the stick out in front of her, closed her eyes, and spoke softly, invoking the Archangel Michael. Next she moved to the West and called upon Gabriel, then Raphael and Uriel in turn.

Her circuit complete, she placed the still burning incense stick in a holder beside the ceramic bowl, drew back the covers, and slid between the sheets. There was no light other than the faded orange of the dying sun, and the glowing tip of the joss stick, burned halfway down. She saw it in the periphery of her vision, smiled, and closed her eyes.

Very gently, the water in the bowl above her head rippled. The motion began in the center, rolling out in rings that matched those embedded in the wooden floor. When the ripple reached the edge of the bowl, it made a soft slapping sound, but Rebecca didn't hear it.

She dreamed.

She woke to the sound of laughter. All around her, women chattered excitedly, bustling about in a rustle of silk and the scents of sandalwood and musk. When she sat up, bells jangled. She glanced down at her ankle and frowned at the delicate band of gold and its noisy bangles. She felt the cool cotton of the sheets she lay upon, and the fresh air blowing over and around her. It was not her room, and it was not her mountains. The air tingled with power, and she knew it for a vision.

The air had a thick, ethereal quality. Rebecca smiled and

rose. She was surrounded by silken draperies. She pushed them aside and stepped into the room beyond. There were at least half a hundred other women, young and old, in various states of undress. The conversation of many more drifted in from doorways leading in three of four directions. In that last direction a larger doorway opened onto a long hall. The entrance was draped with beaded curtains.

Rebecca turned and studied the other women, getting her bearings as quickly as possible. Some washed themselves with the water from metal bowls, and others ran combs through their hair, or sorted through small chests of jewelry for just the right ornament.

She waded through wafting incense smoke and the clutter of toiletries and bed-clothes, stopping now and again to watch as others prepared themselves for whatever was to come. There was never a vision without purpose. She tried to sort the sights and sound and give them a framework to hang on that made sense. It was hot, and it was humid. Sand wisped across the floor, and she guessed she was near a desert, or a beach. There was no taste of salt in the air, but it was moist with humidity. The overall scent of the place was familiar, but for some reason it wouldn't click.

Then one of the other women tripped over her as she stood, taking it all in, and spun back to her.

"Be careful!" she snapped. "There is no time to clean, or change, we must hurry."

The words flashed in and out of focus in her mind, and then locked. The girl spoke Egyptian, but not the Egyptian of Anwar Sadat; it was the Egyptian of Tutankhamen and Cheops. The Egyptian of Alexandria and Cleopatra. Rebecca shook her head once, cleared her thoughts, and then raised her eyes to meet the girl's gaze.

"I am sorry," she said.

The girl smiled. "You must hurry, sister. The King has called for us. There is to be a day on the lake. There will only be twenty chosen. It is a beautiful day, and there will be no work for those who are chosen."

Rebecca followed the girl out of the room and into a long

hall. They moved quickly, and the others closed in around them, laughing and chattering. Rebecca kept her mouth closed and her ears open, and by the time they broke out through the front door and onto the steps, she knew that they'd been summoned for a special service to the King. The King was bored... he required entertainment...and the word was that his advisor, the sorcerer Tchatcha-em-ânkh, had been called upon to provide that entertainment.

The name sent shivers down Rebecca's arms. She was familiar with the popular works of Budge, and she was intimately familiar with the rituals recorded in the various Books of the Dead. She knew the name. She knew his reputation, and had memorized stories of his accomplishments as told to King Cheops—which placed her several dynasties prior to that great Pharaoh's life—and death.

She moved as close to the front of the pack as she could get. The vision was astonishingly clear, but she knew she must play her part. If she wanted to know what it was all about, she would have to become one of the chosen. As they passed a mirror of polished silver, she glanced at her reflection, and was astonished by what she saw. Her face and features were her own, but she was dressed in a very sheer cotton smock. She wore gold at her throat, and on her ankles, and her makeup, while crude and overdrawn, was striking. She wished she could capture the image, but knew her memory would have to serve. She wished that she knew what the others saw, as well. If she had suddenly appeared in their midst, unfamiliar and foreign, they would never accept her—she knew she wore the frame and face of a long dead woman—a woman she would never meet.

As they reached the steps, an aged man, his head shaven and tanned, stepped forward with his hands raised. The women, as one, dropped to their knees. Rebecca joined them, just managing to do so before she was left standing alone. The man was flanked on either side by two young boys with bronzed skin, wearing only short, skirt-like garments and sandals. The boys, like the women before them, were adorned in gold and thick makeup. Each of them held an armload of fine-mesh fishing nets.

Rebecca heard more whispered voices and knew that the man before her was Tchatcha-em-ânkh. He spoke softly, but the words carried, wrapping in and around them, seeming to come from everywhere—and nowhere—at the same time. Even in the eerie, half-life of the vision, he stood out—his countenance was clear, while those around him shimmered in and out of focus.

"You are privileged," he said. "You serve the one King, the son of Ra. It is a glorious day, and some among you will have a special task. It will not be an easy one...you will man the oars on the boat of a God. You will be on display, and you will please. You will be called upon to be beautiful, and to work as a single unit."

He stepped forward then, and began moving among the women. When one met his approval, he bent and touched her head gently. Each time this happened one of the boys draped a net over the chosen. Then Tchatcha-em-ânkh stood before Rebecca, and unable to lower her eyes to his feet, as was expected, she met his gaze fully.

The sorcerer registered shock, just for the shortest of moments. In that time, Rebecca, cursing under her breath, managed to tear her gaze free and lower her head. She waited, expecting the worst. She did not know what would happen if he confronted her in the vision. It would disrupt the flow. She might be trapped, or worse. Her heart slammed in her chest, and she waited, until—like the touch of a fly landing, Tchatcha-em-ânkh touched her head, and moved on. A moment later the cool mesh of a fishing net fell over her shoulders, and the selection was complete.

"The rest of you may go," the sorcerer cried. "Do not despair if you were not chosen. The God shall return, and in that return his dark mood will be lifted. He will smile upon you all. Rejoice. Prepare a feast, and music."

Those not among the twenty drew back in silence, turned, and scurried into the hall behind them. When they were gone, Tchatcha-em-ânkh spoke once more.

"You will attire yourselves in only the nets you have been provided, as if you were a bountiful catch. Make your way to the lake, and you will be led to the King's boat, where you will each take up an oar. Together you will row the God who walks among us about the lake, helping to lift his mood. This is a great honor...do not waste time."

Then he turned, and was gone, leaving them to rise and hurry back to their quarters to change. Rebecca pulled the net from her shoulders and stared at it dubiously. The mesh was fine, but it would be incredibly sheer. She thought about walking among these strangers with nothing else to cover herself, and her pulse quickened.

Play it out, she told herself. *If it wasn't important, you would not be here.*

She hurried after the others, found the bed where she'd awakened, and quickly stripped out of her clothing. Standing naked with only the gold ornament at her throat and the belled ankle bracelet, she concentrated on other things. She drew on the emotions around her—excitement, anticipation, but no shame. None of them was uncomfortable in the near nudity of the fishing nets. If anything, the soft threads excited them. Rebecca did her best to feed off of this, allowing her mind to clear, and channeling their emotions into her expressions and actions.

She knew that she had nothing to be ashamed of, but centuries of ingrained propriety were difficult to slough off. She was a handsome woman. She ate sparingly, walked miles through the mountains each day, and cared for herself meticulously. As with all else in her life, health was a ritual, and one she enjoyed. With the nets trailing over her shoulders and cinched in the center with a bit of gold rope she'd found near her bed, she left the chamber of maidens behind and followed the other chosen down the wide stone steps and into the street that led to the lake. She was certain that they saw what they expected to see— another daughter of the Nile on her way to serve the King. She wondered, though, what Tchatcha-em-ânkh would see...and if he would approve.

She was amused to realize that all of the chosen were virgins. The form she inhabited was that of a maiden. She hoped that Tchatcha-em-ânkh would not have them examined prior to embarking on the day's pleasure, because she wasn't certain which woman he would see—and it had been many years since she fit the description of maiden. She wondered, as well, what he'd seen in her eyes. Did he know? Did he realize another of power had entered his world? Was he threatened, amused—plotting something she could not comprehend? She thought it likely that, at the very least, he knew something was different about her, and so she wondered how he would react, and why she'd been chosen.

They were escorted down a wooden pier by a number of very large, shaven-headed eunuchs. These were so remarkably similar in appearance that Rebecca wondered if they'd been bred to it, or just trained and sculpted to match. She was fascinated by everything she saw—the ornaments, the attire, the immense stone of the buildings. All of it had been dust for centuries. She tried not to let her senses overwhelm her. She concentrated on keeping her footing on the damp pier, and not allowing the meager covering of the fishnet to drop from her shoulders.

The boat was long, like a very large canoe. It was wide in the center and flat, and running down either side were benches, ten to a side. At each of these benches an ornate and gilded ebony oar rested, waiting for one of twenty to be seated and take it in hand.

They were helped into the boat and led to their seats. The Eunuchs paused before each of them, helping to arrange the nets and their hair, positioning them just so to make the perfect aesthetic design—an image to please the senses of a God. Even as her mind rebelled against the objectification of the women, the attention to detail captivated her. The boat was like a huge, many-faceted ritual of which she was but a single part.

The twenty were followed by the boys who had accompanied Tchatcha-em-ânkh. They moved to the front of the boat, where they arranged pillows on a flat seat. Incense was lit in small braziers to either side of the padded seat. Palm fronds were brought and laid to either side and an awning was raised that blocked the brightest rays of the sun.

"He comes," one of the girls whispered.

Rebecca turned her head slowly, watching the pier out of the corner of her eye. A small entourage made its way majestically toward them. Eunuchs flanked the King, and behind him, accompanied by two more of the young men, the sorcerer followed.

King Senefru was young. He might have seen twenty years, and he was slender. Between the eunuchs, if it hadn't been for the golden headpiece he wore, he might have been mistaken for a boy. His brow was creased by a frown, and his steps were hurried. He also wore makeup, more elaborate than that of the boys. His hair was clipped to the length of his shoulders and he wore an amulet of lapis lazuli at his throat. Gold glittered as he moved. It rippled on his robe, in his hair, on his fingers and wrists.

Then the King broke the spell of his own majesty by speaking.

"I hope that you are right," he said peevishly, turning back to Tchatcha-em-ânkh before stepping into the boat. "I have not felt right since rising this morning, and I can't see how riding about in a boat is going to change that."

"You will see, your Highness," the old man replied. A day on the lake, with such beauty surrounding you," Tchatcha-em-ânkh waved his arm to indicate the maidens at the oars, and the beautifully laid out seat awaiting the King, "will do wonders for your spirit. There are many beautiful sights along the banks, and we will see them at our leisure."

Senefru shrugged, nodded, and turned. One of the eunuchs helped him down into the boat, and he made his way slowly forward. As he went, he gazed at each of the maidens in turn. He did not touch them—they were all virgins—but he examined them carefully, checking for any blemish. It was as if he was determined the day would not improve, and wanted any excuse to validate his mood.

When he reached Rebecca, he stopped and turned fully to face her. She kept her eyes respectfully on the boat's plank floor. She felt the heat of the sun beating down on her shoulders through the netting and was suddenly very aware of his eyes, and the fact that she was nearly naked in his presence. He lingered, stepping to one side, and then the other.

"What is it, sire?" Tchatcha-em-ânkh asked. "Does something displease you?"

"No," the King replied, distracted. "I do not know what it is. There is something…"

He shook his head and turned toward the front of the boat. Without further hesitation he made his way to the pillowed seat and arranged himself carefully. Two of the eunuchs took up the palm fronds and began to fan him gently.

"Cast off," Tchatcha-em-ânkh called.

The boat rocked gently and slid out onto the brilliant blue water. Sun rippled on the waves. A short man with a shaven head paced to the center of the boat, taking a position between the rows of maidens. He held a small tambour, which he began, slowly, to tap. It made a susurrus rattling sound. Rebecca and the others took up the oars, dipped them into the water, and within a few beats, they had matched the pace of their strokes to his rhythm.

Rebecca concentrated on the motion. She had rowed before, but never a single oar, and never in unison with others. She didn't want to draw any attention to herself, and it was both easier, and harder work than she'd anticipated. As she relaxed, the light drumming of the oar-master seeped into her consciousness, and her body—the maiden's body—responded. The boat rode light and easy, and the oars, dipping at a leisurely pace, drawing back and rising again, brought them to a slow, but steady pace that ate up the distance with surprising rapidity.

They turned to the left and cruised along the bank. There were groves of trees, and banks of reeds. In the sunlight the distant desert glittered like a sheet of diamonds. It was beautiful, and peaceful, and the King, for all his ire upon their departure, quickly grew calm. He spoke with Tchatcha-em-ânkh, who told him stories, pointed out landmarks, and generally filled in the last elements of a perfect afternoon. Rebecca listened carefully, but heard nothing of importance. She tucked away the names of places and kings, and the anecdotal tales that filled the otherwise silent journey, but she knew she had entered this time—this place—for a reason, and she remained watchful.

Now and then, the old sorcerer turned and glanced at her. She kept her eyes down on these occasions, avoiding direct contact, but she felt his attention like tendrils of spider silk brushing over her skin. More than once a slight shiver threatened to break the perfection of her rowing, and she was certain that—if the old man didn't notice, he at least sensed her discomfort. It irritated her that he was able to affect her control with such small effort.

When they'd seen the sights of the left shore, Tchatcha-em-ânkh directed the oar-master to turn them toward the center of the lake. He said that there were some things he'd like to show the King on the far bank, and wanted to cross as quickly as possible. The squat oar-master changed his cadence to a series of sharp raps. He called out to the maidens on the right hand side to hold tight as those on the left continued their strokes. When the bow was nearly pointed in the direction they needed to go, he shifted back to the steady rhythm with a shimmering rattle of the tambour. Rebecca resumed her steady rowing, and as they progressed toward the lake's center, the beat increased in tempo until they fairly raced across the placid surface of the water.

It appeared they would make a swift, unhindered passage, but it was not to be. A girl near the front of the boat, just to the right and behind the King, faltered. A large horsefly had landed on her hair, threatening to bite. Frightened, she released her oar with one hand and swiped at the offending insect. It buzzed off over the water, but the damage was done. Her oar went dead in the water, then caught the resistance of the lake and slammed back into her chest. The boat's progress was disrupted. They lurched, and spun slightly to the side. The oar-master caught the problem quickly, slowed the rhythm and called out to all of them to stop. The smooth progress they'd been making ceased, and the boat shuddered, unsettling the King on his seat, and nearly tumbling one of the eunuchs into the water.

The girl who'd caused the problem gave a soft cry. There was a clink of metal, and Rebecca saw something strike the side of the boat. The girl reached for it, but her net tangled on the end of her oar, and the glittering object dropped past her grasping hand and splashed into the water beside the boat. The girl brought her hand to her throat and gasped, and though the oar-master called out to them all to resume their efforts, she made no move to return to her oar.

The King, distracted, turned and stared at her. She sat very still.

"What is wrong?" he asked her. "Why have you stopped rowing?"

The girl did not raise her eyes, but neither did she seem cowed by his presence, or his attention. Once again, Rebecca was fascinated. There was some dynamic at work here, some relationship between King and virgins that she did not fully understand, but there was no time to dwell on it.

"My amulet," she said. "It was a gift from my mother, and belonged to her mother before her. It has fallen in the water."

"Then it is gone," the King said. "You must take up your oar so that we may continue."

The girl made no move to comply. Instead, she leaned closer to the side of the boat and peered into the depths below.

Rebecca watched closely. She also watched the King and the old sorcerer. Most of her knowledge of the ancients came from scrolls and books, manuscripts so old they crumbled to dust if handled incorrectly. She did not know how the King might react—what sort of punishment might be forthcoming. She steeled herself for the worst, but it never came.

The King turned to Tchatcha-em-ânkh.

"You were very wise," he said, "to advise me to come on this trip. I am feeling well, and enjoying the beauty, but now we have a problem. This maiden has lost an amulet that is important to her, and she will not row. If she will not row, I fear we will sit here so long that the day will be ruined."

The old sorcerer met the King's gaze.

"It is a problem," he said. "Without an even number of oars on either side, we will not move smoothly, and how would we fairly choose one from the opposite side to excuse from her duties?"

The King smiled.

"I know that you are a very powerful man," he said. "I believe that you can find a way to return this maiden's amulet and restore my tranquility."

Rebecca frowned. The banter back and forth between the King and the old man seemed stilted and formal. It was like a planned script, or something they'd been through again, and again. She concentrated on their words, while willing herself not to turn and stare. She still did not know what would happen if she met the sorcerer's gaze again. If he knew she was there—that she was not the girl she appeared to be—what would he do? What could he do? Would he call her out, or tell the King?

"If it is your wish," Tchatcha-em-ânkh said, "then I will use what small influence I have with the powers of the lake to assist, if I am able."

Senefru turned to watch, not the old man, but the lake. The girl who had lost the ornament, despite her apparent desire to sulk, glanced over as well. All of the girls turned, so Rebecca felt, at last, it was safe to surreptitiously observe

Tchatcha-em-ânkh moved to the side of the boat and stood between the first girl and the bench seat where the King had turned to observe. From beneath his white robe, the old man pulled free a golden scarab pendant that dangled from a strong chain. Rebecca saw a glitter of red, but could not see any details, as the man's back was to her.

She heard a rattle of sound she was certain had come from the sorcerer's throat, but it was not loud enough to hear clearly, or controlled enough to be words. She had heard of exercises used to train vocal cords to operate beyond normal capabilities—and she wondered if she'd just witnessed proof.

Then Tchatcha-em-ânkh began to speak, and the world shifted so quickly and completely that Rebecca nearly cried aloud in shock.

The light from the sun, already bright, turned golden. The air, clear and bright with a hint of the lake's moisture, thickened. It had a taste, but Rebecca could not place it. She turned her head and found the motion uncharacteristically difficult. Tchatcha-em-ânkh had turned, and regarded her with interest.

"Come to me," he said.

Rebecca looked up and down the boat. All the others sat as still as stone, as if they were statues, and only she—and the old sorcerer—existed. With no other clear choice, she rose—again finding it more difficult, the motion slower than it should have been. She crossed the boat, trying not to think of the fact she wore nothing but fishing nets. She met the old man's gaze.

"Who are you?" he asked.

"Rebecca," she said, without hesitation. "I am a seeker."

He nodded, as if her words did not surprise him. He nodded toward the lake.

"It is no small thing that the King has asked," he said. "To retrieve an item from the bottom of a deep lake—twelve cubits, if memory serves—would seem—impossible."

Rebecca held his gaze, and finally, he smiled.

"Observe," he said. "And listen. I do not know you, but I sense your power. Listen, learn…do not forget a detail, because any lost word loses everything."

Rebecca nodded.

"Return to your seat," he said. "They must not know we have spoken."

Tchatcha-em-ânkh turned away from her, and Rebecca hurried, as best she could in the thick, cloying air, to her seat. She gripped her oar, and as she did, the world tilted back. It was like the rush of the downward slope of a roller coaster, and this time she did gasp, but none turned to see why. All eyes were fixed on Tchatcha-em-ânkh as he began to speak.

Rebecca understood some of the words, but not all. She concentrated on inflection and pronunciation. She memorized every tone, every sound and click of the tongue. She concentrated so hard on getting it right, that she paid no attention to what was going on around her. It was only when the girl beside her dropped her oar and covered her mouth to suppress a scream that she glanced up. In that second, her mind nearly blanked.

The water beside the boat had separated. One section, a perfect rectangle, had lifted to a height of at least ten feet above the surface, a thick, wet column, and continued to rise as she watched. She saw fish within that segment of water, and the reflection of Tchatcha-em-ânkh and his amulet, glittering in the sunlight. Though the water rose, nothing dripped or poured from its surface. It might have been formed of panes of glass, or a massive chunk of crystal.

Tchatcha-em-ânkh continued to speak, and Rebecca frantically repeated each intonation, each syllable. She had been trained to incredible feats of memory, but the power and energy crackling through the air stole her concentration.

The slice of lake finally rose to a point where its bottom edge cleared the surface. The sorcerer raised it yet another foot, and then, as if sliding it onto a shelf, he pushed it aside. Rebecca could not help herself...she half-rose from her seat, peering over the far edge of the boat. At the far end of the impossible slit in the water, she saw the bottom of the lake. It appeared dry as bone. Sand actually caught in the breeze, and swirled up to dance in the air.

The King turned, saw her on her feet, and beckoned to one of the eunuchs.

"Bring her to me. We will lower her down to fetch the bauble, and be on our way."

He showed no awe, or even surprise, at Tchatcha-em-ânkh's magic. If anything, he was amused, and seeing the flicker of panic Rebecca had to fight down and control, his smile widened. He was enjoying her discomfiture.

"There is nothing to fear," he said. "You will be down, and then back in the boat within moments. You would not deny the will of your King?"

Rebecca lowered her eyes, crossed the boat, and stood quietly at the old sorcerer's side. Tchatcha-em-ânkh did not glance at her, or at anyone. He seemed in a trance. His lips still moved, but no sound emerged that she could hear. Automatically, she ran through the sounds and intonations of his chant in her mind, once, twice, a third time, and she would have done so a fourth, except that the eunuch took her by her arm and shook her gently. She realized the King had spoken again.

"I hope the heat has not been too much for you," he said.

She shook her head.

"Come, then," he said.

A larger fishing net was lowered over the side of the boat, draping down the perfectly symmetrical wall of water. It unrolled like a rope ladder, and when the top-most edge had been secured to the side of the boat, the King gestured for Rebecca to comb down.

"Don't take too long," he suggested. "Tchatcha-em-ânkh is very powerful, but who knows how long he can hold it?

And there are insects—distractions." The King's smile widened yet again, and Rebecca stared down into the pit below, shuddered, and then, not wanting to appear hesitant, sat on the boat's edge, swung her legs over, and turned, gripping the rope of the net tightly As she bumped into the side of the craft, she was reminded once again of her nearly naked state. Her breasts pressed into the wood, and she felt the King's gaze as he watched, assessing her. She felt, very suddenly, as if she were being offered a test, and that what she did next, and how she did it, was important, though she had no idea in what way, or whether it would be important to herself, or the girl whose place she'd assumed in the vision.

She descended as rapidly as possible. She watched, nervously, as the boat bobbed and floated above her, the side where the net was attached dangerously close to the lip of the strange, impossible pit. She didn't know what would happen if the current, or a strong breeze, pushed the bow over that edge—but she knew she did not want to be at the bottom of the net, or worse yet, still descending it, if she found out.

The climb seemed to take an eternity, though she knew it couldn't have been more than a few seconds. She dropped the last foot or so, expecting to sink into soft, muddy earth, despite the evidence of her own eyes, but it didn't happen. The ground was solid, and she turned quickly. There were plants she'd never seen. There was a tangle of branches wound round and round with some sort of thread. Just beyond it all, she caught a glitter of gold. She walked carefully around the branches, avoided a rounded stone, and bent to pick up the amulet. She felt the net slide from her hip as she bent, and she reached to hold it. There was laughter from above, but it seemed to come from a very great distance.

She picked up the jewelry, turned, and made her way back to the net. The laughter seemed to echo from the walls of water to either side, and a wave of claustrophobia nearly paralyzed her. She placed the amulet gently between her teeth, gripped the net, and began to climb.

Above her, faces loomed, leaning over the edge of the boat, smiling and pointing and laughing with delight. Beside and behind a little, Tchatcha-em-ânkh still stood, arms upraised. She focused her attention on the old sorcerer, ignored the water and the laughter and the voices. She closed her eyes, just for a moment, and repeated the incantation a final time. She climbed, and when she reached the top, strong arms gripped her arms. Someone pulled the amulet from between her teeth.

And then, Tchatcha-em-ânkh glanced down at her and smiled. He dropped his arms and with a terrible roar, the huge rectangle of lake water dissolved. It poured over the edge and back into the pit, equalizing. The boat bucked and rocked, and Rebecca fell back. The last thing she saw was the old sorcerer's eyes. Then the lake closed in over her. The water filled her lungs, and she fought for her breath. She struggled, but the weight on her chest was immense; the thought of the huge block of water settling over her—merging with the lake—pressing her down—drove her to panic.

She grasped at straws of memory. She fought to concentrate and, despite the inability to breathe, she mouthed the words of the incantation, now buried in her psyche. As she pushed the last word from her mind, the last air from her lung—it was gone. All of it. The weight lifted—she was dry—and she came up, gasping for air, to find herself gripping her sheets white-knuckled. She took in such a deep breath she cut off her own oxygen. For the second time in as many moments, darkness threatened to steal her consciousness.

Then, behind her, there was a loud splashing sound. Droplets of water flew from the bowl behind her and dampened her hair, and her neck, her pillows were soaked. Regaining control, she turned and stared. The water in the bowl—what was left of it, was agitated. There were puddles and spills all around it, and Rebecca sat, clutching her sheets, neck craned painfully to gaze at the normally placid pool.

So close. She had lain within her protections. The wards had been set. Nothing had been different, except—he'd seen her. The old man, Tchatcha-em-ânkh, had known her for what she was—known she did not belong. He had been with her in her vision—and so, she realized—he had been within the confines of her protection. It was something to consider in the future and a blessing that she'd not run across a more malevolent power.

All of this flickered through her mind and at the same time, she paid it little attention. She visualized the bowl of water—imagined a chunk the size of a stick of butter being lifted free—imagined it dropping back to splash her and her bed. The words of the incantation were fresh in her mind. She rose, walked the circle around her bed, waving her arm, as if dissipating smoke, and spoke the names of the Archangels in turn, reversing the order of the ward she'd set, until she felt the pressure in the room relax. She crossed the circles to her desk, opened a drawer, and pulled out a leather-bound journal. She flipped it open, and with careful, even strokes, recorded the words as she'd memorized them. When possible she used the Egyptian, but when the words were not as expected, or unfamiliar, she recorded the phonetic equivalents with care. It took her nearly five minutes of deep concentration to get it down to her satisfaction. Then, reaching up to brush the long, dark hair from her eyes, she turned to an old, antique rotary dial phone on the desk's edge...frowned slightly...and reached out. Half a second before her fingers brushed the cool Bakelite of the antique phone's receiver—it rang.

THE FALL OF LITTLE CREEK
A LIGHT IN THE DARK STORY
BY ULFF LEHMANN

"Kid, don't do it," Kerral said again. "They want to screw you over. And will you stop with the drink already? We both know your mood when you're drunk."

Kerral was older than him. He'd seen the hazing that came with being the newest fighter in the warband, had even tried to shield him from the worst. Something Drangar would always be grateful for, but this he had to do. He had to prove to those who tormented him that he was like them—a mercenary.

He took in the older man over the rim of his mug, and tilted the container higher, blocking him out. Instead, mead flooded his mouth, spilling, dripping down his chin onto table and tunic. "You ain't my father," he finally said, burping.

In fact, the young warrior had no father. None he ever knew of, anyway. "I'm of age, I can handle a sword, and we're bloody mercenaries." He arched his eyebrows. "Tuaghal, Una and the others are my *friends*." He burped again.

"Besides," said Tadc, from beside Kerral. "It's easy money."

It was the end of another long day for Mireynh's Marauders. With a sigh, Kerral stood. "Have it your way. Mireynh's taking the company to the winter garrison. You know where."

"Mead!" Drangar yelled, raising his tankard, willfully ignoring the warleader. He was sixteen, an adult for two years— he knew what he was doing.

A heavy hand pushed down his raised arm. "We're leaving, you coming, runt?" Tadc said.

Like everyone in Tuaghal's band of mercenaries, Tadc was a veteran of many battles. He was hardened—like the jagged scars that accentuated his face and form. He was ruthless and bloody well looked the part.

To be in the company of these stalwart warriors was an honor. The fact that they asked him to accompany them on their little expedition to protect a village was a sign that he was finally accepted as a true mercenary. At least, he hoped it was.

For Drangar, this had been a long, slow year of suffering, humiliation, and degradation. Such was the hazing that came with becoming a rookie member in this elite band of warriors. Mireynh's Marauders was one of the most famous mercenary armies in the world, and Drangar had paid his dues. He finally felt like he belonged.

So what if Tadc called him a 'runt'. He didn't mind it. The old warrior was almost two feet taller than him. Truth was, standing next to the man, he felt like a runt indeed.

They set off from Bruidh M'dhain, heading east. At first, the pace was decent, though Drangar could feel his mount trembling with exhaustion long before they reached the inn that first evening.

"What's that say?" Tuaghal demanded. He pointed at the writing underneath the sign of a wolf holding a goat's head in its maws.

"Ask the runt," Lugaid said. "He can read."

Drangar sighed. He should have never proclaimed he knew his letters. Once again the fact that he had been raised in the Eye of Traksor kicked him in the balls.

"Well, Librarian," Tuaghal said, waving him over, "What's that say?"

"It's a piece of wood," Drangar replied. "It doesn't *say* anything."

Why had he used those words? Had he hoped his comrades would laugh? Now that he was accepted among the brethren of warriors, things were different—or so he hoped—so why weren't they laughing?

Only Finnen, who was right beside him, exhaled her amusement, but one look from Tuaghal and she fell silent. The warleader lashed out, slapping Drangar with such surprise force, he damn near knocked out a tooth.

"You little shit, don't you dare get cocky. Understood?"

Biting back tears that were in equal parts shame and anger, Drangar only managed a nod. It was confirmation that he was still *just the runt*.

"I didn't hear you, Librarian!"

"I'm not a Librarian," Drangar pushed back at the man through clenched teeth. His mind raged at the hypocrisy and double standards. He was their equal, now, dammit! A part of the company, a mercenary!

"You're in *my* company," Tughal seethed—and when he seethed, spittle drooled down from the left corner of his mouth, like a ravenous dog. "I lead. What I say is law, and when I call you Librarian, you will answer to it and you will like it, understood?"

Drangar's eyes were level with Tughal. "Aye," he mumbled.

"I did not hear you, runt." His cold stare bore into his newest mercenary.

"Tuaghal," Finnen said. "Give'im a break, already. He's trying to fit in."

If Drangar were to guess, she was in her twenties, closer to his age than theirs. Maybe that's why she spoke on his behalf. Maybe it was because he had taken her place as the runt of this mangy litter.

"He can read, girl, that's why we took him with us in the first place," Sitric scoffed from behind. "Read the bloody sign, boy."

Sitric, like his brethren, was a seasoned fighter. He'd seen his shares of blood and death—women and ale—and had an eye for strategy in warfare. Most of all, Drangar knew that Sitric could always be counted upon to tell it like it was. And so he did...

So that was it? They'd only taken him along because of his letters? Compared to them, he *was* a Librarian, true, but he was no priest of Traghnalach. No, Lesganagh, the god of Sun and

War, was his patron. Drangar gritted his teeth.

"Do what he wants," Finnen whispered, leaning into him.

He turned his head to her and blinked away the tempered tears. Her smile was enough to appease the bruising of his heart against its cage.

"No weapons allowed," he spoke the lettered words to her, but loud enough for them to hear. "Leave them in the stable.— That's what it says."

"Anything else?" Tuaghal asked. "I can count, boy."

Suppressing a sigh, Drangar turned to the despised sign and read the second part. "Any who disobey will deal with the Knights of Kalduuhn."

The mercenaries turned to each other for discourse.

"What's a knight of Kalduuhn?" Tadc asked.

"Never heard of them," Una said. But Drangar had...

"They're the keepers of the law here," Drangar said, regretting it immediately. *They're not going to stop calling you 'Librarian' if you keep talking like one*, he thought.

"Librarian indeed," Tuaghal said with a grin. "You heard the rules, let's get the horses stabled and find someone to take care of our weapons."

This someone was, of course, Drangar. He had barely brushed down his aging gelding when Tuaghal dragged him to the front of the stables. "You'll watch the gear until the local idiot locks them away, understood?" An order.—Spoken by a man who was used to giving orders.

"Yes, Sir," Drangar said, holding out both hands to receive the leader's sword belt and dagger.

"Good boy," Tuaghal said, patting his head.

Drangar resisted the temptation to toss the gear into the muck. Instead, he placed it on the table near the stable's entrance. Some of the others, Sitric first and foremost, did not put their weapons in his hands. They dropped them into the muck at his feet, demanding he bow down to retrieve them.

"Don't fuck with the help," Tadc growled, kicking one of the offenders in the ass. Drangar couldn't suppress the playful smile that curved his lips when the swift kick sent her sprawling. "Here you go, runt," the tall mercenary said, putting his sword and mace onto the table himself. "Don't let them treat you like shit."

Soon he was alone, guarding a table stacked with all kinds of weapons. It wasn't right. It wasn't fair. He was a mercenary just like them. He'd stood his ground in the shield wall, he'd bled alongside them, he'd received his share just like them. Was it his fault he was better with the blade? Was their animosity towards him born from envy? He did his part, was a comrade like Kerral had taught him to be. *In the wall everyone is your sibling, you can't survive the wall without siblings.* Since joining Mireynh's Marauders he'd done everything that was asked of him. Mucking stables, feeding and brushing horses, polishing armor, sharpening blades—everything—all the tasks freshlings were supposed to do, and he had done all without complaint.

Drangar drew his long knife and squinted along its blade in the flickering torchlight. Next, he fumbled for his whetstone and set about uncovering the knife's edge again. Up and down the stone went, along the nicked steel. The motion quelled his anger and drove it to the back of his mind.

"Hey." A voice, Finnen's voice, disrupted his reverie.

Drangar blinked, looked at the knife and stone in his hands and then at the older woman. She carried a covered plate in one hand and a mug in the other hand. Putting weapon and stone away, he returned the greeting—a word for a word. "Hey."

He wanted to say more, but the words only reached his throat before he swallowed them back. He'd never understood why he couldn't just talk to her.

"Brought you this." She handed him plate and mug, pulling off the cover as he took them from her. "Stew and ale. The bread's terrible, so I spared you that," she said. It was her smile that eclipsed his hunger.

"Thanks," Drangar said, putting the mug on the table and digging in.

"I'm sorry," Finnen said, sitting down across from him.

"For?" he asked, chewing.

She paused for a moment, and then met his eyes. "They treated me the same way, you know."

"Oh," he acknowledged the intent of her words. "Well, them being cunts isn't your fault, don't apologize for shit you're not responsible for."

"Still," even if she had no part in it, she was still sorry—for him. "They're being real shitty assholes, even by their standards," she said.

"All right?" He took a pull of ale, not knowing what she was still doing there with him.

"I got the proprietor to send one of his staff out as soon as possible." There it was.

The spoonful of stew in his mouth was forgotten as Drangar pondered the implication. Tuaghal hadn't kept word. *Some leader,* he wanted to say. Instead, stew dribbled down his chin.

Finnen snorted.

He wiped the back of his hand across his mouth, grinning like a fool. Then he remembered. "The gelding can't keep up with the pace. What shall I do?"

"Tell Tadc," Finnen answered. "He sort of likes you, better he tells Tuaghal than you."

"All right," he said, "I'll do that. So, what are they doing up there?"

"What does anyone do when they're gearing up for battle?" she smiled, but it didn't reach her eyes.

Drangar shifted his eyes to the corner of room, looked back at her and shrugged.

"They're eating," she said, "and drinking and fucking. Bloody Una and Tennal practically put on a show in the tavern hall."

Drangar looked down at his plate to contemplate her answer. "Seems more apt to prepare yourself, mentally."

Finnen face fell serious. "This *is* preparing them mentally."

His brows pulled together trying to make sense of her words.

She smiled. "Drangar, when have you ever known a warrior to speak of roses and rainbows?" she started. "Our lives are a gamble *every* time we take the field. It doesn't matter how *prepared* we are or how *strong* or how many. Someone always falls. So, who's it gonna be this time?

"We, marauders, we harden within months among our bretheren. In years, we're practically shelled in steel. Can you dent steel with your hands, Drangar?" Her eyes were cold, and yet the warm coal of emotion burned in the depth of her orbs.

Still, she had more to say, "On the eve of battle a thousand careless thoughts flood through a warrior's mind. And they're not about armor or swords or their numbers or positions or such... You think Una will be thinking of Tennal when she takes the field a few days from now? No. And do you know how I know? Because I've seen the way they look at each other, and there is no love there—not even a little—but there is *need*. A thousand images and voices from the past take over your mind on the eve of battle and you ask yourself *Have I lived? Am I ready to die?*

"So, in these coming days, we live—*fiercely*—it is our way. We eat, we fight, we laugh and we fuck—hard. We live for the day, Drangar, for our last may be near."

He nodded. He understood. "There's one thing I don't understand, though," he said. "Why the Scales are you down here with me instead of up there—*living*."

She shrugged and looked away from him. "I bought you food and ale because you're one of us—a warrior, a brethren—and while we've eaten, I know you hadn't."

He had no idea what he was doing or why he was doing it; but Drangar caught her arm when she stood up and reached for the plate of food he'd cannibalized.

"Please stay." He stared up at her. Immediately, her eyes shot to his as he chucked the plate to the floor beside him and gently pulled her closer.

Finnen was right. Drangar was alone in this world, outside of the Marauders. And if he was going to meet his death within days, he didn't want to spend this time alone and he sure as fuck didn't want to die a virgin.

It was strange. Never having slept with a woman hadn't bothered him before. His mind was always pressed with other things and this was something that could wait. Maybe when he fell in love, maybe she'd be his wife.

But one chat with Finnen had brought a new perspective

to his dismissive attitude towards this particular aspect of life. What had started with a tender kiss deepened into something more desperate—something that gasped for its next breath—Finnen's words had made it so.

That's why she'd said *fucking* not *making love*. This was not a slow process of mutual discovery or spiritual enjoyment, they weren't thinking of pleasuring each other. This was not a gentle act of desire. It was the rough and fierce will to *feel alive*.

At the same time, Drangar wasn't about to lie to himself. He did feel something for Finnen. Maybe he wasn't entirely in love, but given time, thought he could be. The point was… he cared. Which was why this was hard for him. While something buried within him urged Drangar to take her—fuck her—something else held him back. Finnen deserved better treatment. Hers was the kind of beauty that shone from within and draped over from without. Though a warrior, herself, she possessed the rare charm that made men want to write poetry or die protecting it. At least, that's what Drangar saw when he looked at her. She wore warrior marks, well.

It was all he could do not to come in his pants when she'd shed her clothes. She'd shed them fast, as though they were on fire and reached for his. She was practically begging him to fuck her.

Still, he tried to be gentle, to take things slow, but she had him under her and was clearly calling the shots. Desire raced through him and it set his blood on fire. Drangar felt a need to dent the steel shell, to shatter the bloody thing, to feel alive at his very core.

A strong naked woman sat over him, straddling him. He groaned when he felt himself slide into her. It didn't take long before he was too far gone, and so was she.

"Pace yourself," her breaths were labored and driven, "make this last a long while."

Drangar stared at her with wide eyes, taking in the bounce of her breasts, the curve of her waist. He pulled and kneaded her hips and ass, eliciting deeper moans and wilder thrusts. He was learning the language of the Finnen form.

"More," she breathed loudly, "and don't you dare come now."

It was less a threat and more a desperate plea—to be ravished beyond her ability to reason. She just needed to *feel*.

Drangar was about to break; he was losing his mind. Either he got her off him or this was about to end, *now*. His hands were on her hips, holding her in place, willing her to be still.

"Why?" she asked, breathing heavily. "Please," she said, "I need…"

"I know what you need," his level words brought her back to his eyes, "and you'll have it, Finnen." It was a promise that elicited a wanting gasp from the depth of her core.

Drangar switched their position quite suddenly, pinning her to the ground. "Feel me."

He turned her over and pulled her up onto her hands and knees in front of him. She arched her back against him, her naked ass rubbing him as he covered her body with his own.

Drangar traced her scars with his eyes but all he saw was her beautiful, strong body, and all he felt was her soft skin against his own. He could smell her heat—it filled his head with madness and wouldn't let him go.

Grabbing her hips, he pushed her knees apart and she moaned as he slid into her. It was too much. Her groaning, and moaning, her body slamming against his, grinding. He'd wanted—he'd tried to be gentle with her but instinct took over and he lost control. Along with it, he lost any tenderness or gentleness he'd wished to have with her.

Whatever confused feelings he'd had, they were all buried under an avalanche of lust. He gripped her hips and rammed into her hard and fast, she met his motion, pumping her body against his. No! He needed to control this, she had had her way, now he would have his! He held her down and fucked her hard—shoving himself deep into her again and again. Her moans were gaining in time and sound until the lusting cries piqued as he spilled himself into her.

"Scales!" As he continued to gush his seed. They collapsed on top of each other, spent and out of breath.

"Alive?" he asked.

She tried to smile as she stuttered, "Every inch of me is alive."

Finnen rolled onto her side to face him and they both erupted into laughter. In Drangar's life, a life that he had always viewed as one moment of misery followed by the next, this evening with Finnen was a drop of nectar.

A young woman entered and regarded them. Their clothes were scuffed and rumpled, and Drangar was sure his tunic was inside out, but he didn't care. They huddled by the fire and shared stories. To Drangar she said, "Your belt, put it with the others." She inspected the armory on the table. "Guess some of the bastards don't like you very much, eh?—I take care of this, get out—the two of you."

Tuaghal didn't care about the gelding, and late the next afternoon, the company paid the price for that neglect. A goodly ten miles from the next village—well within Chulaghanish territory—the gelding staggered, stumbled, and Drangar barely managed to jump off the saddle before the poor beast collapsed. One final, shuddering breath, a twitch of the legs, and the horse lay still.

"Fuck," Drangar swore.

Sitric growled, "Stupid runt," and rode past him.

"Ah Scales," said Tadc, halting beside him. "The lass told Tuaghal about it, but our esteemed leader said searching for a horse would slow us down."

"Shit," Finnen swore, holding behind them.

"Tuaghal!" Tadc shouted; the leader turned to look.

Eying the gelding, the bastard rode back, glaring. "Waiting for a resurrection, Librarian? Get your shit off the corpse. You can have the ass. Ditch what doesn't fit."

Tadc handed over the reins of the donkey, grimacing. The beast didn't look much better than the gelding. The older mercenary must have seen Drangar's doubt. "The little critter's been with us a year now, always looked so mangy."

Drangar bobbed his head in acknowledgement and began to remove several of the bags lining the ass's back. No sooner had he started, than he heard the loud critical remonstrance that made the hair on his forearms stand straight.

"Not our provisions, you dumb fuck, *your* stuff!" Tuaghal yelled, causing Drangar to stand at attention. Some of the others sniggered.

Was Tuaghal serious? Everything Drangar ever owned was stuffed into those few sacks. He had no home; he had no homeland. This was it, right here; this was all he had. Did Tughal really intend for him to throw away his only possessions?

"This is all I own," he protested. "We can always buy more food."

Drangar could see the line of spittle starting to drool down the left corner of his mouth. *Here it comes.* "This is my company, you pisswit!" Tuaghal spat, "my rules."

Now all but Finnen and Tadc laughed, applauding Tuaghal. *Shitty assholes! The lot of them.*

"Pisswit, that's a new one.

Priceless.

One that'll stay with him forever.

Love it."

Drangar balled his hands into fists; his nostrils flared; his brow clenched. The deep scowl on his lips were testimony to how well he shared their humor. He wanted to lash out; he wanted to bite Tuaghal's head off and feed it to the line of mercenaries always ready to lick his asshole.

Instead, tears of rage threatened to flood the rims of his eyes. Drangar could only do what he always did; he swallowed his anger at the unfairness of it all. His body dropped violently to his knees to rifle through his belongings. He would not open himself to more ridicule by swearing or cursing this injustice.

"Runt, put some of the foodstuffs on my horse," Tadc said.

"The food stays where it is!" Tuaghal snapped.

"Fuck you," Tadc retorted. "You picked up this job, but you aren't my master. You've been treating the runt like shit for months now. The food was paid for with all our money, so I will take my share and have my horse carry it."

Tuaghal's jaw tightened. Drangar eyed a thickening vein in his temple, and for a moment he feared the mercenary would attack Tadc—then him. Steel often repaid humiliation. To his surprise, though, it was Una who reined her horse back to take a pair of sacks off the donkey as well.

Finnen and the others followed, until only one sack was left dangling from the frame straddling the donkey's back. Reluctance was plain on Tuaghal's face, reluctance and *shame*? Still, the older mercenary guided his horse forward. He took the remaining sack, but reined the horse with such aggressive force when he turned about, causing the heavy satchel to slam into Drangar.

"Get your shit packed, pisswit," he growled.

By the time they reached Little Creek, Drangar felt less the outsider than before. Sure, there were many who still shunned him, but with Tadc, Finnen and Una he had some people to spend time with.

It was noon. The clouds were heavy in the sky, and if he were to guess, winter was closer than he had reckoned. It must have been late Chill, or early Cold—maybe. A few children lined the dirt road into the village, staring at them. Here and there, a woman or man poked their heads out of a window or a door to watch their arrival. It wasn't every day they saw a sight like Mireynh's Marauders ride through their streets.

The door to the largest timber frame, wattle and daub building flung wide open and out strode a stout, round-bellied man—a figure far better nourished than the children and people he'd seen. Next to the walking barrel panted a young man. His cheeks flushed red in the chill air. Drangar guessed father and son judging by the similar features. He was slimmer and stronger looking, but younger—much younger. Drangar reckoned he was near his own age.

The donkey looked back at him as if demanding to be free of its load. He obliged, receiving a quick bite on the arm as thanks.

"This is the one I spoke to, father," the younger man said, pointing at Tuaghal.

"So you'll help us with the brigands?" the older asked. "Thank the gods.—Forgive me my manners; I'm headman Amdah, reeve of the Lord Gebennach Duann. Welcome to Little Creek."

"Tuaghal; and we ain't here to trade pleasantries.—Why did

you send for mercenaries? Your son didn't tell me."

Headman Amdah's eyebrows flew to his hairline. "Arvel, you didn't tell them?" he reproached his son.

Arvel could've explained. He wanted to. "But father-," the young man's reply was cut by a crimson heat burning at the side of his face where his father's handprint lay pronounced.

"Foolish boy," the reeve scolded. Addressing Tuaghal, he said, "Apologies for the lack of transparency. Our lord's forces are occupied. All able bodied men went with him. Which is why we searched for you. Heard only good things about Mireynh's Marauders, though the name is a bit unsettling."

Tuaghal looked his son up and down. "Guess Arvel, here, ain't that able in the body, eh?" he said. Even Drangar had to chuckle when the reeve and son shifted in discomfort. "Brigands, eh? Harvest drawing out the rats, eh?"

"Father, will they be-," More crimson heat. Again Arvel was slapped into silence.

"When men talk, children *listen*."

Arvel gritted his teeth and looked to the ground, chastised. Drangar's eye caught the clenched jaw, the locked muscles—he knew all too well each raw emotion coursing through the man.

"The price remains?" Tuaghal asked.

"Aye, twenty suns, plus another ten if you kill the leader," reeve Amdah said.

The Marauders were ten. With Tuaghal taking at least three shares, that still left more than two suns. Enough for another horse. That was, *if* the bastard, Tuaghal, didn't cheat him out of his pay. The donkey bit him again. This time, he punched the beast's nose. *Two suns*, he thought. Soon, he'd be rich.

At nightfall, Tuaghal ordered them to the local tavern to eat and inform them of the situation and his plan. A warm meal, some bread, some watered down ale—Drangar felt better than he had since the gelding had croaked its last. Laden with a wooden plate of stew and bread, and a mug of bitter, he looked around the taproom, searching for a place to sit. To his happy surprise it was Tadc who signaled him, yelling "Over here, Ralchanh!"

Few warriors in the Marauders used last names, that honor

was reserved for warleaders and the warlord. Even fewer among them knew his last name. Of all people, he had not expected that Tadc would be one of them.

Ralchanh. Why would someone like him remember my name? Drangar wondered as he joined Tadc, Una and Finnen at their table. Finnen used her spoon to point at the empty spot on the bench beside Tadc.

"Keep your back to the wall, some fuckers don't like you," she said.

She didn't have to say more, he knew the ones she meant. A few days ago he had tried to juggle sitting on a log by their fire while keeping his food and drink balanced in his hands. It hadn't ended well. Yet, another thing he'd never do again. Now, with plate and mug set on the table, he slid onto the bench. The sheathed sword strapped to his waist thumped against the seat.

"You sharpened that pig sticker?" Una asked.

"Aye," he replied, patting the weapon he'd had with him since his escape from the Eye. "What's wrong with it?"

"Shitty steel," Tadc said, shoveling stew into his mouth.

Una nodded. "Miracle the bugger hasn't broken yet," she added.

Tadc snorted, Finnen chuckled, and Drangar tried to suppress his blush. But the blood crept to his cheeks anyway.

"No worries, runt, we'll find you a proper blade when we're at camp," Tadc said, slapping Drangar's back.

"Silence, fuckers!" Tuaghal's shout drowned out all noise.

The room fell quiet.

The bastard had a smug look on his face; but as his gaze passed over Drangar, it darkened into something sinister. "Two gold suns each, the village promised us as reward to fight off a gang of robbers," he said.

Drangar squinted his eyes. That wasn't what he had overheard. The total was thirty gold, they were ten, Tuaghal was entitled to more; three shares were standard, which left twenty-one gold for nine people to split.

Tadc leaned closer and whispered, "I've seen that look in your eyes before, Ralchanh, don't argue the point. He's pissed off at you as it is."

That's the second time he's called me that. Why the Scales does he remember my last name? The answer was of little consequence. What mattered was that Tadc was on his side. Drangar heeded the man's advice.

"The reeve has no idea how many bastards will attack," Tuaghal continued, "says the number varies. Could be five, could be thirty. We'll have our runners watch the three paths into the village, the rest will wait and rush to form a shield wall to take on the buggers."

"A wall of ten," Una muttered. "Could work, if the bastards are just rabble. We're fucked if they aren't."

"What about if they come from all three directions?" Drangar blurted out.

"Pisswit," Tuaghal growled. "Of course."

"The runt's got a point," Tadc said. "And *you* damn well know it. This place has more holes than Haldain's king by the time the rebels were through with him." A chuckle rippled through the mercenaries.

The veteran went on. "It's got no wall, a few fences, nothing that'll stop a hare, much less brigands. We can't control spit in this place, especially when we don't know whether they have a spy here."

Tuaghal shook his head. "The villagers will help us with them fortifications," he said. "They'll close gaps between houses, rig up some surprises and all that, so the robbers only have the roads."

"Still leaves us with *three* roads through which they can enter," Rathyen said, breaking her usual silence. "We need to control their entrance."

"Block all ways but one?" Tuaghal asked.

It was plainly obvious to Drangar as if the older mercenary had never considered that option. "Some leader," he muttered.

Finnen must have heard him for she chuckled.

"Aye," Sitric said. "Rathyen's right, we need to control the field." Looking over at Tughal, he added, "All this time you had me thinking you'd been Mireynh's messenger-boy. Thought you learned something running for the old man. Where's your mind at, Tughal?"

A lot of the mercenaries questioned where his mind was; but Tuaghal literally jumped for Sitric, grabbed the man's tunic and pulled him off his chair. "Don't you fucking mock me!" he said.

Sitric must have seen it coming because he suddenly had a dagger pressed against Tuaghal's waist. "Picking on the pisswit is one thing," he said, "he hasn't the balls to stand up to you. But choosing to attack someone who's been fighting at your side for years is beyond stupid. Let go, or my collar will be the last thing your hands ever clasp."

The words were ice water to Tuaghal's fiery rage. He came to his senses and released the other.

"Now behave," Sitric said, smiling as he sat back down.

"Wagons," Finnen broke the deathly silence.

"Pisswit's lover is right," Sitric said.

Another insult. Drangar felt as if he was back in the Eye where it mattered not that he had been the most diligent of students. Here he was the youngest, the butt of every joke—always the runt!

He took hold of the tankard and drank. Now they were attacking Finnen as well. *Scales!* he thought. Seething, he emptied the tankard, called for another, shoveled food into his mouth and drank again. Part of him still listened to the plan the mercenaries were forming, a bigger part imagined tearing Sitric and Tuaghal limb from limb.

Sleep came and went as Drangar tossed and turned. Images flooded his mind; images of his clawed hands ripping apart Tuaghal, ripping out the man's guts one inch at a time. He woke staring at his hands in the moonlight, expecting to see blood, so vivid were the dreams that he almost smelled the shit dripping from the entrails.

Over and over—each time a few calming breaths, and he lay back down, only to sit up again as another form of the same blood-soaked nightmare shot through his mind.

The sun was rising as he woke for the fourth time.

"Runt, you all right?" Tadc asked. "You were panting and muttering. Sexy dream?" The older man smirked at him as they washed in the village pond.

"Something like that," he replied.

"Heard the plan?"

"We block all but one path, wait for the brigands, and kill 'em, right?"

"Aye, guess Tuaghal's and Sitric's pissing contest wasn't that important," the other said, chuckling.

"Morning, you bastards," Finnen greeted them, undressing. She jumped into the pond and dammit if she wasn't the very vision of vitality. Drangar stared, growing hard.

"Perfect," he said, realizing too late he had actually spoken the word. And, of course, he wasn't the only one around to hear it.

Tadc laughed as Drangar turned away from the man. Another scarlet tide shoved its way to his face. Good morning, indeed.

"What's so funny?" Finnen asked. He caught her eyes as she looked at his crotch. "Oh," she smiled.

"Aye, methinks he likes you," Tadc chuckled.

Embarrassed, Drangar walked off.

They drafted the villagers to help with blocking two of the roads and every other gap or opening that allowed access to Little Creek. Wagons, wheelbarrows, barrels—even brute logs of uncut wood were piled up to fortify the barricades. The task was complete just a little past noon.

"Pisswit," Tuaghal smirked. By now, the smug son-of-a-bitch was the only one left amused by the insult. Drangar's half-remembered dream from the night before flashed before his eyes. "You're on the roof next to the northerly road. Take your bow, and warn us if they approach from there."

"I'm no bowman," Drangar said. "Can barely hit a barn from ten paces, you know that."

"Good time to learn then, Pisswit Bowman," Tuaghal sneered.

"Fuck you, Tuaghal," Tadc snapped. "The runt said he can't shoot for shit, and you still want him there? You want to get him killed?" he was tired of Tughal's antics. "Aw fuck it! Fight him now, one on one, to the death."

"You're playing wet-nurse to the pisswit, Tadc?" Tuaghal growled.

"You've been acting like a cunt for a week now, Tuaghal, how about you put your money—"

Drangar interrupted Tadc by placing a hand on the man's shoulder. "I appreciate this," he said, loud enough for everyone to hear, "but it's got to be me."

"Oh Librarian Pisswit has got some balls after all," Tuaghal wouldn't stop pushing.

Drangar took a calming breath. *I mustn't lose my nerve,* he repeated in the silence of his mind. The man was twice his age, and had been a mercenary for longer than Drangar had been alive. And who was he but a child compared to him? Sure, the Sons of Traksor had trained him since he could walk, but so far he had only seen two real battles. Did he really stand a chance against Tughal?

Mireynh's code gave him the right to challenge the older man. *Calm,* he reminded himself, he had to stay calm. They were on the edge of battle. It could come at any moment. This just wasn't the right time. Drangar opened his mouth to keep the peace—to dismiss the insult like the thousands before it.

"You've insulted me for the last time, Tuaghal. By the rules of Mireynh's Marauders I challenge you to the death. I shall wait until you have donned your armor, then I will kill you." Instead, that came out.

Tughal dropped his mask of pleasantries, making way for a countenance of hatred. He had never liked Drangar, that was no secret, and now he'd given the older man the chance to kill him. "I need no armor to beat you," Tuaghal said through thin, tight lips. He'd unsheathed his sword just as he'd unsheathed his true face. "I'll end you, now."

This was not the reaction Drangar had expected from the older mercenary. Neither had he thought the man this fast. He was still drawing his sword from the scabbard when Tuaghal charged. Only a lunge to the right, his opponent's left, saved him from being impaled.

Now his blade was free, just in time to stop a downward chop. The blows rained and Drangar gave as hard as his opponent did. Each of them blocked the other's attacks. For a moment Drangar wished for a shield, it would have taken pressure off his sword. The blade was too short for a two-handed grip to be useful, and the hilt barely supported his left hand either.

Anya, his weapons teacher, had once attacked him like this. *"Remember, always keep one eye on your opponent's feet, they will tell you what he plans, and give you the chance to take him down."* The words had barely left her mouth when she had already tripped him, sending him to the ground.

For months, he had bugged her to teach him how, now those painful training lessons ended the duel. Tuaghal went to the ground, and Drangar's blade cut the older man's throat.

"Guess we need to divide the money by nine now," Tadc said.

The others looked at Drangar as if he was Lesganagh's Servant incarnate, and for a moment he felt shame at all their attention. He had only done what was just. All quarrels must be resolved. The duel had done just that.

"Well, runt, all his stuff is yours now," Tadc said. "That includes the chain armor. I suggest you put it on."

They came later that afternoon. From the west. With the setting sun in their backs, they had the blinding rays on their side, and despite the mercenaries' wall holding, the brigands had training themselves and began to rain arrows on them. Tadc had tasked Drangar with taking down anyone scaling their makeshift barricades.

Once or twice he slipped on the blood of the enemy, still unused to the weight of the chain mail and the heavier boots Tuaghal had bequeathed him. Then, from the center of the village, an angry roar sounded, steel clashed on steel and wood. Now was the time to join his fellow warriors.

He rushed back to the village round. The enemy had his comrades surrounded! They stood in a circle, shields outward, back to back, seven warriors against twenty. He saw Tadc take a blow to the helmeted head. For a moment the old mercenary swayed, tried to remain upright. Then he went down.

The rage returned—the furor he felt whenever a brother went down. Kerral had once taken him out of the wall, reprimanding him. He was too uncontrolled for the wall, too undisciplined. Tadc had mocked him, but he'd been kind. Now all control was gone, leaving behind a growing frenzy of wrath and blood.

Another mercenary went down; another brethren fallen.

Drangar went in, howling, barreling into the mob of brigands. If they realized he was among them the moment his blade cleft into the first one's skull, he couldn't tell. It mattered not. His sword stuck, he tore his victim's axe from twitching hands, and chopped into the next in line. The woman fell, almost yanking free his newly acquired weapon. A third and a fourth, one with a spitted, the other with a bashed in face. They all went down.

When the mercenaries saw him rage amongst the enemy, they pushed harder. Blood gushed from a hacked neck, drenching his face. The axe was lodged in the man's spine, so Drangar dove for his opponent's sword and slashed into someone's feet.

He slashed, stabbed, and hacked.

Then it was over.

Tadc lived, the blow had only stunned. Now the older warrior stood, covered in blood soaked mud. Finnen was alive as well and she smiled and laughed as she flung herself at him. They kissed—a taste of blood, sweat and spice. Six mercenaries had survived; it was a much better number to split the thirty gold suns with, but at what cost? With the help of the villagers they carried out the dead and prepared a pyre. Kindling and straw took spark to flame and soon three and thirty, mercenaries and brigands, burned to ash.

Elated, four suns were a big enough fortune, and with Tuaghal's gear and horse, now his, Drangar decided to pay for the night's carousing. He had no idea just how much drink a single gold sun could buy.

"...*will you stop with the drink already? We both know your mood when you're drunk.*" Kerral's words belonged to the past.

He woke; someone was mistreating drums inside his head. Next to him lay Finnen, naked just like him. Had they fucked? Was it good? He smiled, though he remembered nothing. His stomach wasn't as forgetful. Swaying, he got to his feet, stumbled out of the room, tried to get his bearings. Where the Scales was he? A barn? How fitting. The air still carried the stench of burnt flesh.

His queasy stomach rebelled, and he barely made it out, stumbling headfirst into the nearby thornleaf. He didn't care. All that mattered was getting it all out.

He upheaved and spewed, whatever had been in his belly now forced its way back up.

"Ignore him, first the others," the bush said.

"If you say so," the bush answered.

Drangar threw up again.

"Money saved is money earned," the bush muttered.

Drangar vomited a third time.

Water, he needed water, the taste in his mouth was beyond vile. Crawling to the trough he saw someone else had taken a midnight stroll to quench their thirst. "Whatta night," he said, chuckling. "Not that I remember nothing." He remembered Finnen, gloriously naked when he woke up.

His hands cupped water, and the cold liquid trickled into Drangar's mouth. He gargled and spat it out, repeated the process a few times to make sure not a drop of bile or booze or food remained. The smell of burnt corpses didn't make things easy on both him and his stomach. Part of him felt hunger for pork, the other was disgusted that the smell of human flesh actually roused his appetite.

A cool drink of water was surely bound to sate his craving. Only now did he notice that the one he was sharing the trough with hadn't moved at all. *Silly fucker*, he thought, imagining what the bloke would feel like in the morning. "One sore muscle, his whole entire body," he chuckled. It was a funny image, but these folks were his friends, his siblings—brethren. Taking pity on him, he decided to wake him up.

A poke did nothing, so he shoved. The body slid off the trough and fell back-first onto the ground. Nothing. Just silence and immobility. "What the fuck?" Drangar muttered and stumbled over to the other side to wake the man.

Shaking the other's shoulders, he heard a slurping sound.

Moonlight won over the low hanging clouds, and he looked into Tadc's face. The older man's eyes were wide, the gash in his throat even wider.

Drangar stumbled to his feet, leapt back, and fell on his ass. Still, he scuttled backwards, his eyes never leaving the corpse. Someone had killed Tadc! He had to tell Finnen! He had to alert the others!

Rushing back into the barn, he slipped as he reached where they had made their bed. Fumbling in the dark, he reached out to find her body slippery, pawing at her, his hands gliding up her belly over her breasts, to the gash in her throat.

He heard a howl; a wail unlike anything made by man or beast, and realized it was him making those sounds. The world turned black.

When he came to, he was lying in a ditch. The donkey—his donkey—was nibbling at his face. He was cold. Had all this been a dream? Tadc and Finnen couldn't have been dead; he had just had too much to drink, that was all. Struggling to his feet, he noticed he was still naked. There were horses grazing in the field. They looked at him, once, and quickly decided their food was more interesting.

"How the fuck did I get here?" he asked.

The donkey's heehaw was the only answer he got.

Looking around, he saw the village in the east. "Must've walked out," he muttered and began his trek back.

When he reached the first house, he noticed the smell of burnt flesh again. "Have fun in the Halls of the Gods," he muttered to the smoking pyre, then turned towards the entrance to the village.

He took a step back, bumping into the donkey, stunned at a display of nightmares. The reeve's head was on a spear, the weapon's spike poking out of the bald pate. On the other side of the path opposite the reeve's head stood the man's body held up by more spears.

"What the fuck?" Drangar breathed.

A little further down a child of maybe five years lay bisected, the girl's entrails looking like a grisly tether between legs and torso. There were others. Impaled, beheaded, dozens. One woman still clutched her infant child against her, both nailed to the wall by a sword. He saw Una, a look of terror chiseled into her face. Her throat was a mess.

"How?" Drangar stuttered. "What?" he mumbled. He caught his reflection in a window and saw an image straight from his nightmares. This was no dream but him, caked in dried blood and mud. He looked at his hands, red. His arms were the same.

His mind reeled. He couldn't have! How could he have? The image of destruction showed quite clearly he had, but how? No, he refused to believe it. Didn't want it to be true. But, deep down, he knew what had killed them, he *knew*. The deaths of Tadc and Finnen were no nightmare, either, but *why*. Why would he kill *any* of them?

He found the trough and Tadc with the gaping cut in his throat. Inside the barn was Finnen, her throat a gash like Tadc's. *It wasn't me*, he told himself, *it wasn't me!*

"What am I?" Drangar asked. "A mindless beast? A vicious killer? Why?" He looked up at Lesganagh's glowing orb, hidden behind slivers of cloud. "They say you blessed me. Please tell me, o Lord of Sun and War, how could I do this? Is this what I am? A killer? Is this all that I am? I beg you, please tell me. Am I just a killer?"

He expected no answer. The cloud darkened the sun, leaving him in shadow. If Lesganagh said nothing, he knew where he might find answers.

Drangar left the next morning. The village of Little Creek was now ablaze; its people and the mercenaries, his victims, burning alongside the houses and all that had made the place home to those who had died there. He wore his padded tunic, Tuaghal's chain mail, his cloak, and rode the mercenary's horse.

Thirty golden suns lay heavy in his money bag, they had done the job, had defeated the brigands. This was the money they all had earned. His share, four gold, he would keep; the rest would go to the families of the deceased. As for the valuables in the other bag—he would donate those to a temple of Eanaigh, maybe it would do some good there.

"I've come to prove myself worthy of your services," Drangar explained to the statue for the fifth time.

Finally, the thing moved its head and regarded him. "Why?"

At last the dwarf responded. "I need to know if I am worthy... if I'm worth anything at all."

"The Place of Contemplation is to prove whether you want our craft for yourself, if you will honor it, and if you are worthy. This is the contract between dwarves and gods. If mortals want our work, they must prove their worth. Leave your belongings here, only your clothing is permitted. Then enter." The dwarf pointed at the hole in the far side of the wall.

"And then?" Drangar asked.

"You shall contemplate," the dwarf answered, turning away.

Asking anything else seemed pointless. This was the first time this dwarf had spoken more than the one question it had asked at the beginning of each day. "Why are you here?"

He slipped out of his cloak, dropped weapons belt and money bag, and left them lying where he stood. Then he walked through the hole, and entered a luminescent room. Its smooth walls reflected the glow that seemed to come from underneath the floor. Both floor and walls were of a greenish hue. Drangar had no knowledge of stones, would've called any kind of rock just that.

He was alone, in an empty room.

Writing appeared on the wall opposite the door.

"Who are you?"

"Drangar Ralchanh," he said.

"What do you want?"

"Listen, I already told that fellow outside..."

The writing changed. "Who are you?"

"Is this a joke?" he asked. "Fucking Scales."

"Who are you?"

"Drangar Ralchanh."

Time passed. There was food when he needed it, water too. And every day he stood before the asking wall, wondering if it would ask anything else. The more he spoke his name, the more wrong it felt. Ralchanh, the name of a mother he did not know, the name of a father he didn't know either. Who was he? How did he get here? Why was he here? What did he want to live for? Where would he go? Would he sell his honor to the highest bidder? Or would he stand for justice?

The questions were varied yet still the same. Sometimes he was left with his thoughts, staring at the wall, waiting for it to ask.

How long had he been there? His beard said a good long while, fingernails and toenails said the same.

He woke, stared at the wall.

"Who are you?"

"I'm Drangar Ralgon," he muttered. Where the name had come from he didn't know. It just felt right.

"What do you want?"

"To be a better man. To atone for Little Creek."

"You are worthy."

Cookies for the Gentleman

By C. T. Phipps

I live alone. I had a wife, once, her name was Rebecca. You wouldn't remember her, even though she lived right next door to you. You see, she never lived next door to you. Not now. Not ever. One day, you woke up and the next-door neighbors you remember lived there and had always lived there. You don't remember talking with Rebecca, gossiping with her, or the fact she asked you to our wedding.

That's because the Gentleman took her. I see him every night, usually when I can't sleep. I walk out to the window of my apartment and stare out into the parking lot. There, he's always standing perfectly still. I would say he's looking at me but he doesn't have any eyes. At least, eyes I can see. No, instead there are only shadows where his face should be and too many arms where humans have too. He dresses well, in a suit I'm sure someone gave him, but I've never seen his feet.

Sometimes, when I go to sleep, I can hear the Gentleman crawling around my room. He's too tall for it, you see, standing half again as tall as a man and he must slouch over. That doesn't prevent him from moving through cracks and stepping through walls. He plays with my cat, Whiskers, who can see him like me and doesn't seem the least bit afraid.

I wish I wasn't. It's rude and I'm always worried he's going to take offense but it's hard not to be afraid. The Gentleman's shadow brushing up against you makes you unable to move, your hands shaking palms sweaty, and your mouth dry.

I used to be scared of nothing, happy to spit in the face of men twice my size and never losing a fight. That was before I lost half my weight and I ceased to ever sleep completely. He's waiting for me in my dreams too, you know. I won't tell you about what he does there, though it's nothing *un-gentlemanly*. It's just he might hear and decide to visit yours too.

The proper thing is to remember the Gentleman is lonely and the best thing to do is be polite. He doesn't speak, I don't think he has a mouth or a tongue or vocal chords as we know them. However, he *understands*. Don't scream at him, threaten him, or insult him. I made the mistake of doing that when he first showed up in my apartment. I didn't realize it was his and everything which resided in it belonged to him.

That's when he took my parents.

Now-now, I know you're going to say that my parents died when I was very young. They disappeared in a fire and I was moved from foster home to foster home. That's the thing, though, I met with them just a day's prior. They were speaking about my baby brother and how very proud of him they were. It turns out he was never born. The Gentleman left me a picture of him, though, and sometimes brings him to visit.

My brother has no eyes or tongue anymore, only shadows. I think he's happier where he is now.

Now, you can imagine my reaction to all of this. I panicked and pitched a fit, calling the police, the National Guard, the exorcist, and even professors of the occult. Funny thing, no one could remember doing any of that within minutes of me doing it. My wife believed, though, perhaps because the Gentleman let her remember my parents. We decided we'd rabbit for the state lines and go as far West as we could go.

Too bad the Gentleman decided we weren't allowed to leave. I won't tell you what he did to us but there are other places. Merciful God, if merciful he is, has wiped my mind of the majority of the sights I saw but in the corner of my eye I still see the terrible place of all-corners that's all around us. The place where the things which mustn't be and never were stay and I WILL NOT TALK ABOUT IT ANYMORE.

Ahem.

The thing is that the Gentleman only wanted to be loved and I was foolish not to realize that. My wife, on the other hand, comprehended it first. She was foolish about it, though, cutting open poor Whiskers and tossing her parts about around the room. I think she must have read it in a book that people like the Gentleman appreciated animal sacrifice.

They don't.

I still see my wife every day in the bathroom mirror. I don't know if she's actually behind the reflection like Alice or whether whatever was done to her burned an image inside it. She doesn't move, though, only occasionally opens her mouth as if she's trying to say something but can't make it out. Sometimes, I think about asking the Gentleman for her back. I don't think that's a good idea, not since he so dearly loves Whiskers. He was nice enough to return Whiskers to life.

The worst punishment, though, was when I decided to escape the Gentleman the only way I knew how. I tossed myself off the top of our building and hoped to God that I would end up in Hell because surely that would be better than the apartment belonging to the Gentleman. I landed in my apartment, the Gentleman waiting for me.

There is a worse punishment than even the place I WILL NOT SPEAK ABOUT, at least for good Christian folk. A punishment I am even now living and would warn you about, if not for the fact that all will become clear in time.

In the end, knowing I could never escape the Gentleman and that I had been a terribly rude man, I remembered a story of my grandmother. She was from Appalachia, you see, where stories were passed down from mother to daughter straight from Scotland where people came from looking for a new life. All that's forgotten now, replaced with strip malls and gas stations, but she remembered the stories. The stories she'd shared with me.

Oh, I don't know if the Gentleman was a sluagh or a wizard, but I *remembered* the tales. The frightening ones she used to share with me when she babysat, where princesses had their feet cut off for dancing in their glen and peasants' eyes were ripped out for seeing too much.

For a bit of sour milk and some treats, the supernatural would leave you alone for a time. They wouldn't rip your babies from their cribs and leave someone else in their place, they wouldn't skin your husband alive and wear them like a suit, nor would they take you away to the Unspeakable Place. So, I needed to bake cookies for the Gentleman.

Oh, you have no idea what fear and trepidation accompanied this perverse realization. No child hoped to bribe Santa Clause or placate the monster under the bed than I had the terrified realization this was the only way I could get the Gentleman to spare me further torment.

I was not afraid of death, indeed were suicide a possibility I would have welcomed it even then, but the thought of being forced to do my 'penance' was sanity tearing. I hoped, foolishly, that if I managed to placate my new master that he would not make me go through the horrible thing he'd forced upon me.

I'm sure you must think me quite mad or a great liar. Indeed, by the look on your face, I suspect you are already thinking of calling the police or at the very least asking me to leave. A part of you, however small, thinks I'm either telling the truth or more likely deranged enough to believe I am. You possibly think I'm violent. I beg you, however, indulge me a few more minutes. I do not have any ill-intentions to you or your household.

I swear by him. Now where was I? Oh yes, cookies.

The belief that cookies, sugary crumbly pieces of baked flour, could set me free from the hands of a being able to dance between the spaces of God's own kingdom was a mad-mad thought but one I latched on with force beyond measure.

Unfortunately, acquiring them wasn't as easy as it sounds. I had never been a baker and knew precious little about the kitchen my apartment contained. My wife and I subsisted on take-out and sandwiches, ignoring the fineries of the culinary arts.

I also knew, perhaps instinctually perhaps because nothing could be so easy, store-bought cookies would only enrage the Gentleman. Given his earlier actions towards me were spurred on by only, I think, mild irritation, I did not have any desire to test the being's patience further. No, I would have to master the art of cookie making on my own and create such a spectacular confection as to delight the taste buds of a creature with no mouth.

The Gentleman was kind enough to let me out of the apartment for this journey, perhaps sensing I was to make him an offering he'd appreciate. For the past week, I'd been trapped in my apartment with the door to the outside leading to my bathroom and the windows opening up to an apartment identical to my own.

Several times, even, I caught a glimpse of myself entering said apartment only to look over at me as I looked over at him. I feel for my doppelganger and occasionally wonder what he did to incur the wrath of the Gentleman but we were discussing my inability to make a decent tasty treat.

Oh, the *desperation* at the grocery store counter when I realized my escapades had drained my finances dry. I had not been to work in almost a month and overdue bills had long since obliterated my meager savings. At the grocery store counter, I considered killing the woman behind and making away with my supplies before I remembered there was still a little money left on my credit card.

I didn't want to do her harm, of course, but hope is a more dangerous beast than despair. A man who despairs cannot be harmed and, truth be told, I wish I'd fallen to it completely. Unfortunately, I saw an escape and that makes monsters of all us. Whatever the case, I bought enough supplies to bake cookies for an army.

Ugh, you should have tasted the first of my creations. Vile disgusting things with too much sugar and burnt from top to bottom. I spent hours retrying the recipe, reading through the literally dozens of cookbooks I'd checked out of the library as if they were sacred scripture and trying them all. Several times I threw up, having not eaten in days only to fill my belly with sweet but nutrition-less confections.

I didn't sleep for almost two days until I came up with something I believed which would satisfy the Gentleman. It was hubris, of course, a madness shared by Perseus and other great heroes who thought they could walk amongst the gods without being struck down.

Oh the agony! The pain! The terrible *things* he did to me. It was minor compared to my penance but so much more *physical*. All the torments and fires of hell could not match the Gentleman's wrath he inflicted on me without saying a word. Even now I feel like crawling into a ball and crying, I who used to brag about my ability to take a punch without flinching.

Where was I? Oh yes, the Gentleman did not care for my cookies.

At all.

A more foolish individual might have concluded that it was the fact I was offering him cookies and not something more substantial that offended him. Since that time I have occasionally been allowed to walk the crossroads with the Gentleman and I have seen what other people have left for him: gold, shoes, wild flowers, infants, and the hearts of young women. The Gentleman seems to prefer the flowers, putting them on his lapel as one might a boutonnière but is indifferent to the others.

The cookies, though, I was sure were the key to his heart.

I drank myself silly that night, indulging two bottles of whiskey the Gentleman had allowed me to purchase that I threw up before they killed me. I could sense the Gentleman was growing bored with me and that terrified me more than the prospect of his wrath. You see, across the hall, there was a happy couple much like my wife and I had been. Arguably, they were more so because they had a young five-year-old daughter.

Now they don't. They never did, citing the expense and hardships of raising a child. I think the Gentleman must have taken a fancy to her and brought her with him to the nameless realm he calls home. Perhaps her young developing mind is not so caught up in the mundane aspects of things like physics, cause and effect, or people should have all of their parts when they speak. I like to think so, the other option is simply too terrible. In the old stories, the Gentry simply cooked and ate the children they took.

It would be a mercy compared to the alternative.

I poured over my recipes as a deranged alchemist, tasting the cinnamon and sugar each to see what might have been the problem. I tried combinations which ranged from the ghastly to the sublime, struggling to see where I went wrong. My landlord gave me an eviction notice during this time, only to be replaced the next day by a kindly old woman who said I could stay as long as I desired. I do not like her very much, she has no shadow and I can see things moving under her skin when she thinks I'm not looking.

Whatever the case, I was halfway to embracing whatever punishments the Gentleman could devise when inspiration struck me like it must have struck Edison when he created the light bulb: the milk! The Gentleman was a creature beyond the scope of time and space; he wouldn't want cookies made with artificial ingredients. No, he would want *raw* milk for his cookies and the drink to wash it down. Straight from the cow and fresh! I seem to recall having heard raw milk was much tastier, simply possessing a higher possibility of germs.

Finding a dairy willing to cater to my unusual request wasn't that difficult. Many of the local farmers resented the government's regulations against raw milk and were willing to sell it to me in bulk, especially once I revealed my willingness to pay exorbitant sums from pawning my wife's jewelry. Adjusting my recipes to the new, stronger taste, took some work but I could tell I was on the verge of something masterful.

By that point I hadn't eaten or drunk anything but my creations in days but determination kept me alive, determination or the will of the being who was now the arbiter of my fate. Whatever the case, I finished a batch of what I felt were the single greatest cookies ever made by man well after midnight and laid them out with a fresh glass of raw milk by my doorstep. From there, I climbed into my bed and collapsed.

I had hoped, rather foolishly in retrospect, the Gentleman would let me die. I never entertained any foolish notions of him returning my parents or my wife, such thoughts had long since left my head with the idea the Gentleman cared about such things as humans might. I'd compare him to a lion amongst gazelle but lions are closer to humans than the Gentleman. Better to compare him to a star or a gaseous cloud than anything which evolved on planet Earth.

Instead, I simply lay there, unable to sleep. I felt the

Gentleman creep into my room and pick up the plate from the ground. I could imagine his sickly, spider-leg-like fingers lifting each of the cookies up and making them disappear into the shadows. I doubt, now, the actual composition of the things mattered to him. He could have eaten the molten metal of the Earth's core without grimacing. No, instead, it was the suffering and desperation of my struggle to please him that made the cookies good.

You see, he really is just lonely. Once he finished the plate, making it disappear along with the glass, I knew he would never be satisfied with simply one order. From this day forward, I would be expected to prepare my magnificent feast of wafers every night. They would all have to be as perfect as this batch, never the slightest mistake or error. I do not know if the Gentleman will allow me to age but I do know I am still expected to do my penance.

Yes, my penance.

I mentioned it earlier, that terrible thing that is worse than the place of all-corners. I tear up and scream inside every time I think of it. Yet, as bad as it is, I promise you I would return to it rather than do this. I have no choice, though, because if I didn't comply things would get worse. I don't know how they would get worse, I lack the imagination, but I know in my withered belly and sleepless mind they would.

The Gentleman is lonely you see and he has a delightfully karmic sense of justice for those who are rude to him. I was terribly rude to him and the only way to pay him back for my discourtesy would be to find him new friends. People who could show him the love and affection he so richly deserves.

I've chosen you. Now, now don't panic. Your friend panicked. What friend? Oh dear, this is going to be a long story.

Cookie?

THE MORAS CHAMPION
BY MICHAEL R. BAKER

Talmoc's pursuers awaited him atop Hawk Point. Outnumbered, there was nowhere left for him to run. Or so they would think.

Perhaps now, I will get what I crave. The lord of Nightenmarch had been killed so easily by Talmoc's hand. He wanted a true challenge.

Five of them stood silhouetted on the hill-top, and one was unmistakable. *Lazil. The Brazen Call.* Light glittered off the smoky edge of the champion's greatsword, dancing on the blood-laden sky.

Mistress, the blade that spilled the blood of a thousand foes.

It will be mine if I win tonight, Talmoc thought. It was a big if, of course, but what was life without a little risk? He quickened his pace, his feet slipping slightly on the dirt path winding upward, slick with rain.

He glanced over his competition. Besides Lazil, two of his brothers wore little armor. The ones in the back had bows. Nightenmarch Rangers. They hadn't seen him yet, instead focused on Ymer Forest off to the east. Its gnawed depths shivered, an ancient fog hanging low over its natural ally. Its shadow masked his own footsteps.

As Talmoc expected, Lazil was the first to spot him. *They move fast.* In moments, Talmoc was surrounded.

He ignored the flattery of lesser fools, focusing his attention solely on the only man who mattered. Lazil, the aged man of a thousand wars, wore a solemn expression, iron eyes of cold.

"Good evening gentlemen," Talmoc said.

Lazil met his courtesy with his eternal stone. "Talmoc. You shall go no further tonight."

"Not in this world." The lion-haired man next to his superior drew his weapon. "Tonight you die." His bronze, double-handed battle axe had streaks of old, dark blood down the edge of the blade.

"I didn't find you on the fields of Urnzur." Talmoc ignored the others completely. *Fucking gnats.*

"We were not there," said the warrior monk on Lazil's left. "Justice warrants our blades more." In his hands coiled a fearsome, two-handed battle staff. "That justice being your head, Talmoc."

"How noble of you. Yet when your kin called for war against the might of Beruno, you didn't join them." Talmoc nodded to Lazil. "Why is that, Lazil? You belong to the Western Realm, do you not?"

"You address him by his name!" one of the rangers snarled.

"Easy, sir," The Brazen calmed his sheep with a bronze smile. "King Jalid has forty thousand men to fight for him, Talmoc. The loss of five men won't hurt him."

"Quite. I know of your deeds well, Lazil, but I'm afraid I don't know the names of your companions," Talmoc said. None of them offered a name.

"Quit your stalling, Talmoc. You know why we're here."

The second ranger drew his bow. "You stand guilty of murdering Lord Haldon of Nightemarch."

Lazil stayed them with a calm hand. "We discovered your foul crime, and so we have you." A gleam of life entered his eyes, two chips of ice; an iron wreath of judgment. "You must pay for your crimes."

Talmoc laughed aloud. The wind would carry the song of this coming battle for miles around. *Let it. Let the gods hear my victory.* "If I wanted to cover my tracks, even your blessed rangers wouldn't be able to find me, I promise you. I *wanted* you to find me, Brazen."

"Say what you mean, Talmoc."

"I gain nothing from defeating the weak." As soon as the words left his mouth, Talmoc pondered his meaning. He had never said anything truer. In a swift movement, he drew his trophy blade, Nightmare. Its obsidian edges glowed a malevolent smoke. The monk shied away from its sight.

"A monstrosity!"

"How did he get that?" The rangers muttered, no longer as cocky as they were. Lazil did not back away; he was no coward. He took a step forward, Mistress in his embrace.

"You carry such arrogance in your words, Talmoc." Lazil raised Mistress with both hands. "You struck down Lord Haldon and slipped away into the night like a snake. It matters not whether you planned this meeting. The ending will be the same. Surrender now, or you will most certainly die."

He gives me a choice. "Humor me. What happens if I surrender?"

"You'll be dragged back to Nightenmarch, where you'll receive the Son's Justice."

Talmoc laughed in his face. "You're going to have to kill me. If you can."

Whatever trace of warmth in Lazil's face curdled into an iron fury. "Then you'll die here, your corpse feeding the crows. You chose this fate, Talmoc."

Talmoc swept Nightmare around him in a semicircle, his eyes darting between his opponents. The rangers had recovered from their moment of weakness, their hands reaching for arrows from quivers. "My knees will never bend."

Lazil's gaze wavered, a drop of sympathy. "Then this ends." His voice echoed a tinge sadness.

Talmoc slashed at the air with Nightmare, uttering the words of a dead god. *"Kilzarchit."* The tongue of old Valia was still potent. A burst of dark, smoldering energy came with a flash of light, and the two rangers crumbled. Their bows clattered to the ground as they clutched their faces, screaming.

"Obe! Saneor!" The foolish lion screamed, taking his eye off Talmoc for a split second. *I know your names now.* Talmoc charged as the rangers collapsed, their faces blistering and peeling from the dark spell.

"Fool!" Lazil roared, as he and the warrior monk charged in for the kill. Talmoc weaved through them, intent on killing the axeman. Nightmare parried the first lazy cut by the monk and deflected Mistress as Talmoc struck, piercing the lion. Black, oily liquid welled from the wound, spattering the fog-like blade. It cackled in the night, crackling.

The monk's eyes were wide with fear, dropping his staff. He was next. The next slash by Nightmare, and his head was taken off his shoulders in a rain of blood and gore. The screams of the two rangers rang in Talmoc's ears, sweeter than any music he'd heard in inns. The sound of blood and his enemy's pain were his songs. Only Lazil remained, who moved out of his deadly range, Mistress tightly wielded in both hands. *How does that feel, Brazen? To be covered in the blood of your companions.* The two warriors locked eyes. Lazil stared right back, his gaze burning into his own.

"So it comes down to this," Lazil declared. The two circled each other, scoping one another for an opening. The Legend's movements were quick and fluid, not once giving a weakness to strike. However Talmoc could see the doubt in his eyes, the tension of a soldier hardened by years of bloodsport. *He fears me.* Elation filled him.

Lazil struck first, trying to feint out Talmoc with an uppercut to the legs, but Nightmare parried and Talmoc survived, weaving behind him to attack next. He was tiring now, and holding up the great black sword was harder than it was before. The aftershock of the dark spell rampaged through his body. *Nightmare cannot be used again.* Its foul workings required a sacrifice of life-force, beyond his current talent. Talmoc knew that.

Lazil's speed and reflexes were incredible, and Talmoc smiled despite himself as the two men exchanged blows. Nightmare and Mistress clashed, the lady's dance against the demon sword, neither getting an advantage. The two men came apart once more, panting for breath. Lazil's heavily-lined face was shining with sweat, pain of forty years on his back. They circled each other again, both under the glinting moonlight. *Oh dance with me this night, my good man.* How did that song go again?

"You joke easily for a dead man," Lazil panted. His steel eyes had a slight twinkle to them, hiding under the duty. He thrust forward, bringing Nightmare to battling height to stop Lazil's desperate attack. The two blades came apart, their union broken again. Nightmare hissed in response. *It's time to end it. He knows it too.*

"You cast foul magic, Talmoc. You'll die soon enough." The Brazen grunted, stern in his reproach. Talmoc flashed him his sweetest smile.

"No rules in war. That's why I live, and your companions are dead at my feet. Now, for your Mistress. It's time I take her."

"Then you shall have it, serpent." The two came forwards once more, and this time, Talmoc knew there was no turning back. Again and again the two swords crossed, so quickly it became a blur, as lady pushed for a breakthrough. One slash grazed Talmoc's shoulder, but it brought the great champion's swing out of balance, and Nightmare found its mark, biting deeply through chainmail and plate, deep into Lazil's guts. He dropped to his knees, his eyes rolling back in his head gasping for breath. Blood trickled from the corners of his mouth. Mistress fell from his fingers onto the ground.

Panting hard, Talmoc pulled Nightmare out of the wound he made in the Brazen's stomach. But, the energy was spent, the evil glow ebbed away and left it dormant. Talmoc gasped, feeling his own strength wane, and his own knees buckled; were it not for him supporting himself on his sword, he too would have fallen. *Its too much. The blade's magic is still draining me.* Tears streaming from his eyes, he crawled to Lazil, still alive, but defeated. His eyes were open, gray and glassy with shock.

"Damn you, sorcerer!" His last hiss rattled deep into the night.

Talmoc staggered over his fallen prey. The two rangers now lay still, their faces unrecognizable, a black, ripe mess. Talmoc grabbed Lazil's chin, forced him to meet his eyes. The steel still lived, but fading fast. The great man's eyes dilated, then went still.

"We'll meet again in the paths of the Mora I'm sure, Brazen. Farewell."

The great champion, defeated by a smelter's son. Talmoc bellowed his triumph for the heavens to witness. Only silence greeted his victory. Mistress lay on the grass, dusty and chipped. When he picked it up, he saw a solid bend in the steel, where it had clashed with his Nightmare. *A fine prize. And yet...*Talmoc killed the Lord of Nightenmarch in a heartbeat. He too was rumored to be a great man, a warrior for the ages. Haldon died in less than an instant, blubbering for his life.

Talmoc took a deep breath. No, tonight was a victory, and a glorious one at that! He had taken on five great warriors, one the most prolific swordsman of the Western Realms, and defeated them all. His shoulder burned, a twinge. *Not wholly unscathed.* His satchel of herbs was in his cloak pocket, ready. But first, he had to loot the dead. It was against the wishes of the gods, but why deny him the right to his victory?

There was some gold, a couple of handsome crafted ivory daggers belonging to the two rangers. One had a particularly appealing bow made of hornwood. Talmoc took it all, including the quiver full of arrows. He was no master marksman, but there was always a time to learn. By that point his wound was stinging, so he took a rest and removed his shoulder plates to inspect it further.

Only a graze. He had to take care of it still, less corruption from the dark gods set in. The Flame always sought to take over its disciples. He had no knowledge of healing magic, so he had to rely on other skills. He took out some herbs from the satchel, ground them up with a stray rock and wrapped it in torn cloth to make a makeshift poultice to wrap around the minor wound. With that taken care of, it was time to address the fallen Brazen. Talmoc was tempted to strip the corpse completely. But he had fought bravely. No, let him go to the Octane's halls of glory in his likeness. He deserved to reach the Mora a whole man.

Talmoc turned his attention to the monk. *Nothing.* The warrior order of Altnor were fearless men indeed, sentenced to a lifetime of suffering. Then he paused. There was something in his robes, a scrap of parchment? *No.*

Curiosity getting the better of him, Talmoc dug it out and unfolded it. On it were hastily scrawled words.

Dearest Ibrim.

I don't know when this will reach you, but I hope they arrive soon. We need you. Things are growing, a shadow in the dark over in the Maldir Mountains. Two of our Order have gone missing, Brothers Sandar and Coulm went into the ruins, not to be seen again. We have been investigating the stalkings of a madman who has been delving in the mountains; we saw him enter our domain many days ago. It is imperative whatever foul power lies in that ruin is found and destroyed. We need to investigate immediately. I fear it is Jatar. Please, come west to me. I will be waiting at the inn of Kaimist; the Ale of Drinkers. It is vital we do this, for the Order of Altnor.

May the light of Altnor pray on you.

Yours

Grandmaster Albrich, Champion of Altnor

Jatar. That word rung a bell. Some of the elders called it a demon. But there was no fear, only excitement. It was a spirit from what Talmoc knew, though he had little knowledge of the finer details. This Order of Altnor was another story.

Talmoc paused, frowning. Some invisible force was holding onto him, something powerful. It was more than just an interest, it was a hunger. A desire. He had to find out more. Then it hit him. He knew then what to do.

Standing above the fallen monk, Talmoc opened his left palm, his eyes closed. *Ibrim, that was his name. He didn't die nameless at least.* That was a man's worst fear. One who died without a reputation in this world was no man at all. He knew how to find out more knowledge. His memory sorcery could be just the thing. Remembering the struggle of learning the old, powerful art under the Syndicate, Talmoc smiled, and spoke a word.

"*Soulsternis.*" The old Valian words cracked from his tongue in shattered ice, forcing the corpse's mouth open. Tears split his lips spilling blood, then wider and wider, splitting his cheeks wide open. A light, silvery substance oozed out of the wounds of Ibrim, molding together into a bubble, wider and wider until they smothered his corpse.

"Let me find what I'm looking for," Talmoc muttered. Already he could feel the strain in his eyes. Flashes of speech and images fired in the bubble before him, indistinguishable at first. *Come on, come on.* It was getting harder and harder to hold onto the thoughts. Then he caught a glimpse of two men talking in grey, flowing robes which fell to their feet; something he could use? Then snatches of speech. Talmoc listened hard.

"The Order....we must ride with "

"Alberich of Brotherhood, he knows about the Jatar. Go to him at once, in Kaimist."

"No Unuch!. I must obey my Lazil's words first."

Then it was done, the bubble distorting out of shape and evaporating. Talmoc sat down hard on the sweet-smelling grass, the coppery smell of Ibrim's blood on his fingers. *Maybe that was undeserved. A sully, for one of your Order to have your bodies befouled by such trickery.* A tingle of remorse mingled with his curiosity now. But there it was again, that force, tugging at his adventure. Talmoc couldn't put a finger on it.

He knew one thing for certain. Whatever path lay ahead, Kaimist was the best place to begin.

"What you having?"

Talmoc's eyes itched. He fucking hated places like this. The fumes from the tavern's billowing fireplace was hot and smoky, making his eyes sting.

"Finest of your spiced wine. Whatever you have, I don't care." He hurled a handful of coins on the table. *Just don't bite the coins, dear woman.* Talmoc made a mental note to toast the great men who paid for his board.

She accepted the coins. Nobody questioned cheap money. "Everything seems to be in order."

What did you expect? It was as though everyone thought Talmoc to be some rampaging murderer with a magical sword.

Warm, friendly smells of woodsmoke and roasting meat was a welcome bereave from the rain. Many small tables made of polished oak were cramped in the room, many seating patrons nursing bronze-colored tankards, or gambling with dice and playing with those stupid black cards called Kis. What a dumb name. He'd never played it. Gambling with cards was for lesser men. He gambled with his very life every day.

"Boy! Bottle of the Harcour wine for this gentleman. NOW!" The innkeeper snapped to someone out of sight, the force in her voice made a couple of surly patrons wince. Talmoc only smiled. Hurried footsteps scrambled upstairs. "I swear, that boy's too slow sometimes. Needs to be beaten to learn his way," she muttered, shaking her head. "Anything else, sir?"

Sir? Talmoc kept his face neutral. "A room, if it's possible." He already had food at his table. A wooden platter bearing a feast of heavy rye bread, salted cheese, black pudding and smoked mutton. *Poor fare for a poor people.* He found the inn in the village of Stemar, six days ride from Kaimist. It was a shit-hole. Regardless, it was filling, which was all Talmoc wanted. He was a wanderer and a cutthroat, not a pampered prince.

The innkeep flushed pink. "Not sure if we have any more rooms, sir. There's been some trouble with the baron's men, and-"

"Would this help?" Talmoc threw another coin purse on the table, bulging with coppers. She took it with trembling fingers. "You may as well take it. I need a place to stay tonight and rest my bones. I'd take any room. Any."

The poor woman looked like she'd never seen money in her life. "Only the room below the boiler remains. And I can't charge this much for it. You'll sleep poorly."

"No need," Talmoc smiled. "But if it makes you feel better... how much is the boiler room?" It would surely be noisy and cramped, but better than outside. *And should any danger come, better these people die before I do.*

"Two Senns for the night, five for two, and an extra for each consecutive night you spend," she replied. The dull way she spoke it was a drone, a rehearsed one. *What kind of life would that be?* A scrawny lad appeared from around the corner, holding out a dusty bottle with a faded label. The words *Halmoc's Refuge* were barely readable in faint black ink.

"I'll only need one night, then I'll be on my way again." Talmoc gently took the coin purse back from the woman, feeling the smooth mouse skin. Opening the drawstring, he emptied and counted seven little copper coins, handing it to the innkeep. "There you go."

She bowed her head in acceptance and turned to address one of the other patrons, who was singing a loud, crude song about a rat. *An honest innkeep, that's new.* Talmoc knew many who would have taken the full purse and told him to piss off. They tended to become the dead ones.

Talmoc weaved his way through the tables and found his own seat again. Comfortable, he raised the bottle of spiced wine to his lips and tore a chunk of black bread with his hands. The taste of ginger and nutmeg flooded his mouth; a warming treat. Now he could feel the strain of the day's efforts in his body. His eyelids were drooping. He needed sleep, but first came idle listening. *You never know what you might hear.*

Someone had gone travelling into the Kilto ruins far to the east of Magenor and found ancient Mammoth bones, so large that he could ride his horse through the skeleton. He was laughed at by his peers. *Mammoths.* That must have been from the older times, when the Mammoth King still raged in the Magenor. He was asking for help to travel back to the ruins and bring the bones back to the city markets, but was shot down in a gale of laughter, and he stormed out of the inn in a rage. The Mammoth King was an old legend, even before the death of the Valian gods...

Talmoc slipped and nearly banged his head to a few muffled guffaws from onlookers. *Time for bed.* Taking the directions of the innkeeper, he headed down a flight of stairs and opened the first wooden door on his left, feeling the hardwood underneath his sandals. The panels creaked as he entered the cramped, dark space. The sound in the ceiling was loud and obnoxious, like pigs fucking.

Well, you get what you're paid for. The bedding was clean, and the mattress was reasonably comfortable. Taking off his clothes leaving him only in his thin undergarments, Talmoc covered himself with his thick traveling cloak; the sheepskin would keep him warm. He disarmed himself of his main weapons; Nightmare emitted a strange chanting from deep in its blade. Talmoc regarded it curiously. *What's up with you?* The whispering stopped.

He kept his trusted butcher's knife close though. *Just in case.* His eyes drooped....

He awoke with a start. He couldn't see a thing, his head on fire. Pain, blazing pain, laced every inch of his body. Then came a burst of blinding light, so potent his eyes burned to even look. He kept his eyes shut. Then he heard it, a great and mighty snarl in the air.

"Hear my call, mortal." He stood upright, bolt awake.

"You are weak. Right now, your enemies surround you. But you have potential. Such...delicious potential." There was a relish in that voice, so powerful, almost lustful. A heavy weight pressed over his eyes, forcing them shut.

"Who are you?" Talmoc shouted. *Such power.* He felt himself shaking. "Only a coward talks in thin air. Show yourself!"

"This little man has a fight in him!" The voice mocked. "I trust you haven't forgotten your ways. You left all your home and worldly past for war. I have much use for people like you, Talmoc. A champion."

A champion? "Who are you? Declare yourself!"

"Soon," crooned the disembodied voice. "I need people like you."

"I do not fear death," Talmoc declared, even as he stood there powerless, weaponless. The malevolent voice laughed again.

"You challenge, me mortal, without hope of survival. I like it. I have seen into your soul, Talmoc. I see your potential, your divinity, your *hatred*. If you want to find me, there is a caravan outside your world right now, making its way to Kaimist. They want to destroy me, but you cannot destroy an idea, can you? Find them, and come to me. Now wake up! Stumble in the mist no longer, and become a champion of the Mora."

Talmoc hit his head on the wooden beam, hanging low above him to the sound of the boiler's rumbling; a beast without its meal. *Fuck.* He was drenched with sweat, but he remembered the spirit's words. *A caravan.*

So be it. It could be just what he needed. Packing up his things, he walked out of the room and into the main bar. The innkeeper was behind the counter, her glossy black hair matted and forlorn. There were still patrons inside the inn. *Did I even sleep?* But he no longer felt tired. A power was sustaining him. Opening the wooden door out into the town square, he stepped out into the cobblestones. It was dark out, the sky painted inky blue.

Far into the heavens, he could see the constellation of Carbturbis. *The Sword of the Octane.* The village of Stemar was a small one, a trading post under the control of Lord Jaqtir. Talmoc knew the old bastard well, had even served him for a while. A few tired guards patrolled the streets but fortunately ignored him.

He found what he was looking for: a group of people on horseback talking to a guard.

"We need more men for the task ahead; we have reports of demon worshippers." The speaker was a particularly tall bald man, his head covered by a straw-colored hood. "Can you spare any men? You will be richly rewarded." He had a cold, blunt way of speaking. *Yenick. He's from Yenick.* Talmoc inched closer.

"None here." The guard tried shooing them away with a dismissive wave of his spear. "We've had attacks on the outpost by bandits. You'll find no help here, I'm afraid."

"This is important." The second speaker was a woman, fingers curled around the reins of her steed.

"I cannot help you," the guard repeated. "I am sorry."

Talmoc decided to intervene. "I'm available if you need assistance." Everybody turned to look at him.

There was a tight-lipped sneer in the sentry's face. "There's your help I see. Now be gone."

The bald man scrutinized Talmoc with suspicious eyes. "Can you fight?"

Talmoc gestured at his clothing. "I'm still alive if that's your concern."

"He looks strong enough," said the woman. "We are heading

towards the outpost of Kaimist, to purge a demon's crypt."

"Tira, we know nothing about this man!"

"He looks experienced enough, brother. And we'll need the steel," Tira shot back, not once turning her gaze from Talmoc. Finally, their leader spoke.

"He'll need a horse. Can you ride?"

"Well enough." Talmoc shrugged casually. The guard cut in then.

"Go to the stables outside the gate, Lancem can see to it. Tell them I sent you. Name's Pengnor. Now leave. It's past curfew." The guard stalked away, leaving Talmoc with the monks.

"You'll do then. Come, we have no time to waste, It is five days ride to Kaimist, Do you have a name?"

"Talmoc."

"Good." The bald man gestured casually to his brothers. "I am Brother Aram. These are Tira, our shield-maiden, and my fellow brothers, Unuch and Samuel. You do your duty, and you will be richly rewarded."

A shiver ran down Talmoc's spine, and he heard a whisper again, cold and brutal. *Oh you shall be, mortal. Lead them to me. My game has begun.* He struggled to keep his face calm and normal. "Very well then."

"Good. Then we ride."

"There. You see the ancient markings?"

Talmoc craned his neck to see where the monk was pointing. The five wanderers trotted their horses up the dirt path slowly into the hamlet of Kaimist, so not to wear out their steeds. The cliffs here were worn brown teeth, a light rain falling on their faces. If he squinted, he could make out the stone slab carved into the rock.

"Aye I see them. What is that tablet?"

"An old relic. Kimist is an ancient place, built during the age of Altnor." Aram shifted in his saddle. "Our ancestor was a great king, dedicated to pursuing the meditation of the Octane and defending its people from the curse of the world. That tablet bares our ten tenets, the eternal laws we follow until the day we join him in the Mora."

You're tied to your god, like all faiths.

"So tell me, wanderer. Where you come from? How did you come across us?" Brother Unuch sat brooding on his horse, his hard-little eyes boring into Talmoc with ill-repressed suspicion. The others had been wary of him, but shared their food and warmth with Talmoc amiably enough. Unuch was a huge, scathing brute, covered with coarse, stinking hair and didn't talk much. When he did, it was a scowl. Not once did he offer to share his provisions with Talmoc.

"If you were listening, Brother Unuch, you would have known all about him," Tira scolded. She nodded to the soldier guarding the set of wooden gates leading into the village, who granted them access. She had her long red hair tied back in a ponytail this morning, her freckled face dirty and unkempt.

Entering the village, Talmoc was unimpressed by what he saw. It was small and badly kept, with small stone buildings on either side of a single dirt street. Far above them was the foreboding rock face; the mountain of Chillbrak, Great words had been carved into the rock in a language which Talmoc didn't understand.

Samuel saw him looking. "It's ancient Valian, back when the old Dynasty held power across all of Uldur." They dismounted, Talmoc feeling the squelchy mud under his boots. Three young boys in white robes hurried to take the bridles, leading the horses away.

"So, where is he?" Unuch grunted. "I desire me some infidel bones."

"Patience," Brother Aram growled. "There he is." A heavy footed male dressed in a flowing black cloak walked towards them, leaning heavily on a walking stick. Only when he got closer did Talmoc notice the aura radiating from it. *A sorcerer then. Interesting.*

"You are late, soldiers." His heavy, jutted jaw stuck out under a disjointed, bulbous nose, cheeks covered with gruesome, deep scars. He too was bald.

"Father Alberich." Aram bowed.

Alberich's eyes turned to Talmoc. "And who is this one?" He grunted. "A volunteer?"

"I found Ibrim during my travels, sir. I'm sorry to say but he's dead. I...found your letter." Talmoc shoved the parchment in the elder brother's face. The leader's eyes narrowed, snatching it out of Talmoc's hand. *Why did I say that.* He heard a snigger, and wheeled round. Nobody was laughing. The monks were giving him cold, hostile looks.

"You had this information and didn't tell us? Why?" Tira's sword was in her hand, but Samuel held her back.

"He may have had his reasons, Tira."

Alberich held up a calloused hand for silence, still reading the letter. "How did he die? How did you get this?" Clearly, he was used to being obeyed without question. Talmoc tried not to smile.

"I was traveling from Nightenmarch, when I came across two bandits harassing him. I killed both bandits, but he died from his wounds. I checked his letter and traveled up north to Stemar. That's when I came across your comrades." The lie came easy.

"May our vigilant Altnor watch over his soul," Tira whispered, looking down at her feet. Alberich squinted curiously at his writing, then back at Talmoc. "Seems like you'll do. You have my thanks. Your name?"

"Talmoc."

"You wear two swords."

"I like having both hands free to kill."

One of Alberich's henchmen snickered, the head monk giving him a cold look.

"I see." Alberich hunched closer, those watery eyes scrutinizing and scraping. "We're here because we have a possessed man in the crypts. Well, you read my letter to my agent," He went on, waving a hand airily.

"I need more to go on then that."

Alberich shrugged. "Not much to tell. The place was abandoned, none of us go near it. That's when we heard of the madman. We need to go in. You shall go with Brothers Samuel and Unuch." He paused, pursing his chapped lips together. "Should you do your duty, you will be paid well. How does three hundred Senns sound?"

That was a handsome price. "Seems good to me. I need more information."

"You're hired muscle, not one of ours," Alberich snapped. "It's all you need to know." Talmoc glared right back at him. "Still, I appreciate you for coming here, when it isn't your fight. When you find out more, leave the house immediately and find me. Do not attempt to talk to the entity, whatever it may be." The other two bowed low and hurried off, leaving Talmoc in the company of Samuel and Unuch. Alberich stalked away.

"Let's go," barked Unuch.

The three walked along the street, Unuch breathing down Talmoc's neck. *Do they expect me to run after all this way? On* his back, he felt Nightmare shiver with anticipation. He had no idea what to expect when he entered that house. Again, that irresistible force was driving him on, and like a sheep following its shepherd, Talmoc followed. *It will all make sense I'm sure.*

They walked down the hill with stone dwellings flanking the dirty path, some with white-robed men and women kneeling on the ground at the doorways praying, some working in a large open space on the left, weaving.

Nearby, a couple turned over a dead calf over a spit. *Fuck, that smells good.*

They went under a creaky wooden bridge, and beneath that, carved into the rock was a tunnel, leading deep into the mountain.

"In there," Samuel whispered. Unuch took the torch off the guard at the entrance.

Inside, the corridors were pitch black stone, and dripping with mildew. They walked in silence for a while, Talmoc feeling the tunnel wind left and right, the flames licking the walls, tasting the dew.

"The house is close by," Unuch's voice wavered slightly in the echoing path. "Alberich thinks it's demon worship. Could it really be Jatar?"

"Who knows?" Samuel shrugged. "Let's just...let's just get going."

They don't speak of it, Talmoc thought. *They fear him.* They came to a halt at a heavy stone door carved in the right hand side. The tunnel continued onward for some time ahead, swallowed by darkness.

"They lead into our crypts. Some say the body of Altnor himself lays in there. We can't go in though, forbidden," Samuel scratched the back of his neck with a free hand. "Shall we go?" He hesitated.

"Craven. He'll die by my hand," Unuch snarled, panting for breath. The light flickered, showing his pustule-covered face, cheeks dripping in sweat. Unuch shoved his way into the room. Breathing deeply, Samuel followed him in.

Slowly, Talmoc got used to the darkness. The room was small, and barren, nothing inside but a few rotting pieces of wood. The floor was cold stone drenched with a glutinous red fluid. *Blood.* Then they saw the bones, littered everywhere. Two skulls, pale yellow. Pieces of rotting flesh hung from the eye sockets.

"Altnor preserve us!" They drew their swords. The door slammed shut, blocking their only means of escape.

"No!" Unuch snarled, running to it and pushing on the door. It wouldn't budge. Then somebody cackled from ahead. He wheeled round, wielding his blade. A discarded lamp rose suddenly into the air, hovering. With a beam of glowing light, it burst into flame, revealing a passageway.

"Show yourself, madman! You die today!" Samuel brandished his sword.

The voice. The same one as in Talmoc's dreams. *"Let us begin. Kill them. Crush them all!"*

Samuel uttered a low, feral moan, weak as a kitten, as Unuch spun round.

"We need to get out of here!"

Nightmare chanted in Talmoc's grip, vibrating hard and glowing a violent purple. It had never reacted like this before.

"Kill or die. Only the victor leaves this place alive. But what's this? My blade?" The voice chanted, the giggle shrill and childlike, echoing ever deeper around them. Unuch let out a howl of rage, feral. Talmoc readied himself for a fight, but it never came. Unuch charged at Samuel.

"It's you!"

Samuel didn't even raise his weapon to defend himself. In a single stroke, Unuch's sharp blade took off Samuel's sword arm, sending both it and the sword flying in a wave of blood. Samuel fell to his knees with a scream, not even as Unuch turned round, recognition dawning across his bloodlust. Talmoc stayed calm. Unuch's cold eyes hardened.

"No. *You're* the enemy!"

Too late for you. Talmoc charged. "That was your mistake." Nightmare slipped through the man's open grasp and pierced his chest in a fluid movement. Two more quick stabs, and both men lay dead on the ground, blood pooling at their feet. *So easy,* Talmoc mused. *Now how do I get out of here?* He was still locked in.

"I've come. I know you're here. I've answered your call!" Only silence met his declaration. "Show yourself!" Talmoc screamed into the dark, spit flying from his mouth.

Something on the floor scuttled. Unuch's corpse floated into the air. His eyes, blank in death, burst into life. The man's bowels loosened in death, the smell of shit rank in the dusty tomb. The corpse's mouth tore open and began to speak.

"Welcome Talmoc. It's a shame I cannot see you face to face but I cannot manifest physically in this realm. This mortal will do. It has been long since I've seen such talent. Disposing of such honorable men. *Delicious.*"

Talmoc stood his ground, aware of how dry his mouth was. Slowly, he lowered Nightmare. "The monks mentioned a madman."

"Oh yes, *him,*" The disembodied voice was bored. "I promised him power, but it seems I drove him mad with my visions. He died some time ago. He ripped out his own guts with his bare hands, poor thing. I made him think he was being possessed. Weakling." The puppet threw its head back and laughed. "No loss. But you are different. And you wield my weapon too. Nightmare." Uluc's head lolled from side to side. "It has been a long time."

The pommel grew white hot. Talmoc dropped it, cursing, only for it to hover upright in front of him, glowing red. "This is yours?"

"In a manner of speaking," said the bored voice. "The First Ones stole it from my vaults during the rebellion, right before they escaped. I've been watching you ever since you plucked it from its resting place."

"That was a long time ago." Talmoc stared at the body. "Who are you?" The necromantic monk began to giggle.

"Who am I? I am only a small prince amongst the Flame's realm. But you can call me Jatar. The Scourge, I am called to some of you little sky-dwellers. Little nobles, I think that's what you lot call yourselves in the land above. I..." The puppet convulsed, vomiting from its putrid mouth. The air stank with blood, so thick Talmoc nearly retched. "Heheh...you know the legends of creation of course?" It began to sing;

"And the Octane of old, and new, called into the power of the Balance, and so the great Shadows of the world were thrown back, their blades and corruption receding, as the world breathed life again."

Talmoc felt his strength leave him. *So it was all true.* "There are more of you?"

"Too many. Your realm should be ours, but we're forbidden to enter it thanks to the powers of the First Ones. My brothers and sisters bicker endlessly on how to proceed. The fools." Jatar's sneer was cold and harsh. "The Flame does not care though, and neither do I. We are all his children. We will be one eventually. Time is nothing to us."

"I've had enough of your games." He turned to leave, but the passageway was still blocked. "Let me out."

"You cannot bargain with me, Talmoc. Besides, I'm here to help you. This is what I desire. I want to see Alberich destroyed. I want to see his faith burn before his eyes, before he joins me, and swears off this Altnor forever. Can you do this?"

Talmoc felt his lips twist into a sneer, almost controlled. "Very well. Since you give me no choice, I accept. How do I proceed?"

"Lure him here. You will show him the true meaning of the word pain." A creak of open rock scraping against stone, and light filtered into the room again. Talmoc was free. "Go. Find him. You'll find a way, I'm sure. And Talmoc...do not betray me."

Talmoc fled the tunnel, heart hammering in his chest. The guard moved to join him, white.

"What happened?"

Talmoc grabbed his shirt. "They're all dead!" He shook him. "It's the Jatar...he's killed them all. I only barely escaped..." He made his voice waver, feel the tears in his eyes. "We need Alberich! Your *leader!*" The guard was young, his face green with fear.

"He'll be at the inn. Come, we need to hurry!" Talmoc panted, injecting the fear into his voice. He wasn't even faking it this time.

The guard quickened his pace to match his. Bursting through the door of the inn, they found Alberich sitting alone, nursing a cup of wine. Talmoc hurtled towards the elder brother.

"What happened? Where are the brothers?" Alberich's eyes widened, stone melting.

"It's Jatar, or whatever his name. The madman attacked, killed Unuch and Samuel. I only just managed to kill him, then I heard the chanting...the terrifying chanting..." Talmoc paused. The demonstration of the things power made him sick. He pushed his honor aside. *This is me or him.* "I managed to break free, run away, but it's still down there. It was issuing a challenge. I heard its voice. It mentioned you by name, Alberich." On his back, Nightmare stayed dormant.

"Very well. The demon wishes to challenge me, I will face him."

"But sir-" the guard began, but Alberich bullied over him, grabbing a war staff from the corner.

"You, you'll come with me," he ordered Talmoc, who nodded, eyes wide. "I shall purify that ruin in Altnor's name." He stalked out of the inn, and Talmoc followed. *That was easy.*

The chamber was exactly the same as it was when Talmoc had left it, although Unuch's corpse no longer floated. He lay still, drained and withered. *It's as though he's been dead for weeks.* The air was thick with dust, but heavy with something else, a foul presence. *He's here. Waiting.* Alberich drew his staff to killing height. "Draw your weapon," he said curtly.

As predicted, the slab closed in on them, bringing them into darkness. Talmoc drew Nightmare. Still it lay dormant. *Now, we shall see.* He took deep breaths, waiting. Then he heard Jatar.

"Ah yes, my adversary." A flicker, and the room burst into light, their own torches snuffed out at the same time. Alberich stepped forward, whipping his warstaff around his fingers.

"Jatar! You will leave this place.!" He took a step closer, then another.

Talmoc didn't see the spikes coming. He yelped and jumped aside as great bladed spikes came out of the floor with a grinding noise. Alberich responded only a second too late; his fingers grasped one of the spikes and came away bloody. Like an embalmed tomb, the spikes encircled Alberich, pinning him in place. He struggled to get to his feet, but the trap made it so he was forced to kneel.

"What is this? I won't be quelled by this, Jatar. I've defeated you before!"

"Oh yes. But now I have a new power by my side." Jatar cackled, and the bodies on the ground came back to life, rising into the air. Alberich's mouth opened in a sob as the two fallen monks flanked him on each side. Talmoc took a step closer to the cage. Alberich's eyes widened.

"You!" The cage began to twist, the bars curling around Alberich's arms to pin him in place. The path to him was open. "Fucking traitor!" His bare arms slowly turned red, the blood running down his body in rivulets.

"It's time for the breaking," Jatar's voice boomed. The corpse that was once Samuel limped slowly over to Talmoc, holding out a large, rusted club. Talmoc took it, the metal warm to the touch. It purred.

"No ... Samuel, what you doing? This is blasphemy!" Alberich moaned. He began to cry.

"He can't hear you, old man. Now Talmoc. Beat him." Jatar commanded. The fire returned to Alberich's eyes as Talmoc advanced, mace raised.

"You'll never defeat me! And you, when this is done, you will burn!"

With a smile on his lips, Talmoc held the mace high above his head. Samuel and Unuch's rotting eyes bulged, lips torn wide as they urged him on in Jatar's voice.

"I am your god now, Alberich."

The first blow collided into Alberich's left shoulder with a sickening crunch: it exploded in a gout of pus and blood. Alberich screamed in pain, letting loose a barrage of abuse. The chanting grew louder around Talmoc, echoing.

"Shatter his pulp!"

"Excellent!" Jatar shouted above the man's screams. "Again! Again. *Destroy him.*"

"I will ... never give in," Alberich sobbed. *The Elder Brother, reduced to a squalling infant.* Talmoc readied another blow.

Not his face. Not yet. Jatar's voice was silky in his ear. *Crush him. I know just the place.*

The second blow caught him between the legs. Alberich howled, blood flowing freely.

Just as well the Altnor Order are celibate, Talmoc thought with a chuckle.

Again and again the blows rained down, on his legs, his arms, his body. Bones snapped, hilt of white poking through his limbs, ribs tracked like snapped branches. Despite it all, Alberich was still alive. Finally, his face remained.

"End it. Burst him like an orange. A *blood orange.*" Jatar jeered. Talmoc brought back his arm for the final swing. Alberich started crying, his voice faint.

"No more ... no more. I give. I submit to you."

"You offer me yourself?" Jatar demanded. His puppets repeated it, their voices hoarse in the flickering light.

"Surrender. Surrender. Choose. Choose!"

"Yes. I am yours ... Master." Alberich murmured pitifully. *He's broken.*

"End him." Jatar sneered, dismissive. Talmoc readied for the final blow, staring into Alberich's dead eyes. There was nothing left.

"Excellent work, my champion," Jatar murmured as Albernich slumped to the ground, his once handsome face now an unrecognizable pulp. The two reanimated brothers fell to the ground discarded.

"You sound unimpressed," Talmoc said shortly. He inspected the cudgel, smeared with blood and bits of brain. He threw it to the ground.

"Not at all. People just bore me, and he was weak. But you did as bid. Your reward." Suddenly, the exit cleared again.

"You will have to fight to escape. The Order will fight to avenge their leader. They are coming."

It was only then Talmoc realized what was missing. *Nightmare.*

"Here." Jatar's voice was soft.

A sword appeared in front of Talmoc; one he knew well. Nightmare, in all its glory, but it was different, its blade shorter, thicker.

"Take it."

As Talmoc's fingers wrapped around the hilt, something heavy wrapped around his body. He was encased in obsidian black, heavy armour from head to toe, his gauntlets clamping into his skin. He gritted his teeth with the pain, great long talons bursting from his fingertips.

"Nightmare, restored to its own glory. Your power is mine. Go into the world. Kill in my name, and your boon will be infinite," Jatar crooned in his ear. Loud voices were coming from outside, panicked shouts.

You brought them. You planned this. Talmoc should have been angry. Instead, he smiled. Inside his new skin his body began to burn. *The price,* he knew it. No matter.

He had come this far, after all.

About Our Authors

Michael R. Baker studied history at the University of Sunderland, and it only took five years for him to find a use for his degree. Alongside his passion for storytelling and worldbuilding, Michael is a video game writer by trade and a cartographer in his spare time.

Allan Batchelder is the author of Immortal Treachery, a series of dark fantasy books that culminates in Book Five: *The End of All Things.*

C. H. Baum is a diabolical mortgage professional. By night, he dons his superhero outfit (made up of exactly one pair of worn underwear) and goes to bed early, ensuring that he gets a full eight hours of sleep. All this discipline keeps him refreshed and ready to wrestle with your loan application. He lives with his two boys and his stunningly beautiful wife in Las Vegas, Nevada. What happens in Vegas, usually happens without him. He loves to write, ride his bicycle, make furniture, and read. He does all that while avoiding pickles, eggplant, and hummus; because everyone knows those things are just gross. Other works by him include *Gods of Color* and many more to come.

Matthew P. Gilbert, in addition to being a fiction author, is a professional video game developer; a veteran; a columnist for his local newspaper; and the father of three wild boys and two wild girls. He was born and raised in Woodbury, GA, and has been on watch for zombies ever since. He is the author of the Sins of the Fathers Series, which you can find at https://www.aethonbooks.com/matthew-p-gilbert

You can follow him on Facebook (https://www.facebook.com/mattgilbertwriter), Twitter (@AmrathOfNihlos), and on his personal site, http://www.nihlos.com/

Matthew Johnson is a current student in the MFA Creative Writing program at University of Riverside Palm Desert. He has published stories in both fantasy and horror genre, *Lazarus Rising*, a zombie play, and is currently working on two novels and another play. He resides in Riverside California with his wife, director and actress Wendi Johnson, and his two loveable puppies. You can find more about his works at www.matthewjohnsonauthor.com

S. D. Howarth spends daytime as an I.T. Manager at a civil engineering consultancy where he is banned from using humour. At night, he deserts wife and children to edit scrivenings in the attic. His first fantasy novel *The Tryphon Odyssey* will soon be inflicted on an unsuspecting editor and *Halidom* has evolved into a steampunk side project. The Angry Cumbrian may be found on Facebook and Twitter.

Christopher Keene has quite the backstory. Growing up in the small town of Timaru, New Zealand, Christopher Keene broke the family trend of becoming an accountant by becoming a writer instead. While studying for his Bachelor of Arts in English Literature from the University of Canterbury, he took the school's creative writing course in the hopes of someday seeing his own book on the shelf in his favorite bookstores. He is now the published author of the *Dream State Saga*, as well as his new fantasy epic, *A Cycle of Blades*. In his spare time, he writes a blog to share his love of the fantasy and science fiction genres in novels, films, comics, games, and anime at www.fantasyandanime.wordpress.com

Paul Lavender has been lied to all his life. He thought he was born in Gateshead, England when really, he was born in Newcastle-upon-Tyne. This may seem like a small thing (the two places are about 200 yards apart) but it means Paul is a true Geordie. Of course none of this matters as he now lives in Worcester with Sam, his very supportive wife, and Ryan their son.

When he was younger, Paul was heavily influenced by the dark arts of comics, RPGs, fantasy novels, power metal and computer games. It really is amazing that he's turned out so well adjusted. You can find more about *The Orcslayers* at http:// pslavender.wixsite.com/the-orcslayers

Frank Martin is a comic writer and author that is not as crazy as his work makes him out to be. He writes and produces the biblical mythology comic series *Modern Testament*, which features a wide ensemble of artists throughout its four volumes. His most recent novel, *Mountain Sickness*, was published last year by Severed Press. Frank currently lives in New York with his wife and three kids. www.frankthewriter.com

Richard Nell mixes his love of history and ideas with fantasy because reality could use some sprucing up. He's the author of dark, epic fantasy Kings of Paradise and Kings of Ash, and a new gritty flintlock series starting with The God King's Legacy. He hopes you like them. Check out his website here: www.richardnell.com

Martin Owton is a UK-based writer and the author of two published books *Exile* and *Nandor* in the Nandor Tales series, the world in which this short story is set. He is a member of the Gravity's Angels (formerly the T-Party) writing group in London. He holds a PhD in Chemistry and in real life is a drug designer for a major pharma company. www.martinowton.com

C. T. Phipps is a lifelong student of horror, science fiction, and fantasy. An avid tabletop gamer, he discovered this passion led him to write and turned him into a lifelong geek. He is the author of the *Bright Falls Mysteries, Cthulhu Armageddon, Lucifer's Star*, The Supervillainy Saga, *Wraith Knight*, and others. He is a regular blogger on "The United Federation of Charles" http://unitedfederationofcharles.blogspot.com/

Michael Pogach is the author of the dystopian thriller Rafael Ward series: *The Spider in the Laurel* (a Kindle Book Award finalist) and *The Long Oblivion*. His work has been hailed as "refreshing" and "gritty and graphic." He lives in Pennsylvania with his wife and daughter, and he swears he is totally almost done writing the third Rafael Ward novel. You can catch up with him at michaelpogach.com or on Facebook and Instagram.

Jesse Teller fell in love with fantasy when he was five years old and played his first game of Dungeons & Dragons. The game gave him the ability to create stories and characters from a young age. He started consuming fantasy in every form and, by nine, was obsessed with the genre. As a young adult, he knew he wanted to make his life about fantasy. From exploring the relationship between man and woman, to studying the qualities of a leader or a tyrant, Jesse Teller uses his stories and settings to study real-world themes and issues. He lives with his supportive wife, Rebekah, and his two inspiring children, Rayph and Tobin.
https://jesseteller.com/
https://www.facebook.com/PathtoPerilisc/

Ulff Lehmann has spent quite a while waiting on his Midlife Crisis and decided he won't go there. For the past two decades he has been developing the stories he is now publishing. Born and bred in Germany, Ulff chose to write in English when he realized he had spent most of his adult life reading English instead of his mother tongue and brings with him the oftentimes Grimm outlook of his country's fairytales to his stories. A wordsmith with a poet's heart, Ulff's goal is to create a world filled with believable people.

Damien Wilder is a critical care worker by night and a fantasy author full-time. He lives in the southern U.S. with a supportive family who put up with endless book talks. In his non-work and non-writing hours, he's playing D&D, going on adventures, or trying to get a few hours of sleep. To keep up with his writing, follow him on Facebook or on Twitter @ AuthorDWilder

David Niall Wilson is awesome. He has been known to edit, design, and write books simultaneously while carrying on Facebook chats with authors. He runs the publishing company, Crossroad Press, that will one day take over the world and believes that a time traveler named Frederick Douglass will be our salvation. You can find him at http://www.davidniallwilson.com or on Facebook and Twitter

Curious about other Crossroad Press books?
Stop by our site:
http://store.crossroadpress.com
We offer quality writing
in digital, audio, and print formats.

Enter the code FIRSTBOOK
to get 20% off your first order from our store!
Stop by today!